HAIKA
SORU

THE FUTURE IS JAPANESE

THE FUTURE IS JAPANESE

EDITED BY NICK MAMATAS AND MASUMI WASHINGTON

HAIKA
SORU

SAN FRANCISCO

THE FUTURE IS JAPANESE

Cover art by Yuko Shimizu
Design by Fawn Lau

HAIKASORU
Published by
VIZ Media, LLC
295 Bay Street
San Francisco, CA 94133

www.haikasoru.com

Library of Congress Cataloging-in-Publication Data

The future is Japanese : stories from and about the land of the
rising sun / edited by Nick Mamatas and Masumi Washington.
    p. cm.
ISBN 978-1-4215-4223-2
1. Japan—Fiction.   2. Science fiction, American.   3. Science
fiction, Japanese.   4. Fantasy fiction, American.   5. Fantasy
fiction, Japanese.   I. Mamatas, Nick.   II. Washington, Masumi.
PS648.S3F893 2012
813'.0876—dc23   2012008381

The rights of the authors of the works in this publication to be so
identified have been asserted in accordance with the Copyright,
Designs and Patents Act 1988. A CIP catalogue record for this
book is available from the British Library.

Printed in the U.S.A.
First printing, May 2012

CONTENTS

Foreword

When I started looking through the stories from Western writers on my desk, I took my pencil and marked the Japanese names and terms that appeared a little off to my Japanese eye. "That's not a Japanese name…" I'd note, or "The spelling of the term should be…" But soon, as I got into each story, I threw my pencil aside. *Forget it.* They're all right just how they are. We know *Tagomi* doesn't sound like an ordinary Japanese name, but that didn't hurt *The Man in the High Castle*.

Later, a translation for one of the Japanese stories landed on my desk, and I started reading. Soon, I got a strange feeling… *Wait. This story can be understood much more clearly in English than in Japanese. What happened?* It was as though the story had been waiting to be in English a really long time.

I enjoyed the privilege of being the first reader for all the fantastic works created in the spirit of cross-cultural understanding. This is the moment when we've truly met one another on the same page. Then, what's on the next page? More stories! I hope we can continue to explore this joy of reading together.

Thank you very much to all the contributors and translators who participated in this anthology. And special thanks to our copy editor, Rebecca Downer, who has worked tirelessly on every Haikasoru title.

—Masumi Washington

Introduction—Revolving Around a Rising Sun

A few years ago, when I accepted a job editing Haikasoru, an imprint of Japanese science fiction, fantasy, and horror, I had little idea of what to expect. There had been some anthologies of Japanese SF in translation, but they tended to concentrate on the historical. Like many people, I'd guessed that Japanese SF was heavy on the cyberpunk, with yakuza heroes and flickering neon everywhere, characters motivated by *bushido,* with the occasional "socially relevant" story about Japan getting its economic revenge on the US for the Second World War and subsequent occupation. I was wrong. Happily, gloriously wrong.

Japanese science fiction is just like Western science fiction, in that it is hard and soft, dark and whimsical, rigorous and fantastical. Indeed, there are few fans of Western SF as enthusiastic as Japanese SF writers. The Japanese know much about science fiction as it is practiced in the West; Westerners still know too little about Japan. Video games, manga, and anime have filled the knowledge gap, but not completely. My own inaccurate vision of Japanese SF actually came from American science fictional visions of Japan— the neon and the economic rivalry were Western preoccupations.

Then there's the problem of Western writers appropriating Japanese cultural concepts and stereotypes of Japanese behaviors and using them as the building blocks for alien species. Reading about Japan in the West is often like looking at a funhouse mirror through a kaleidoscope.

The Future Is Japanese is an attempt to bridge the gap between Western and Japanese SF and fantasy. Many of our Japanese contributors wrote pieces specifically for this project—their work is appearing in translation here before being published in their native language. And the Western writers, many of whom have some personal connection to Japan, pulled out all the aesthetic stops. Yes, there are virtual worlds and *kanji* and even a squadron of giant *mecha*, and the stories are as authentic as they are fantastical. SF writers have always explored strange new worlds—with *The Future Is Japanese*, we explore our own.

—Nick Mamatas
San Francisco, California
February 2012

Mono no Aware by Ken Liu

The world is shaped like the kanji for *umbrella*, only written so poorly, like my handwriting, that all the parts are out of proportion.

My father would be greatly ashamed at the childish way I still form my characters. Indeed, I can barely write many of them anymore. My formal schooling back in Japan had ceased when I was only eight.

Yet for present purposes, this badly drawn character will do.

The canopy up there is the solar sail. Even that distorted kanji can only give you a hint of its vast size. A hundred times thinner than rice paper, the spinning disc fans out a thousand kilometers into space like a giant kite intent on catching every passing photon. It literally blocks out the sky.

Beneath it dangles a long cable of carbon nanotubes a hundred kilometers long: strong, light, and flexible. At the end of the cable hangs the heart of the *Hopeful*, the habitat module, a five-hundred-meter-tall cylinder into which all the 1,021 inhabitants of the world are packed.

The light from the sun pushes against the sail, propelling us on an ever-widening, ever-accelerating, spiraling orbit away from it. The acceleration pins all of us against the decks, gives everything weight.

Our trajectory takes us toward a star called 61 Virginis. You can't see it now because it is behind the canopy of the solar sail. The *Hopeful* will get there in about three hundred years, more or less. With luck, my great-great-great—I calculated how many "greats" I need once, but I don't remember now—grandchildren will see it.

There are no windows in the habitat module, no casual view of the stars streaming past. Most people don't care, having grown bored of seeing the stars long ago. But I like looking through the cameras mounted on the bottom of the ship so that I can gaze at this view of the receding, reddish glow of our sun, our past.

"Hiroto," Dad said as he shook me awake. "Pack up your things. It's time."

My small suitcase was ready. I just had to put my Go set into it. Dad gave this to me when I was five, and the times we played were my favorite hours of the day.

The sun had not yet risen when Mom and Dad and I made our way outside. All the neighbors were standing outside their houses with their bags as well, and we greeted each other politely under the summer stars. As usual, I looked for the Hammer. It was easy.

Ever since I could remember, the asteroid had been the brightest thing in the sky except for the moon, and every year it grew brighter.

A truck with loudspeakers mounted on top drove slowly down the middle of the street.

"Attention, citizens of Kurume! Please make your way in an orderly fashion to the bus stop. There will be plenty of buses to take you to the train station, where you can board the train for Kagoshima. Do not drive. You must leave the roads open for the evacuation buses and official vehicles!"

Every family walked slowly down the sidewalk.

"Mrs. Maeda," Dad said to our neighbor. "Why don't I carry your luggage for you?"

"I'm very grateful," the old woman said.

After ten minutes of walking, Mrs. Maeda stopped and leaned against a lamppost.

"It's just a little longer, Granny," I said. She nodded but was too out of breath to speak. I tried to cheer her. "Are you looking forward to seeing your grandson in Kagoshima? I miss Michi too. You will be able to sit with him and rest on the spaceships. They say there will be enough seats for everyone."

Mom smiled at me approvingly.

"How fortunate we are to be here," Dad said. He gestured at the orderly rows of people moving toward the bus stop, at the young men in clean shirts and shoes looking solemn, the middle-aged women helping their elderly parents, the clean, empty streets, and the quietness—despite the crowd, no one spoke above a whisper. The very air seemed to shimmer with the dense connections between all the people—families, neighbors, friends, colleagues—as invisible and strong as threads of silk.

I had seen on TV what was happening in other places around the world: looters screaming, dancing through the streets, soldiers and policemen shooting into the air and sometimes into crowds, burning buildings, teetering piles of dead bodies, generals shouting before frenzied crowds, vowing vengeance for ancient grievances even as the world was ending.

"Hiroto, I want you to remember this," Dad said. He looked around, overcome by emotion. "It is in the face of disasters that we show our strength as a people. Understand that we are not defined by our individual loneliness, but by the web of relationships in which we're enmeshed. A person must rise above his selfish needs so that all of us can live in harmony. The individual is small and power-less, but bound tightly together, as a whole, the Japanese nation is invincible."

"Mr. Shimizu," eight-year-old Bobby says, "I don't like this game."

The school is located in the very center of the cylindrical habitat module, where it can have the benefit of the most shielding from radiation. In front of the classroom hangs a large American flag to which the children say their pledge every morning. To the sides of the American flag are two rows of smaller flags belonging to other nations with survivors on the *Hopeful*. At the very end of the left side is a child's rendition of the Hinomaru, the corners of the white paper now curled and the once bright red rising sun faded to the orange of sunset. I drew it the day I came aboard the *Hopeful*.

I pull up a chair next to the table where Bobby and his friend, Eric, are sitting. "Why don't you like it?"

Between the two boys is a nineteen-by-nineteen grid of straight lines. A handful of black and white stones have been placed on the intersections.

Once every two weeks, I have the day off from my regular duties monitoring the status of the solar sail and come here to teach the children a little bit about Japan. I feel silly doing it sometimes. How can I be their teacher when I have only a boy's hazy memories of Japan?

But there is no other choice. All the non-American technicians like me feel it is our duty to participate in the cultural-enrichment program at the school and pass on what we can.

"All the stones look the same," Bobby says, "and they don't move. They're boring."

"What game do you like?" I ask.

"*Asteroid Defender!*" Eric says. "Now *that* is a good game. You get to save the world."

"I mean a game you do not play on the computer."

Bobby shrugs. "Chess, I guess. I like the queen. She's powerful and different from everyone else. She's a hero."

"Chess is a game of skirmishes," I say. "The perspective of Go is bigger. It encompasses entire battles."

"There are no heroes in Go," Bobby says stubbornly.

I don't know how to answer him.

There was no place to stay in Kagoshima, so everyone slept outside, along the road to the spaceport. On the horizon we could see the great silver escape ships gleaming in the sun.

Dad had explained to me that fragments that had broken off of the Hammer were headed for Mars and the moon, so the ships would have to take us further, into deep space, to be safe.

"I would like a window seat," I said, imagining the stars streaming by.

"You should yield the window seat to those younger than you," Dad said. "Remember, we must all make sacrifices to live together."

We piled our suitcases into walls and draped sheets over them to form shelters from the wind and the sun. Every day inspectors from the government came by to distribute supplies and to make sure everything was all right.

"Be patient!" the government inspectors said. "We know things are moving slowly, but we're doing everything we can. There will be seats for everyone."

We were patient. Some of the mothers organized lessons for the children during the day, and the fathers set up a priority system so that families with aged parents and babies could board first when the ships were finally ready.

After four days of waiting, the reassurances from the government inspectors did not sound quite as reassuring. Rumors spread through the crowd.

"It's the ships. Something's wrong with them."

"The builders lied to the government and said they were ready when they weren't, and now the Prime Minister is too embarrassed to admit the truth."

"I hear that there's only one ship, and only a few hundred of the most important people will have seats. The other ships are only hollow shells, for show."

"They're hoping that the Americans will change their mind and build more ships for allies like us."

Mom came to Dad and whispered in his ear.

Dad shook his head and stopped her. "Do not repeat such things."

"But for Hiroto's sake—"

"No!" I'd never heard Dad sound so angry. He paused, swallowed. "We must trust each other, trust the Prime Minister and the Self-Defense Forces."

Mom looked unhappy. I reached out and held her hand. "I'm not afraid," I said.

"That's right," Dad said, relief in his voice. "There's nothing to be afraid of."

He picked me up in his arms—I was slightly embarrassed for he had not done such a thing since I was very little—and pointed at the densely packed crowd of thousands and thousands spread around us as far as the eye could see.

"Look at how many of us there are: grandmothers, young fathers, big sisters, little brothers. For anyone to panic and begin to spread rumors in such a crowd would be selfish and wrong, and many people could be hurt. We must keep to our places and always remember the bigger picture."

Mindy and I make love slowly. I like to breathe in the smell of her dark curly hair, lush, warm, tickling the nose like the sea, like fresh salt.

Afterward we lie next to each other, gazing up at my ceiling monitor.

I keep looping on it a view of the receding star field. Mindy works in navigation, and she records the high-resolution cockpit video feed for me.

I like to pretend that it's a big skylight, and we're lying under the stars. I know some others like to keep their monitors showing photographs and videos of old Earth, but that makes me too sad.

"How do you say 'star' in Japanese?" Mindy asks.

"*Hoshi*," I tell her.

"And how do you say 'guest'?"

"*Okyakusan*."

"So we are *hoshi okyakusan*? Star guests?"

"It doesn't work like that," I say. Mindy is a singer, and she likes the sound of languages other than English. "It's hard to hear the music behind the words when their meanings get in the way," she told me once.

Spanish is Mindy's first language, but she remembers even less of it than I do of Japanese. Often, she asks me for Japanese words and weaves them into her songs.

I try to phrase it poetically for her, but I'm not sure if I'm successful. "*Wareware ha, hoshi no aida ni kyaku ni kite.*" *We have come to be guests among the stars.*

"There are a thousand ways of phrasing everything," Dad used to say, "each appropriate to an occasion." He taught me that our language is full of nuances and supple grace, each sentence a poem. The language folds in on itself, the unspoken words as meaningful as the spoken, context within context, layer upon layer, like the steel in samurai swords.

I wish Dad were around so that I could ask him, How do you say "I miss you" in a way that is appropriate to the occasion of your twenty-fifth birthday, as the last survivor of your race?

"My sister was really into Japanese picture books. Manga."

Like me, Mindy is an orphan. It's part of what draws us together.

"Do you remember much about her?"

"Not really. I was only five or so when I came on board the ship. Before that, I only remember a lot of guns firing and all of us hiding in the dark and running and crying and stealing food. She was always there to keep me quiet by reading from the manga books. And then…"

I had watched the video only once. From our high orbit, the blue-and-white marble that was Earth seemed to wobble for a moment as the asteroid struck, and then, the silent, roiling waves of spreading destruction slowly engulfed the globe.

I pull her to me and kiss her forehead, lightly, a kiss of comfort. "Let us not speak of sad things."

She wraps her arms around me tightly, as though she will never let go.

"The manga, do you remember anything about them?" I ask.

"I remember they were full of giant robots. I thought, *Japan is so powerful.*"

I try to imagine it: heroic giant robots all over Japan, working desperately to save the people.

The Prime Minister's apology was broadcast through the loudspeakers. Some also watched it on their phones.

I remember very little of it except that his voice was thin and he looked very frail and old. He looked genuinely sorry. "I've let the people down."

The rumors turned out to be true. The shipbuilders had taken the money from the government but did not build ships that were strong enough or capable of what they promised. They kept up the charade until the very end. We found out the truth only when it was too late.

Japan was not the only nation that failed her people. The other nations of the world had squabbled over who should contribute how much to a joint evacuation effort when the Hammer was first discovered on its collision course with Earth. And then, when that plan had collapsed, most decided that it was better to gamble that the Hammer would miss and spend the money and lives on fighting with each other instead.

After the Prime Minister finished speaking, the crowd remained silent. A few angry voices shouted but soon quieted down as well. Gradually, in an orderly fashion, people began to pack up and leave the temporary campsites.

"The people just went home?" Mindy asks, incredulous.

"Yes."

"There was no looting, no panicked runs, no soldiers mutinying in the streets?"

"This was Japan," I tell her. And I can hear the pride in my voice, an echo of my father's.

"I guess the people were resigned," Mindy says. "They had given up. Maybe it's a culture thing."

"No!" I fight to keep the heat out of my voice. Her words irk me, like Bobby's remark about Go being boring. "That is not how it was."

"Who is Dad speaking to?" I asked.

"That is Dr. Hamilton," Mom said. "We—he and your father and I—went to college together in America."

I watched Dad speak English on the phone. He seemed like a completely different person: it wasn't just the cadences and pitch of his voice; his face was more animated, his hand gestured more wildly. He looked like a foreigner.

He shouted into the phone.

"What is Dad saying?"

Mom shushed me. She watched Dad intently, hanging on every word.

"No," Dad said into the phone. "No!" I did not need that translated.

Afterward Mom said, "He is trying to do the right thing, in his own way."

"He is as selfish as ever," Dad snapped.

"That's not fair," Mom said. "He did not call me in secret. He called you instead because he believed that if your positions were reversed, he would gladly give the woman he loved a chance to survive, even if it's with another man."

Dad looked at her. I had never heard my parents say "I love you" to each other, but some words did not need to be said to be true.

"I would never have said yes to him," Mom said, smiling. Then she went to the kitchen to make our lunch. Dad's gaze followed her.

"It's a fine day," Dad said to me. "Let us go on a walk."

We passed other neighbors walking along the sidewalks. We

greeted each other, inquired after each other's health. Everything seemed normal. The Hammer glowed even brighter in the dusk overhead.

"You must be very frightened, Hiroto," he said.

"They won't try to build more escape ships?"

Dad did not answer. The late summer wind carried the sound of cicadas to us: *chirr chirr chirrrrrr.*

> "Nothing in the cry
> Of cicadas suggest they
> Are about to die."

"Dad?"

"That is a poem by Bashō. Do you understand it?"

I shook my head. I did not like poems much.

Dad sighed and smiled at me. He looked at the setting sun and spoke again:

> "The fading sunlight holds infinite beauty
> Though it is so close to the day's end."

I recited the lines to myself. Something in them moved me. I tried to put the feeling into words: "It is like a gentle kitten is licking the inside of my heart."

Instead of laughing at me, Dad nodded solemnly.

"That is a poem by the classical Tang poet Li Shangyin. Though he was Chinese, the sentiment is very much Japanese."

We walked on, and I stopped by the yellow flower of a dandelion. The angle at which the flower was tilted struck me as very beautiful. I got the kitten-tongue-tickling sensation in my heart again.

"The flower..." I hesitated. I could not find the right words.

Dad spoke,

"The drooping flower
As yellow as the moon beam
So slender tonight."

I nodded. The image seemed to me at once so fleeting and so permanent, like the way I had experienced time as a young child. It made me a little sad and glad at the same time.

"Everything passes, Hiroto," Dad said. "That feeling in your heart—it's called *mono no aware*. It is a sense of the transience of all things in life. The sun, the dandelion, the cicada, the Hammer, and all of us; we are all subject to the equations of James Clerk Maxwell and we are all ephemeral patterns destined to eventually fade, whether in a second or an eon."

I looked around at the clean streets, the slow-moving people, the grass, and the evening light, and I knew that everything had its place; everything was all right. Dad and I went on walking, our shadows touching.

Even though the Hammer hung right overhead, I was not afraid.

My job involves staring at the grid of indicator lights in front of me. It is a bit like a giant Go board.

It is very boring most of the time. The lights, indicating tension on various spots of the solar sail, course through the same pattern every few minutes as the sail gently flexes in the fading light of the distant sun. The cycling pattern of the lights is as familiar to me as Mindy's breathing when she's asleep.

We're already moving at a good fraction of the speed of light. Some years hence, when we're moving fast enough, we'll change our course for 61 Virginis and its pristine planets, and we'll leave the sun that gave birth to us behind like a forgotten memory.

But today, the pattern of the lights feels off. One of the lights in the southwest corner seems to be blinking a fraction of a second too fast.

"Navigation," I say into the microphone, "this is Sail Monitor Station Alpha. Can you confirm that we're on course?"

A minute later Mindy's voice comes through my earpiece, tinged slightly with surprise. "I hadn't noticed, but there was a slight drift off course. What happened?"

"I'm not sure yet." I stare at the grid before me, at the one stubborn light that is out of sync, out of harmony.

Mom took me to Fukuoka without Dad. "We'll be shopping for Christmas," she said. "We want to surprise you." Dad smiled and shook his head.

We made our way through the busy streets. Since this might be the last Christmas on Earth, there was an extra sense of gaiety in the air.

On the subway I glanced at the newspaper held up by the man sitting next to us. USA STRIKES BACK! was the headline. The big photograph showed the American president smiling triumphantly. Below that was a series of other pictures, some I had seen before: the first experimental American evacuation ship from years ago exploding on its test flight; the leader of some rogue nation claiming responsibility on TV; American soldiers marching into a foreign capital.

Below the fold was a smaller article: AMERICAN SCIENTISTS SKEPTICAL OF DOOMSDAY SCENARIO. Dad had said that some people preferred to believe that a disaster was unreal rather than accept that nothing could be done.

I looked forward to picking out a present for Dad. But instead of going to the electronics district, where I had expected Mom to take me to buy him a gift, we went to a section of the city I had never been to before. Mom took out her phone and made a brief call, speaking in English. I looked up at her, surprised.

Then we were standing in front of a building with a great American flag flying over it. We went inside and sat down in an office. An American man came in. His face was sad, but he was working hard not to look sad.

"Rin." The man called my mother's name and stopped. In that one syllable I heard regret and longing and a complicated story.

"This is Dr. Hamilton," Mom said to me. I nodded and offered to shake his hand, as I had seen Americans do on TV.

Dr. Hamilton and Mom spoke for a while. She began to cry, and Dr. Hamilton stood awkwardly, as though he wanted to hug her but dared not.

"You'll be staying with Dr. Hamilton," Mom said to me.

"What?"

She held my shoulders, bent down, and looked into my eyes. "The Americans have a secret ship in orbit. It is the only ship they managed to launch into space before they got into this war. Dr. Hamilton designed the ship. He's my...old friend, and he can bring one person aboard with him. It's your only chance."

"No, I'm not leaving."

Eventually, Mom opened the door to leave. Dr. Hamilton held me tightly as I kicked and screamed.

We were all surprised to see Dad standing there.

Mom burst into tears.

Dad hugged her, which I'd never seen him do. It seemed a very American gesture.

"I'm sorry," Mom said. She kept saying "I'm sorry" as she cried.

"It's okay," Dad said. "I understand."

Dr. Hamilton let me go, and I ran up to my parents, holding on to both of them tightly.

Mom looked at Dad, and in that look she said nothing and everything.

Dad's face softened like a wax figure coming to life. He sighed and looked at me.

"You're not afraid, are you?" Dad asked.

I shook my head.

"Then it is okay for you to go," he said. He looked into Dr. Hamilton's eyes. "Thank you for taking care of my son."

Mom and I both looked at him, surprised.

"A dandelion
 In late autumn's cooling breeze
 Spreads seeds far and wide."

I nodded, pretending to understand.

Dad hugged me, fiercely, quickly.

"Remember that you're Japanese."

And they were gone.

"Something has punctured the sail," Dr. Hamilton says.

The tiny room holds only the most senior command staff—plus Mindy and me because we already know. There is no reason to cause a panic among the people.

"The hole is causing the ship to list to the side, veering off course. If the hole is not patched, the tear will grow bigger, the sail will soon collapse, and the *Hopeful* will be adrift in space."

"Is there any way to fix it?" the captain asks.

Dr. Hamilton, who has been like a father to me, shakes his headful of white hair. I have never seen him so despondent.

"The tear is several hundred kilometers from the hub of the sail. It will take many days to get someone out there because you can't move too fast along the surface of the sail—the risk of another tear is too great. And by the time we do get anyone out there, the tear will have grown too large to patch."

And so it goes. Everything passes.

I close my eyes and picture the sail. The film is so thin that if it is touched carelessly it will be punctured. But the membrane is supported by a complex system of folds and struts that give the sail rigidity and tension. As a child, I watched them unfold in space like one of my mother's origami creations.

I imagine hooking and unhooking a tether cable to the scaffolding of struts as I skim along the surface of the sail, like a dragonfly dipping across the surface of a pond.

"I can make it out there in seventy-two hours," I say. Everyone turns to look at me. I explain my idea. "I know the patterns of the struts well because I have monitored them from afar for most of my life. I can find the quickest path."

Dr. Hamilton is dubious. "Those struts were never designed for a maneuver like that. I never planned for this scenario."

"Then we'll improvise," Mindy says. "We're Americans, damn it. We never just give up."

Dr. Hamilton looks up. "Thank you, Mindy."

We plan, we debate, we shout at each other, we work through the night.

The climb up the cable from the habitat module to the solar sail is long and arduous. It takes me almost twelve hours.

Let me illustrate for you what I look like with the second character in my name:

It means "to soar." See that radical on the left? That's me, tethered to the cable with a pair of antennae coming out of my helmet. On my back are the wings—or, in this case, booster rockets and extra fuel tanks that push me up and up toward the great reflective dome that blocks out the whole sky, the gossamer mirror of the solar sail.

Mindy chats with me on the radio link. We tell each other jokes, share secrets, speak of things we want to do in the future. When we run out of things to say, she sings to me. The goal is to keep me awake.

"*Wareware ha, hoshi no aida ni kyaku ni kite.*"

But the climb up is really the easy part. The journey across the sail along the network of struts to the point of puncture is far more difficult.

It has been thirty-six hours since I left the ship. Mindy's voice is now tired, flagging. She yawns.

"Sleep, baby," I whisper into the microphone. I'm so tired that I want to close my eyes just for a moment.

I'm walking along the road on a summer evening, my father next to me.

"We live in a land of volcanoes and earthquakes, typhoons and tsunamis, Hiroto. We have always faced a precarious existence, suspended in a thin strip on the surface of this planet between the fire underneath and the icy vacuum above."

And I'm back in my suit again, alone. My momentary loss of concentration causes me to bang my backpack against one of the beams of the sail, almost knocking one of the fuel tanks loose. I grab it just in time. The mass of my equipment has been lightened down to the last gram so that I can move fast, and there is no margin for error. I can't afford to lose anything.

I try to shake the dream and keep on moving.

"Yet it is this awareness of the closeness of death, of the beauty inherent in each moment, that allows us to endure. *Mono no aware*, my son, is an empathy with the universe. It is the soul of our nation. It has allowed us to endure Hiroshima, to endure the occupation, to endure deprivation and the prospect of annihilation without despair."

"Hiroto, wake up!" Mindy's voice is desperate, pleading. I jerk awake. I have not been able to sleep for how long now? Two days, three, four?

For the final fifty or so kilometers of the journey, I must let go of the sail struts and rely on my rockets alone to travel untethered, skimming over the surface of the sail while everything is moving at a fraction of the speed of light. The very idea is enough to make me dizzy.

And suddenly my father is next to me again, suspended in space below the sail. We're playing a game of Go.

"Look in the southwest corner. Do you see how your army has been divided in half? My white stones will soon surround and capture this entire group."

I look where he's pointing and I see the crisis. There is a gap that I missed. What I thought was my one army is in reality two separate groups with a hole in the middle. I have to plug the gap with my next stone.

I shake away the hallucination. I have to finish this, and then I can sleep.

There is a hole in the torn sail before me. At the speed we're traveling, even a tiny speck of dust that escaped the ion shields can cause havoc. The jagged edge of the hole flaps gently in space, propelled by solar wind and radiation pressure. While an individual photon is tiny, insignificant, without even mass, all of them together can propel a sail as big as the sky and push a thousand people along.

The universe is wondrous.

I lift a black stone and prepare to fill in the gap, to connect my armies into one.

The stone turns back into the patching kit from my backpack. I maneuver my thrusters until I'm hovering right over the gash in the sail. Through the hole I can see the stars beyond, the stars that no one on the ship has seen for many years. I look at them and imagine that around one of them, one day, the human race, fused into a new nation, will recover from near extinction, will start afresh and flourish again.

Carefully, I apply the bandage over the gash, and I turn on the heat torch. I run the torch over the gash, and I can feel the bandage melting to spread out and fuse with the hydrocarbon chains in the sail film. When that's done I'll vaporize and deposit silver atoms over it to form a shiny, reflective layer.

"It's working," I say into the microphone. I hear the muffled sounds of celebration in the background.

"You're a hero," Mindy says.

I think of myself as a giant Japanese robot in a manga and smile.

The torch sputters and goes out.

"Look carefully," Dad says. "You want to play your next stone there to plug that hole. But is that what you really want?"

I shake the fuel tank attached to the torch. Nothing. This was the tank that I banged against one of the sail beams. The collision must have caused a leak, and there isn't enough fuel left to finish the patch. The bandage flaps gently, only half attached to the gash.

"Come back now," Dr. Hamilton says. "We'll replenish your supplies and try again."

I'm exhausted. No matter how hard I push, I will not be able to make it back out here as fast. And by then who knows how big the gash will have grown? Dr. Hamilton knows this as well as I do. He just wants to get me back to the warm safety of the ship.

I still have fuel in my tank, the fuel that is meant for my return trip.

My father's face is expectant.

"I see," I say slowly. "If I play my next stone in this hole, I will not have a chance to get back to the small group up in the northeast. You'll capture them."

"One stone cannot be in both places. You have to choose, son."

"Tell me what to do."

I look into my father's face for an answer.

"Look around you," Dad says. And I see Mom, Mrs. Maeda, the Prime Minister, all our neighbors from Kurume, and all the people who waited with us in Kagoshima, in Kyushu, in all the Four Islands, all over the earth and on the *Hopeful*. They look expectantly at me, for me to do something.

Dad's voice is quiet:

"The stars shine and blink.
We are all guests passing through,
A smile and a name."

"I have a solution," I tell Dr. Hamilton over the radio.

"I knew you'd come up with something," Mindy says, her voice proud and happy.

Dr. Hamilton is silent for a while. He knows what I'm thinking. And then: "Hiroto, thank you."

I unhook the torch from its useless fuel tank and connect it to the tank on my back. I turn it on. The flame is bright, sharp, a blade of light. I marshal photons and atoms before me, transforming them into a web of strength and light.

The stars on the other side have been sealed away again. The mirrored surface of the sail is perfect.

"Correct your course," I speak into the microphone. "It's done."

"Acknowledged," Dr. Hamilton says. His voice is that of a sad man trying not to sound sad.

"You have to come back first," Mindy says. "If we correct course now, you'll have nowhere to tether yourself."

"It's okay, baby," I whisper into the microphone. "I'm not coming back. There's not enough fuel left."

"We'll come for you!"

"You can't navigate the struts as quickly as I did," I tell her gently. "No one knows their pattern as well as I do. By the time you get here, I will have run out of air."

I wait until she's quiet again. "Let us not speak of sad things. I love you."

Then I turn off the radio and push off into space so that they aren't tempted to mount a useless rescue mission. And I fall down, far, far below the canopy of the sail.

I watch as the sail turns away, unveiling the stars in their full glory. The sun, so faint now, is only one star among many, neither rising nor setting. I am cast adrift among them, alone and also at one with them.

A kitten's tongue tickles the inside of my heart.

I play the next stone in the gap.

Dad plays as I thought he would, and my stones in the northeast corner are gone, cast adrift.

But my main group is safe. They may even flourish in the future.

"Maybe there are heroes in Go," Bobby's voice says.

Mindy called me a hero. But I was simply a man in the right place at the right time. Dr. Hamilton is also a hero because he designed the *Hopeful*. Mindy is also a hero because she kept me awake. My mother is also a hero because she was willing to give me up so that

I could survive. My father is also a hero because he showed me the right thing to do.

We are defined by the places we hold in the web of others' lives.

I pull my gaze back from the Go board until the stones fuse into larger patterns of shifting life and pulsing breath. "Individual stones are not heroes, but all the stones together are heroic."

"It is a beautiful day for a walk, isn't it?" Dad says.

And we walk together down the street so that we can remember every passing blade of grass, every dewdrop, every fading ray of the dying sun, infinitely beautiful.

The Sound of Breaking Up by Felicity Savage

The last time I'd eaten at Yasukuni Bar de Café, I'd ordered the sweet potato Mont Blanc. This time I picked the castella with natto ice cream. The waitress took our order and glided away over the Pacific, chiming softly. Overhead, a Zero fighter strafed a swarm of UFOs.

My target had made a big effort with his appearance—false eyelashes, decals on his toenails, the works—but nothing could disguise the scared look in his eyes.

I felt sorry for him. Now that we were face to face I could see he was physically harmless, biceps like chopsticks. We could have done this at his place, where he would be more comfortable. It had been mean to drag him out. But we were here now, so I might as well get it over with.

"This is goodbye," I said. "It's better to end the relationship before anybody else gets hurt. Sorry."

"I understand," he said to the horizon.

I had to make sure he really did understand. "She doesn't ever want to see you again. She's divorcing you today. She's also unfanning you and canceling your access to her WORLD. And I know you wouldn't do this, but don't try and stalk her under a false identity, because she's got your ID from the time you killed her."

He flinched. He wasn't eating anything, just cradling a durian soy frappulatte. I used my OPU toolsuite to check for incoming packets. He was streaming a slasher-kei opera while we talked. He and his wife were both into slasher-kei, only he hadn't known where to draw the line.

He watched me chasing my ice cream around my plate. "When I was little," he said suddenly, "natto had a smell. It doesn't anymore. I wonder why?"

"Maybe people didn't like it," I said, shrugging. I seemed to remember that too, now he mentioned it. A dollop of natto on rice fresh out of the cooker before school. A smell of fermentation.

A big gray battleship chugged past our island. A caption popped up against the sunset to identify it as the *Yamato*, Marshal Isoroku Yamamoto's flagship, on its way to Midway. Wherever. I just liked it here for the sea. They did a great job with the waves lapping on the beach. You could fool yourself that if you went down to the water-line, you'd really get wet.

I finished my dessert—I might as well, since I wasn't paying for it—and we deboxed. The waitress zipped down the aisle, bowed from her thoracic hinge, and debited the bill from his Life Support account. I also got her to log the visit on my reward card. I knew I'd be back. We walked toward the exit between the rows of boxes. From outside they looked grotty, covered with printscreens for assisted-suicide services and meds for noncompliant personal-ity disorder, which had been the hot disease at least six months ago. Clearly, the Yasukuni Bar de Café had problems attracting advertisers.

Outside, segway cops patrolled the asphalt in front of the main attraction, a building with red pillars and curly-edged roofs encased in a transparent polythene tent. We put our masks on. There'd been a fallout warning today.

He stopped beneath the giant torii gate on the way back to Kudanshita station. "What about the kids?" he said. "What's going to happen to them?"

My client had specifically instructed me to tell him the truth about this, if he asked. I'd been hoping he wouldn't. "They've been liquidated," I said. "Sorry."

"No. No! Ayumi's about to start first grade. Tomitake's only three. You can't just snatch their lives away from them like that!"

"She's their mother. It's her right." He was crying, his mascara dripping onto the pink-skull-patterned fabric of his mask. I didn't feel sorry for him anymore. "Anyway, you should have thought of that before you killed her," I said.

"But she asked me to," he whispered.

I called my client while I was on the train. She wanted to know if he'd asked about the kids, and I said he had. "Good," she said vindictively. "I want the asshole to suffer."

"He started crying when I told him."

"What a loser," she said, echoing my own thought from earlier. "Who cries over virtual kids?"

More people than you'd think, actually. But I only said, "I'll expect my fee to show up in my account today. That's not a problem, I hope?" As always, I got a tiny low-down thrill when I mentioned getting paid for my services.

"It's already there," she said. "I really appreciate your hard work. I'll be sure to recommend you to my fans if anyone needs a proxy."

I was still thinking about her husband's last words—*but she asked me to kill her!* Breakups are always more complicated than they look from the outside. I wondered which of them was telling the truth and felt something complicated—disappointment and relief mixed up—at the thought that I'd never know.

"By the way, what does he look like?" she said before we hung up. "I've never met him."

I'm a professional proxy. To get my license, I had to pass the National Examination in Compassion and Warmheartedness (Level 1). Most of my coursework was obvious stuff dressed up in jargon, but a few parts really struck me, such as the module about *meiwaku*. It said, "The Japanese dislike causing other people meiwaku. Such is our reluctance to inconvenience others that many of us prefer to suffer in silence…" blah blah blah, and then there was this bit: "The comparatively low divorce rate (80 percent of Japanese physical marriages and 27 percent of virtual marriages last more than one year) is often attributed to this national trait."

When I screened that, I knew I was going to specialize in proxy breakups.

It's bullshit about meiwaku, of course. But check out those statistics. Forty-six point five percent of *all* marriages last less than one year! And the beautiful thing about divorce is that you still need the other person's signature and stamp, even if the marriage was virtual. So there's a lot of demand for what I do. In fact, I make almost as much money as I could claim from National Life Support for sitting on my ass all day. And I kind of enjoy the frugal lifestyle, actually.

I had a few hours to kill before my next appointment, so I stopped off in Shinjuku for a makeover. There's this one place I really like, on the forty-second floor of the You-Vie building, that has a little zoo in the lobby. Sometimes I just sit and watch the butterflies and birds and things. But I'd been up all night engineering contacts, and I was looking grotty, so I went straight into surgery.

I like to look different for each appointment, when possible. Some guys will photograph you on the sly and run an ID search using facial-recognition tools. I'm a jump ahead of them. This time through I had my lips plumped, my cheeks lifted, and some new hair extensions put in. As I got back on the train, the numbness was fading into that tingly phase.

There are more faces on the street at night, fewer full-body masks. People want to be seen, especially in Roppongi. You can feel that old-time glamour in the air. Neon, smiles, the smell of shwarma. But I wasn't going to get to eat a fancy meal at someone else's expense, not tonight. I was breaking one of my own rules: I was going to meet a target at his place. This guy lived on the 244th floor of the Roppongi Space Needle, so I figured it was all right.

"I'm here on behalf of your wife," I said. "Sorry to have deceived you." I'd made contact with him by pretending to have a skinship fetish, operating off a tip from my client—his wife—that he liked that kind of thing. As a matter of fact, that was why she was divorcing him. It had taken a couple of weeks before he revealed interest and agreed to meet me, so I'd thought maybe she was wrong. Uh-uh. He'd met me at the door stark naked. I stood in the *genkan* without taking my shoes off and said, "She's through with you, and she's not interested in discussing it. I just need your signature and stamp here, please." I usually tried to soften the blow for them, but his nudity was so disrespectful I couldn't be bothered to be Compassionate or Warmhearted at all.

"Ah-huh," he said. "I see. Did she say why?"

"Yeah, because you're a pervert." I gestured at his crotch. His penis hung in a clump of black hair like a little brown *mochi-iri kinchaku*.

He looked down sadly at himself. "I never tried to have sex with her," he said. "I'm not one of *those*."

"No, you're even sadder than that."

"I guess I am." He sighed and climbed into a pair of sweatpants.

He said over his shoulder, "Come in for a drink. I want to hear her side of the story, then I'll sign your paperwork."

Well, you hear about girls getting attacked by sex maniacs. And it now occurred to me that maybe the line between skinship and sex wasn't as bright as I'd assumed. On the other hand, I had my professional pride: I hate failing a client. And I was curious to see inside his apartment. I could see from the door that it had at least two rooms.

Three, it turned out. I started to wonder what his scam was. National Life Support pays out the national *average* income, which would not cover so much as a unit bath in the Roppongi Space Needle.

He gave me a can of blueberry juice from the fridge. "So, do you do this for a living?"

"Yeah," I said, a bit defensively.

"Not many people bother to work for a living nowadays."

"There aren't many jobs that need doing."

"By people."

"No."

"Still. You could just claim Life Support. Why don't you?"

"Look, I know I'm weird, okay? I just happen to like doing a job and getting paid for it. Same as you like getting naked and rubbing yourself against other people. Everyone's weird in their own way."

"That's not true." He looked at me in a way I didn't like, as if he were seeing through my makeover habit to whatever I would have looked like without all the surgery. "Not rubbing, actually. For your information. Just sort of…holding."

"Ugh," I said, and a burst of music played. He grabbed a gadget off the table. A phone. Wow. I hadn't seen one of those in years.

"Yeah. No. That's not good…Yeah? On my way now."

He disappeared into the bedroom.

"I've been called out. Sorry. Can we finish this on the way?"

"To where?"

He came back out tying a necktie around the collar of a Y-shirt. He was wearing a suit. I hadn't seen one of *those* in…God, since I was a kid. My dad used to wear a suit to go to…*the office*. That was what we called it, *the office*.

"Hey," I said. "You work for a living too, don't you? Asshole."

"We weren't talking about me."

I followed him down to the building's carpark. A Tata Buzz glided out of the darkness, making a throaty engine noise. We got in. The car rolled up the ramp and straight onto the elevated highway. Tokyo stretched to the horizon, a dim grid of energy-saving LED streetlumes, dotted with a few sparkling islands. My guy switched on the interior light and flipped through the divorce paperwork. "I'm not signing this," he said.

"You have to."

"I don't *have* to do anything. Neither do you."

The car exited at Kokkaigijidomae. We passed the Diet building and pulled up outside a nondescript office block on Sotobori Dori. My guy worked for the government. He was a civil servant. I remembered my father saying that civil servants had the best jobs of anyone. That was in the days before National Life Support started and suddenly there was no reason for anyone to have a job at all. Most of my teachers quit. My father stopped going to the office. We were happy at first, but then my mother broke up with us and went to be a biobot developer in China. She died in the Rongcheng nuclear accident. A while after that, my father hanged himself in the bathroom. He left a note saying that he wasn't worried about leaving me because he knew National Life Support would take good care of me.

As we walked toward the doors, my guy squirted me a security code via my public inbox. The guards scanned us through. Inside the building, men in suits were running. Some of them had guns. I thought nothing of it, probably because I'd seen so many guns in people's WORLDs…and then we plunged through another set of doors, big wooden ones with rosettes on them, and we *were* in someone's WORLD. Had been all along, perhaps. The seamless intro had fooled me.

"Well, this is kind of pathetic." Hands on hips, I surveyed the twilit countryside spread out below. We seemed to be standing on the parapet of a castle built on a craggy outcropping. Flat farmland stretched to a line of distant hills. I could just make out the familiar triangle of Fuji-san, the sun still bright on its snowcap. "Are we actually still in your car? Or still in your apartment?"

A cold, fresh wind licked at my face.

"This isn't a virtuality," my guy said. "It's 2417 AD."

"Oh yeah? Because it looks like an out-of-the-box WORLD set in the Warring States Era."

"Have another look." He pointed toward the hills. I saw motion along a distant crease in the fields, too fast to be a column of horses. The tops of trucks zooming along a sunken road. Farther away, something flickered brightly, burning.

"They ambushed Supply Convoy Number 313 thirty minutes ago." Another suit was briefing my guy. "We've secured the area and are evaccing casualties."

"Retaliatory measures?"

"Not yet. We're waiting for a decision."

"I'd better take a look at the damage. Do we have control of the local airspace?"

"Yes sir, we do. They do not appear to have surface-to-air missiles at this time."

"Right, right. That comes earlier." My guy frowned at the distant flames. "Get a chopper ready then."

"Can I come?"

"No." He was different now, distant. *Working.* "Stay here."

"He cares about me," I explained to the people who were left on top of the gatehouse. "He wouldn't want me to get hurt." I'd analyzed the security code he sent me, using the basic suite of tools in my onboard processing unit. It identified me as his "secretary." Whatever. I didn't know what a secretary was supposed to do, but complaining seemed like a good start. "Why is my OPU running so slow? I'm only getting, like, gigabits per second."

They exchanged glances. "Limited bandwidth on this side, miss."

I rubbed my fingers over the top of the parapet. Gritty yellow stone. Licked them. Taste of dust. In the west, the sun was slowly sinking. I love sunsets, all the yellows and the reds, like an oil painting by Mother Nature. But this one looked like an amateur effort, just a few lemony veils of cloud drifting above an orb too bright to look at. "What's with the sky?"

"It's the air, miss. No pollution out here."

I felt cold, and not just because of the wind. "This really is the twenty-fifth century, isn't it?"

"Yes, miss."

I wanted to go home. I'd spent my whole life chasing reality, trying not to get sucked into a WORLD-based existence like most people, but now I didn't want this to be real.

The problem with reality is it doesn't care what you want.

I spotted a trapdoor in the roof and went for it like a mouse diving into its hole. Inside, the gatehouse was less castle-y, with ordinary stairs and wide gray corridors, more evidence that this was real; if it was a WORLD they'd have kept it authentic. Two of the people from up top followed me, a female suit about my age and an older guy in a coverall that said *NaLiSu* on the pocket. The female suit led the way down through several levels where people in military uniforms were working at desktop computers and out to a big yard surrounded by a sloping drystone wall.

Trucks rumbled in through a security chicane with two hairpin bends that hid the world outside the gate. Each one stopped for about a minute in the chicane, then got directed into one of the big hangars inside the yard. There were a lot of other buildings too. It was all very administrative and functional-looking.

"They do it with lasers," the older guy said. "I don't know the details, but it turns out light can bend space. And once you can bend space, that bends time. It's all in Einstein."

"What's Einstein?" I said.

He gave me a pitying look. "Died about a hundred years before you were born. See," he said to the female suit. "This is what you're creating. Plundering the future to keep your kids spoiled and ignorant."

"What's that smell?" I said.

The female suit said, "Exhaust fumes. These trucks run on gasoline. We can't risk letting the downstreamers steal our battery technology."

The older guy sniffed. "In the next century upstream, they've already got it. We take it off them. But it's not going to be easy."

"What's in the trucks?"

The guy had crooked, discolored teeth. "Rice, mostly."

Little black shapes fluttered across the darkening sky. *Bats.* I'd seen virtual ones before, but these were real. There was something exuberant about their flight that just couldn't have been generated by an algorithm. And green stuff grew in the cracks between the stones of the wall. The truck engines made the same noise that you'd expect, but throatier, louder, because it wasn't electronically generated to prevent collisions—it was real.

I looked at the female suit. Her neat, practical look made me feel embarrassed by my pink hair and temp-tats. "How do I get a job here?"

She laughed. "You can't. We're closing this era down."

"Moving upstream," the older guy said. "Getting too hot in this century."

"He comes from the twenty-seven-hundreds," she said. "Started out as a supplier, jumped to the logistics and procurement side. That's one way to get a job with us. Be born in the future."

She was sneering at me. Looking down on me because I was

a noob. For some reason, I could take it from the old guy, but not from her. "Well, screw you," I said. "You're only a gofer anyway." I wandered away from them across the yard. The trucks had stopped coming in. The human staff banged the gates shut. It was getting dark.

While we were talking, I'd had my OPU working on an environmental analysis of my new "secretary" identity. I was using harvested processing power, which constrained me to a rate hardly faster than the public datarate here. But I had some black-hat tools purchased from contacts in the New SSR, and these now spat out preliminary results telling me that I had access to a bunch of self-explanatory facilities such as "Dining Hall," as well as something called the Mallett Gate, which did not show up on the map the tools helpfully pushed onto my left retina.

The noise of a helicopter announced the return of my guy and his companions. His nice shirt was smudged and dirty. He smelled like burning.

We ate in the dining hall with the day-shift staff of the Kanto Collection Point (KCP), which was what this was. My heavy consumption of onboard power had given me a ravenous appetite, but the food would've tasted good anyway. Real baked fish, real leafy greens, and rice that made me feel like I was six years old again. None of it was tank-grown or reconstituted. It came from the farms here which supplied the goods we trucked through the collection point and back home to 2082.

"We can't take too many more losses like today," my guy said. "The instability premium is cutting into our margins."

"They've got it worse in Kansai," the old guy said. "The downstreamers there are using suicide bombers."

I said, "What've they got against us?"

I'd already picked up a lot from listening to people. KCP was located in the same place where the Tokyo city government offices stood in our own century. That's why the view from the gatehouse had looked familiar. But the whole expanse of land that I knew as Tokyo, a city of sixty million, had reverted to wasteland partially reclaimed for farming. It was scary to imagine what might have caused that to happen. Maybe another big nuclear accident. Maybe a war. Maybe it was scheduled to happen the day after I got home.

My guy picked a fishbone out from between his lips. "Well, it's not just rice," he said. "We collect all kinds of commodities. Minerals. Biomass. Timber. Natural gas from the Sea of Japan—*that's* a security nightmare. The downstreamers in this era haven't got the technology to hit our drilling platforms, but we've got the commies from our own century on our asses, trying to expand their catchment areas. All the same, the goods get through. Everything we need to keep society functioning, really."

"The future supplies the difference between what we produce and what we consume," the female suit said. She'd gotten a bit drunk on *shochu* during the meal; her face looked softer, kind of confused.

"But we don't produce anything at home," I said. "Unless you count virtual stuff."

The old guy cackled. "Exactly."

My guy said, "We pay for everything, of course. But for some reason, they always end up hating us." He helped himself to some more shochu. "The Mallett Gate was invented in America. A lot of the early users ended up taking one-way trips to, like, extinction events two billion years downstream. They thought it was a wash. Time travel as Russian roulette. It was us that refined the technology, fine-tuned it. Japan has always been poor in natural resources. That's often driven us to take desperate risks...Pearl Harbor, Midway. That didn't work out. But this did. With the flick of a switch, we were suddenly the richest country in the world."

He looked wistful. "Unfortunately, the technology leaked, and now everyone's got it. So we're still stuck in a competition for resources… in the future."

"Started off in the twenty-ninth century," Kurosumi-san said. "Go any further downstream than that and you run into an extinction event presumably caused by a meteor strike. That was forty years ago. Ever since then, we've been hopping upstream a few decades at a time. See, when we go *upstream*, they don't know we're coming."

I nodded slowly. "But what happens when we go so far upstream we bump into ourselves coming the other way?"

"Ah, well then we're screwed," my guy said. "But we can get another generation out of the system at our current pace."

"And then what?"

He refilled my cup. "Kanpai."

The downstreamers were shooting at us. Apparently they did this a lot, creeping up close at night. The sky thundered. Our soldiers were shooting back. I covered my ears as my guy dragged me toward the gatehouse. "The demographic bulge," he shouted at me.

"What?"

I cowered against the clammy stone wall. I felt like I needed shelter, even though I wasn't really in danger. My guy swung in close, facing me, one arm braced over my head.

"National Life Support was supposed to produce a demographic bulge!" he shouted. "To reverse the graying of society! To expand the workforce so we could keep the whole thing going! Hasn't happened! We don't even have enough people to defend our downstream facilities! Those are biobots up there! I was being ironic!"

He grabbed my hand and tried to hold it. I pulled away. "If this is some kind of an elaborate pickup line, forget it! I'm not interested in breeding! Ugh!"

"Not that." He swayed closer to me so he was speaking into my hair. His breath smelled of shochu and his voice sounded like he was crying. "Be my proxy."

"What?"

"It happens in 2106, according to our latest timeline. You'll see. You'll know what you have to do."

Incoming! A huge slug of data landed in my inbox, trailing a long tail of links. Phraud alarms blinked on my left retina like tracer fire. Then everything went black.

Two Years Later

"Everyone clear on what they have to do?" I looked around the hollow at the faces of my friends. Hard, weathered, young faces striped with camo cream mixed from charcoal and potato starch. No one said a word. These were the pick of the New Edo samurai: they'd been fighting the upstreamers half their lives, and now, for the first time, they had a chance to defeat them. Every line of their tense, squatting bodies screamed *ready for action*. I nodded, pleased. "If there are no more questions, then let's get moving."

We walked in single file, our guns and equipment tied down so nothing rattled, utilizing upstreamer asphalt where it was safe, cutting across country in other places, making for the obscenely bright glow of KCP. I mentally reviewed my own plan for the upcoming action. I hadn't even told Tomoki how I hoped it was going to play out.

As if my thoughts had summoned him, he moved up from the rear of the column. "If anything happens to either of us tonight…"

I spoke past a sudden lump in my throat. "Your mom and dad will take care of Michiyo. She'll grow up to succeed where we failed."

Mentioning our daughter, just six months old, made me question what I was doing. Made me remember my own parents, who'd both left me, as I was leaving Michiyo tonight. "But we aren't going to fail."

He nodded, his face shadowed by the scrub woods we were moving through. "Asuko…"

That's my name. Asuko. I never told it to anyone before. *Tomorrow's child.* Ironic, huh?

I tripped on a chunk of centuries-old debris buried under the dead knots of winter grass and kicked it, upset. We were walking uphill in the region that had once been known as Shibuya.

"When the upstreamers are gone for good," Tomoki said, "we'll rebuild." He squeezed my hand. "This will be a city again." He had grown up as a slave on one of the upstreamers' vast collective farms in what had formerly been Saitama Prefecture. He'd never heard of any such thing as a city until I told him what Tokyo used to be. I had actually described a WORLD set in the early twenty-first century that I used to visit a lot: the incessant construction and development, the commercial bustle, the warmth of neighborhood communities that interlocked like links in a fence keeping out the night. Maybe it was just some WORLD-designer's dream, but it was the kind of dream this ravaged century needed.

We called a final halt on the bank of the Kanda River, almost within earshot of the blazing-bright towers of KCP. I gathered everyone close.

"The guy who sent me to you," I said, "wanted me to act as his proxy. See, back upstream, I was licensed as a kind of relationship expert. I had qualifications in compassion and warmheartedness." Knowing me, they snickered at that, as I'd hoped they would. "He sent me out to spread the word that we, I mean the upstreamers, were withdrawing. He wanted me to break up with you. To say goodbye, no hard feelings, it wasn't you, it was us."

The river gurgled over the shallows we would shortly be fording. My men squatted as still as stones.

"Well, I was like, screw that. I don't owe you anything. So I just shared the data he gave me with you...and the rest you know. We've stepped up our campaign. Killed hundreds of them."

I reached blindly for Tomoki's hand. Now came the hard bit.

"But I didn't tell you everything."

Assaults tend to succeed or fail in the first thirty seconds, and this one was no exception. We blew up the gates using a grenade launcher captured from the upstreamers themselves. After that it was no contest, since I had the security codes to dismantle the KCP biobots. The codes were two years old but still worked piecemeal, leaving fatal gaps in the perimeter defenses. Our guns did the rest. Amid the clamor and carnage, I wondered again why that guy had given me the codes. I imagined, or remembered, a voice from somewhere: *They asked us to kill them.*

Maybe *that's* what he'd really meant when he asked me to be his proxy.

In which case, I was two years late getting on the job. I'd taken time out to fall in love, have a child, and find out what being human really meant.

Now it was time for me to act on that knowledge.

Takagi-san, a huge samurai in particolored scrap-metal armor, emerged from the gatehouse waving his gun triumphantly. The building was clear. I ran inside and up the stairs. At every turn I had to jump over the bodies of office workers sprawled in their gore. We hadn't spared a single soul. This time, the upstreamers would not be coming back. But I knew that already.

Reaching the command center on the third floor, I tried to open the blastproof door with my security codes. Nothing happened. "Shit!" The base network had gone down. I could not transmit any data.

Tomoki materialized at my side. "Stand back," he shouted, and fired a full magazine of armor-piercing rounds into the door. I hit the floor as ricochets screamed around the corridor. Raising my head I saw the door sagging on its hinges. I also saw Tomoki's lovely smile.

"Get out," I shouted, my hearing shot. "Get everyone out. The whole gatehouse is the Mallett Gate."

"I'm coming with you," he said, and our hands touched just as the building seemed to twist on two axes at once, spinning sickeningly as if gravity had gone on vacation. I knew what was happening. They were shutting down the Mallett Gate from the other side.

I felt my OPU reestablish a connection with the national internet for the first time in two years, and time stretched as I fought the operators. I jammed everything I had learned into the maw of the program that crunched time and space. I told them about breaking my ankle in the woods and being rescued by villagers who lived off the grid…about pain and recovery: swimming in the river, working in the fields, helping to build really useful things with stolen parts…about holding and kissing the person you love. I gave them a whole WORLD based on my experiences, designed over the last two years with the sensory-conversion software that every kid in my own time got preloaded. The twisting and spinning slowed as the unseen operators, humans and AIs alike, took the bait.

Somewhere along the way I lost Tomoki. But I'd been going to lose him anyway. Him and our daughter and everyone.

I sat up, aching all over, in a rectangle of dusty sunlight. Several men and women in lab coats and masks were staring down at me. Someone was screaming in the background. One of the men frantically pushed buttons on a piece of equipment that looked as jerry-rigged as anything we used to build in the twenty-fifth century.

I knew roughly where and when I was: America, sometime in the 2060s. I had seized control of the Mallett Gate and gone back as far as possible, to the end of the line, the day the very first working prototype was built.

"Hello," I said. "I'm Asuko." They weren't Japanese. They didn't understand me. I spoke on anyway. "I'm canceling your experiment." I stood up and pushed the prototype, knocking it over. Glass crunched. Next I pulled my twenty-fifth-century pistol out of my waistband and fired at the researchers, dropping each of them in turn with body shots. It felt as if I were shooting the people I'd loved. By changing the past, I would change the future. I'd never be able to return to my own time, let alone the twenty-fifth century. But with luck, my actions would help to head off the nuclear war that was scheduled to kick off in 2106. And somewhere, somehow, I prayed my daughter would have a chance to grow up. Through my tears, I said, "This is goodbye."

Chitai Heiki Koronbīn by David Moles

There used to be a snack bar or a kebab shop or something at the side of the hangar. It's scrap now, a shapeless pile of fiberglass and corrugated tin, broken pieces of brown and white signs advertising *döner* and currywurst. Some of the plastic chairs have survived though, and now Jacob drags three of them through the green-uniformed cordon of nervous Ländespolizei into the rain shadow of the hunched Colombine and Pantalon. Maddy takes one without a word and sits, or rather sprawls, knees wide like a salaryman on a late train, looking out at nothing. After a moment the black figure of the Scaramouche crouches down beside the other two robots; the cockpit opens, and Abby slides down to join Maddy and Jacob.

"Captain Asano says the transport's almost here," she announces.

Maddy nods.

Jacob says, "Tanimura get any?"

"She didn't say."

Jacob is still wearing his helmet. He takes it off now and flings it across the tarmac. Some of the Ländespolizei look round at the clatter and then hurriedly away. Without his big Malcolm X glasses Jacob's face looks naked. Maddy and Abby can see that he's crying.

Abby goes and retrieves the helmet and sets it down at Jacob's side. Then she draws the third chair up next to Maddy and perches there, her knees drawn up to her chest. In the white chair, in her black Nomex suit, she looks very small.

"You got a few of them, Maddy," she says after a moment. "Didn't you?"

"I got one or two," Maddy says, her voice sounding flat, echoless in her own ears.

Abby looks over toward the hangar, the second ring of Ländespolizei, the green tarps and trailers of the field hospital and the makeshift morgue.

"That's something, I guess," she says.

Maddy doesn't answer.

The transport comes in, low and heavy, roaring down the length of the runway so the wind of its passage rocks the trailers, rips tent pegs from the ground, and sends the Ländespolizei scurrying to secure the tarps. It slows and turns down at the far end and taxis slowly back.

A squawk comes from Jacob's helmet. Abby lifts her own to her ear, says something quietly into the microphone, then listens. She looks over at the others.

"Tanimura's gone," she says.

"What?" says Jacob. "They got him?"

Abby shakes her head. "No," she says. "He's AWOL. Asano wants one of us to go look for him."

"You're kidding," says Maddy. "Isn't that her job?"

"He's taken the Pierrot too," Abby says.

Maddy stands up. "Fine," she says. "I'll go."

She doesn't bother putting on her own helmet, just climbs back into the Colombine's cockpit, closes the hatch, powers up the instruments and screens, plugs the IV into the cannula in her hip. She waits for Jacob and Abby to get the Pantalon and the Scaramouche moving, follows them up the ramp into the transport.

"All right," she says into the helmet, as the crew locks the Colombine into its cradle. "Where's he gone, Disneyland Paris?"

Asano's voice, coming from the helmet, is reedy and strained.

"He's gone into the zone," she says.

The secret robot base was an old oil platform somewhere north of the Arctic Circle. Officially it was the United Nations Provisional Containment Authority Northern Hemisphere Rapid Deployment Facility, but after six weeks in the British Columbian woods at the United Nations Provisional Containment Authority Pacific Region Candidate Induction Centre Camp Chilliwack, Maddy had had enough of UN word salad, and when Abby had called it the secret robot base, Maddy had picked the name up and made it stick. The walls of the base were white-painted steel that flaked in places to reveal an older layer of nicotine yellow and occasionally bits of faded Russian stencil. The UN had rubberized the floors and put in new signs in English and Japanese, but to Maddy it still felt like they'd gone back in time, or like they were on the set of some old war movie like her dad was always watching on the History Channel, *Top Gun* or *Blue Submarine No. 6* or *The Final Countdown*. She liked that. Jacob said the gray glop on the ceilings was asbestos and it was giving them cancer.

They would come back from one of their thirty-hour Rapid Deployments to the edge of—but never into—the Canadian zone, or the European zone, or the zone off the coast of the Philippines in the South China Sea, and the doctors would strip Abby and Maddy and Jacob out of their Nomex pilot suits and decontaminate them and flush the zone drugs out of their systems and put them through a battery of medical and psychological and parapsychological tests that would have been humiliating before Camp Chilliwack. Likewise before Chilliwack Maddy would have been self-conscious about being undressed and prodded in front of Abby and Jacob, would have been conscious of Abby's bony nakedness and Jacob's invasive gaze, but now it was just Jacob and Abby, and Jacob's gaze wasn't invasive, just exhausted, and Abby's naked body wasn't remotely erotic, just tired and bruised, and Maddy could care less what she herself looked like. If the doctors put Tanimura through any of this they did it somewhere else.

In three months at the secret robot base Maddy had had exactly one conversation with boy hero Shinichiro Tanimura. It had gone like this:

Tanimura (English strongly accented, eyes behind his unkempt black bangs never lifting above Maddy's none-too-impressive chest): "You lived in Japan."

Maddy:「東京。三年間。」(Tokyo. Three years.)

Tanimura:「日本語上手だね。」(Your Japanese is pretty good.)

Maddy (lying): "I don't understand."

She'd understood fine. She just didn't want to make friends with Tanimura. Which raised the question of why she'd felt it necessary to show off by speaking Japanese in the first place when Captain Asano had introduced them, and Abby had asked Maddy exactly that when Maddy had told her the story.

"Competitive much?" Abby had said, and Maddy had given her a withering look; but Abby tended not to notice things like that. And Maddy had to admit—to herself, anyway—that Abby was probably right. But she was getting that geek-boy crush vibe from Tanimura, or thought she was, and she wanted to shut that down right away. She wasn't here to be Tanimura's friend, and she certainly wasn't here to be his girlfriend. As far as Maddy was concerned, she was here to be his replacement.

Maddy and Abby and Jacob were American. Almost everyone else on the secret robot base was Japanese, apart from a few of the doctors that had followed them from Camp Chilliwack, who were Canadian. They were Japanese because Tanimura was Japanese, and until the Camp Chilliwack graduates had turned up, Tanimura, and Tanimura's shiny white robot the Pierrot, had been the only thing standing between the enemy coming out of the zones and the human race.

There had been twenty-seven test candidates at Camp Chilliwack and five of them had graduated. Of the twenty-two who hadn't, four were dead and seven would need serious medical attention for the rest of their lives. Of the five who had, two had been killed the very first time they were Rapidly Deployed: Hailey Peterson had died trying to save a busload of Taiwanese schoolchildren who shouldn't have been anywhere near the operational area, and Oscar Jara—who was a soldier, and at twenty-three the oldest of them by five years, and who Maddy privately thought should have known better—had died going after Hailey. Hailey's body had been sent back to Ontario and Oscar's to California, and the Docteur and the Arlequin to wherever dead robots went.

The Colombine and the Scaramouche and the Pantalon came back in one piece, and Maddy and Abby and Jacob did too, more or less. They got better at what they were supposed to be doing. The zones got bigger, the things coming out of them—crawling out of them, usually, crawling and dying, but not always—got weirder, and Maddy and Abby and Jacob killed the monsters and turned back the machines and they stuck to the mission and none of them died. They stood for press photos, with Captain Asano just out of frame; they got crayon robot drawings from schoolchildren in Nunavut and Poland and Hong Kong. Abby said they were saving lives and giving people hope. Jacob said they were saving a lot of property.

The showers in the secret robot base were new and Japanese, but as industrial as all the rest of it, with spray nozzles in worrying places, oversized controls suitable for clumsy gloved hands. Maddy made sure the cannula in her hip for the zone drugs was sealed, turned on about half the nozzles, made the water as hot as she could stand it; wet her hair, scrubbed at her shoulders and upper arms. Coming back, maybe it was the disinfectants, maybe it was going off the zone drugs, something made her itch all over. She was breaking out again. She lathered her hair, rinsed, rubbed in conditioner, leaned her forehead against the smooth ceramic of the cubicle wall. She closed her eyes and saw the enemy.

Back at Camp Chilliwack Abby had made a game out of the enemy recognition cards they'd all been given. It was a sort of mah-jongg or gin rummy, except instead of making sets by number or suit you had to make them by the shared characteristics of the enemy machines. This one, a thing like a walking mushroom that a UN committee or computer had named the AG-7 *Grauekappe*, Abby classified "bipedal." As she did this one, the dumpy, vaguely human-oid AM-3 *Zwerg*. But the *Grauekappe*, at forty meters plus, was also "gigantic" and so could make a set not only with the *Zwerg* but also with the MC-11 *Wiatrak*, spindly and three-legged. Or so Abby had said as she took the trick.

It had seemed funny at the time, and probably served the purpose the cards were meant for, inasmuch as it helped the test candidates of Camp Chilliwack memorize the different shapes and sizes. But even back then Maddy had seen that what the otaku-obsessive cataloguing mostly did, the profusion of numbers and abbreviations and code names that might have come out of Jacob's anime collection, was mask UNPROCON's ignorance regarding the zones and regarding the enemy, an ignorance that was deep and practically total.

Now behind Maddy's closed eyes, the alien shapes moved gray and blue between white stuccoed houses, were chased across the Colombine's screens by cursors and reticles. She remembered looking down into a railroad cut overhung with green under a gray sky, a parked string of heavy freight cars, angular black metal forms folding and tearing like foil as the *zwergs* and *hryuks* slammed through them, tumbling along the cut away from Maddy's fire. Remembered the shadow of the *grauekappe* above her, and then the shocking brightness of its weapon, the way it cleaved in an instant through rock and vine and concrete, shearing away a building-sized chunk of city so that for a moment Maddy saw pipes and wires and foundations and bedrock, before a water main exploded into a linear cloud of steam and Maddy was throwing the Colombine forward into the cover it gave, down onto the tracks, the cockpit at the Colombine's heart spinning like a hamster ball to keep Maddy upright as they rolled, and then they were down on the tracks and Maddy's finger was on the trigger, cutting down the smaller machines with the Colombine's rifle, sticking to the mission, finishing the job. Saving the world.

She'd turned back to the *grauekappe* then, four times the height of the Colombine, not an opponent but a rude adult about to stomp flat child-Maddy's robot sandcastle; and she'd aimed the Colombine's rifle at the glowing blue eyes beneath the enemy machine's spreading mushroom-cap, watching the white light of the beam weapon building in its shocked round O of a mouth; and Maddy had been surprised to realize that even though she might be about to die she was happy.

And then the Pierrot had been there, in the way, Tanimura getting up in the thing's face, spoiling its shot and Maddy's too, and the *grauekappe* had leapt backward, strangely graceful, three times its own height from a standing start, over a tall building in a single bound and gone.

Maddy opened her eyes. She rinsed the conditioner from her hair and turned off all the taps. As she squeezed the water from her hair she heard the locker-room door open and close.

She came out to find Captain Asano at the sink, washing her hands.

"Maddy-san!" In the mirror Asano saw the toothbrush Maddy was holding, and said, "Sorry. I'll only be a moment."

"It's all right," Maddy said. "I'll wait."

Asano finished what she was doing but made no move to turn around. Her English was much better than Tanimura's. It was Asano that relayed the orders, Asano's voice Maddy and Abby and Jacob heard in their helmets when they were on an operation; it was Asano who had drafted the letters to Hailey Peterson's parents and Oscar Jara's wife, though they'd gone out over the signature of some UNPROCON undersecretary. Abby had helped her with those.

When the Camp Chilliwack graduates had first arrived at the secret robot base Asano had already been there, and when she'd introduced herself to them Maddy had thought she was in her mid-twenties, but now she thought that had been makeup. Thirty? Thirty-five? Older? The pale UN blue wasn't a flattering color. Now Maddy realized she didn't really know what Asano's job was either. Radio operator? Translator? Babysitter? Object of vaguely Oedipal desire for Tanimura, picked out by UN psychologists after watching even more giant robot shows than Jacob?

That thought was cruel, and immediately Maddy was ashamed of it. Asano looked tired. There was nothing particularly wrong with the figure under the baggy fatigues; nothing particularly sexy about it either. It wasn't as though Asano was parading around the base in a sports bra and and Daisy Dukes.

Still. Maddy would bet any amount of money that the body under the blue cloth was what Tanimura thought about when he was trying to get to sleep at night. Or had been, till Maddy and Abby showed up. Even if the UN hadn't planned it that way.

Asano's eyes met Maddy's in the mirror, and Maddy had the uncomfortable feeling that Asano knew what she was thinking. She flushed. She wondered if the UN knew she was a dyke, if that was in a file somewhere and Asano had read it.

"You lived in Japan," Asano said.

Maddy thought better of busting out her schoolroom Japanese this time and just nodded.

"How did you like it?" asked Asano.

Maddy shrugged. "It was all right," she said. It had been, apart from the first few months. And the last few.

Asano said, "I was there at Aoyama Gakuin when you took the preliminary tests."

Maddy remembered the tests. There had been a lecture hall and about three hundred Japanese teenagers in it, faces lit by laptop screens; the twenty or so expatriate kids there to take the English version had been corralled by the UN organizers, herded into a smaller lab with older desktop computers, tested on math and physics and logic, then on coordination and reflexes and spatial relationships, then on stranger things. Maddy remembered an even smaller room, part of the music school maybe, with a grand piano under a dust cover, where a middle-aged black man with a British accent had sat her in a sort of reclining pod like a first-class airline seat, covered her eyes with opaque red goggles, played low-frequency static at her through headphones for half an hour, and afterward brought out a flat, Victorian-looking box of wood and glass and asked her to pick individual butterflies out from a dusty collection. There had been some Japanese in UN uniforms watching while she did that; maybe one of them had been Asano.

"I'm sorry," she said. "I don't remember."

"It's all right," said Asano.

As far as Maddy knew, she was the only one, Japanese or expat, out of the three hundred-odd who'd taken the test that day to make it through to advanced testing. She wondered if Asano had remembered her.

Asano turned around at last. "Can I ask you a question?" she said.

Maddy shrugged again. "I guess," she said.

"Why are you here?" Asano asked.

Maddy stared at her for a long moment. They'd asked her the question, in various forms, three or four times in the course of the testing, and she'd given the kind of bullshit answers somebody in one of her dad's movies would have given: *blah blah* make a difference, *blah blah* save the planet. After a while they'd believed her, maybe, or maybe by then they'd just put enough money and time into her that they'd stopped caring why she was there so long as she did what she was told. And she could say the same thing now and it might even be true, but it would still sound like bullshit.

She just didn't want to get into it, the tangle of frustration and ambition and loneliness and credulity and outrage that had brought her here, that had made the Colombine seem like a better idea than graduating high school and going off to college or joining the army or just hitchhiking to Rhode Island and getting a job as a waitress, and she didn't want to get into it with Asano, and she particularly didn't want to get into it with Asano when she was standing in a bathroom on an oil rig in the Arctic Ocean wearing nothing but a towel and dripping cold water on her shower shoes.

Instead she asked, "Is it true that in Shenzen, last year, Tanimura ran away, and you had to drag him back?"

"Where did you hear that?" Asano asked.

Maddy didn't answer.

Asano sighed.

"Tanimura-kun…It hasn't been easy for him," she said. "Be good to Tanimura. He could use a friend."

"I'm not here to be anybody's friend, Captain Asano," said Maddy.

Thinking: No, you're here to be Tanimura's fucking backup band.

Asano said something to herself in Japanese that Maddy didn't catch a word of, and shook her head.

"What?" said Maddy.

"It isn't fair," said Asano, "what they're doing to you."

"We're saving the world," Maddy said. "No one told us it was going to be easy."

Asano put a hand on Maddy's damp shoulder.

"Maddy-san," she said. "The lady robot pilots in those anime Jacob likes to watch—they die. A lot. That doesn't have to be you." She let the hand drop. "気を付けて、ね?" she said.

And she left.

Maddy went to the sink, turned on the water, took out her toothbrush. 気を付けて. She knew that one. *Be careful*. As if she'd be here at all, if she was.

Maddy's parents had sent her to a therapist for a little while, when they were still living together, before the divorce was final. The therapist, a gray-haired, soft-spoken Chinese-American, had taught Maddy a breathing and meditation exercise that was supposed to reduce anxiety. He'd told Maddy to imagine a room, a quiet room somewhere deep in her mind, with a door she could close, leaving on the other side of it everything she was afraid of or angry at or that she just couldn't control—not to wish those things away or imagine them gone, but just to put them aside for a little while, put herself beyond their reach.

Maddy had imagined not a room but a beach, the ocean to her right and to her left a field of grass-topped dunes, herself seated comfortably on a rock. The door was there, in front of her, standing free on the pale sand, its white paint and the brass of its knob shining in the sun, and the world was still there on the other side, the noise of it just barely audible beneath the sound of the surf and of the wind in the grass.

Now Maddy was there, and the noise behind the door was louder, much louder; something was rattling the knob, trying to jiggle the old-fashioned key from the lock. Sooner or later something was going to break through.

Maddy, watching the door from her perch on the rock, discovered she was fine with that. Sooner or later something was going to break through; all right, it would break through. And when it did, Maddy was going to kick the shit out of it.

The drop goes wrong. Maddy knows it's going wrong as soon as the Colombine tumbles out of the back of the transport, curled fetal in its packed ball of parachutes and airbags, the cockpit whirling like a fairground ride to keep Maddy upright. Maddy and the Colombine fall out of the sky into the European zone, and every screen in the cockpit shows nonsense, then goes solid blue; the motors steadying the hamster ball seize up for a stomach-twisting moment, then let go, leaving Maddy turning slowly head-down as the Colombine continues to fall. She has time to decide that whatever's happened to the screens has done for the parachutes and the airbags as well, and that she's going to die; and that while she doesn't especially want to die, there's nothing she can do about it; and that she ought to have some last words, except there isn't anything she particularly wants to say to anybody; and that that's kind of sad.

And then the parachutes open. The Colombine lands, hard. Maddy feels its knees take most of the impact, feels it throw out one arm as it comes down in a crouch, but the screens stay blue and the controls, when Maddy works them, do nothing. The Colombine's alive, but the cockpit is dead.

Maddy levers the cockpit open with the emergency bar and climbs down, leaving the Colombine kneeling in the shadow of a house-sized boulder. The ground is cracked black rock, sloping up behind the Colombine to a snow-covered ridge, its top only a few hundred feet away. As she comes out into the sun Maddy finds grass and tiny white flowers, and a steep slope down into a narrow valley with across it another ridge, not as high as this one, its slopes lined with dark evergreens, pine or fir or something; Maddy's never been good with trees. The sun is redder than it should be—that's a zone thing—but it's warm, and Maddy sits down and takes off her helmet, and after a little while she lies down in the grass, looking up at the sky, cold blue with white clouds.

She's somewhere in the Alps, or what used to be the Alps, German or maybe Austrian. She can't say more specifically than that. She figures she's at least ten miles inside the zone, maybe more. They say the zones are bigger on the inside than on the outside, that it takes longer to walk out of a zone than it took to walk in. Maddy doesn't know how they know that, how many people have walked into a zone and then back out, but she supposes it must have happened a few times. They say the laws of physics are different in the zones, that that's why people who stay in the zones without the drugs get sick, why the living things that come out of the zones die so easily and the machines are so hard to kill. It doesn't, to Maddy's mind, adequately explain why those machines can only be stopped by teenagers with giant robots, but it's a fact that tanks and planes didn't do so well, so maybe it's true; and whatever's going on in the zones it's fucked up Maddy's GPS along with everything else.

She can feel the Colombine there where she left it, out of sight on the other side of the boulder; she's found she knows where it is, always, without thinking, the way she knows where her left hand is. She's never told the UN doctors about this, never talked about it even with Abby and Jacob, though she assumes they feel the same connection to the Scaramouche and the Pantalon. Maddy's part of the Colombine now and it's part of her: a mute external body, androgynous at best despite the name, sort of butch even, the long-limbed strength and slightly inhuman proportions of an El Greco saint in thirty feet of blood-red machinery, but part of her.

The Colombine is a weapon.

The Colombine is Earth's last hope, or nearly.

The Colombine is a job.

The Colombine is Maddy's other self.

The Colombine is broken.

If Maddy's anywhere near the war she can't hear it. She tries putting her ear to the ground like some kind of hunting elf in one of Abby's fantasy novels but feels stupid immediately, and stops. Now, her face turned back to the sky, she closes her eyes and hears the wind down in the valley, and somewhere a trickle of water. It would be so easy to fall asleep here. Maddy tries to remember the last time she fell asleep in the grass, and can't.

She's not going to sleep here. If she does, something will come along and step on her, or the drugs in her system will run out, or the zone will find some other way to kill her. Maddy gets up.

She follows the sound of the water up out of the cleft and across the slope, scrambles over some rocks, comes down into a space like a shallow bowl, where meltwater from the ridge has formed an oval pool about fifty yards long, ringed with gravel and gray mud.

There is a girl there.

She is squatting at the edge of the pool, all knees and elbows, trailing the fingers of one hand in the water. Maddy knows instantly that it's a girl, though she can't then say, and won't later be able to say, how she knows; and Maddy knows instantly that it/she is not human. She is dressed from head to foot in something dark blue and mirror-glossy, so that Maddy can see the clouds above and the rippling water below reflected in it. It rises to cover her head as well, and drops to cover the hand that's not in the water, so that only the skin of her hand and of her too-round face is uncovered; and that skin too is blue, or bluish, or maybe a pale gray made blue by the blue around it.

The alien sees Maddy and instantly she straightens up, a quick, birdlike motion, and the glossy blue runs swiftly down her bare fingers and across her face, leaving only the eyes, not the inky black of a cartoon alien's but large and round and bright like the eyes of a lemur. Standing, she's even more obviously inhuman, her torso too long, her hips and shoulders too narrow, her waist nonexistent. But there's something beautiful about her all the same, beautiful and strange, the more so as she seems to relax, and the armor or whatever it is withdraws again from her face and hands. It's hard to read that strange face, but Maddy thinks she looks expectant, or maybe a little puzzled.

Maddy comes down to the water, sliding a little on the loose rocky ground, and the alien stays where she is; then when Maddy stops about ten feet away she comes closer, one pale blue-gray hand extended, long fingers splayed. Maddy tugs off her right glove and raises her own hand to match the alien's. There's the tiniest crackle of static electricity as their fingers meet. Maddy laughs.

And then the alien's head clicks round to train those wide eyes on something over Maddy's left shoulder, and she grabs Maddy's hand in a cool, strong grip as if by reflex; and then as Maddy turns to see Tanimura, frozen at the top of the slope, the alien drops Maddy's hand as quickly as she took it. Her attention flickers from Tanimura to Maddy and back, her strange face agitated and unhappy. And then she jumps away, that blue armor flowing over her, mounding into strange forms that disguise the thinness of her body, opening out around her head like an umbrella or the brim of an enormous round hat, so that Maddy can no longer see the bright eyes.

Then she's getting bigger, somehow, as she retreats, heavier, wider, taller, impossibly tall, tall as the icy ridge, so that Maddy has to tilt her head back to take the blue shape in. And as Tanimura scrambles past her down the gravel slope and out into the water, hands outstretched, crying, the alien jumps back, seeming to hang for a moment between the snow and the sky, and Maddy recognizes the shape now, from the railroad cut and from Abby's card game, and the broad cap tilts back and Maddy recognizes the eyes and the mouth that she'd been so sure meant death; and then the alien is gone.

Tanimura is still moving, still wading out into the pool; it's almost up to his waist. Maddy wonders if she's going to have to drag him back. And then he stops, suddenly, and turns around, and sloshes his way back to the shore. He squats down and puts his head in his hands. After a little while he looks up.

"ばか," he says.

Maddy knows that word. *Dumbass.* Or something like. But she doesn't think he means her. Maybe he means himself. Maybe he means it's a dumb-ass situation. Or a dumb-ass world. She can't say she disagrees.

The Colombine's cockpit stutters to life as soon as the Pierrot comes near. Together Maddy and Tanimura make their way down off the mountainside, find a road leading out of the zone, and follow it till they find a stretch of autobahn long and straight enough for the transport to land. Maddy speaks briefly to Asano over the radio; she doesn't say anything to Tanimura. She hasn't figured out what she wants to say.

Aboard the transport, the Colombine secure in its cradle, Maddy powers the cockpit down again and sits in darkness. The amphetamines they gave her at the start of the mission are wearing off; she can feel it.

She closes her eyes. She wishes she had a home, so that she could feel homesick for it. In the dark, she sees the alien girl.

Back at the secret robot base she finds Tanimura in his cabin. It's not the *hikikomori* rathole she's been expecting. Apart from a few books, a Sony laptop, and a scattered deck of the recognition cards, there's no real sign anybody lives there. Tanimura is sitting on the bunk, playing some game on his phone, or maybe texting somebody. He stops when Maddy comes in.

"I figured it out," she says. "On the way back. She thought I was you, right? You met her before. That's why you ran away. But I bet they can't tell us apart, and she thought I was you."

Tanimura doesn't say anything.

"It's all a lie," Maddy presses on. "Everything they've told us about the zones, about the enemy. Isn't it? Maybe they're not lying to us on purpose, but it's all bullshit. They don't know anything. You and me, we know more than they do."

Tanimura just looks at her. Maddy can't tell if he understands her or not.

"Look," she says. "I want to help, okay? Who is she? What's her name?"

"Name?" Tanimura says.

"名前," Maddy says. She goes to the desk, finds the card, holds it up. "Hers."

Tanimura looks at the card, then up at Maddy.

"*Grauekappe*," he says levelly. "AG-7."

Maddy stares at him.

"Okay," she says, dropping the card to the floor. "Fuck you too."

She can't get into the hangar. She wants to climb into the Colombine's cockpit and put six inches of red metal between herself and the world, but they aren't going to let her do that. She goes to the simulator room instead, and climbs up into one of the big white boxes and closes it and sits there unseeing as the computers run it through its routine, never touching the controls, so that she dies again and again; and then she wipes her eyes and opens the box and gets down.

The Indifference Engine by Project Itoh

Translated by Edwin Hawkes

We straddle over the twenty or so corpses that are scattered about on the red clay and reach the top of the hill.

I imagine for a moment that I'm looking down on a huge ocean that's reflecting back the stars of the night sky. The blue-black vista is sprinkled with glittering clusters of light.

It's not really water I'm staring down at though, and I know it. Those lights are people. That distant twinkling is people cooking, studying; it's families gathering after a long day.

That light. That warmth. I take a deep breath. The acrid gun smoke all around us, the smell of burning flesh, the stench of blood and guts, of shit and piss that's seeped out of the dead bodies— it all merges into one. For a moment it seems that I can also smell the scent of the living as it drifts over from the glittering mass of light in the distance.

I sense wild animals watching us, warily keeping a safe perimeter. They're biding their time, waiting for their opportunity to chow down on the mangled corpses we've so casually scattered about the place. When the white men first came to this country they were shocked at how you only needed to step beyond the narrow

confines of the city before the feral underbelly of this savage continent exposed itself.

Forward march! I call out, my voice calm.

Some of the guys are taking their time, others are impatient
to get going. We each advance at our own pace. No need to bother
anymore with the pretense of trying to step in time.

Fat, thin, lanky, short—we all start moving. Walking, climbing
down the slope.

The gentle breeze that meets us carries with it the bustling
smell of life, and we advance.

I think back to the day the war ended. At the exact moment I
heard the orders for ceasefire, the tip of my AK had been shoved up
against my friend's head.

This fucked-up situation had come about due to a terrible coincidence. Earlier that day orders had come down for us to kill everyone
in the encampment. Not just the SLF fighters and their command-
ers, but every last one of the children and women too, even the
pregnant ones. Our ambush was a success, and we captured the
frontline base with only five or so casualties on our side, but then
we were faced with a lot of Xema women—the womenfolk of our
tribe. Kept women for the enemy leaders—bed-warmers, there to
be used and abused at a moment's notice.

The SLF—the Shelmikedmus Liberation Front—were from the
Hoa tribe.

That's why our orders from above were to massacre the girls
along with the rest of them. We couldn't risk trying to mount a
rescue mission. The Hoa who managed to escape would have had a
field day. The shit they'd talk about us. Even more importantly, if any
of the girls were with child, their babies would be tainted by Hoa

blood. Just thinking about it gave me the creeps. The very idea that womenfolk from our tribe could have their children.

That's how they do things, we'd been taught over and over by our leaders. They pollute our bloodlines with their filthy blood, and at the rate they're going it won't be long before they manage to wipe the Xema tribe from the face of the African continent. The Hoa abduct our womenfolk so that they can eradicate the Xema.

I shuddered. Just thinking about a Hoa face made me feel sick. Ugly eyes so far apart, big flat noses. Just like toads. The white men in the Peace Corps apparently can't tell them apart from us. That pisses me off, it's ridiculous. Nothing on Earth is uglier than a Hoa. As for me, I almost felt that we'd be doing the girl prisoners here a favor by killing them—at least they'd die with their honor intact and wouldn't have to suffer the indignity of whelping ugly Hoa brats.

So orders came down to kill them all, and that's where it all went tits up.

Ndunga had become separated from his younger sister a few years ago, and it turned out she was among the unlucky ones held captive in the base. Ndunga discovered this fact during the battle and decided to take it upon himself to go against orders and try and rescue her. Well, he failed. The captain shot her dead himself, so I hear, though I wasn't there to witness it. Our platoon moved out as soon as we set fire to the village that had been serving as their outpost.

It was after we'd reached a safe distance and had stood down that the shit really hit the fan. We had our debriefing by the riverbank as we drank and refilled our canteens. Our leaders wasted no time in getting straight into the postmortem for the battle. Had any of our soldiers wasted any bullets on unnecessary fire? Had we let any standards slip? And just at the end of all the usual debriefing schtick, Ndunga's name was dropped like a bombshell.

The captain hauled Ndunga out in front of all of us and denounced him. This traitor put the whole company at risk, and what's more he conspired to pollute the Xema bloodline, we were told. Ndunga didn't even make the slightest effort to justify himself by explaining that the girl was his sister. The captain proceeded to kick seven shades of shit out of my comrade and then pointed at me. He's your friend, he said, and you should take care of this. That's what the captain said to me. You know what to do, don't you, asked the captain. And, of course, I did. Since joining the army I'd seen no end of cowards and traitors be executed.

That said, I'd never actually killed one of my own comrades with my bare hands, let alone a comrade who I also considered a friend. Ndunga had joined the SDA around the time I had. Both of us had seen our villages burnt to the ground and our fathers, mothers, friends—everyone we had ever known in our lives before the war, in fact—murdered. Ndunga had thought his sister dead right up until the moment he discovered her in that Hoa base. All the people he once knew—from the moment he was born right up until the moment he began his military career—were all dead, vanished from this world.

Well, anyway, I got up, and, anyway, I lifted my gun, and, anyway, I had it trained on Ndunga's head, but I found that I lacked the strength in my finger to pull the trigger.

I was trembling. It was like that moment three years before when I first killed a man.

I vaguely remember hearing the captain saying that if I couldn't pull the trigger I'd be executed alongside Ndunga. But I was so zoned out in terror I wasn't even sure if that's what I really heard. My fingertips were going numb. My confidence in my ability to ever be able to pull the trigger was seeping away rapidly.

At that very moment I heard a soldier's voice in the distance. War's over, came the cry. Central command's declared a ceasefire, all troops return to base.

I looked toward the voice. It was Muriki from Comms, waving his arms. The war was over—but I felt neither joy nor relief.

None of us did. Not one man from the once thirty-strong company.

Truth be told, none of us really knew how we were supposed to react to this new development. I seem to remember we all just stood there, slack-jawed. Probably 'cause we all found it so hard to remember how we'd passed our days back before the war started. Now what, seemed to be the prevailing sentiment. Apparently the thought of what we'd do once we'd gotten rid of all the Hoa bastards had never crossed our minds.

A shot rang out.

I turned around to see a wisp of smoke rising from the muzzle of a handgun. While I was at it I looked in the direction the gun was pointing, to see the head of my comrade. It now sported a small reddish-black hole in its left temple and a bright red mass of blood and brains spurting out of its right temple. I noticed something weird: Ndunga's eyes were staring straight into mine, even as he lay there, spread across the ground. Probably a coincidence, but I've never been able to shake off that mental image since. Why, why. Why did I have to die.

"The war may be over," the captain had said, returning his gun to his holster, "but we're still an army here, and military rule has to be followed. Protocol is protocol." The captain sighed before turning away, and it occurred to me that he wasn't addressing this comment so much to me as to Ndunga's corpse.

Earlier that day the Government Forces, the SLF, and the SDA—that's us, the Shelmikedmus Democratic Alliance—had agreed on a multilateral ceasefire, brokered by the white men from the Netherlands, the country that used to rule this land. And because the Americans had for some time been using its weird technology to support that unholy union of blood-traitor Xema and filthy Hoa fucks that now called itself the Government Forces, it was a major embarrassment to the Americans when the Dutch negotiators apparently emerged from nowhere to conclude a quick and effective three-way armistice.

Perhaps that was the reason why there were so many American troops stationed in our capital, Heaven City. To try and convince themselves that they had been the real peacemakers after all.

People were thronging the open-air stalls at the crossroads, and these bizarre black machines were floating overhead, flying saucers with fans grafted onto them. Now and then one would take off like a low-altitude airplane. They were not quite big enough to fit a person inside them, but they were incredibly fast. Then there were robots trundling along on their thirteen legs, looking and moving like some sort of insect, not that you could find an insect that muscular and powerful anywhere in the natural world. Thinking about it, there weren't really so many Americans here as it seemed at first glance, not in the sense of actual American people. They were around, of course, the American soldiers, but even these were matched one for one by their various machines. It had always been this way, even during the war. At least it had been whenever we'd been up against the Government Forces backed by their US technology.

The Government Forces had sent these machines into battle with us on occasion. Our main enemy might have been the dirty SLF bastards, but the Government Forces—Xema and Hoa working side by side—had been our enemy too. I'd heard there had been a time when we Xema were forced by circumstances to ally with them, but apparently a cowardly betrayal from their side had put paid to that idea. Must've been down to the Hoa section of the Government Forces. Not only were they ugly and brutish, they had a treacherous streak running through them a mile long, the Hoa, so it must have been their fault. Anyhow, the Government Forces would beg, borrow, or steal these half-living-half-machines from the Americans so that they could throw them in our paths, these mechanical freaks that sported miniature cannons and machine guns and could move of their own accord and would flock together to gang up on you. They moved like living creatures on their thirteen legs, and then they'd do something so quick, the sort of strange maneuver that only a machine can make, and they would be behind us, bearing down on us. I could barely count the number of my comrades that were killed by the things.

The subhuman thugs that were the Hoa, and inhuman beasts employed by the opportunistic Government Forces. That's what we'd been up against, and in the course of fighting them, can you blame us if we started to think that we were the only ones who were normal, human? If we didn't win and drive the Hoa out decisively, our country would be lost. I'd been bombarded with this message so incessantly that I believed it with all my heart—at least, I did at the point the war ended.

"You've had a tough time of it, haven't you?" the white doctor said, looking at me with pity.

Now, I didn't particularly have anything against this white man, but I wanted to yell at him anyway—butt the hell out of what doesn't concern you.

Anyway, there had been this incident, and after that these white doctors had descended on our school one day and started interviewing all the so-called problem children one by one. I say "school," but it was really some sort of fancy-schmancy institute, designed to prepare us for the brave new world with no more war. The House of Smiles. Awful name, awful place. The adults who ran the institute preached all kinds of shit at us, enough to make you want to puke. The war is over, they would say. Gone is the necessity to fight and hate each other, they would say. So stop hating the Hoa and learn to study and work alongside them, they would say.

Fuuuuuuuuuuuck that.

I—we—weren't going around killing the Hoa out of "necessity." Oh no. "Necessity" never came into the equation. It's not as if we were being forced to bear some great cross called "necessity" or anything. We didn't grin and bear it out of "necessity." No. What had happened was we had completely transformed into children who knew nothing else, who couldn't conceive of doing anything else. They were going around killing us, so we needed to go around killing more of them. That was the setup. How the world worked. Necessity, or duty, or anything else you wanted to call it, didn't even come into the picture.

So, the institute. Hoa were walking around freely. The same Hoa who had raped and murdered my mother and sister were walking around without a care in the world, and we were being fed this malarkey about how we shouldn't hate them or want revenge. So I decided one day that I would just think of our new instructors as machines. Heartless, unthinking automatons. Made in America. Just like the floating fans that hovered overhead in the alleyways, or the thirteen-legged freaks that pursued us when we retreated into the caves to escape from their armored vehicles. They were machines that looked and sounded alive at first glance, but a closer inspection would reveal they were empty on the inside.

I was in a foul mood. I didn't have any of the Khatsticks I'd become so used to chewing on the battlefield, nor any dope. We used to use gunpowder in a pinch, snort that when we were out of the good stuff, but now that they had taken away our guns and ammo we couldn't even fall back on that. Even a smidge of gunpowder would have been enough to zone me out. Enough to ignore the fact that a Hoa bastard was sitting right next to me. As it was, though, I was full to the brim with rage and pent-up frustration.

So long as I was in such a state, throwing me into a classroom along with a bunch of Hoa and telling me to get along nicely was a recipe for disaster. You might as well have ordered me to flip out and start mowing down my classmates with a machine gun.

All things considered, I reckon I did pretty well to hold out for a whole month.

Now, there was no doubt at all about the fact that these guys had attacked Xema villages, burnt them to the ground, killed our people, violated our women. They wouldn't have been here otherwise. The House of Smiles was specifically for former soldiers. If they were Hoa and they had been soldiers, it was inconceivable that their hands weren't steeped in the blood of a thousand rapes and murders.

So when I noticed a bunch of them in the corner pointing at me and laughing, I knew the time had come.

I'd been preparing for this moment, this instant, for some time: I'd taken pains to make sure I always had a sharpened pencil on me. I'd known this moment would come sooner or later, and that it was my destiny. No questions asked.

When the moment finally came I was relieved.

I didn't even need to harden my resolve. My body moved naturally, and I found my target, in the form of the back of the hand of the disgusting Hoa nearest to me.

"Mondays are bad enough as they are," I said, driving the point of the pencil deeper and deeper into the gaping and bleeding wound, "without having to look at your ugly fucking face."

The Hoa squealed like a pig, but I knew that was just an act. The captain had told us as much. Hoa don't feel any pain.

Just as I thought of the instructors as robots, the Hoa were basically just machines too. Sure, they showed all the outward signs of experiencing pain—they writhed around in agony, with tears and snot and drool streaming from their faces—just like we did, but that was no more than an act they put on to try and manipulate us, designed to try and make us feel sorry for them. In reality, they couldn't feel any pain at all. The captain once said to me that they were more or less like zombies. After all, if the Hoa bastards could feel pain there's no way they could have done the things they did to your father or mother or sister. It's only because they don't know what pain is that they can't imagine what suffering might feel like to other people, and that's how they could go around killing people without blinking—that's what the captain told me. And I found his logic pretty convincing.

"Hurts, does it? Of course it doesn't, right, you little Hoa fuck!" I shouted, driving the point of the pencil down further.

The classroom erupted in a melee, and a number of my friends rallied to my side. I pierced the Hoa's body over and over with my knifelike pencil, stabbing him with deadly accuracy, opening up more and more holes in his body. Not to be outdone by us the Hoa started flocking round, but without AKs this couldn't truly be called a real battle. We pushed, we shoved, we shouted at each other. When the dust was settled, though, not a single one of the happy inhabitants of the House of Smiles had died. Our little war just petered out.

I guess I'll be kicked out of this place now, I thought to myself.

I wondered where I was supposed to go next. Heaven City was already bursting at the seams with beggared children. I'd seen desiccated little corpses left lying there where they died in the street, unable to find any sustenance for themselves. Some were Xema children, others were Hoa, and sooner or later I would be joining their ranks. The people at the House of Smiles talked grandly of the day we would "graduate," but they couldn't keep us from knowing about the harsh reality of what was waiting on the outside.

If I'd still been a soldier I would have been able to obtain food by raiding Hoa villages, but the problem was we'd had our AK-47s taken away from us. Even though the war was now over—or rather, because the war was now over—we'd been plunged into a world of misery and hunger.

Surprisingly enough, I wasn't turfed out of the institute.

White men came. No—there had already been a few whites in the school. More accurate to say a new contingent arrived. They looked like doctors. A number of expensive-looking shiny black vans pulled up inside the grounds, and men in bright t-shirts and sunglasses poured out of them. The black vans had a large logo—a pretty cool design, if truth be told—plastered on their sides: "CMI."

I'd forgotten the name of the doctor who I found standing right in front of me at that moment, but I remember he said that he'd come to heal our hearts. So he must've been a doctor.

"What's CMI?" I asked, not even attempting to hide my wariness. "Are you anything to do with the SLF?"

"No, nothing to do with the SLF, son. Having said that, we're not related to the SDA either," the doctor answered calmly. "You used to be a soldier with the SDA, didn't you?"

"What's CMI?" I asked again. I didn't want any more of his sympathy or pity. I was tired of talking about my life as a soldier. And I was sick of this casual, meaningless sympathy, given so freely and worth so little, from these people who never once in their life had had to worry about where their next meal was coming from.

"CMI stands for 'Combat Medical Instruments.' It's English. If you translated it into your language, it would mean something like an organization for helping people with the problems they suffer from after battle."

"Yeah, I speak English. Not difficult words, though."

"Of course you do, son, forgive me. I see from your file you wanted to be a doctor? Your grades at school were top of the class too—you're quite the bright young man, I can see."

This blatant attempt at buttering me up pissed me off. "So what is it exactly that this CMI does?" I asked.

"Well, as I said, we try and help soldiers who have been hurt, in body and in mind. We also inoculate soldiers against anxiety and depression by giving them a little shot to the heart."

"A shot to the heart…"

"That's right. A jab, a shot. With the technology we have these days, we're not just limited to administering our injections intravenously. We can also give a little shot straight to the heart." The doctor looked into my eyes. "You'll find out soon enough for yourself."

Condescending fucker. Keeping things from me.

"So, why exactly have you CMI guys come here?" I asked.

When the doctor next spoke it was with the same calm tone of voice, but this time laced with a hint of pride and conviction. His voice now had the same determined quality as we'd had when we used to chant our SDA slogans. And I recognized that gleam in the eyes.

"We're here to put a stop to war in this country once and for all."

"The war's already finished," I said.

"Well, then. Let me ask you a question. Has the war finished for you?"

That stopped me short. Why was this doctor trying to stir things up, I wondered. The teachers here had been banging on about just the opposite. The era of hatred was over; the era of war was over. We weren't supposed to hate anybody anymore. We weren't supposed to kill anybody anymore either—that's what they had told us. Even though these adults knew full well that our lives so far hadn't exactly been picnics in the park, they had somehow managed to convince themselves that all they needed was to repeat these platitudes over and over, like a broken record, and all the bad things in our lives would somehow magically disappear. I wanted to stab the shit-spouting teachers over and over with a sharp knife, a scenario I'd daydreamed about many times. But externally I always ended up putting on a show—a brave face, stoically holding back my tears.

"All the people here say the war is over," I said. I doubted that I sounded convinced, or convincing.

"All the people here don't really believe that though, do they?

Not for a second," the doctor continued. "Surely you've worked that out for yourself by now?"

Perhaps it was Ndunga's battlefield execution just after the end of the war that had stripped me of any illusions. I seem to remember agreeing tacitly, unquestioningly, with the captain's pronouncement that protocol was protocol and that military order needed to be upheld. I was devastated that my friend had been killed, of course, but there was no denying that he had disobeyed a direct order. Regardless of whether the fighting was due to continue or not, the fact was that he had to be punished.

So that's how the war ended. Five seconds before my best friend died.

At least, that's what everyone kept on saying. That the war had ended. But, I wondered, how was I going to put an end to my own personal war?

Let me tell you how my war started.

I was on my way home from school, two rivers and a mountain away. Around the time I'd crossed the second river I noticed a plume of smoke rising from my village. As I got closer, the smell closed in on me. Not the usual smell of goat droppings or plants or animals, but a revolting stench. Before I knew it I had discarded my bookbag by the wayside, and I was running toward my village.

I stopped in my tracks at the entrance to the village to behold houses reduced to ashes and corpses scattered about the place. There were limbs piled up next to the chopping block where we cut our firewood, and the evil SLF were responsible. Later on I learned the full extent of what exactly they had done—after all, I ended up doing more or less the same thing myself to the other side. But at the time I couldn't even register what the mound of severed arms and legs, piled up like so much kindling, even was.

Overcome with dread, I rushed like a lunatic toward the place where my house once stood.

So, first there was Mom. I wasn't so concerned with the fact that her shirt was ripped to shreds and that her face had been beaten so badly it was a swollen mass. Mainly because she was prostrate and there was blood flowing copiously from the numerous open wounds on her back. The earth around her had drunk her blood and was stained reddish black. Next to her was Sis's body. Or rather Sis's corpse. My clever little sister Minnu. There was a bullet hole decorating her broad forehead. The SLF barbarians had repeatedly and mercilessly used her prepubescent body as a fucktoy. She wasn't even ten years old. Unlike Mom, Sis had been stripped completely naked, and semen was still dribbling from her spread-eagled crotch.

I'm pretty sure I fainted right then and there. It was too much to take in.

I wonder how long I lay there unconscious next to the dead bodies of my family. Eventually, though, I heard some voices, men's voices, register amidst the fog of my mind.

I still had no real idea what was going on, but I found myself gently propped up by a man in military fatigues. How ya holdin' up, kid, he asked, and then something else: Sorry, if only we'd got here sooner we wouldn't have let the SLF do this, get away with this.

The man held me up as I staggered out of the house to survey the scorched village. Mom was dead. Sis was dead. After having their last scraps of dignity ripped from them and after suffering more than any woman should ever have to suffer. Pop was gone too. Also killed, no doubt. M'tougwai from next door, who used to help me with my homework as if he were my brother, had his arms chopped off and his chest was riddled with bullets.

No one I had ever known was alive anymore.

And that's how I became a soldier with the SDA. So that I could see to it that every last one of the SLF was annihilated.

"You're absolutely right that a ceasefire has been declared, of course," continued the white doctor. "The Dutch managed to get the SDA, the SLF, and the Government Forces to agree on that. Now, do you know what 'DDR' means?"

I shook my head.

"It stands for Disarmament, Demobilization, and Reintegration. Basically, it's about getting former soldiers like you back into normal life. It's a vital part of ensuring that a war is well and truly over."

Bile rose up in me. DDR…particularly the last part of it. Reintegration…integration…Were we now supposed to somehow get along with the fucking Hoa? The words made me almost dry heave. Integration…If it came down to it I'd rather go down, AK-47 blazing, taking as many of those little shits down with me as I could before the police ended me. Rather that than be "integrated."

The doctor carried on speaking, blithely oblivious to the rage that was seething inside me. "So, let's see. The decommissioning of the weapons has started properly, hasn't it? You were given a sledgehammer so that you could destroy your AK-47 with your own hands, weren't you? And then you were freed from the army."

"Fired. Not freed."

"Come now, son, you weren't the only one who was 'fired,' as you put it, were you? Soldiers from all sides were 'fired,' young and old. Your new country only needs a small standing army, after all. That's what we mean when we talk about demobilization. A country at peace has no need of so many soldiers, and besides, children shouldn't really be fighting in the first place."

"I don't know about your country, Doctor," I replied, "but in this country, what 'should' happen and what does happen are two different things."

"Well, then," said the doctor, "I guess you could say I'm here to make sure that what 'should' happen does actually happen."

We were bussed over to the ruins of a place that had once been a five-star hotel somewhere in downtown Heaven City. American and Shelmikedian armored vehicles were parked outside, and both countries' national flags were flying. Next to these flags was another flag with a picture of the earth wrapped in a ring of leaves, and next to that yet another flag, this one with angels of yellow and cream and brown holding hands and forming a circle around the earth.

"What's that flag there?" I pointed and asked as I got off the bus. The doctor, who had gotten off right behind me, peered at it and replied, "That's UNICEF. It's an international organization dedicated to protecting children around the world."

Hmm, great job you're doing there, I thought but didn't say. I continued my questioning. "And what about the one next to that?"

"Oh, that's what's called an NGO. It's not a national or international organization, exactly. It's more like a civilian organization here to try and help the people of this country get back on their feet."

"What about this CMI that you're from, Doctor? Don't you have your own flag?"

"No, we've been hired in by MSD—that's short for *Monde Sans Divisions*," the doctor explained. "That's what this NGO is called. And we come under their banner."

The hotel had been abandoned during the war, and with no guests or even a skeleton crew to maintain it, it was now in a real state: a crumbling husk of a building with an empty, cracked swimming pool that now functioned as a giant trash can. Looking at the pool now it was hard to imagine it ever being full of water. It was as if the rectangular hole was the obvious thing to expect there, a natural part of the landscape.

As such it was hard to imagine that inside would be much better. It looked like these guys had set up camp here a few days ago. Cardboard boxes were scattered all over the place. The hotel was made of stone, like all the fanciest places were once upon a time, but right now it was a dump. The soles of the doctor's shoes clattered on the marble floor as he walked along.

"You'll have to excuse the mess," the doctor said with a hint of apology in his tone. "But up until three days ago there was even a pack of wild dogs roaming about the place, running through the corridors and guest rooms."

So what's happened to them now, I asked, and the response I got made me laugh.

"We got rid of them, of course. We had to make this place safe for you guys."

Safe. What a word to use. Up until recently there wasn't a single place in this country you could have called safe.

There were twelve of us in total who had been brought from the school, and now we were escorted into a large room. As I looked at a mural on the crumbling wall I thought what a beautiful room this would have been only a short while ago. It had a skinny guy in the middle who was glowing, with his arms outstretched, and around him were a bunch of men. It must have been painted by some of those Christians who used to run the country. It looked like the guys in the painting were at a dining table or something, but for some reason they weren't gathered around it but rather lined up neatly on one side. Each to their own, I suppose, but it seemed like a strange way to eat dinner to me. It almost made our own gatherings around the campfire chewing our Khatsticks seem normal.

Anyway, the room we were now in, it was full of lots of weird-looking chairs.

Almost like the robots used by the American forces. They were brand-spanking-new shiny, and I imagined that they were ready to grow a pair of legs and walk off at any time. The strangest parts of them, though, were the bucketlike contraptions attached to the tops of the chair backs.

"What are those things that look like buckets?" I asked, pointing at one.

"Well, after we've given you all your little shots, we'll just need you to put them on for a little while and take a little nap," the doctor explained. "Goes without saying they're perfectly safe, of course."

"Why do we have to put them on?" I asked.

"These are the things that are finally going to bring your war to an end," the doctor said. "As I said before, as long as you do this you'll be able to stay part of the program. You won't return to the House of Smiles, of course, but you'll be able to carry on your studies in peace at another institute nearby, and you'll be well looked after."

That's why I was here, after all; that's what was on offer. It was just me and my ilk who had been brought here from the House of Smiles. In other words, kids who had joined the SDA after they'd had their family and friends killed by the Hoa. We weren't the only kids who had joined the SDA, remember—some kids signed up because it had been the only way to get a full belly. But none of those kids were here with us in the hotel today.

"You keep on talking about this injection. What is it exactly?"

"Well, you remember how we were talking about the shot to the heart that we could give you? This is it."

"How does it work?"

"How does it work?" The doctor laughed nervously. "Uh, that's not the easiest thing in the world to explain, but I suppose I could try. You know what the brain is, right? It's the part of us that controls how we think or feel."

"Have you ever seen a brain, Doctor?" I asked him.

"No, well, I'm what you call a nanomachine technician. I'm not a brain surgeon."

Nanomachine, schmanomachine. This much I did know—I'd seen enough brains to last me a lifetime. Even if I'd never seen a whole one intact, as they were always messed up and spilling all over the place. What right did this guy who hadn't even seen a real brain have to lecture me about how they worked?

The doctor just carried on, though, completely unaware of how much of a fool he looked in my eyes. "To get a bit more technical, the procedure's called *Geistesgestaltbedeutungseinsatz-existenzlokalisierungsveränderungsausführung*. All you really need to know, though, is that we lightly, uh, modify your brain, so that you end up looking at the world in a slightly different way. We call it the Indifference Engine."

At the time I wasn't thinking too hard about what the "slightly different way" could mean. I am who I am, after all, and it's hard for a person to get his head around the idea that he could be any different from who he is.

I was more interested in asking whether the procedure had been tried out on anyone else. "I'm not being used as some sort of guinea pig, am I?"

"Not at all. There are plenty of people in my home country who've already had the same operation as the one you're about to get. They all chose to have it—it's an elective procedure. And even here in your country, there are quite a few adults who've had the operation and are working to make the world a better place. Take microfinancing, for example—oh, I guess you wouldn't know what that is, would you?"

"Not exactly," I replied.

"Microfinancing is where you lend money to people who just need a tiny bit of capital to get a business off the ground: seed money, it's sometimes called. Now, normally, the condition of the loan is that the person who borrows the money has to pay it back and then some. After all, the lender is entitled to make some profit, right?"

"I guess so," I said.

"Well, this extra amount is what we call 'interest.' Now, the NGO that employs us makes these sorts of loans to people who want to start businesses, but they give them a choice. The borrower can choose to pay back the money with interest, like with a normal loan. Or they can choose to have the shot to the heart. Many people go for the shot. Most of the traders you saw back at the market have already had it, for example."

This I didn't know. Still, I couldn't quite shake off a niggling feeling that there was something not quite right about all this, even if I wasn't the first to have the operation. It still felt like I was somehow being hoodwinked.

The doctor addressed the whole lot of us now. "Anyway, come on now, guys, the sooner you take a seat the sooner we can get you all home," he said, almost cajoling us into the chairs.

What did he mean by "home" anyway? We'd lost that to the Hoa many years ago. Not just "home": our villages had been wiped away completely. Where exactly was I supposed to go? As long as the war continued, I always had my company. That had been my home. War had been my home. What about now, though? Was the House of Smiles supposed to be my new home?

The doctor just didn't get it. I ignored him as he droned on and slipped into one of the chairs, which turned out to be surprisingly comfortable. I decided to focus on the reality in front of me—if I went through with this, at the very least I'd be good for another meal.

We were moved again.

To the east side of town this time, to a building that had a big billboard displayed up top reading Seeds for a Brave New World. This new building was closer to a residential area, and people from the neighborhood had come out to watch our arrival. Their stares were full of curiosity—and hostility.

When I realized I wasn't going to have to deal with those Hoa I had fought with, I breathed a sigh of relief. Half the class I was now with were guys who had fought alongside me back at the ruckus, the other half I didn't recognize at all. We all seemed roughly the same age, and I figured the others had probably been involved in similar incidents elsewhere. I doubt they'd thought to use a pencil like I had, though.

Something seemed strange when we entered the classroom. It was almost as if my field of vision had been wrapped in a warm, fuzzy blanket. At that moment I hadn't yet realized what had happened to my mind.

"I'm Ezgwai," said the softspoken boy who was sitting next to me.

"What did you do to make them send you here?" I asked by way of introduction.

For a second he looked as if he'd been slapped, but then he laughed. "You don't beat around the bush, do you?"

"We're all here for a reason—we're troublemakers. I just figure same goes for you guys," I said.

"Touché. I'm sure you've probably worked it out by now, but we've just been moved here from a place called the Second Chance Rebirth Saloon, over on the other side of town," Ezgwai answered.

"You guys ex-soldiers too?"

"Yep."

"Huh. So you were a soldier too, huh? Like me."

At this point Ezgwai seemed to bite down on his lip. As if he'd just remembered something he'd rather forget.

"My family were all killed," Ezgwai said. "My ma, pa, gran, my brother—all of them."

"What about your village?"

"Gone, I'm guessing. It was burnt to shit last I saw it. Most of us were killed, but I was one of the 'lucky ones' taken prisoner."

An orphan. Just like me. He too had seen his house put to the flame, seen the piles of arms chopped off by the Hoa machetes like so much firewood. We were hardly the only ones here who'd seen such atrocities firsthand, of course, but nonetheless the shared experience seemed to act as a bond between us.

"My family was murdered too. Same goes for everyone else in our class."

Ezgwai nodded in silent acknowledgment. There wasn't any more to say on the subject, and the conversation tapered off into an uncomfortable silence. Unable to bear it any longer, I decided to change the subject completely.

"Did you guys go to that weird hotel too?" I asked.

"You guys too, huh?" Ezgwai actually seemed surprised about this. "Yeah, we were made to sit down and put those barrel things on our heads after being pumped full of stuff."

"D'you know what they actually did to us?" I asked, my voice trailing off.

Ezgwai shook his head. "You?"

"Nah. One of the doctors did try explaining, but…"

"Forgot what he said, huh?"

I shook my head. "Something like that. There was this ridiculously complicated foreign word. Something to do with cutting something off or blocking or changing or something, I think. A million times more complicated than our classes here."

"I wonder if the teachers here would explain it to us if we asked them," Ezgwai said.

"Yeah, I wonder. I get the sense they're keeping something from us," I said.

Just then a teacher came into the room. A fat lady wearing a pearly white short-sleeved shirt. I wonder if she'd been raped too, I thought to myself. I couldn't imagine that there were many women left in this country who hadn't been raped at some point or another during the war. I'd done my fair share of rape after all. When we raided Hoa villages. The captain had said he'd kill me if I didn't, so what else was there to do? I was shit-scared the first time, but once I'd done my first I realized there was nothing to it, really. If you needed to empty your bladder you pissed in a toilet, and if you needed to empty your balls you raped a woman. So it went, and so I did what needed to be done.

But I did wonder which tribe would have had this fat woman. The Hoa? Or would it have been us Xema?

And that was when I started to realize that something was not quite right.

"Good day, gentlemen. Welcome to the place where you will prepare for a new chapter in your lives," said the fat lady.

Gentlemen. I looked around, surveying the others who were in the room.

"You have all been granted a new ability," Fatty continued. "An ability that will stand you in good stead for the future of our country. This new ability is already commonplace in Europe and America, and I guarantee you that it will free you from the shackles of hatred that are currently holding you back."

Her voice was soft, gentle, brimming with hopefulness—and gave me the creeps.

I leaned in toward Ezgwai. "They just don't get it, do they? I mean, it's not as if they don't know what we've been through."

Ezgwai suppressed a laugh. "You said it, bro. I do see where they're coming from, though. That sooner or later we're going to have to let it go, or we'll never be happy. Otherwise we'll never have peace, I guess."

"What about our mothers and sisters? They'll never be happy. Do we let that go too?"

"No, that'll always be with us," said Ezgwai, his face suddenly a picture of desolation. "And even when I know in my head that sooner or later we're going to have to let bygones be bygones, whenever I actually see someone who used to be the enemy...I see red. I feel like I'm going to explode with hatred. But what can I do? I don't have my AK-47 with me anymore, and even if I did, if I killed someone I'd just be imprisoned for murder. It's not like it used to be, when you could kill all you wanted."

"Well, we might not have our guns anymore," I replied, holding up the pencil I'd been given, "but this baby here can go a long way in a pinch. Trust me, I know."

Ezgwai and I became tight.

We lined up for rations together, and we helped each other out with our homework. He was a real good guy, was Ezgwai. He had his head screwed on too and was always there to calm me down whenever I was about to flip out over something. You could have called us opposites—could have, that is, if we hadn't shared the uniting factor that we'd both been driven into the army when our families had been killed.

Our actual classes were more or less identical to those we'd had back at the House of Smiles, with one key difference: the teachers seemed awful keen on speaking to us individually. Do you like it here? Anything that's annoyed you or made you feel angry recently? There seemed to be a constant barrage of questions like these. And there always seemed to be a white doctor by the teacher's side, tapping away at their keyboard.

"So, can you tell me why you're feeling grumpy?" Fatty asked me one day.

I nodded. "I guess 'cause I got no Khatsticks or gunpowder."

"That's the reason, is it?" Fatty gave a sympathetic nod of her head. As if to show she understood my pain. All this did, though, was piss me off even more.

Fatty continued regardless. "We call those sorts of things drugs. If you carried on using them you would have destroyed your bodies."

"I feel so irritable without them though," I said.

"And what about your friends? Have you noticed any of them fighting? Anyone you particularly don't like?" Fatty continued.

"Fighting?" I asked. "Not really—what do we have to fight about?"

Fatty and the white doctor exchanged glances. Then she smiled at me again. "Looks like we're making progress." She rubbed her eyes. And then I realized it was to wipe away her tears. She seemed deeply moved by something.

"By the time you young men become fully fledged adults this country should be a wonderful place again. A gentler place where the terms 'Xema' and 'Hoa' are nothing but irrelevant old labels. Even though at the moment it might seem like all you can think about is hatred, it won't be long before you breech that final frontier. You'll explore strange new worlds together. You boys are our hope incarnate, you are new life. We adults have been irredeemably corrupted by our hatred. But you're different. You'll be able to leave this place and boldly go where no man has gone before. You'll found new civilizations, a new Shelmikedmus."

With that, Fatty rose from her seat and enveloped me in her ample bosom with a tight hug.

The main feeling I experienced at that moment, with my face pressed into her massive tits, was an uneasy sense that something wasn't quite right about what she had just said. I wondered from where this woman's hopes and dreams were springing. Personally, I'd seen too much—and done too much—to expect anything good from this world.

I had settled into life in Brave New World after a fashion. Things were much easier now I didn't have to live side by side with Hoa. Back when I was at the House of Smiles, all I could think of during lessons was the fat jugular running down the neck of the Hoa bastard sitting next to me and ramming my pencil right into it. It was far too febrile an atmosphere for their lectures about how we should all get along in peace to have any effect at all back then.

In fact, they often had the opposite effect, stirring things up even more.

I was a part of the community now, though. Ezgwai's serene demeanor was a calming influence on me. Ezgwai was so gentle, so thoughtful, so considerate, that I often thought it a miracle that he ever survived in the army.

Ezgwai always spoke steadily. Deliberately. Whereas most of us soldiers had become used to barking at each other, fighting to get a word in edgewise over the din of gunfire. The result was that even when the battlefield was a distant memory, we were still used to shouting over each other all the time.

"I am," was Ezgwai's simple reply when I asked him if he was deliberately trying to go in the other direction by speaking quietly and slowly. "When I'm shouting and spitting words out like there's no tomorrow, I can't help but feel I'm back on the battlefield. So I decided to make a conscious effort to speak calmly at all times. I guess I kind of hope that it might catch on, in time."

And catch on it did before too long. Whether or not it was all down to Ezgwai's deliberate efforts, it wasn't long before everyone at the institute had stopped shouting all the time and started speaking much more calmly. Including me. Once this happened, it became possible for us to start thinking of the institute as a place where you could actually relax, chill out.

Not only that, it was much easier for me to relax because I hadn't seen a single Hoa from the moment I arrived at Brave New World. At least, it was easier to relax right up until the moment I discovered we had been living a lie.

"Bro."

I'd been standing in line in the mess hall one day when Ezgwai spoke to me. Standing there with my enamel bowl, waiting patiently for my state-mandated ration of synthetic meat. The real stuff was way out of our league pricewise, I'd heard—real meat something only the white man's countries could afford. After all, they could even afford to use stuff like maize and wheat as fuel for their cars and airplanes, apparently. Hard to believe you could really power a car on food.

"Whassup, bro?" I replied. Then I noticed Ezgwai's face was something real strange. Warped, twisted, like he wanted to cry and was suppressing something incredible.

"I heard that you took part in the raid on Minga Village," he said.

"Hey, why are you asking me about the war all of a sudden?" I asked. "And who told you that anyway?"

Ezgwai dropped his container and brought his face right up close to mine. I could feel the breath from his nostrils on my cheek.

"Thankwa told me. Thankwa from the same company as you," he said.

I'd fought alongside Thankwa in the same company for a long while. I suppose you'd call him a comrade. He'd been one of the first to join in the melee when I sprung that Hoa bastard with my sharpened pencil, and naturally he'd been sent here with me.

"Bro. Please. Just tell me. Were you or were you not part of the raid on Minga?" Ezgwai asked.

I'd no idea why he was being like this. "Calm down, man. We're talking about an op from three years ago, you know?" I said. "Yeah, I remember, that village was a key point in the Hoa supply lines. Quite a battle. Yup, it's coming back to me now."

Then Ezgwai fell dead silent, his gaze fixed on mine. It was as if he'd forgotten he needed to breathe. His eyes were unnaturally wide, and his teeth were gritted behind his tightened lips.

"Minga Village was my home," he said.

I didn't understand. I looked into his eyes, which were now filmed over. How would Ezgwai have been living in Minga? Minga didn't have any of our captives…

Then it hit me. The true meaning behind Ezgwai's awful, twisted face.

And what his face *didn't* mean.

"Ezgwai…what tribe are you from?" I asked.

But I already knew. I knew then why I hadn't seen any Hoa since arriving here. While we were at it, what tribe was Fatty from? Hoa and Xema were different species. Hoa were subhuman. The Hoa had completely different faces from us Xema. Didn't they?

But the reason I hadn't seen any Hoa since arriving here was simple: I could no longer tell who was Hoa and who was Xema.

That's why I had automatically assumed that everyone here was Xema like me. It hadn't even occurred to me to wonder what tribe people were from. I'd been lulled into a false sense of security, and that's why I'd just presumed that Ezgwai must have been Xema too.

Don't answer my question, I prayed in my heart, even as the words were escaping my lips. But there was no going back.

Ezgwai gave an unearthly yell and jumped me.

I had no time to react or hit back. The back of my head smashed into the floor, almost knocking me out. But fortunately (could you call it fortunately?) my eyes remained open, and I was conscious that Ezgwai was on sitting on top of me, fist raised up high.

His fist came down, burying itself in my face.

I tasted blood in my mouth. Before I had the chance to recover from the surprise attack another blow rained down on me, and this time smashed into my left temple. I was reminded of the time the captain fired that bullet into Ndunga's head.

"I was born in Minga!" Ezgwai yelled through his tears. A fist came down for the third time, shattering my nose. I heard the crunch from inside my skull, and the next second blood was pouring out my nostrils. "You killed my family!"

Another blow was flying toward the right side of my face. At this rate I was going to be smashed to a pulp. I'd better play my cards right, I thought to myself. Better try and avoid the next blow.

"I'm a Hoa! A Hoa man!"

And then, somehow, I managed to raise my right arm to deflect the incoming fist, and at the same time shoved Ezgwai off me with my left arm, and used all my pent-up energy to spring up onto my feet.

Ezgwai landed on his ass, and I used the opportunity to get the hell out of there. I had no intention of fighting after taking the hits I'd taken, and anyway I needed a moment to figure out what had happened to my head. And when I say "what had happened to my head" I wasn't talking about what Ezgwai had just done to me with his fists. I figured it had to do with when I was back at that ruin of a hotel, when the white doctors injected me with something as I wore that bucket on my head.

"Why? Why are you a Xema?" came an anguished cry from Ezgwai, already in the distance. I hardened my heart. I wasn't going to listen; I needed to block his voice completely.

Driven by something primal, I ran straight out of the mess, and before I knew it I found myself outside the institute too. I was terrified of returning. I couldn't tell the difference between Xema and Hoa there. Between friend and foe.

In other words I was out of my mind. After all, it didn't even occur to me at that moment that there was no reason things should be any different in the outside world.

I had nowhere to go.

I'd been effectively confined to different institutions ever since the war had ended and I was released from the SDA, so I had no real idea of the geography of the city. Or rather, I had no real idea of the important things: safe places to go to make myself scarce, or places I could go to scrounge a bite to eat.

There were plenty of children who didn't make it into an institution. Not just children, of course, but adults too. But the children, well, they had formed themselves into gangs and roamed the city's slums. They kept their AK-47s well out of sight from the occasional American patrols, and sold Khatsticks just as they did during the war.

At this moment it seemed to me the most unlucky thing in the world that I'd been "rescued" by an institution, because it meant I hadn't had the opportunity to join one of these gangs. That's how it seemed to me right now anyway. I didn't know the layout of the town, how it had changed since the war ended, who lived in which sector, who ruled the streets where. I had no idea about any of the things that actually mattered.

In other words, I was fucked.

When I tried to root through a pile of trash to see if I could find anything useful, I heard someone shout, "You piece of Xema shit!" Before I knew it I was surrounded by kids. Orphaned Hoa children, I guess they must have been. I couldn't help but think how full of energy and life they seemed.

Now, because I'd spent so much time in institutes, my garbage-foraging skills were distinctly lagging behind those who'd had more experience in it. But that was the least of my worries. There was a pecking order to the various dumps and skips that littered the town. There were turfs, patches, cribs, and the best spots, those with the juiciest hauls, were all taken. I didn't know this at first, and almost died when I tried to approach a spot that was already spoken for—by Hoa.

Sharp kicks. Feet digging into my gut. I hold my breath, and now it's fists, flailing, coming at me. Now it's my jaw that's smashed. My face is slammed, I fly back, and now a leg is pinning my chest down. I'm forced down into the pile of trash.

"Easy, guys, easy. We're ruining good food here. Throw this punk off the heap."

Someone gives orders, I'm hauled off the trash pile and bundled down onto the road beside it. And that's where they properly put the boot into me.

Who said that wartime hatred was dead?

Every kick digging into me felt like payback for each bullet I fired during the war. But how was I supposed to avoid this? I had no way of telling whether I was on Xema turf or Hoa. And I had no way of telling in the future. I could always have gone up to the gang first to ask them which they were, but doing so would have put me at a fifty-fifty risk of being half killed. Killed, maybe even.

The orphans of this town weren't done with their war yet. They were fighting over the castoffs and the scraps of "generosity" shown by the white men and the rich people of the city. They weren't quite shooting each other up to protect their neighborhoods and their sources of sustenance, but otherwise it was just like before.

Are you Xema or are you Hoa? This question was now more important than ever. If you wanted to eat, that was.

For a while I was so desperate that I thought about raiding a store, but I had no gun and no comrades to help me. In any case, I wouldn't have been able to tell whether I was attacking a Hoa- or Xema-run shop. It wouldn't have been right to raid Xema.

The upshot of all this was that because I was now the proud owner of a brain that had no way of telling the difference between one tribe and another, I also had no way of finding a way to eat. I grew thinner and thinner.

After a while, I grew accustomed to my new, emaciated state, and could even contemplate it objectively. I was able to compartmentalize my raging hunger, push it to the back of my mind where it no longer bothered me, even as it gnawed away inside me. Yes, it was like I'd been shot through the heart, all right. I'd had my birthright taken away from me: the ability of anyone born in this country to instantly distinguish between Hoa and Xema.

Anyway, I was lying by the side of the road, about to waste away, when a voice called out to me.

"Long time no see."

I heard this voice call to me indistinctly, far far away from a place that could have been called consciousness. *Who is it?* Even the thought was too much for me. I was fading away, after all, getting smaller and smaller until soon I'd be dwarfed by a single grain of sand and then, finally, disappear into nothing. I'd been collapsed here for the last few days with this single thought spinning round in my mind. Even opening my eyelids was a herculean task. Everything was too much for me—I was almost past caring.

"Hey, can you hear me?"

Maybe I can't, I thought. *What can I hear, what could I hear?* I didn't rightly know anymore.

"Carry him, will you?"

I was lifted up. Up, up, like a fluffy cloud floating away in the sky.

At some point in time I was laid down on something. Somewhere softer and much nicer than where I was before.

"Feeling any better yet?" It was my old captain. He handed me a bowl of soup.

I had only ever seen the captain in combat fatigues, but even though he was now wearing the sort of leather jacket white men wore, he was instantly recognizable by the gold chains and other wartime bling he used to wear. Also unchanged was the holster strapped to his waist, gun-strap open, so that he was always ready to draw and fire at a moment's notice.

The big difference was in his eyes, in his manner. He'd gone so soft it was almost uncomfortable. Almost like he'd become one of those Christian priests.

I nodded and took the bowl of soup.

"This ain't your government-approved synthetic rations, you know. This here's real beans and real meat," the captain said.

I wolfed the soup down. A few short days ago I'd been on the brink of starvation, and now I was in an empty warehouse in the middle of the slums, being pampered back to health. Nothing we had to eat at the institute ever tasted as good as this.

The captain attended me himself. When some of the food I was cramming down spilled down me, he gently wiped it off.

"Looks like you've had a rough time, huh, kid?" The captain smiled his new saintly smile and then sighed sorrowfully. "What's the point of this newfound peace if my boys are suffering so badly under it, that's what I say. This city, this whole country, is still proper messed up. But I'm real glad I could take care of you at least, kid."

The captain's eyes were gentle, full of fatherly love. Bizarrely, I was reminded of the fat lady back at Brave New World. The generosity of spirit. The unquestioning, unconditional love. All the warmth and human kindness that I'd forgotten how to feel and couldn't imagine myself ever feeling again.

In spite of this kindness, though, there was no doubt I was in a dark place. A suspicious place.

There had been a number of guys taking care of me these past few days, and I'd peered into their faces to try and glimpse a hint as to whether they were Hoa or Xema. Nothing doing.

When the captain asked me how he came to find me half starved by the side of the road, I answered him truthfully. That I had run away from the institute. That I'd had their shot to the heart.

"Boy oh boy, you've had it rough," the captain said, placing his hand softly on my shoulder. "But that's all behind you now. As long as you're here you'll never have to worry about where your next meal is coming from, or about stupid squabbles between Hoa and Xema."

My dark suspicions came rushing forward again. I needed to ask a question but could barely get the words out. "Are you telling me that there are Hoa here, Captain?"

"Well, well. It seems this shot to the heart really works, huh?" The captain laughed as if we were enjoying a joke together. My heart sank. "You remember the man who brought you food and looked after you while you were collapsed these past few days? Hoa, ex-soldier. His face is about as Hoa as it comes, in fact."

My hackles rose. *A Hoa nursing me! For days!* The anger and hatred in my mind flooded through my body.

"Come with me. I'll show you what it is we do here." The captain beckoned me to the door. I managed to calm down enough to take a gulp of air, and steadied my breathing, willing myself to calm down. I got out of bed and followed the man who had once been my captain.

Khatsticks.

We used to chew them on the battlefield all the time. They numbed your senses and stopped you from having to dwell on things.

I'd been convalescing in an officelike room these past few days, but when I'd left the room the rest of the warehouse turned out to be a giant Khatstick factory. The floor was lined with rows of tables, each one a workstation for women and children standing and working in silence. Hoa or Xema, I couldn't tell. They were taking the green powder made from the dried and pulverized leaves, turning it into sheets, rolling them up, and cutting them into small sticks that at first glance could have been cigarettes but in actuality were made of far stronger stuff.

"It's all about business," the captain said with a satisfied smile on his face. "We want to expand our field of operations, but there are people who want to get in our way. Bad people who are holding us back. I think it's fate that we came across you when we did. You were a first-class soldier during the war. You fought well for the Xema. So how about doing the same for us here?"

"You mean you want me to become a soldier again?" I asked.

"Hey, it's a cushier gig than fighting in any war!" The captain put his strong arm around my shoulder. "We're minting it at the moment, so you'll never have to worry about food, and you get all the Khatsticks you want, on the house. Perk of the job, you might say."

In other words, my former captain had made it big as a drug dealer. Khatsticks were stupidly addictive—after you'd chewed one once you were sure to want more, and the withdrawal symptoms were something else. When you ran out you became irritated and nauseated. And even if you knew what it did to you, you ended up chewing it anyway, as it was the only way to get through the war. It had become a necessity, not a luxury. The reason I was constantly in a foul mood back at the institute was because I was craving the stuff with all my heart and soul—and body.

During the war we were all doped to the eyeballs on the stuff. We chewed away before a battle, we chewed away after a battle, we chewed away twenty-four-seven. When we ran out of the leaf we used gunpowder as a poor substitute. Vile stuff. No way you'd snort that normally, unless you needed your ersatz kick.

Then the war finished and we soldiers were let go. What this meant was that all the soldiers who'd gotten themselves addicted or who had had addiction forced upon them were suddenly cut off from the source of their addiction. In an instant, Khatsticks had changed from being a ration vital to everyday function to a luxurious vice. Funny how something can go from frivolous to essential at a moment's notice, depending on which way the wind is blowing.

"The ignorant white fools are trying to put pressure on the new government to outlaw the stuff, of course," said the captain. He was animated now, almost as if he were acting out a part in a play. "But the fact is this city's overflowing with people who need the stuff, who rely on it. This new government won't give them what they want. They're too worried about what the white man would say. So that's where we come in. Think of what we're doing as a sort of public service."

I surveyed the faces of the people working on the shop floor.

Hoa? Xema? I walked up to one of them and stared straight into her face from point-blank range. Still nothing. I just couldn't tell.

"The woman you're looking at? She's Hoa. A valued member of our staff. Part of our family," the captain told me. I looked at her again, trying to sniff out even a hint of a clue that would give away whether she was Xema or Hoa: her pupils, nose, her forehead, the thickness of her lips. I stared and I stared. Perhaps she felt uncomfortable, I'm not sure, but suddenly she turned to me without warning and answered a question I hadn't even asked.

"I'm glad I found this place," she said with a smile, her hands continuing to work away all the while. "I earn a decent wage and can feed my family well on it. Mr. Entoleh there is a fine gentleman, he looks after all his workers good and proper. This one time, my boy was sick in bed with a fever, and when Mr. Entoleh heard about it he went out of his way to bring the boy some medicine. He came himself, personally! Right over to my house, even though I'm a Hoa!"

"Well, we're all in this together, after all," said the captain. "It's the least I could do for one of my best workers." He spoke calmly and with an apparently unshakeable confidence.

Mr. Entoleh. I realized that I had never known the captain's real name up until now. During the war we only ever called officers by their rank.

The man who had ordered our company of children about during the war, telling us to kill this person and burn that village down to the ground, that man was now making a different sort of killing altogether by selling Khatsticks on a grand scale. Not that this was the part that bothered me. Khatsticks may have been illegal or whatever, but there were plenty of people who needed them and wanted them, and anyway, shit on the white man's law and his government lackeys. No, what bothered me was the other thing. The fact that, for me, the war was still not over yet.

"But, but…there are Hoa here!" I couldn't stop myself from blurting this out.

Captain Entoleh made a big show of shaking his head theatrically. "The war's over, kid. In order to do business we all need to get along. Try talking to one of the Hoa guys sometime. You'll find that they get it. The fact is, there's no real difference between them and us."

No real difference between them and us.

The words stabbed me deep. I remembered words this man had shouted at us before our assault on Minga Village, before countless raids on Hoa villages. They're different from us. They're not human. *So kill, kill, kill them all.* Then he'd give us a swift slap on the butt to send us into the thick of it.

"But we were fighting the Hoa for ages! You were the one who taught me about all the terrible things the Hoa did before I was born, Captain!"

Entoleh shook his head as if he were indulging a petulant child. "I did what I had to do to get you to fight."

"Are you saying you lied to us, Captain?"

Entoleh frowned. "No. They weren't lies. What you were taught was real history. History from the SDA perspective. In order to fight, you need history. People need to know why they are fighting, what they are fighting for."

"So you made up some bullshit history just so you could get us to fight your fucking war!" I was shouting now. This man in front of me, all the adults, had poisoned my mind, getting me to do their dirty work for them by spinning me their lies. The Hoa started it. Hoa don't feel pain, that's why they're so cruel themselves. My friends and I bought it hook, line, and sinker: my friends who fell all around me in battle.

"As I said. They weren't lies." The man who had once been my captain raised his voice and rubbed his eyes with his fingertips as if he were now dealing with some wearisome episode. "What you have to understand is that no one had any conception of a history between us before the war actually started. Not us Xema, not the

Hoa. Until the war began, no one cared less what sort of history their tribe may or may not have been shouldering. It's only when we constructed a concept of history that the Xema started to hate the Hoa. And vice versa. History is just a backdrop to pin your wars on, nothing more, nothing less. Wars don't start because of history, but you do need history to start a war. You need a pretext to fight, to find a way, however tenuous, to differentiate yourselves from the other side. And not just history either. The same goes for countries. Even tribal distinctions such as Xema and Hoa, all artificial constructs. You can even take this to its logical conclusion—even distinctions between 'you' and 'I' exist only to make war possible. Think about it. In order to kill each other, the 'each' needs to be distinct from the 'other.' Wars don't start because 'you' and 'I' hate each other, oh no, that's the wrong way round. Better to say the very concept of 'I' exists purely in order to fuel war."

"You think your fancy fucking speeches somehow make everything all right?" I screamed at him to try and cut through his bullshit. The factory workers, who had up until a minute ago been absorbed in trying to make their quotas, all stopped still. Their eyes surreptitiously flicked toward us. "They don't. They don't, and you know it, Captain. All you're really saying is that you made up some crap so you could get us to kill each other."

I pressed my point. I was now completely playing the part of the stubborn child refusing to listen to what he was being told. I didn't understand a single thing this man was saying to me. "I" and "you" only exist so we can go to war with each other? That was crazy…I'd never fought with Mom, not really. Only a little with Sis. Sure, I argued with Pop all the time, but that sure as hell couldn't be called war.

"Okay, well, do you know what? Let's go with that. You got me." Entoleh spoke as if he were resigning himself to something, but then continued, "So, do me a favor, kid, and stop taking everything out on the Hoa, stop flipping out and attacking them every time you see them, stop getting angry at them or blaming them for everything. I'd much rather you blamed me. Just remember, we Xema speak the same language as they do; we eat the same food. We just look a little different, that's all. Just keep telling yourself that everything we taught you was all lies, and you'll see there's no logical reason why you should hate them anymore. Much more important to move on and concentrate on surviving in this new world. Working side by side for a better future, if that's what it takes."

Should hate them? The man who used to be my captain was now spouting such shit that I was rooted to the spot in dumb amazement.

Did this man really think we hated the Hoa because we "should," because we had some sort of logical reason to do so? What a fucktard. The reason I hated the Hoa, why I hated them all these years and would continue to hate them, was because there was nothing else I could do. They killed my family, Mom, Sis, Pop, and there was no other way I could live except to hate them. The question of what I "should" or "shouldn't" do never came into the equation. If it were just a matter of deciding what I "should" do, why wouldn't I have done it by now?

Most of all, though, the thing that was the funniest and the most fucked up was the fact that this man sounded exactly like the fat-bitch teacher back at the institute. This man who had ruthlessly and indiscriminately mown down women and children on the battlefield was now spouting exactly the same sort of platitudinous crap as she did. "Working side by side for a better future" my ass.

I considered the man in front of me. All it would take would be for me to reach out toward his holster and grab his gun, I was sure of it. That barrel that was covered in engravings, not that this made it any more practical, although it was cool…

All I needed to do was take the gun, pull it out, and shoot him. I could do it, I realized—but then it hit me that I had absolutely no desire to kill. Sure, I'd had a rush of blood to the head a minute ago, but now that was subsiding I realized what an insignificant speck of fly crap this man was in the grand scheme of things.

Besides, if I were to kill him, I'd be shot to shit by the guards patrolling the perimeter. He wasn't worth it.

"I'm really sorry, Captain," I said honestly, "but I don't think I'm going to be able to stay here after all."

I went back to living on the street.

I wandered the city aimlessly, taking care only to avoid any place that looked like it might be somebody's patch. I briefly considered returning to the institute, but the idea of having to spend my days surrounded by people when I had no idea whether they were Hoa or Xema was just too unbearable.

After a few days like this I was back to my former physique. I could feel my ribs jutting through my skin. My joints ached and I felt weak all over. *Well, I guess this is it, I'm going to waste away now,* I thought to myself as I meandered toward the center of Heaven City.

Faces, faces, faces with their white eyes, looking at me. Were they Hoa? Xema? I still couldn't tell, of course. Kids would stop their begging when I passed by, looking up at me, checking out who it was invading their patch.

If I were to start looking for food or alms around here I'd be surrounded and lynched in no time flat. I was starving, parched, and was withering under the cruel sun. The city gave me no shelter, no comfort, no sustenance. I was a cipher, a ghostly figure, probably. Not that I was the only such specter in this town.

Then I smacked into something.

"Hey, watch where you're going, kid." The speaker was carrying a gun and wore a flak jacket adorned with pockets. An American soldier.

I stumbled backward from the impact. I tried to catch my

balance but my legs were too weak to support me. My knees crumpled like paper. I must have been a truly pathetic sight as I folded up and landed on my ass.

"Jesus Christ, kid. Look at the state of you. Are you okay?"

The American soldier helped me up. He really was something else in his camouflage gear, his flak jacket and his big gun. A model soldier. *I wish I'd had all this back when I was fighting*, I thought to myself for a moment. This was a different sort of cool from the carved gun that the captain had. The latest. The best. The soldier helped me up, but it still took me some time to find my footing again; that's what happens when you're so low on energy, I guess. Sorry, it's just 'cause I haven't eaten for days, I said, or rather I tried to say—I had no idea whether my parched vocal cords had been able to get the words out.

"Don't sweat it, kid. Take this," the American soldier said, and handed me a bar of chocolate. FIRST STRIKE, it said on the plastic wrapper. Cool. The American also gave me his canteen full of water to swig on. I gulped it down greedily. Just like I had at the captain's hideout. Like a dog, like the dog I had become.

I noticed the evil stares I was getting from the kids who claimed this territory, but there wasn't exactly anything they could do when faced with an American soldier.

"I need to get out of here," I begged the soldier. I needed him to get me out of this place, or else the moment he left I'd be a sitting duck.

"Why's that, kid?"

I'm not allowed to beg for scraps here, I explained, and then the rest of my story started pouring out almost of its own accord. I'd already told most of my story once before, to Captain Entoleh, so I knew how it went already. This time, I was able to tell it even more fluently.

The American seemed to understand. He escorted me out of the area.

We found ourselves by his barracks, and we sat down next to them. I dived into some more candy and water. The soldier asked me who I was, and I gave him my real name. I'm Williams, he told me in return.

"CMI has done all sorts of stuff to my brain too," he said. "Stuff that stops me from stressing out when I'm in combat, or after I return home. Some of the guys don't like the idea of being interfered with this way, of course. As for me, well, I'm not crazy about it, but I guess I see why they do it. Probably a good thing on balance."

My hand holding the candy bar stopped midair. So this guy also had doctors mess around with his mind, huh? How, exactly, I asked? There's no way of telling what sort of "shot to the heart" somebody has had just by looking at them, of course. It's not like losing a leg or an eye.

"Huh, well, let's see. Before I go into battle I get this little jab that stops me from feeling pain. It works on my brain. Now, if this jab really stopped you from feeling pain at all, then if you took a bullet you might not even notice that you were wounded, right? You could end up bleeding to death over what should have just been a flesh wound."

I nodded.

"So what happens is this," Williams said. "When a bullet hits you, it registers in your mind that you're hurting—how do I say this—it's a bit like 'knowing' in the sense of knowing what's happening in a book you're reading, or a conversation you're having. You follow, you know, you process it, you just don't end up rolling around in agony. That's the sort of thing we get injections for."

"So you know that you're in pain, you just don't feel pain," I said.

"Exactly, kid. You're quick on the uptake. You put it far better than I do. It took me almost two months to get my head around it." The American kept a straight face as he spoke. No hint of a smile. It seemed so weird he could talk about this with such clinical detachment, such a lack of emotion.

I thought about what Williams had just told me. If American magic was capable of such weird stuff, then it must have been easy for them to make it so my head couldn't tell the difference between Xema and Hoa anymore. I could still tell the difference between individual faces. Who's who? It was just that when I saw someone for the first time, I couldn't tell whether they were Hoa or Xema—that was all. The most natural thing in the world to anyone born and raised in this country, and I couldn't do it.

Was this what they meant by "indifference"?

This was crazy. Did they really think that by removing the target of my hatred, my hatred would just disappear? That the world would suddenly somehow become a peaceful place? Who came up with this scheme? Was it the new government? The Americans? Our teachers? Who could have honestly thought that this would solve anything?

"It's the NGOs," Williams said. "Who're behind these mind-changing programs, I mean. It's a popular school of thought in Europe and America at the moment. The idea that all the world needs is for people to stop treating different races differently and then we'd have a perfect world where harmony and equality prevail. And once people believe in an idea strongly enough, they'll do anything to try and make their ideology become reality."

"Are there wars between different tribes going on back in your country, sir?" I asked.

"No, no, nothing quite as drastic as that. There are plenty of people who'll point out that there is still a sort of low-level discrimination that hasn't yet completely disappeared, though. And it's usually those people who put themselves forward for the mind-altering surgery. So that they can make a dramatic statement to the world. To tell us all they are not prejudiced—and to wear the fact like a badge of honor. And it works. It helps these people get ahead in life, get a promotion at work. In some companies, at least. These people get stuck in their grassroots volunteering on Sundays, they sort their trash and their recycling religiously, they attend their monthly counseling sessions faithfully, they participate enthusiastically in consumer focus groups and the social progress debates of the day, all while keeping a meticulous log of their social virtue so they can brandish their good citizenship credentials at a moment's notice.

"Hardly surprising that it's these people who are the most enthusiastic about the idea of fiddling about with people's brains to make it so they can't distinguish between different races anymore. It's almost become a prerequisite to being a 'good person,' someone society can trust. And I guess that some bright spark at some NGO somewhere had the idea that this sort of social engineering could be taken and transplanted into some other country where different tribes were killing each other. Figured it would somehow bring about peace."

I could hardly follow half the things he was saying, but one thing did stand out: this man's home country was, all things considered, a pretty peaceful place compared to ours. It had to be, for people to have the time to worry about whether they should or shouldn't go in for an operation that would make them utterly unable to distinguish between races.

Try that in the war here so that you couldn't tell the difference between Xema and Hoa. You'd be dead before you had time to blink.

"Yeah, my country is hardly the theater of war that your country's been these past years," Williams said, almost as if he were apologizing for the fact. "Sorry to put it so bluntly."

"So what gives you the right to come over here and impose your values on us?" I asked him. "This is a war zone here. Not being able to tell the difference between races can get a person killed."

"The war's over though, isn't it?" the American replied, a trace of doubt lingering in his voice. "We ended it, didn't we?"

I wanted to shout at him—not just to say it was the Dutch and not you arrogant Americans who ended the war, but to scream that for me the war wasn't yet over—but I knew it would be pointless. We were just doing what the president of this white man's country was telling us to do, after all. Forget your hatred. Forgive the crimes of those who murdered your family. And this is what we were being forced to do in reality: not a single Hoa had been tried for his crimes, and they were all going about their business in Heaven City as if nothing had ever happened.

Now, of course everyone wants peace. Believe it or not, I myself didn't particularly enjoy the act of fighting—not at all, in fact. But there was really only one answer you could give when the white man came to your land and told you that all you now had to do was to forgive the people who raped the shit out of your sister before killing her. The answer being:

Fuuuuuuuuuuuck that.

I thanked the soldier for the food and said goodbye and walked away. After a while I looked back to see one of those flying fans floating just above the American's head. This machine, oh so clever and oh so soulless, was surveying the land below it, master of all it could see, camera and machine gun both ever ready.

I needed something done about my messed-up head.

I cut across Heaven City, making a beeline for Brave New World. As I walked I found myself gradually getting used to the reality that I could no longer tell the race of the people whose faces I was passing. I thought of my surroundings as being part of a dream and focused my attention on the soles of my feet. This became my whole world, the only thing that was real. The grains of sand underfoot. The twinges of pain whenever I stepped on a sharp stone.

I felt the pain, savored it like I savored the feeling of the sand, and by the end of the day I was back at Brave New World.

"Anybody home?" I yelled out.

Brave New World was a burnt-out, blackened husk. Walls had been ripped down and doors smashed in.

The sight itself was nothing new to me. I'd seen it countless times. In villages I had raided. When my own village was attacked. All of them had been like this. The only difference was that here there weren't actually piles of severed limbs or corpses strewn about the place, stripped naked and desecrated. Otherwise, it was pretty much the same—blood spattered about the place, and signs that machetes or some such had been used to tear the place up.

"Is that you, Enza? You decided to come back, did you?"

I spun around to see where the voice was coming from. It was Fatty, my old teacher. She looked half dead.

"What happened here?" I asked.

"It was awful," she said in a choked little voice. She collapsed in a heap on the floor. "There was a riot. You know how they say suspicion breeds suspicion? Well, that's exactly what happened here. After your incident, when you ran off, there were similar incidents, almost every day. Things got worse and worse, and before we knew what was going on, Ezgwai managed to get hold of a machete and smuggle it in. You can imagine the rest…"

She pointed toward one of the classroom walls, and when I looked over there I saw a machete firmly embedded in it. It was lodged deeply into the wooden surface, with a long hairline crack running up the wall from the point it had made contact.

Ezgwai did this? Gentle Ezgwai? For a moment I refused to believe it—I couldn't believe it—but then I remembered the look on his face when he jumped me. It was the expression of a Hoa soldier who had killed and killed and would kill again. Not unlike me, in fact. A mirror image.

"Why don't you just fix all our heads up so that everything goes back to normal? Surely that would solve all your problems?" I asked.

Fatty flashed a wry smile. "You really want to go back to the way things were? All that hatred?"

This time it was my turn to almost laugh. "What, you think that just because you've messed around with our minds a bit we've stopped hating each other?"

"No," said Fatty, "but if we were to go back to the way things were, how long would it take before you started drawing up battle lines again? Us and them? Then you start killing anyone on the other side. You know what I think of that? Fuuuuuuuuuuuck that!"

Hang on a second. Wasn't that the sort of thing I was supposed to say?

Then I realized that the fat woman in front of me had fallen into the same sort of trap that I had. She'd been living with the illusion that all she had to do was pull the wool over our eyes and peace would naturally come of its own accord. The illusion that all you had to do was to strip away the labels "Hoa" and "Xema" and people would stop hating each other. Her *fuuuuuuuuuuuck that!* was the inevitable, gut-wrenching response of her illusions being shattered into a million tiny pieces.

"In any case, the white men have all evacuated," she continued. "The NGO, whose pet project this was, was involved in some sort of scandal back in its home country. Before any of us knew what was happening, the donors all pulled out and the program was completely derailed. Apparently the NGO is going to 'consider its options' back in the safety of its home country. There's no one left in the hotel, and as for the CMI, once the funding dried up, do you think they hung around for any longer than it took them to pack away their precious equipment?"

So we'd been abandoned.

Abandoned in our own messed-up minds.

A strange calm descended on me. I'd come a long way to reach this point, and only now did I truly feel I had been released. Hoa and

Xema were nothing to me now. The empty slogans that the white man and his lackeys such as Fatty here used to spout endlessly—the time was now ripe for me to embody them with my own flesh and blood. I knew the way it had to be.

I yanked Ezgwai's machete from the wall. It had been stuck so firmly in there that I had to pull real hard. For a moment I thought I had dislocated my shoulder.

And then it was time for me to do what I had to do. Before I left the city. This fat woman's corpse would serve as a beacon to signal the beginning of my struggle. I was no longer thinking in terms of the war that had not yet ended for me. Rather, I realized that everything that had come before was nothing more than a dry run for the real thing that was now about to start. If you really wanted to call that my postwar period, fine, but as far as I was concerned that was now well and truly over.

I approached the fat bitch from behind and brought my machete down on the nape of her neck. Her spine may have been protected by her blubbery skin, but I knew I'd still be able to shatter it in one blow. I could see it clearly. Just as I could see her fat skull perched on top of that spine, smugly smiling away.

Three years have passed since then, and now we're finally about to return to the city.

There are glittering clusters of light up ahead; it is the light of people going about their daily business. The scent of the living drifts over. The city in the distance is like a starry sky reflecting on a large body of water. We pick our way over the twenty or so corpses of Government Forces troops lying on the ground and reach the top of the hill, surveying the night vista in front of us, taking in the smells.

I'm going to let the people of this city know that the war isn't over yet. Not for me.

The war isn't over. Because I myself am the war.

It's going to be hard to convince them of this fact with mere words, so I'll have to use my AK-47 to persuade them. I'm sure they'll get the message.

Just before my bullets pierce their hearts.

My mind makes no distinction between Xema and Hoa. Same goes for most of the other guys here. I'm sure some of the guys here used to be in the SLF and would have done all sorts of terrible things to Xema women and children. But I forgive them. After all, they could no longer tell the difference between Hoa and Xema either.

Our army transcends tribalism, transcends race. Not like the uneasy alliance of Government Forces troops who spent half their time watching their own backs, constantly suspicious of each other. With us, it's only when we actually tell each other that we even get to know what tribe our comrades are from. So we don't. We've managed to become a true band of brothers.

You see, it seems I wasn't the only one who found he needed to leave the city fast after losing the ability to distinguish between Xema and Hoa. Some of us banded together, looked out for each other, managed to arm ourselves, and then we started raiding caravans and traveling groups of foreigners. Before long we were strong enough to start attacking villages, and whenever we did we always welcomed their children into our ranks. We traveled far and wide, across the breadth and depth of Shelmikedmus, steadily expanding our influence as we did so.

And now, here we are.

I wave at my comrades, my friends, behind me. Even in the darkness I can tell that they're all smiling.

We're bearing down on Heaven City. All there is left to do is head down the wide road taking us into the city and then we, the outcasts from Heaven, will kill everyone and everything in sight. The people of the city who made us what we are today. The people who drove us out of Heaven. The white man is afraid of us now. He's long since left the city from one of its ports. There won't be a single American soldier or a single machine waiting to greet us.

We march.

We advance.

We bear down on the shining lights.

The scent of life, of culture, of peace.

Once upon a time we wanted all of this for ourselves. Wanted it desperately, but couldn't have it.

Not anymore, though. Now we're going to destroy it all. And we're going to enjoy doing so.

Some of the guys are taking their time, others are impatient to get going. We each advance at our own pace. Fat, thin, lanky, short— no need to bother anymore with the pretense of trying to step in time.

All we need now are our AK-47s. They're there for the taking, scattered all over the place. All you need to do is pick one up and prove to the world that you are who you are.

Go on. Pick it up. Pick it up and join our ranks.

We're almost there now. Coming with us? Get ready for the ride of your life.

(First published in SF Magazine, November 2007)

The Sea of Trees by Rachel Swirsky

Not ten minutes in, I spot yellow electrical tape strung through the trees. Recent, not tattered. I grab, hold on hand-over-hand as I scramble over roots and rocks. Good to have a touch-connection to the way out. If you don't know the way back, the trees might lure you and keep you.

The forest is all shadows. Clinging mist damps the sunlight. Light penetrates at strange angles, casting a glow over lichen-covered roots, shredded bark and rotting logs.

To the left: a rope suspended from a branch that's too weak to support a man's weight. Hung by someone stupid or indecisive or playing a prank. Hope that's not all I'll find today.

To the right: a second tape trail branching into the shadows.

Better stick to the trail I'm on for now. Hope it pays off.

A few meters later: a woman's compact on the ground. Kick it; watch it bounce end over end, mirror flashing. It leaves an indentation in the soil. It's lain undisturbed awhile. Good. Makes it more likely I've gotten here before the suicide watch. I slip the compact into my pack.

I'm feeling really good right now. This is a bingo. Can already see *yurei* shadows hiding behind trunks. Not long dead, this one, not with ghosts still gathering.

The scent of mandarin oranges precedes a yurei flashing next to me. She's all floating with no feet. Her Edo-style white burial kimono casts a shadow on the lichen.

Black hair sweeps to her waist, equally covering the back and front of her head. Impossible to locate her face. Tendrils curl toward me entreatingly.

This yurei's been around as long as I have. Likes jokes. Minor pranks. She's harmless.

"*Your life is a precious gift from your parents,*" she says. "*Please think about your parents, siblings, and children.*"

"*Ha.*"

She's quoting the signs that are posted at the edge of the forest in a weak attempt to turn back the suicidal before they add to the body count among the trees. Who gets this far to be stopped by a sign?

Tendril of hair grasps my shoulder. I bug-shudder it off. "*You know that's not why I'm here.*"

"*Don't keep it to yourself,*" she says, still quoting. "*Talk about your troubles.*"

"*Only trouble I've got right now is where to find good scavenge.*"

The yurei rotates slowly in the air. A raven lock gestures down the trail I've been following.

"*Thief-girl.*" She uses her derisive pet name for me. "*That one's got nothing. Couldn't even take a train back to Tokyo.*"

Another tendril points back to the tape fork.

"*That one came with everything he's got. Red tent under a big tree.*"

Her tone is too helpful. Suspicious. This yurei likes barbs and mischief. She's not sugar unless she's hiding something.

"*Not gone yet, is he?*" I ask.

Ends of her hair curl up in a shrug. "*Neck's broken. Wait ten minutes.*"

All right. I open my hydration pack. Drink.

Yurei keeps floating by. Can't tell where her eyes are behind all that hair, but she's watching me.

"*You want something?*" I ask.

She bobs silently.

Sigh. "*Go ahead.*"

She floats closer. Tendrils of hair reach out like tentacles. I grit my teeth as she feels my face like a blind person. Hair feels like hair feels, but this hair moves like hair shouldn't. Body knows that. Body does not like being touched by the dead.

The scent of mandarin oranges lingers as her hair withdraws. "*Just wanted to remember,*" she says. "*What it's like. To touch skin that wants to live.*"

I wipe my mouth, reseal the hydration pack. "*It'll be ten by the time I get there. Thanks for the tip.*"

You can call this place Aokigahara or you can call it Jukal, the sea of trees. Either way, it's haunted.

The forest grew 850 years ago after an eruption of Mount Fuji. Green things sank their roots after the lava cooled.

The woods are very quiet. Little lives here except for ghosts and people on their way to joining them. Wind scarcely blows. Mists hang. Overhead, branches and leaves tangle into a roof underneath which the world is timeless and directionless.

Everything is trapped.

Everything is waiting.

A pair of tennis shoes, sitting alone.

Pants, voluminous over leg bones.

A suicide note nailed to a tree: "Nothing good ever happened in my life. Don't look for me."

The yurei, watching.

The man hanging above the red tent smells like the shit his bowels just released. He has three gold teeth, an expensive watch, brand-name trainers, and a pack of money. I'm unclear on the point of taking cash into the forest, but people do what they do.

Good scavenge, that's sure. Most people have nothing when they come here to die. Easier to feel empty when your bank account's the same.

Scissors, nail clippers, a comb. Copy of Wataru Tsurumi's *Complete Manual of Suicide*. Half of everyone who comes here carries that. Stupid book. Stupider people. Can't even reject their lives without instructions.

I'm about to toss it back when I hear a crunch in the undergrowth. Nearby.

Damn it.

Snap to my feet. Pull on my pack. Now I notice what greed blinded me to: where are the yurei around this fresh death? Other living people must be on their way. Scared the ghosts off.

That yurei must have known. She trying to get me caught?

The suicide watch is not going to be friendly when they realize I'm looting. I scramble, searching for a tree to climb. No way they won't have heard me by now, but some are superstitious, might put noises down to yurei without really looking.

I hear the smack of someone tripping. The swearing that follows is in American English.

"Damn it to bugfucking, motherfucking hell!"

I can see her now. American tourist wearing a downy red sweatshirt over jeans with sandals of all stupid things. Half-empty hydration pack hangs from her backpack. Either she can't ration or she's been hiking awhile.

Young. Maybe fifteen, sixteen. Makeup and clothes are all-

American, but can't conceal Japanese eyes. Probably another fucking Nisei looking for her roots.

I push into the shadows, thinking I'll wait her out, but it turns out that despite being clumsy and unprepared, she's not stupid.

"*Sumimasen*," she says. "*Eigo hanashimasuka?*"

She wants to know if I speak English. I have no intention of letting her know I do. "*Gomen nasai. Eigo ga wakarimasen.*"

"Figures," she mutters. "Just another slant-eyed motherfucker with half a brain."

I can't stop my snarl in time. She cracks a grin.

"Ha! Thought you did!"

No point denying it. "What do you want?"

"I'm lost."

I point over her shoulder at the tape path. "You can get out that way."

She squints. "I recognize you. In town. I stopped to use my phone. You were on the corner."

"Sorry, wasn't me."

"Someone pointed you out. They said there aren't many women who spend time up here. They said an *onryo* follows you around."

People should set up shop and charge for gossip the way they toss other people's stories around. Everyone figures it's fair game if there's a ghost.

I gesture at the trees. "You see an onryo?"

"They didn't say it followed you all the time."

I cross my arms. "What do you want?"

"I need to find a yurei."

I point to the newly hanged man. "Wait around."

"No. I need to find a particular yurei. I need to find my father."

Here's the thing about me: I came to Aokigahara when I was twenty-two, the year my onryo came for me. I've been here seven years since. Sure, I leave the trees, but I'm always here.

I make my living scavenging. Selling valuables. Or, most of the time, not finding anything valuable and then hunting down buyers with too much death on their minds, people who want to thrill themselves with a hint of the haunted by buying detritus that once belonged to a suicide. Combs. Glasses. Rope from a noose. Remnants of lives abandoned.

I don't need much to live, but I earn less. That's why I listen when the American girl caps her plea with, "I'll pay."

"How much?"

The figure she names is enough to buy a day or two in the forest looking for a ghost.

I won't even have to find her father. Just spend some time searching, then turn up any ghost at all. She'll never tell the difference.

Still, I can't help pressing further. See what she's made of.

I sling my backpack off my shoulder. "Sounds like a deal."

She smiles. Gestures to herself. "I'm Melon."

I give her an oddball eye. She laughs.

"Mom thinks nature names sound Japanese."

I exchange mine. "Nao."

"Cool. Where do we start?"

"Nowhere today. It's getting late."

It's early evening; we could go a couple hours. But I want to stop here.

I unpack my sleeping bag. "I'll be fine on the ground."

She nods.

I add, "You take the tent."

I grin as I point. The red tent still smells like the sweat and piss of the man swinging from the tree. The girl looks up. His shadow falls over her, black as bruises. She swallows fast.

Breaking her gaze from the dead man's eyes, she crouches to unzip the flap.

"Look comfy?" I ask.

She glances back. Her too-earnest American face has a closed, hard set.

"Looks fine."

She crawls in. I'm not unimpressed.

Two AM. The ghost hour.

The whistling of wind wakes me. The sound comes alone, unaccompanied by breeze.

Then she's there. My Sayomi. My onryo.

Dead lips on mine. Cold fingers stroking my thighs. Prehensile tendrils of hair circling my waist, teasing my nipples, trailing my spine.

Creep-shudder, gullet to gut. Body does not like being touched by the dead.

But my Sayomi. Body likes being touched by my Sayomi.

Timeless at twenty-one. Smooth-cheeked, willow-bodied, bloodlessly pale. Eyes shining with tears a decade old.

A long skirt flows to her ankles, Western-style but cut from white-flowered silk. Low-cut lace shows the apple-tops of her breasts. Lipstick stains her mouth; she opens to moan; blood-color smears her teeth.

She dressed up to die, my Sayomi.

Ashen tongue in my mouth like a cold lump of meat. Hair busy undoing the zip of my jeans, her obi-style waistband. Night air breathes cold on flesh usually hidden.

She pushes me to the ground, roots sharp in my back. Sayomi on top of me. Her hair parting my lips. Her fingers inside me.

I moan.

She always makes me moan.

The creeping horror of her hair. The unchanging beauty of her face.

My body tightens. That moment, near arriving. Her unfinished business with me nearly resolved.

It takes a great deal of will to shove her away before it comes.

She screams. Her hair ties itself in angry knots. I squirm out from underneath. Her fingernails claw the dirt where I've been.

Someday, I won't get away.

Someday I won't want to.

I gain my feet. Her hair stretches for my wrists and ankles. Her eyes are wide and guileless even as she tries to drag me down.

It would be so easy to give in.

Clouds shift. Across her moonlit face, a shadow swings.

I look up. The hanged man. Socks on his dangling feet, robbed of their expensive trainers.

The red tent. The American girl. I'd forgotten where I was.

Desire vanishes.

Sayomi pounds her fists on the air. She screams again. This time, the sound dissolves her. It becomes a windless whistle as she blows away.

Back in the silence of the sea of trees, all I can hear is my ragged breath.

I pull up my jeans. The girl's face peeps through the tent flap. I politely look away, but she won't give me the courtesy of silence.

She asks, "Was that the onryo?"

I shrug. She knows it was.

"Why is she a pile of bones?"

I sigh. "There's an old ghost story. A lonely scholar lives in his house, pining away, until one day a beautiful woman visits at night. He lets her in. They make love. In the morning, she leaves, and the scholar gets sick. Every night after that, she comes to him. They make love, she gives him pleasure, and he gets weaker."

The girl's watching eyes are bright like Sayomi's, but tearless.

"One night, the scholar's worried neighbor looks through the window," I continue. "He sees the scholar in bed with a skeleton. He tells the scholar what he saw, and that night, when the ghost arrives, the scholar knows what she is. But he doesn't see a pile of bones. When he looks at her, he sees a woman."

"What happened to the scholar?"

"He died."

Silence. Then, "What does your onryo look like?"

I shrug again.

"Did you know her? When she was alive?"

That's enough. I don't listen to whatever she asks next.

A girl may love a girl, but eventually both become women.

One goes to university in America. The other studies in Fukuoka. Each misses the other, but one is distracted by learning English and sunbathing by Lake Michigan and eating cafeteria lunches. For the other, Fukuoka is what Fukuoka has always been, but drained of joy. Joy that will never return for girls who've grown into women.

Even across the boundary of life and death, flesh may yearn for flesh. But when the dead pleasure the living, they pull them to their side, as the ghost woman pulled her scholar.

As a ghost, Sayomi doesn't talk, but just before she died, she sent an email. I didn't receive it until after she was gone. Sometimes it feels as if it were written by her ghost.

Come to Aokigahara, she wrote. *We'll finish things there.*

I wake before the girl does.

Three yurei gather around the hanged man. Clawed hands emerge from hair-veils to peck at the corpse. Spectral fingers leave no marks, but the man's body swings back and forth despite the lack of wind. Slowly at first and then faster and faster. The branch creaks as if caught in a hurricane. The yurei make noises I've never heard. Part shriek and part scratch, simultaneously the sounds of predators and of terrified things.

I pull the girl out of the tent. Gesturing for silence, I point to the ravenlike yurei. The girl's not stupid; she follows my lead, packing without a word. We back away, careful not to make noise with our feet.

When we're a distance removed, she asks, "What was that?"

I feign nonchalance. "Don't know."

Hope she'll think I'm saying *Don't know and it doesn't matter* instead of *Don't know and I thought I knew everything about yurei*.

Not sure she buys my dismissive shrug. She keeps her own counsel for once.

When she does talk again, it's about something else. She pulls a photo from her pack. "This is my father."

I expect a generic, smiling face, but the photo shows a corpse. Dried flesh on bones. A tidy button-down drapes over shoulders that look like a coat hanger. Hair clumps on remnants of scalp. Part of the nose and cheek remain, but not enough to make a face.

She points to the background. "See those rocks? I thought maybe you'd recognize them."

Tourists.

"It's a big forest," I answer.

"Not that big."

"Big enough."

She should know what I mean without my having to tell her: with all the ghosts here, the sea of trees is as big as it wants to be.

The girl looks like she wants to stomp her feet. "Then how are you going to find him!"

"Wander. Watch the trees." She still looks pissed. I add, "If we keep going deeper, he'll find you."

If he wants to find her.

If someone else doesn't find us first.

She bites her lips. Gazes abstractly at distant trees. "Do you think he'll talk to me?"

"Yurei like to talk."

I shouldn't say more since her optimism is what's paying me, but I can't stop myself.

I add, "No telling what he'll say."

We're still in familiar forest. I can navigate. Would be better to follow tape trails, but I don't want the strange yurei to find us too easily.

Once we're moving steadily, the girl starts talking.

"My mother met my father while she was backpacking the summer after college. He was older than she was. They didn't stay in touch, but she had his name. Last year when I turned sixteen, she said I was old enough to figure out for myself what to do with it. So I tracked down his family. They told me he'd died, but they wouldn't say anything else."

"He committed suicide," I assume.

"The suicide watch found him here." Melon's voice is thick. She tugs the strap of her backpack so she has an excuse to hesitate. "They sent me photos."

"What makes you think he became a yurei?"

"I read online that the first night after they bring the bodies back, someone from the suicide watch sleeps next to them. In the morgue or wherever they take them. To make sure their souls can rest."

"No one slept next to him?"

"I don't know. I didn't ask. But in the photo of him, of his body... you can see that he's been...that's he's already..."

"Rotted."

She stiffens. Doesn't protest. "No one slept with him then. On the real first night."

Quiet, there, in the sea of trees. Just me and her. Me and her and her sadness.

I ask, "Did he know about you?"

"Mom told him. Before I was born." Her tone changes. Last night's hard look returns to her face. "I know what you're asking. No. He never tried to get in touch with me. It doesn't matter. I care even if he didn't. I have to know where I came from."

I don't think much of Melon's reasons, but I like her conviction. I also like the fact that even though I can see she's tired and sore, she hasn't complained.

"Why do you speak English?" she asks.

"I went to college in America."

"Where?"

"Northwestern."

"Oh!" she says. Then, quietly, "I've read a lot about Chicago."

Something mournful there. Something unsaid. Maybe something to do with why she's seventeen and hiking alone half a world from where she grew up, searching for a father she never knew.

I'm so grateful that she's keeping something to herself for once that I leave it alone.

We're past where most suicides go, but we find footprints so I stop. Gives the girl a chance to rest. Gives me a chance to keep my profits up.

Result: a bag half buried between roots. I shake off loose soil. Dig through canned food and hygiene products.

The girl asks, "Why'd they bring all that in?"

"Some people stay a long time before they do anything."

"Saying goodbye to the world?"

"Or making up their minds."

At the bottom of the bag, a *mokume-gane* wedding band. Dirty. Sized for a small man or a large woman.

The girl watches the light pick a glint from beneath the grime. "How sad."

I push the ring into my pocket.

Melon continues, "It makes sense to want to say goodbye to the world before you leave it."

Mist drifts through motionless leaves. Trees creep slowly, invisibly, toward the masked sun.

"This place is like a graveyard," she says.

"Whole world is. At least here, it looks like what it is."

We go on. Evening draws closer. Silent and navy instead of silent and white.

I almost lead the girl toward a cave I know when I feel sudden trepidation. I stop abruptly. "Shh!" I hiss to forestall the girl's question.

A yurei, crouched between trees. He hovers midair, hair parting over his nose and sweeping down in two dark curtains. His exposed jaw stretches all the way to the ground: a gaping maw the size of a door. Black, open, waiting to swallow us into hungry dark.

I pull the girl backward for several meters before I dare turn. We move swiftly through the trees. Takes a while. Navy turns darker. Still doesn't feel safe.

The girl gets sick of following. Demands, "Where are we going?"

I look back through the dark, toward where the mouth gapes. Yurei like ravens. Yurei waiting to swallow us down.

I've lost my nerve.

"We should get out," I say.

"Why?"

"Something's wrong. Something's bringing out the darkest."

In the last light, she looks lost and lonely. Her voice is all breath. "Maybe it's me."

Melon's stupid and young and American. Annoying as she is, I can't imagine what about her would draw darkness from ghosts.

Chill on my nape, though. Says maybe I'm wrong.

Melon asks, "Can you get us out this late?"

It's almost black. Moonlight casts faint silhouettes across nearby trunks.

We're far away from electrical tape and signs entreating us not to end our lives.

I could get us out. I think. But I don't want to be wrong.

"We'll talk in the morning," I say.

Moonlight reveals her guileless grin.

Two AM.

The sound of wind without wind.

Sayomi.

Me on the ground in my sleeping bag. Crisp, night smells. The girl nearby.

Doesn't matter who's watching. Nothing stops Sayomi's devouring kisses. Hair embraces me. Meat-lump tongue laps at my lips. She wants to pull me out through my mouth. Fill her ribcage with my heart. Fill her bones with my marrow.

I want her too.

Legs scissoring. Pelvises matched. Lips to lips. Pleasure fluttering. Hovering. Rising. I should go with her. I should let her make me come. I should come; I should go; at least then I'd be somewhere.

No. Not now. Not tonight, with the girl watching. There will always be another night to let Sayomi suck me down.

I shove Sayomi away. She screams. Hair lashes my face, leaves stinging marks that will last till morning.

"No." I shove again.

Hair winds around my throat. Pulls tight. An ethereal glow

lights the whiteness of her skin. Her teeth are bared, her weeping eyes bloodshot. She strains as her hair cinches tighter.

Throat hot. Lungs searing. I'm suddenly hyper-aware of air on my face, on my thighs—air I can't breathe.

Sayomi's never gone this far before.

Even as her hair strangles me, strands of it separate to move beneath my waist. The burning cinch. The gentle stroke. Each sensation sharpens the other.

My vision sparks. Blue. White. Fading. Can't even struggle.

A rock streaks past Sayomi's cheek, clatters on the ground behind her. She can't be hurt like that anymore, but she recoils with surprise. Her hair withdraws from me, moving reflexively to protect her like a shield. I can just make out Sayomi's eyes behind the veil. Angry. Betrayed.

Air chokes my throat. I grasp my neck. Pain all the worse now that I have oxygen to feel it.

Hands on my back, checking to see if I'm all right. Melon's hands. "Nao!" she exclaims.

Sayomi looks down at us and screams again, that hair-to-heel scream that scatters her into the night.

"I tried not to watch," Melon says.

I clutch my burning throat.

"Her bones are white. I thought you had to be dead a long time for your bones to bleach like that."

Her voice trembles. Her eyes are afraid. Maybe she's realizing the danger now. These aren't American ghosts you can banish with water and chanting. They're yurei. They take what they want.

I knew Sayomi was dead as soon as I read her email. She was long gone by the time I arrived in Aokigahara.

I've spent years reconsidering all the times we'd spent together after I left for school. The phone calls made when one or the other of us should have been sleeping. The emails complaining about classwork. The summer after my second year when I came home and we went hiking but we got too tired to climb and so we laid down near the mountain's base instead, holding each other's hands and watching the sky.

I should have heard the plaintive tone in her voice on the train heading back. "You'll always come back for me, won't you?" She was staring out the window, not even able to look at me. I hadn't understood what that meant.

I didn't give her what she needed then so I give her what I can now. Not much: a few kisses, a nightly embrace.

Until I can muster more.

The girl and I are both awake by dawn.

She's angry that I still want to go back. "I need to find my father! You deal with ghosts all the time. I thought you were an expert!"

"That's why I know when to leave."

"You can't just stop! I'm paying you!"

I laugh.

Angry surprise lights her face. American girl, used to money buying power. She doesn't expect *dismissal*.

"This is my only chance! I have to fly back to Nebraska on Tuesday. Who knows if I'll ever get back? I have to find my father! Please! You owe me. You wouldn't even be here if I hadn't rescued you last night!"

I wait for her to run out of shouting.

"I'm heading back," I say. "Come with me or go alone."

Her face goes blank, caught between pride and fear.

I throw her a bone.

"Maybe we'll find your father on the way out."

When we glimpse sunlight, the trees thicken.

Down past the rocks, the trees thicken.

Along every path, the trees thicken.

Each time, I turn heel and try another way. My heartbeat goes faster. My mouth dries. I tell myself I'm only lost. I'll find the way.

But I already know. There is no way.

The trees have claimed us.

I don't tell Melon. It would only scare her. She'll eventually work it out.

Maybe by then I'll know what to do.

The girl's frightened inhalation warns me to halt.

I'm about to step out from underneath the canopy's shadow. In front of us, a lightning-struck tree has fallen across its sisters, creating a small clearing.

Encroaching on its boundaries, dozens of yurei. Flocking. Screeching.

It's daytime, but shadows swarm around the ghosts, creating temporary dark. Some hold torches aloft in locks of their hair. Firelight picks out undertones of blue and green in their white kimonos. They swoop and dart like carrion-eaters, all suddenness with no grace.

Leaders emerge into the clearing. Pass through. There are many, many more behind.

The girl trembles. Goosebumps prick my skin.

Any moment, they could smell us. They may already be watching behind their hair. Clawed hands could part their veils at any instant.

Hundreds stream by until, at last, the grimacing legion is gone, shadows and firelight with them, leaving behind mist and silent trees.

The girl starts forward into the clearing. No! I throw my arm out to stop her. She cringes as she glimpses what I've seen.

One last yurei sitting on the lightning-charred stump.

The air is so cold. My exhalations are ice.

The yurei's scent drifts toward us.

Mandarin oranges.

Relief instantly warms me. "Don't worry," I tell the girl. "I know this one."

The yurei's head rotates toward our approach. Her body remains motionless. If she had a living neck, it would snap.

"*Thanks for your advice the other day,*" I say acidly in Japanese.

"A moment, please!" she replies in English. "Consult the police before you decide to die."

The girl gasps. Her expression shows fear.

"Don't worry," I repeat. "This one always quotes the signs. She thinks it's a joke."

Melon trembles. She braces her hands protectively across her stomach. I think but don't say, *You're the one who wanted to meet a ghost.*

"We can't get out," I tell the yurei.

She switches to Japanese. "*All roads lead to Aokigahara.*"

Melon breathes raggedly. I can't tell how much she understands.

"Hardly anything leads to Aokigahara."

"*All roads lead to death. Aokigahara is death. All roads lead to Aokigahara.*"

"*You are not being helpful!*" I reply angrily in Japanese.

"*The forest wants you.*"

"*I've been here a hundred times! Why does it want me now?*"

I glare at the yurei. I know her pricks and pranks. She's keeping something to herself.

The girl breaks in, using halting Japanese. "*Please! I need to find my father. Can you help me?*"

The yurei turns again, that neck-snapping turn. "Your name is Melon."

Her English is very bad.

"Yes," Melon says. She's afraid, but it doesn't silence her.

The yurei calls back to me, "*You come a hundred times alone and once with this one. What do you think is different?*"

Melon looks between us, confused. The Japanese is too fast for her. "Please," she repeats. "My father's name is Manabu. He died here."

"Why should I help you?" the yurei grumbles. She adds in Japanese, "*She doesn't have anything I want.*"

"*She has the same thing you get from me,*" I say. "*She has skin that wants to live—*"

The words aren't entirely out of my mouth before I realize what the yurei is implying.

I gape at Melon. "What did you really come here to do?"

Melon hasn't understood our words, but she knows how to read my shocked eyes. She tenses. I move forward to catch her, but I'm too late. She flees.

The yurei rises to watch her go. Her hovering form casts a sharp shadow across the lightning-struck log.

For a moment, I'm too confused to pursue. Everything is going wrong. The trees closing in. Sayomi refusing to let go.

"*One girl wants to die,*" the yurei says. "*One girl is marked by a ghost. Both belong to us.*"

"*What do I do? How do I get out?*"

"The trees have been waiting to claim you. They won't let you out while they're feeding on her."

"Then I'll chop them down! Damn it! What do I do?"

The yurei says nothing. She won't help. She got what she wanted yesterday and now she's watching her prank play out.

Damn her. I run past, following Melon.

"Please reconsider!" the yurei calls after me. *"Think of your family!"*

Melon's still walking when I find her, but she's turned herself in circles and hasn't made it far.

She jumps when she feels my hand on her pack. She struggles to keep me from pulling it off, but I'm stronger and her straps are loose.

Inside: gear, clothes, hygiene items—and there: I rattle an enormous bottle of analgesics.

"What's wrong with you?" I ask. "Why do you think you need these?"

I push the lid down and twist. Throw the open bottle. Pills rain down in a hyperbola.

I grab another. Melon fights me for it. I twist free of her grip. Scatter another pill rain.

"Do whatever you want!" she shouts. "You think I need pills? Look where we are!"

Bottle of vodka at the bottom of the pack to wash it down. I dump it. Make some mud.

Melon stomps off. Leaving her pack behind. Leaving me behind. I jog after. Catch her in a couple steps.

"Poison's not even a good way to do it. Stick to rope. It's faster."

"Thanks for the advice."

"I'm not giving you advice! How old are you? Sixteen?"

"Seventeen."

"What the hell is wrong with you at seventeen that you think you need to come here?"

She whips around to face me. The ferocious movement makes me stagger back.

"You think I can't have problems because I'm seventeen? My mother ran off. Okay? She ran off to Chicago when I was seven and left me in Omaha with my grandparents. They don't even like kids. Last year, she comes home just long enough to give me my father's name. Only time I've seen her since I was twelve. So I take the money I've been saving for college and I buy a trip here. To meet my father's family. But they don't want me either! Who am I to them? Some kid from another country? I'm here to find my father!"

Spit from her shouting lands on my face. I'm too stunned to answer. Not used to people emptying themselves. Not to me, the woman with the onryo who spends too much time with the dead.

At last, I think of words. "You think you're going to find family here?" I gesture at the trees. "Make a family of ghosts?"

"Why not? You're fucking one."

She can see that hurts. She's happy to have landed a punch.

"Leave me alone," she says.

"The trees won't let me." I hate to say it, but it's true. "I already half belong to them. They won't let me leave without you."

Doubt flickers across Melon's face. She didn't intend to force me to die with her.

I push at her weakness. "Your father. Will you promise not to kill yourself if I help you find him?"

She hesitates. Nods. I can see from the flicker in her eyes that it's not a real promise. She'll still kill herself to stay with him if she can.

As long as she's with me, I've got time to convince her otherwise.

We retrieve her pack and walk in silence.

The girl's shoes squeak as we walk uphill. Our unwashed smell clings to our clothes.

Why do I care if Melon dies and takes me with her? I've been here seven years, flirting with death. Letting death kiss me. Waiting for her to bring me to a height I can't safely leap down from.

I always knew Sayomi would take me eventually, but not now, I never wanted it now. Seven years of soon, later, someday.

Maybe I never wanted to die at all.

We tread on springy feathers of lichen. Creepers wind around tree trunks like yurei hair, beautiful and confining. Fingerlike branches point in a thousand different directions.

Between trees, a shadowed mass blooms where there should be day.

The horde of ghosts.

I grab Melon's elbow. I know where to find her father.

Ghosts' shadows blacken the narrow, winding twists between trees. We run toward them as they stream toward us. Within moments, we're engulfed in dark.

I scream into the mass of ghosts. "We're looking for her father! You know where he is!"

Torchlight illuminates Melon's upturned face. She's all flickers and contrasts.

Something changes in the flow of ghosts. They move around us as if we're an island, leaving an empty space. A yurei floats into the opening.

Melon's father.

He wears the button-down shirt from the picture, faded and grayed. Too-long slacks drape over his feet—if he has feet. Empty cuffs hang two feet above the ground.

He doesn't have tumbling hair like traditional yurei, but what hair he has obscures his eyes. Impossible to tell where he's looking. What he's thinking.

"Manabu?" Melon's voice shakes.

The ghost's words scrape against each other like pumice stones. "*I was alone.*"

"Speak in English?" Melon pleads.

"*They didn't think I could do it. They thought I was a coward.*"

"Please. I know you used to speak English with my mother. She can't even say *domo arigato*."

"*No one would hire me. I spent all day in the park.*"

A wind that affects nothing else blows around him. His clothing streams away from his body. Sometimes it presses tight against him, revealing the outline of his skeleton. His hair remains motionless, concealing his face.

I shout at Melon, "He's not even listening to you!"

She ignores me. "I'm your daughter! From America! I knew you'd understand me. You know what it's like to be alone."

"*I told my mother I'd talk to her landlord about the plumbing. She said I didn't have anything else to do. She pestered me until I said yes. She called my cell phone while I was sitting in the park. 'Why haven't you done it yet? You can't even talk to the landlord.' She didn't think I could do it. She thought I was a coward.*"

"Please! I don't understand! Talk to me in English!"

"*I had an interview that day. Maybe I'd have gotten the job. Who knows? I went to the landlord. I told him to fix my mother's plumbing. He said he'd get to it. I slammed him against the wall and told him, 'Get to it now.' He didn't think I was a coward then.*"

"Your...your mother's toilet...?"

"*He said he was going to call the police. I told him, 'Go ahead.' They* could find me in the park. I left his house, but I didn't go to the park. I bought a train ticket instead."

I grab urgently for Melon's hand. "He's stuck! Listen! It's what they're like. They're fixed…fixed on loneliness, on kissing someone, on playing games…"

"*I was alone. They didn't think I could do it.*"

Her father has reached the end of his story that is also the beginning. He's repeating himself now, but Melon's still listening to him, not me. Yurei stream around us, their hair growing longer and shorter as the torchlight flickers.

I have to do something to get her attention.

I fumble in my pocket. The mokume-gane wedding ring. Polished by my worrying fingers, it glistens. I hurl it toward the yurei.

They descend, magpies after something shiny. Claws emerge from hair. Wordless, screaming voices rise.

"You see?" I shout. "That's all they are! Picking after scraps of lives *they chose* to leave behind!"

One snatches the ring. It disappears under the veil of her hair. Others screech.

Melon's father drones. "*They thought I was a coward. No one would hire me.*"

I rip open my pack and pull out the trash. Scissors, nail clippers, comb, compact.

I throw them toward the trees. Where each item falls, flocks of yurei descend.

"*I spent all day in the park. I told my mother I'd talk to her landlord about the plumbing.*"

"It might make sense to kill yourself if you thought it would stop the pain. But look at them! It doesn't stop! It just keeps going!"

"*She said I didn't have anything else to do.*"

"There's no family here! Look at them!"

Two yurei attack each other in the air. Their claws rake toward each other's throats.

"They'll tear each other apart for a shred of something living!"

"She pestered me until I said yes. She called my cell phone while I was sitting in the park. 'Why haven't you done it yet?'"

It's not enough. Melon's gaze is still on her father. Full of longing. Full of hope.

I grab for a side pocket of her pack. She wrenches away, but I snatch the zipper. Open it, pull out what I saw her tuck there: the photo of her father's corpse.

I throw it at the ghost's feet. At once, he falls silent. As he recognizes himself, he becomes an arrow of greed and obsession. He dives to retrieve it, Melon forgotten.

"Do you see?" I ask. "Do you understand?"

I see the moment when Melon's gaze hardens. She turns away from her father. I grab her hand.

Wordlessly, we run through firelit dark, terrain rough beneath our feet. We stumble over roots and rocks. Barely manage not to fall.

The howling yurei horde pursues. I pull more trash from my pack. Strew it behind us. It slows them down, but they're still too close.

Melon shrugs off her pack. Abandons it.

I follow her lead and throw the expensive stuff. The trainers from the hanged man. A fan of money.

Our temporary lead widens. We glimpse sunlight through the trees. Burst into day so bright it makes us blink.

The shadows speed behind us. We've nothing else to throw.

From ahead, a drifting scent: mandarin oranges.

There she is, floating above the fork of a tree, the twisted thing that tangled me in this. I want to snarl. I want to punish her. But she's our only chance.

"Please!" I shout. "We need to get out!"

She doesn't rotate toward my voice. Was already facing us. Was probably watching all along.

She asks, "*The usual price?*"

"Yes!"

She floats toward us. Dread pricks the back of my neck.

"*Why are you helping now?*" I ask.

"*Now there are two of you to pay.*"

In front of us: her hair extending toward our bodies. Behind us: the yurei horde blocking out the light. Her hair reaches us before the horde does. Wraps us in its cocoon.

Tendrils tangle my eyelashes. Intrude into my ears, my nostrils. Horrible bug-shudder of dead-touch all over. Inescapable. We're buried alive in her hair.

Joy sparks her split ends like static electricity. Will she ever let us go?

Eventually, the hair unwinds. I can move my fingers. My limbs. She unveils my sight last. The yurei horde is gone, passed while we were hidden.

"Thanks," I say.

There's acid in my tone. It's hard to thank someone after they risk your life.

Gratitude in my tone too. Hard not to be grateful after someone saves you.

She floats a meter away from us. Her hair is back to its normal length, sweeping to her knees, no longer voluminous enough to engulf two people.

"*Consider your parents, your siblings, your children,*" she says. "*Tell the police about your troubles.*"

A lock of her hair separates from the rest. Points to a gap between trees.

"*End of a tape road there,*" she says. "*It'll get you out.*"

She rotates to watch us leave.

"I wonder who she was," Melon says. "Maybe she's from old Japan. Like her kimono."

"Hard to say."

"Maybe she's the first one who died in the forest."

"Maybe."

Melon and I sit in the parking lot. During the day, it's filled with tourist buses. Now, no one else is here.

We'll go back to town soon. Now we need rest.

"What am I going to do?" Melon asks plaintively.

Hard to answer a question like that. So painfully honest.

"You should call your grandparents."

"They don't care."

"They might."

She shakes her head. Looks away.

"Someone will care."

Her voice is quiet. "Yeah, right."

She inhales raggedly as if she's going to cry, but she doesn't. She doesn't say anything either.

Speaking feelings is hard for me, but I try. "You'll be happy. Someday. Even for a few minutes. It's more than the ghosts get." Remembering what the yurei said in the forest, I add, "All roads lead to Aokigahara. You may as well walk slowly."

The words leave a too-sweet aftertaste. Sentimental. But they make Melon smile.

Maybe a little sweetness will keep her from dying so young.

Isn't that why I've spent seven years in Aokigahara? Wishing to stop a girl from dying young?

We sit quietly for a few more minutes before we walk to town. I sit by while she places an international collect call to her grandparents.

Two AM.

Wind whistles without blowing.

My Sayomi.

She coils hair around my wrists. Draws me closer.

She's different. Almost transparently pale. So cold that her embrace is like spring rain: sudden, drenching, cold.

Hair strips my clothes. Winds between my thighs. A humid smell rises between us. Tears and desire mingle on our skins.

She opens me. Begins her caress. Cold: both shocking and exquisite.

We half-embrace, half-struggle on the floor of my single room. Same as we've been for seven years. Caught between yearning and anger.

Does she blame me? For leaving? For failing to see what I should have seen?

Do I blame her for drawing me back? For tangling me in death while I still lived?

I push my fingers between her thighs. In her midst, a spot of warmth. She tenses as I find it.

Hair simultaneously pushes me away and draws me closer. Its tips tie themselves in knots. Sayomi's expression is furious, rapturous, relieved.

All things I'm feeling too.

My tongue, melting her ice.

Her cold numbing my lips.

We shiver together as she comes.

At the apex, she screams. For once, it's not rage. It's consummation. It's expiation. It's catharsis.

As the sound dissolves her, I know she won't return. Her ghost form dissipates, leaving behind only bleached, white bones.

My Sayomi.

I curl myself around her skeleton. It's no longer as cold as ice, only as cold as death.

I sleep there, on the floor, with what's left of her, just as the suicide watch sleeps beside the bodies they bring back. For one night at least, someone must stay to console the newly dead. To ease their loneliness as best we can before morning.

When we have to go on.

Endoastronomy by Toh EnJoe
Translated by Terry Gallagher

People complain, but nobody goes out there. It's just like wondering where to go. Or asking whether to go anywhere, and if so, where to. Like pointing down the tracks, which seem to go on forever, and asking, that way? Or pointing back over one's shoulder, and saying, that way. Or stretching out your arms and asking, which way?

Our very small village is situated somewhere in a vast plain that seems to go on forever. The tracks run straight, right up against it. They come from over there and disappear off in the other direction. There isn't even a proper train stop. Children run after the trains and wave at the trainman who heaves off supplies. The supplies hit the ground hard and roll and roll, and the stuff inside is often strewn around.

"So, don't you think, it's just like where should we go, isn't it?" Leo says, perched on the rooftop, picking up the apple I had just tossed aside. The earth is a sphere, and if you look at it from far away, it's just like a point. You can't move around on a point. So there's no point in going anywhere. That is Leo's bizarre logic.

"If you really want to go somewhere, you have to believe in the

Flat Earth Theory," Leo goes on. It is just like Leo. The plain goes on without limit, and no matter how far away you get to look back at it, it is still a plane. If space is like that, it doesn't matter where you think about going, it's all the same.

I climb to the top of the ladder and sit a little ways away from Leo. Leo is lying on the slate roof. Leo sets the apple aside and drinks lemonade from a bottle. The night sky spreads overhead like an overturned sugar bowl, as far as the eye can see, with the moon looking down on us like a big eyeball. The old man says this night sky is like the terrain of old. The old night sky used to be like the terrain is now. No doubt, looking at it like this, it feels like your body is floating up toward the night sky and somehow falling toward it at the same time.

I reach out for the hand-crank radio. Noise is mixed in with the audio. It is the language of some foreign country, like music, but random mutterings, flowing smoothly, then pausing abruptly, then flowing again. It is said to be a radio broadcast from the moon, and the radio waves are certainly coming from the moon, but no one can understand what is being said.

This is what we do every night, look at the celestial bodies like this. All the light in the sky is starlight, and the earth too is a celestial body, so it is natural. If all things floating in space are celestial bodies, then we too ourselves are celestial bodies.

On the giant moon floating overhead, a pupil is visible, black and sucking in all the light. The strands of light make a pattern like a retina across the surface of the moon. It is said to be a vast city, but no one really knows for sure. People say all kinds of things about it: that rabbits live there, that crabs built it, that nine million grandmothers live there. I like to think it was built by our ancestors, but the history of our village is silent about the city on the face of the moon. I cannot imagine our descendants traveling to the moon. Likewise, I cannot believe our ancestors went there either.

Sitting here silently looking at the moon like this, sometimes I think it gives a big wink. I think it is trying to tell us something. I think it is looking back at us.

A big-screen sky full of stars. Few of the constellations are familiar to us. The ancient constellations are becoming lost, intermingled with the countless stars that are newly appearing. It is getting hard to point out particular stars. If you point at a star and say, "That one!" no one can tell which one you mean. No one can sit in the orbit of another. Even as we're sitting there saying "that one" and "which one?" we forget most of the names of the stars and constellations, and there are just too many newcomers for us to give them all new names.

We give names willy-nilly to arrays of stars, but they are just names, capricious. The constellation Lion covers half the sky, roaring. Whether it is the same as the ancient constellation known as Leo is anybody's guess.

Of the few that are certainly still the same, the ones that everyone knows, even today the constellation Orion looks to the right, his belt of three stars slopes up to the right, twinkling, and from it hangs his club.

"Anytime now Orion should be turning," Leo predicted, and so for several nights in a row we came out to look up at the night sky.

"What do you mean, 'turning'?" After years of experience listening to Leo, I have learned that when Leo starts saying things I don't understand, I should ask the meaning of the words Leo uses.

Leo makes a stern face and answers seriously. "It means he will turn from looking right to looking left. Or of course the other way around."

"Huh?" I say blankly, and start packing the radio, apple, cookies, cold-weather gear, and lemonade bottles in the backpack. Whatever the logic, once Leo decides something, there is no shaking that hypothesis.

Now Leo stands up and points straight at the night sky, yelling merrily, "Look, look!" Rocking a lemonade-addled head, Leo is doing a dangerous dance on the rooftop.

"He's looking left!"

Orion floats expressionlessly in the night sky.

"Looks the same to me," I say matter-of-factly. Just saying what I see. Orion is still looking to the right, in a muscular pose.

"The stars seem to be moving more quickly than usual."

"No way," Leo says, snapping fingers sharply, in effect telling me to pipe down.

Brushing off the pants' seat, knitting brows, and then slowly relaxing them again. Leo stares intently at Orion and says, "Orion has no front or back!"

A name meaning "lion" seems entirely fitting for someone shaking fists and standing all hairs on end because the constellation Orion will not look straight in this direction.

This village is very close to the end of the earth.

That is the conclusion both Leo and the old man on the other side of the tracks have reached. More precisely, they have concluded this village is one-fifth of the way from the end of the earth. Probably that means it is about one-fifth of the way from the end along the tracks that run from the center of the earth to the end.

The old man is someone who was driven out of town because he once drunkenly espoused subtraction in the town bar. As is written in the holy textbook, our creator the watchmaker made this world using natural numbers and addition alone. But from this performance we can conclude that math was not his best subject. That is why this world is rife with errors, and these mistakes do not cancel one another out, they simply get added together, giving birth to even bigger mistakes.

Now, if this were just change back from a bill we were talking about, there might still have been room to rethink things, but the old man was on a tear and started going on about dividing one fraction by another.

Division of fractions was the forbidden knowledge that destroyed the ancient world.

Subtraction and multiplication are the work of man. If the old man had quit there he might still have been okay, but as the overzealous people began to practice division of fractions, the end result was a giant tower of mathematics, and the ancient world was irreparably ruptured. As the word *fraction* suggests, the world itself had been fractured. Of course, I have no idea to what extent this fable reflects reality.

It was the decision of the village council that the possessor of such heretical ideas must never again cross back to this side of the tracks, and since that time the old man has remained on the other side, sleeping in a shack that is little more than a pit dug out of a garbage heap. He is somehow a distant relative of mine, and to Leo he is a friend, or a teacher, or something.

"What I mean to say is…" was the old man's pretentious pet phrase. "Let's assume you happen to be alongside the tracks, waiting for the next train, with a stupid look on your face." His eyes clouded by alcohol, he gazes at my face as if to say, "Got it?"

"Which direction will the next train be going in?" the old man asks.

I answer that the probability of a train heading left would be the same as a train heading right. But the old man, his breath reeking of alcohol, belches, "I thought so too. But I was wrong."

Leo is in the habit of gathering up liquor bottles thrown from the train and giving them to the old man in lieu of tuition. One day as Leo was doing this, the thought came: once Leo finally reached the tracks and was waiting for the next train to come, there were far more trains heading for the end of the earth than in the other direction.

"Now it seems so obvious!" Leo and the old man had tried many times to explain this to me, but they had never succeeded. But thanks to this, although I still did not understand at all, I had at least memorized the explanation.

"One line of track crosses before us. Many trains are positioned in various places along this track, and they travel at random in one direction or the other. If a larger number of trains are positioned to our left, there is a high probability the next train we see will be heading to the right," is how I put it to them, and Leo and the old man both nod.

"So why is it that from this, you know where this village is located?" I ask them every time, and every time they look perplexed.

"What do you mean, 'why?' It's just as you just explained. A middle school student would understand," says Leo—who would be about the age of a middle-schooler by the old way of reckoning—with a deeply quizzical look. And I, who should also be a middle-schooler, continue to recite from memory sentences I only halfway understand.

"In other words, as one approaches the tracks at random, if one knows the probability that a train will be heading to the right or the left, one can deduce one's own position along the line."

"Is that it?" I ask, and Leo and the old man nod solemnly.

They are unable to comprehend how someone might be able to recite the explanation in this way and still not grasp the underlying concepts. I am simply parroting by rote, and I end up thinking I really am no better than a parrot.

"It's called the Elevator Paradox," the old man says, shrugging his shoulders, using his usual locution. The two of them devised on their own this method of deducing the location of the village, but the old man later found the same ideas recorded in ancient texts. At some point in the past, someone named Elevator had stumbled upon this idea and had attached his own name to the principle. Of course, the old man could not be sure that Elevator was a person's name. There was also a theory it was the name of the mathematical tower that towered toward the heavens and incurred the wrath of the watchmaker. Or perhaps its patron.

"Probably everything is like that."

The things people are capable of imagining were all imagined long ago. All has already been written. That is what the old man told me, with a wan smile. "But this time is so fantastic," says Leo beside him, nodding eagerly.

"The forecast for the lunar eclipse has arrived," the old man says.

"Oh, I want to see that," I respond, without enthusiasm.

Through a gap in the roof of the scooped-out shed, the round moon looks down upon us.

Observing the celestial bodies and calculating their orbits through the sky is a secret hobby for Leo and the old man. Even if they didn't try to keep it a secret, though, the only other person within earshot is me.

Strewn on the desk in the tumbledown shack are a slide-rule and a hand-cranked calculator; the floor is covered with a pile of punch cards and other stuff. The old man says understanding the movements of the celestial bodies requires first a knowledge of the basics of science. The reason for this is simple. Points move in a vacuum, that is all. The stars themselves have no insides and no emotions. They conform faithfully to strictly defined rules, they never complain, they move mutely along. Or at least that was the case a long, long time ago. Now might be a little different.

That is what those two say to those of us here now, unable to tell anymore from one day to the next even whether Orion is looking to the right or to the left. Like children learning to write their letters, who often confuse p and q, b and d. Our minds are swiftly deteriorating, and we can no longer even grasp that we no longer even know what we really are. We call ourselves "humankind," but we are reverting to childhood's end. By now we should be crawling out of our cradles, but instead for some reason we find ourselves crawling back into another one.

To understand the movements of the constellations, first one has to understand what a constellation is. Leo and the old man, however, do as they please, saying that constellations can be said to be looking left or right. Of course, there is no reason why stars should be moving around like that; what's moving is just what's in our heads. Those who would observe the celestial bodies must begin by facing that that lies within themselves. What a vexing universe we inhabit. To understand how steadily stupid we are becoming on a daily basis, one need look no further than that idiot Leo. Today once again Leo is standing beneath the full moon, lemonade in one hand, observing Orion while trying to make me understand.

"What I mean is, if there is a universe where Orion is looking to the right, and a universe where Orion is looking to the left, we could say we live in a universe somewhere in between."

"By the same logic as the trains…" I start to say in desperation. One can deduce one's position along the tracks by counting the number of trains going from right to left versus the number of trains going from left to right. That's how we know that our town is one-fifth of the way from the end of the earth. To me, Orion always looks like he's looking to the right, but if someone were to ask me what that means, my confidence would crumble. If all the b's and d's in the world were switched, and then if the mechanisms inside my head that recognize a b as a b were also switched so that b seemed like d, I would never even be able to notice the change.

The astronomy that Leo and the old man are constructing is based on a similar kind of substitution, and it has grown into a giant sophistry where the microcosmos that exists in our heads is linked directly to the macrocosmos of the universe. Their view is that a human-scale process of substitution is now under way, and their evidence for this is the Orion that can change his orientation and the full moon that winks. If things that by rights should not be possible actually occur as if they are natural, the assumption that these things should not be possible must be mistaken. It could be either the stars or us that's crazy, or of course it could also be both.

We are already on our way to becoming unable to distinguish *b*'s from *d*'s, and we are unable to grasp the wave of change that is threatening to envelop us. That said, the problem is really one of perception; the unseeable is unseeable, and there is nothing we can do about that. At least, I can't see it. These two are the only ones in town who actually perceive the changes taking place, and one of them is the town drunk and the other a mere child.

From sane to crazy, the change is slow. And what is sanity then? Someone who was once sane and turns crazy still thinks of himself as sane. A sane person who is going crazy, and during that process continues to assert that he is still sane, is in a way affirming his insanity. If, up in the sky, hung an insanity in the shape of the moon, it would still stare down on those of us on the face of the earth.

"Regardless of the veracity of your logic..."

"It is verifiable," Leo responds curtly.

"But you need some proof!" I say.

"Our understanding of the turning of Orion has reached a point where we can predict its frequency," Leo says.

"That's not what I mean. You need some objective proof! I only see an Orion looking to the right."

Leo points at the moon.

The old man was just a child when the city on the face of the moon first appeared, shouting in its sleep in radio waves. And actually, that was just a memory of the old man's. Everyone else says the moon has always looked just the way it does now.

"Somebody else has started to be able to see the city on the moon," Leo says.

"Who? Just tell me, who?"

"This is still just a hypothesis," Leo says, uncharacteristically timid. "Whales, maybe, or porpoises. Or perhaps squid or lichens. Or Antarctic krill."

Hmmm, I say, trying to look profoundly impressed. Recently I have begun to suspect that lemonade might have an intoxicating effect on certain people.

"Don't you realize that the human senses are more subtle than our thoughts?" Leo grumbles, looking somewhere beyond me with that look that dreamers get in their eyes. For a second I think that Leo, who could see Orion left-right-reversed, might be seeing me front-back-reversed.

"People's understanding of nature is flawed," Leo continues with a shake of the head, addressing no one in particular. "But something has begun to understand nature better than people are able to."

Leo is flapping the arms wildly, and the lemonade bottle falls to the roof, disgorging its contents. In accordance with the laws of nature, it rolls off the edge of the roof and disappears into the darkness.

"Empires and dinosaurs have their similarities." Leo has begun to cross to the far side of the fine line between genius and insanity and continues to spout random chains of thoughts into the empty air. "Just as the world once viewed by the dinosaurs has disappeared, the world viewed by empires has also disappeared."

I can hardly tell if Leo is whispering something or just breathing heavily.

"It could be that the human race is being expelled from its current cognitive niche."

The human race has evolved to the point where it can comprehend the process of evolution. Though it may seem natural now, this is something that is anything but self-evident. Even if one is completely unaware of evolution, the process of evolution proceeds anyway. Trains run without having any awareness of logic, and we humans are able to think about things. The day we become unable to think about things unless we know how we are supposed to think about them, that will definitely be the day we no longer have time to think about anything.

The term *cognitive niche* is also something the old man dug up from the ancient texts; it is not a new invention. For something to be cognizant of something else is about as natural as for something to eat something else. Living things compete with one another for limited resources. This is the way it is, so that in the daisy chain of edible objects, one finds the most suitable niche of prey species among the many possibilities, and pointless competition can be averted. If two species exist that eat the same things and have the same fighting skills, they will not be able to occupy the same niche. They will have to settle in different locations, to enhance the efficiency of the whole. Of course, this expresses the process in reverse: the less effective one will be forced to go on a drastic diet, and it will starve to death. Or it will simply be eaten. Isn't it obvious?

Applying this idea to the cognitive process, one arrives at the idea of the cognitive niche, which is where we say, "This means that." A person looks at an apple, a bat looks at an apple, a donkey, a dog, a cat, a chicken can all be friends and observe apples—that is when the apple really starts to shine. That's the way it is, so that an apple can really feel more like an apple. Someday I'd like to ask Leo or the old man what that really means.

We are the ones who took the places of some newcomers who were already occupying this niche. That is the opinion of the pair who are able to see Orion turn. Those two, who can observe Orion look to the left, think human consciousness is moving into a niche that was previously occupied by some other life-form. Or else this:

the human cognitive process is invading something somewhere, rendering the transformation of our consciousness inevitable.

Our capacity to process information does not extend to fully processing the data input by our sensory organs. Right now, in the night sky above our heads, countless stars are shining. I can look at each one individually like this, but I cannot remember them all individually. If one of them should be extinguished tomorrow, or if a new one should be added, I wouldn't notice. And somehow or other I think that is how the number of stars increased so dramatically, while we were not paying attention. I live my life unaware of the hairs that are quietly saying sayonara to my father's scalp, until one day I notice that his hair has grown very thin. As I grow, my eyes get higher above the ground, but I can't say I've noticed that as it is happening.

We waste information, letting it flow from right to left without really processing it. It might move us a little bit, emotionally, but that's about it. With all that freely leaking information, people say something else is chowing down on it. Something that is better than people are processing it.

Two species in the same niche is one too many.

For ordinary thinkers, doubting one's own thoughts is probably the sane thing to do, but Leo and the old man are powerful thinkers, and they can't abide that kind of sanity. They are the kind of people who can look at a nonsensical universe and remake astronomy itself.

"But matter is solid," I argue back lamely. Even if most people think the earth is flat, that doesn't make the earth flat. "But it does look flat," Leo says. Or one might think earthquakes result when the earth's crust slips on the sweat of the elephants that are holding it up. "We are free to sense whatever we want. I'll give you that," I say. But Leo says that is not the case. "Sensations are not like thoughts. We are not free to believe we did not sense whatever it is we just sensed," Leo says.

"We can only think that we sense it by mistake," Leo says. "If there is such a thing as detecting the existence of molecular particles, or sensing the effects of evolution, that is just a mistake. 'Molecular particles' and 'evolution' are just words that were created to help us understand. They are something we recognize, not something we perceive. It is because we cannot sense them that we thought them up. But if we feel them as actual sensations, that fact itself is unassailable."

"But matter is solid!" I repeat, without any intention of fooling anyone. "Or numbers are," I add. Even if humans get so stupid they can no longer count any higher than three, that doesn't mean numbers don't exist anymore. This is not a matter to be decided by majority rule. I would rather believe it is something that is not to be decided at all.

"Well, so, how about that then?" Leo is pointing quietly to the sky.

Today again there is a huge full moon, and the pupil defined by the city on the surface of the moon is quietly gazing down upon us. Even I can certainly see that eye. And it certainly seems to be winking.

According to Leo's record of astronomical observations, the length of time Orion faces left is gradually growing longer.

This is an indication, in other words, that our universe is gradually approaching either the edge of the universe or the center of the universe. Not right away, of course, but bit by bit, something is about to happen. At least in Leo's mind, that is. Even the two of them have no idea what might happen when we reach the edge of the universe. The old man is fine as long as it happens while he is still alive. He has terrible shakes from not drinking, but even he does not know if that day will be in the near future or in the distant future.

The old man asks, grumbling, if I am alone today. I pick up a whiskey bottle and show it to him.

"Couldn't you at least tell me what it is you expect to happen?"

"But that's why I'm thinking like this, so's I can understand what's going to happen."

I take the bottle and grip the hand of the old man, who is buried beneath a pile of calculator paper.

"This idea about Orion switching around is just some fantasy the two of you have."

The old man eyes both me and the bottle, and clucking his tongue he says, "I do not deny that possibility. If someone were to say it was just a coincidence that only me and Leo can see it, there's nothing I can do about that. Some fantasies can be contagious. Synchronization is a basic strategy of living things."

The old man squints to check the label on the bottle and then shakes his head as if to say he has no interest.

"What is it that you want to know?"

"About the moon."

"The moon, eh?" the old man says. Folding his arms and shifting his weight to his rickety spine, he slides down the pile. "The logic should be very simple. Grand phenomena can only be achieved through simple logic."

"Simple," I mumble, not really speaking, but he ignores me and smiles a slightly awkward smile. It seems a pleasant enough expression, but at the same time it is ominous.

"Even now you want to hear some outmoded term like 'quantum mechanics'?"

"No, not at all."

"Well then." The old man smiles and coughs. "No matter how you slice it, that was never anything more than a figure of speech. The truth is really very simple. Through the act of someone observing something, that something exists."

Lifting his heavy eyelids as high as they can go, he stares at me to see how I might respond.

"That sounds to me like a pretty arrogant way of thinking."

"Precisely." He nods with an air of satisfaction. "But it is only arrogant if we think it is only humans who have consciousness at their disposal."

Silently, I begin to count the crevices carved in the old man's face. He asks me, "Why is it we should think that only humans possess consciousness?"

"Because we are the ones who sense things."

"Hmmph," says the old man, putting on his thinking face. "What about the idea that it has been observed that we believe we sense things?"

"Well, I sense that I believe that we are here talking and that we are moved to speak words."

The old man, seeing that his sneak attack has been thwarted, blows his nose and waves his hand to indicate I should go away. I am sure he is thinking that I am right. I leave the whiskey bottle on the desk.

At one time, everyone thought that what had hardened into a single eye and floated up into the sky was the moon that looked down upon us.

Whether the retina of the moon that had been created in this way was the product of our awareness and aspirations, or that of the squid or Antarctic krill or arachnocampa that would someday take over the cognitive niche that we have slid down into, is something we will never have any way of knowing.

I realize this discussion has become a bit involved. We are cognizant of the eyelike moon. But it could be that really it is the moon that is cognizant of us, and that moon is something that somebody else cogitated. It has been observed that we believe we are observing the moon.

And why should it be that that someone did not cogitate us

directly, but rather did it through the moon of all things. I would like to ask that someone directly, but the address to which such an inquiry should be sent is unknown. It is also most highly probable that they did not waste a minute thinking about us. They probably just wanted some kind of machine that would be able to see them objectively.

As I try to arrange these various things—if they are like that, then we must be like this—into some sort of coherence, all sorts of contradictions come burbling up. Our universe has this sort of a form, like a piece of knitting where the first stitches were somehow wrong. And just as everything is spinning out of control, the whatever machine keeps going blithely around and around. The blind watchmaker made it just to see what he could do, and now it keeps on recreating itself, to the point where it is no longer clear if it is a watch or just what kind of machine it is. Only the parts made now and then by the watchmaker himself resemble timepieces.

As for the reality of the guys observing the moon, as they are now, I can add one sleuthlike observation: what makes Orion appear reversed is looking at the celestial sphere from the outside. It's not that the moon is floating outside the celestial sphere on which the constellations are plastered, but if you think about it that way, the constellation Orion cannot be observed from anyplace else but Earth.

But I'm sure that Leo and the old man realized all this a very long time ago.

I find it a little bit amusing that those who put that city on the surface of the moon by thinking it, and who are now looking down on us, seem to have imagined the celestial sphere or something like it. When I think that their astronomy must be a little different from ours, a little thrill runs through me.

Any fairy tale like this can go from the dull to the endlessly complex, but that would be a pain, so I'm going to stop. Well, I'll go just a little further. That full moon that is looking at us was in all probability born somehow from the dreams of humans and other things like that; it was created from the unconscious of those of us who recognize a need for a transcendent or transcendental overseer. Just like thinking that by observing that moon we bring it into being, we are also observed by the moon we are observing, and we find that to be reasonable, or something like that. I think humans are nothing more than a highly overvalued delusion.

Actually this isn't even really a fairy tale, it's more like a load of hogwash. Just what we perceive as fairy tales and what is mere bunkum depends to a great extent on our own process of perception.

The old man pops his head down through a door-shaped aperture, and shouts at my back, "Don't forget!"

"Don't forget what?"

"That you came to see the lunar eclipse!"

Only then do I remember that Leo and the old man have been working on those calculations. That had been a formal pronouncement of theirs, I concede. In a universe that has lost its sanity, they have discovered laws that govern this activity, and they have predicted the next manifestation. The logic of delusion is incapable of predicting actual results, but if Leo and the old man's astronomy correctly forecasts this lunar eclipse, then it must contain at least some part of the truth.

Of course what I expect, though, is that the eclipse will not come about as forecast and that Leo and the old man's astronomy will be cast aside.

Of course there is no reason why the lunar eclipse predicted by Leo and the old man's endoastronomy should be known to the other local residents, so the town is in a bit of an uproar. For this to come up all of a sudden, it is easy to see why they might think the end of the world had arrived.

"First time in fifty years, right?" the old man says. Out of the old man's shack we have brought every cushion we could find, and we lie out in the grassy field of the night. We can see Saturn's rings around the round moon.

"No matter what anyone says, Saturn can't be there, can it?" I complain to the old man, but Leo kicks me in the side and I shut up. Saturn's rings are slowly sliding above the moon, and Saturn itself is slowly starting to cast its shadow on the moon.

"Pretty much as predicted, right?" the old man says.

"Right," Leo responds.

As the two of them exchange remarks matter-of-factly, once again I doubt, from the bottom of my heart, their sanity. I am in denial of something I am witnessing with my own eyes.

"Actually, something is not quite right. If we are saying that Saturn has now interposed itself between the earth and the moon, we should have been able to see it approaching before this," I say.

"But we have been seeing it. For weeks. For a long time now." Leo's reply makes me forget what I want to say. But the next words after that practically make me stop breathing.

"Even before that, we should have been skeptical about the fact that the moon we see is always full."

This is information I am simply letting go of. The moon revolves around the earth, and the earth revolves around the sun. This is just common sense. The moon we see is always full. That too is common sense. There is no connection between these two pieces of common sense, but for whatever reason, we still hold them both to be common sense. The bridge binding these two islands of common sense has been washed away by the senses, and now there is no more connection.

As Saturn gradually obscures the moon, it becomes a black disk exactly the same size as the moon, creating a crisply defined corona facing in this direction. From the far side of the tracks, flames blaze up, and shouts can be heard faintly from the direction of the village. The light of the moon fringes the black disk. A terrestrial blaze threatens to obliterate our horizon. Our village, said to be one-fifth of the way from the edge of the earth. The group of us, hoping to become merely those observed by a universe possessed of a different consciousness.

"Are you coming with us?" Leo asks.

But that is impossible.

With the universe now looking like this, there is no way anything more can be done. This is now a universe that is apparently making a showy display of crushing the laws of physics, and unquestionably even the concept of numbers is perhaps on the verge of collapse. And Saturn is the adversary. Can there still be room for human thought in a thinking universe where our adversary might even be a living being? I think not.

"You're wrong. We can definitely solve this," Leo says, still looking up at the night sky.

A strong statement, without foundation, and extremely paradoxical. We are seeking, using our own logic, to know the mechanism that will expunge our own logic itself. This is not a matter of translating some foreign language into our own language. It is very nearly an attempt to translate our own language into some foreign language we ourselves cannot comprehend. Actually, it is more serious than that. We are not translating some language of aliens. We are almost trying to bury our own language within a circumstance where only alien language exists. Just thinking about it makes my head spin.

"There is no way we can do that."

"Quit your bitchin'."

At some point the old man got up, and he is looking down on us.

"Aren't you two a pair!"

"What's that supposed to mean?" I start to say, but before I even get to the end of the sentence, Leo leaps up and shouts, "What's that?" The old man crouches lightly and, in a surprisingly swift martial arts move, avoids Leo's kick.

Not that anybody had tried to hide it. Just, nobody had thought to mention it, thinking it had nothing to do with the current storyline. It's just that in the language of the country of Leo's ancestors, no one thought it strange to give a name meaning "lion" to a girl.

"No matter what anybody says, that's just how it is. Nothing in this world is more effective than simple things."

The old man is even now attempting to whistle, and Leo stares hard at him before turning on her heel to walk away. Squaring her shoulders and jerking them up and down, Leo waves her arms in rage and sets off at a clip, as if to cross the unending dark plain on her own. She heads away from the town. At a right angle to the tracks.

"Aren't you going to chase after her?" the old man says.

"This isn't like that, at least I don't think it is," I respond.

The old man makes a face as if to say, "What an idiot," but I ignore him.

"What will happen if I don't go with her?" I ask. I can't even see left-facing Orion. I am not even fully aware of how completely deceived I am by crazy nature. This is not a problem of thought. It is not even a problem of feelings. It is merely a problem of awareness. I am simply not one chosen in this way by this universe.

"Shouldn't you be asking what will happen if you do go along?"

"So, that way, I suppose."

The old man says to me disparagingly, laughing: "The two of you are going to have to work this out. Find the being that is now newly occupying the cognitive niche formerly owned by human-kind, and then I don't care if you fight or if you negotiate or if you find some way of living in a new niche. Or you can look for a law to destroy the law itself. It will be a great adventure."

"I have no interest in great adventures."

The old man points his chin out toward the plain. "That girl does…"

My shoulders droop as I let out a sigh.

Beneath the eclipse, a small shadow stands imposingly like a temple guardian, shaking its fist repeatedly at the sky.

I raise my eyes with bated breath. All I see is a blank space. Right where Orion should be. Where Orion should be there is a blank space. Only Orion's space is completely erased. Not that there is a space there. What I notice instead is merely a vertical alignment of stars. Although I'm not sure that "merely" is the right word here.

This may be the moment at which I really enter Leo and the old man's "club." Which is like getting into some club of social insects, or batlike aliens, or the somehow super-intelligent. Two people might share a delusion, but if three are involved it's something else entirely. Isn't there an aphorism like that?

My mind is desperately searching for some reason why Orion should choose this instant to show me its turned form for the first time, but this effort fails to bear fruit. It may be nothing more than coincidence, or it may have something to do with Saturn interrupting the moon's gaze. The moon looks down upon us even in the daytime, so the likelihood of the latter is extremely low. Saturn's shadow may have obscured what sanity remained in my heart, perhaps that is it. Saturn is the ruler of melancholy, and perhaps what I am experiencing now is a concealing of the crazy moon in my heart. Thinking is futile. Even more so thoughts that are realized because they are observed by the moon. This is the point where ordinary logic ceases to function, and the only thing to do is to create new logic.

Once this is seen, resistance is pointless. We are what we are. Existence, as we know it, is over.

The filthy words Leo spat at Orion appear to have been carried by the wind and reached their destination, however faintly. I record them here, cleaned up just a bit.

"You just hang on there a minute, I'm coming to show you what's what."

Now I know the reason why I am able to see Orion turn. I think it cannot be understood, actually, but if you look, you can see it. That self that is there within my body, transmitted in an unbroken chain from ancient times down through the ages in my cells, just rips right through thought and discovers a new niche, and then, of its own accord, starts to recognize it. I choose myself, and I know that I do so. At least in that sense, it is I that has to choose something.

I can see Orion as he slowly shakes his rough club at Leo.

My body leaves my head behind.

"Leo!" I cry out, and I start to run across the endless plain. Her fine, small body is starting to stir, somewhere way out there. Whether she is looking this way or that way, it is too dark for me to tell yet.

"Wait for me!"

I'm on my way there to you.

In Plain Sight by Pat Cadigan

Goku Mura thought the old lady probably wouldn't have fallen for it if the scammer hadn't had the bright idea to use the term "Easter egg." Emmy Eto, as she was known to her neighbors in the retirement community, was one of the last of the generation who had actually used the antiquated term. She was in her mid-nineties, which also made her old enough to remember Japan as it had existed physically, before quakes and tidal waves had reduced it to fragments that would have been uninhabitable even without the radiation. He didn't want to think it made her more gullible.

He had no idea why Doré Konstantin had sent the case to him. For one thing, he hadn't laid eyes on her in several calendar-months—more than two, fewer than six? Seven, for sure—which Konstantin said was a lot longer in AR time. Dog years, she called it. Although he had seen her in AR during that time, but only just barely—a flicker in the corner of his eye, too fast or too far away, but recognizable as Konstantin if only by the empty spot she left behind. *Hello too busy talk later,* he supposed, and marveled at how she managed to do it in Augmented Reality as well as Artificial Reality. The deregulation of Augmented Reality in the US had been a legal shit storm, leading to what Goku thought was the single most awe-inspiring piece of legislation of the last century: *legal reality*. He'd been dying to talk to Konstantin about it, but he'd been too busy even to send her a smart-ass remark.

Maybe that was why she'd sent him the Emmy Eto case, so he'd have to get in touch just to ask wtf. He read through it to make sure he wasn't missing anything, but it seemed to be nothing more than what Konstantin called straight-up bunco—despicable but hardly a job for I3. The local law machinery could run it on autopilot: the prosecutor would claim two counts of special circumstances, saying Eto had been targeted not only because she was elderly and more vulnerable but also because she was Japanese. That made it a hate crime and therefore under federal jurisdiction. The prospect of facing a federal judge was usually enough to make offenders and their (usually) court-appointed lawyers amenable to a plea bargain, which was heavy on plea without much bargain. The DA simply removed the special circumstances charge. Relieved felons went off to serve sentences barely lighter than what they could have expected after a jury trial, thinking they'd been given a break, while overworked prosecutors were even more relieved to have saved themselves the trouble of working up special-circumstances briefs that were all too likely to be shit-canned by equally overworked federal judges with no room on their twenty-four-hour dockets.

The only thing slightly out of the ordinary about it was how the scammer was refusing to sit up and beg like someone who had seen the error of her ways, even just for the time it took a judge to gauge the sincerity of her remorse and pass sentence accordingly. She was a piece of work named Pretty Howitzer, not just legally but from birth. With parents like that, Goku Mura thought, she'd never stood a chance. Her record backed that up—a long list of unremarkable misdemeanors and felonies, suspended sentences, sentences commuted to time served, sentences reduced because there just wasn't room in the correctional facility, along with a number of dismissals and DTPs. A Decline To Prosecute usually meant lack of evidence or witnesses or both, though one was also marked TFB, which, Goku discovered after a little digging, stood for Too Fucking Boring.

Too funny to ignore, he thought and phoned Konstantin.

He got one of her detectives instead, the one with the mutton-chops. It took him a minute to remember her name: Celestine.

"Jurisdictional nightmare," Celestine told him cheerfully. He'd never been a fan of facial hair on women or men, but something about her smile always gave him a lift.

"International?" He shrugged. "You guys handle international all the time."

"In AR, sure. But this is also AR+."

"What difference does that make?"

"It's both Artificial Reality *and* Augmented Reality, with offline interludes, all crossing international borders. Our DA took one look and decided it was someone else's headache. I gotta say, though, I didn't think you'd be the lucky winner."

"I didn't know Konstantin was sending things out for the district attorney's office these days."

Celestine's cheerful smile faded. "Uh, say again?"

"I got the case from Konstantin, not the DA."

Now her face lost all expression. "Hang on." She started paging through something on her desk just below camera range. It was almost half a clock-minute before she looked up again. "The DA's office says it's on record as exported to I3 twenty minutes ago. They're also saying this must be a world record for turnaround."

"I guess so," Goku said, "because it got to my inbox twelve hours ago. You guys using neutrino mail?"

Celestine shifted uncomfortably. "Well, someone's clock is off, maybe on this end. Somebody screwed up with the time zone or something."

"I've never heard of that," Goku said, "but as Konstantin always says, stranger things have happened." The detective all but flinched at the mention of her name. He started to get a bad feeling. "Could be her joking around."

"It's not Konstantin," Celestine insisted stonily. "And if it's a joke—hell, I can't think of anyone that tasteless even in the DA's office."

"Something happened." Goku kept his voice even as a small, dense knot of dread formed in the pit of his stomach. Civil service: bureaucracy relieved by sudden incidents of homicide. Konstantin had laughed at that one till she cried.

"She got shot."

Shot. Shit. Shooting the shit, she got shot. He forced the thought away. "How?"

"Sniper. Right in the eye."

"Around the turn of the twenty-first century," Lieutenant Bruce Ogada said as he and Goku sat in the empty waiting room, "someone had the bright idea to take a laser pointer and aim it at the night sky." His dry, matter-of-fact tone reminded Goku of the last international economics report he had endured, minus the ambiguity. Ogada was dressed in a standard suit and tie. His one concession to his own comfort had been to remove his jacket and lay it over the arm of his chair; he hadn't even loosened his tie, and his white shirt seemed as crisp and clean as if he had put it on only minutes earlier, fresh from the store. *Fresh from the showroom*, as Konstantin would have said had she been there, Goku thought, wishing she were with an intensity that under other circumstances he might have tried to tell himself was surprising.

He made himself sit up straighter in the peculiar chair. It was a weird piece of furniture, too large for one person and not big enough for two, making it impossible to rest both elbows at the same time without them being absurdly akimbo. The arms were thin, squared-off tubes of metal too uncomfortable to lean on anyway. It was a style of chair Goku had never seen anywhere except in waiting rooms, usually the kind that people didn't want to be in—assuming there was any other kind. He was only in this one because he'd been turned away by the smiling gorgon at the entrance to Intensive Care. One visitor at a time, and even if her lieutenant hadn't been visiting at the moment, his name wasn't on the approved list. He'd have to see Lt. Ogada about that, if he cared to wait. He had, barely pausing to get a cap of the gorgon. The projection was completely opaque even as close as twelve inches, and its features had an authentic quality that suggested there was a real, possibly unwitting, model.

"A thin red beam of light going straight up into the dark, all tight and narrow and focused, must have been fascinating," Ogada was saying. "'Look at me, I've got a lightsaber a hundred miles tall.'" He leaned forward, elbows on his knees, hands loosely folded. "One night during one of these do-it-yourself light shows—and I'm just guessing now but that's how things like this usually happen— somebody noticed a plane flying in the vicinity and thought, what the hell. That's what you do with a laser pointer—you point."

Goku nodded, although Ogada wasn't looking at him.

"When the beam hit the cockpit, it blinded the pilot. Temporarily, of course, although there were a few cases of burned retinas." He looked over at Goku, eyebrows raised, a man about to reveal a criti- cal detail. "Didn't show up till a few days later. Pilot'd get a strange feeling in the eye, have a doctor check it out, and there it was." He gave a short, soundless laugh. "A little round spot. Like a cigarette burn. Aiming a laser pointer at aircraft became a serious crime. Committed by morons, since it was easy to trace a laser beam back to its source."

He let out a breath and sat back in his chair; it was similar to Goku's but smaller, with padding on the arms. "The statute's still on the books because, believe it or not, every so often, some idiot gets the brilliant idea to go outside and wave a laser pointer around. The aviator lenses most cockpit crews wear inflight usually protect their eyes so they don't get burned, but sometimes, if a beam hits just right—excuse me, just *wrong*—it can actually fuck up the lens in a way that affects the pilot, or whoever. They get dizzy, disoriented, even have seizures." His gaze had drifted away; now he looked at Goku again. "I don't suppose any of this is news to you."

Goku shrugged. "I'm not familiar with *every* country's aviation laws."

"You probably never leave home without your state-of-the-art safety goggles, just in case lenses aren't enough. Or is that too low-tech for Interpol 3?"

Goku's half smile was wry. "We have a small collection of old hardware, kind of an in-house museum—CB radios, break-glass fire alarms. Black lights. Modems. There's even a Zippo lighter with a military insignia. I think it's the US Marines Corps but I'm not sure. Maybe it's just the army."

Ogada's face was expressionless, and Goku suddenly felt ashamed of his feeble attempt at humor. He was formulating an apology when Ogada spoke again.

"I know I3's been trying to recruit her." His face still gave no hint of emotion. "And before you ask, no, she didn't say anything about it. She never mentioned you at all—I mean, not so much as a vague reference. As if she weren't even aware of your existence. Which was how I knew. She didn't want to give me an opening to ask any questions she didn't want to answer. I know how she thinks."

"She always said no."

Now Ogada's eyebrows went up again. "Did you ask her if she was thinking about it?"

Goku hesitated, unsure of what Ogada was getting at. "I *had* asked her to think about it."

"But did you ask her if she *was* thinking about it?"

"Well…" Goku shook his head slightly. "She didn't say she wouldn't."

"Yeah. That's what she didn't want to tell me, that she was thinking about it. She didn't tell you that either. She just said no every time you tried to recruit her." Ogada gave a short laugh. "I keep forgetting you're not from around here."

Goku smiled a little. "I was thinking the same thing about you," he said, "until I remembered where I was." Pause. "Look, I didn't know anything about what happened till one of her detectives told me, the one with the—" he made a widening gesture on either side of his face with both hands.

"Celestine," Ogada said.

"Right. And the only reason I called was to ask about a case. I thought I'd got one of hers by mistake."

Ogada looked at him sharply. "Which one?" It sounded more like a demand than a question.

Goku gave him the gist.

"Oh, that one." The lieutenant shook his head. "Jurisdictional nightmare. We voted it off the island. Something my father used to say," he added in response to Goku's puzzled look. "Case too small for you guys? Well, don't worry—the minute Pretty Howitzer finds out 13's interested, she'll probably lie down and plead like she should've done in the first place."

Goku decided against mentioning the contradictory information as to how it had come to him, at least for the moment. "Right now, I don't give a shit one way or the other. I came to see how Konstantin's doing."

"No change from yesterday or the day before or any other day in the month since it happened," Ogada said wearily. "I stop in two, three times a week, sit next to her, tell her I'm eating lunch, and suggest she lose some weight."

"Why would you do that?" Goku asked, drawing back slightly.

"I figure that'll get a rise out of her if nothing else will. So far—"

He got up and put on his jacket. "No joy. We'll get your name on the list, maybe you'll have better luck. But not right now. You might as well come back to the precinct and question What's-Her-Name Howitzer, she's still in Holding. You guys got this case a lot faster than usual."

"So I've heard," Goku said.

Pretty Howitzer was a type that Goku privately classified as cute. He couldn't decide how much Japanese there was in her lineage—more than a fourth, possibly more than a third, but certainly not more than half. The jailhouse lenses dulled her eyes a bit, but he could still see they were closer to gold than brown, and there was a sprinkle of freckles across the bridge of her turned-up nose. She was also very petite, more so than he had realized from her mug shots.

But the most striking thing about her at the moment was her relentless nail biting, which did nothing to undercut her blasé attitude. Someone had once told him that for some people, nail biting had nothing to do with anxiety—it was merely a neurological glitch, possibly a half-baked form of OCD or even Tourette's. Pretty Howitzer made it look like self-indulgence; the longer she chewed on herself, the more relaxed she seemed, awkward as it was with the handcuffs.

Goku found it hard to watch, and there was nothing else in the small interrogation room to draw the eye. The observation window was camouflaged as bare wall, so there wasn't even a mirror. Anyone with the slightest tendency to claustrophobia would have a rough time in this room. He remembered Konstantin's partner, Taliaferro, who worked out of an office on the roof. Too long in here, Goku thought, and he might have to join him. Assuming Taliaferro was still getting away with it now that Konstantin was benched.

"So you're the big bad I3 agent," Pretty Howitzer said, removing her left index finger from her mouth briefly. "Thought you'd be taller. Or maybe it's this room." She dipped her head like she was afraid something would fall on it and looked from side to side. "Is it me or is this a goddamn shoebox?"

"It's you," Goku lied, mildly surprised at how confident he sounded. "Shit doesn't get a whole lot deeper than this—well, not while you're alive anyway. So if you feel like the walls are closing in, it's because they are."

Pretty Howitzer rolled her eyes. "If that's a mixed metaphor, you're not even trying."

Several sharp retorts jockeyed for position in Goku's mind, but what he heard himself say was, "Get your fingers out of your mouth."

To his surprise, she obeyed. "Yeah, sure. Sorry." The handcuffs rattled as she wiped her fingers on the front of her pink coverall. According to some expert, the color supposedly made prisoners feel physically and mentally less powerful. Pretty Howitzer looked like she was wearing a playsuit. "Most of the time, I don't even know I'm doing it."

"How do you cope in AR?" Goku asked. "Going without for hours must be real hard on you."

"I don't have to go without anything." She looked down and to her left for a moment at something only she could see. Goku did likewise, but if her lenses were tapped, he wasn't getting a copy. Civil service: he'd probably have to fill out eighty thousand forms in triplicate for a transcript. Which he could expect to receive in four to six weeks. "When they deregulated AR+, I sent a basket of flowers and a box of chocolates to my congresspeople," Pretty Howitzer was saying. "And I can't even vote." Her upper body rose and fell with a deep sigh that was somehow both wistful and satisfied. "I don't remember the last time I was stuck playing indoors."

"Well, it's the end of an era for you, Ms. Howitzer." Goku leaned on the bare metal table between them and then was annoyed to find he had to pull his chair in farther. The legs shrieked on the floor, and he had to suppress the urge to pick the thing up and throw it across the room. "You don't get AR or AR+ in prison. It's just ground floor all day, every day, day in, day out. But the good news is, you can bite your nails whenever you feel like it. All the way down to your elbows, if you want."

Pretty Howitzer wrinkled her cute little nose. "You talk like my grandfather. And that's not a compliment. I hated that old f—"

"Get your fingers out of your mouth."

She made a small, jerky movement, obeying reflexively before realizing she didn't have her fingers in her mouth. "Hey!"

He grinned broadly without showing his teeth. "That why you've been picking on the old folks, because you hate your grandfather?"

"Oh, are you actually a head doctor? You gonna psychoanalyze me, figure out how I went bad? You want to put in some buttons, turn me good?" She wrinkled her nose again. "For. Get. It. Not giving up *my* free will, not for a hundred times what I took off that old bat. I'm pro choice all the way. I do whatever I choose to do, not because someone else controls me—"

"Get your fingers out of your mouth."

Again, she started to obey before realizing she didn't have to; he felt a surge of spiteful joy. "You fuckin' cops," she growled, infuriated. "Think you're so genius—"

"I'm an Interpol 3 agent. I can show you my *credentials*," he said, inflecting the last word carefully to trigger it.

She started to answer, then froze for half a second. Her eyes took on a brief faraway look before she closed them and moved her eyes from side to side a few times to dismiss the image he'd sent her. "If I want to see your fucking *credentials*, I'll—oh, shit." She squeezed her eyes shut, pressing her thumbs against them.

Goku managed not to laugh. "That was your own fault. The way you said *credentials*."

Again she stared distantly at nothing before she clapped her hands over her eyes. "Cut it out, asshole!" She knuckled her eye sockets.

"I'm sorry, that really *was* an accident," he said, meaning it. "It's a tone-of-voice trigger. If you can keep yourself from mocking me for at least two clock-minutes, it shouldn't happen again. I don't think. I don't know what the system is here for jailhouse lenses."

"Just proves my point." Pretty Howitzer's glare was slightly bloodshot. "Agent's just a fancy name for cop and I3 agents are just *free-range* cops. You're only interested in crimes in places you want to go so you can get a free paid vacation. Don't give me that look. It's true, everybody knows that about you *agents*." Abruptly, she heard the way she'd said the last word and froze, looking dismayed. But *agents* wasn't a trigger word. Today.

"I have to say, I'm gobsmacked." He couldn't help chuckling now. "That you would think *I* actually *want* to come *here*."

"Gobsmacked?!" Pretty Howitzer threw back her head and hooted at the ceiling; the acoustic tiles swallowed her voice so quickly, she sounded almost staccato. The effect reminded Goku of a story he'd read long ago, about a man whose job involved cleaning leftover sounds out of empty rooms. Years later, he had started out in I3 doing something that he sometimes thought of as (vaguely, faintly) similar, just as a way to relieve (albeit very slightly) the stultifying tedium of surveillance.

"Do you ever hear yourself! 'Oh, I *say*, old chap, I'm utterly *gob*smacked by the *whole bloody business*.' What's that accent about anyway?"

"What accent?"

"Oh, *veddy* funny, old chap, *veddy*, pip pip cheerio and all that rot! Come on, what's with you?"

Goku couldn't help laughing. "Nothing. What's with you, besides too much vintage TV?"

"Hey, *I'm* not puttin' on an accent."

"Neither am I. I was born and raised in England."

"Yeah? You do all that English stuff? Boarding school? Uniforms? Cricket, rum, sodomy, and the lash?"

Is this the vanguard of a new, more educated offender? he wondered, amused. "You'll have lots of time to read about the lives of English schoolboys in the Mid-Atlantic Prison library."

"*What?!*" Pretty Howitzer's cute jaw dropped as she lost whatever cool she'd still had. "*No!* You *can't!* I didn't *kill* anybody, I didn't use a *weapon*, I didn't even make *threats!* I'm a US *citizen*, you *can't* sink me, you *can't!*"

"I can. And the US apparently thinks it would be a good idea since they signed off on it."

Her eyes moved rapidly as she searched for a pop-up that Goku knew wouldn't be on her lenses. "Show me!"

"Paperwork's still on the way," Goku said smoothly, unsure if that were true. "*Real* paper. Sinking anyone, even a totally unapologetic and unrepentant career criminal like yourself, is serious business. Has to be done with hardcopy."

"Who says I'm not apologetic?" Pretty Howitzer sat up straight and folded her cuffed hands on the table. "I *said* I was sorry! I *always* say I'm sorry! Look it up, it's on the record!"

Goku leaned one elbow on the table and covered his mouth with his hand, as if he were thinking hard and not hiding a grin.

"Besides, *I'm* as much a victim here as Auntie Emmy," she added, looking down her nose at him, or trying to. She came off more like an insolent child than a high-mileage felon, which Goku suspected was how she had managed to go as long as she had without doing any serious time.

He filed that for later consideration, along with *Auntie Emmy.* "What do you mean, *you're* a victim? You knowingly sold a trusting old woman an invisible bag of vapor—"

"I didn't *knowingly* do anything! It was *supposed* to be the *real deal!*"

Now he did laugh, a loud, hard, sarcastic sound that had little humor in it and was gone quickly, without even a hint of echo. The effect bothered the fuck out of him, Goku thought irritably. "There's nobody—that's capital No, capital Body—who would believe for one second—that's capital One, capital Second—that you really, sincerely believed—"

"Okay, so *you* don't believe me, but I swear, so help me freakin' gods of techno—"

"—one hundred percent genuine—"

"—only because I *knew* it was the real thing—"

"—out door, egress, exit, whatever con artists are calling it these days—"

"I believed it because I tried it and it fucking worked!"

Goku stared at her for a long moment. Then he laughed again. "Whew, for a second there, the look on your face—you almost had me. Do you practice in front of a mirror or is it just plain old hardcore desperation? Don't answer that," he said as she opened her mouth. "I think maybe you need some alone time in a holding cell to give your situation some serious thought. But just to make sure you don't get too bored, I'll tell the duty officer to load some brochures for you." He stood up, paying no attention to her protests. "About the programs and facilities available at Mid-Atlantic. Underwater correctional institutions are the most advanced and best equipped in the world. You get used to the emergency drill fast, I've heard. They've got education programs from the top schools, your Ivy League, Eton, Cambridge—and I mentioned the library, didn't I?"

As soon he stepped into the hallway and closed the door behind him, her pleading cut off as if someone had flipped a switch, and the ambient noise of the police station suddenly assailed him. A bit disconcerted, he leaned against the wall for a moment; funny, he thought, the way you never noticed how much things echoed under ordinary conditions. Not to mention how much difference there was between quiet and the absence of sound.

The flicker at the left-hand edge of his vision came just as he thought of Konstantin, two separate things happening simultaneously. His initial reaction was reflexive now, a mental smile coupled with mild embarrassment for still not having reciprocated. It took a full clock-second for him to remember that according to what both Celestine and Ogada had told him, nobody had received any messages of any kind from Konstantin for at least four weeks; nobody could. Therefore, nobody had.

The flicker sure seemed like her, though. Even considered in the context of what he knew, there was a Konstantin-ness about it that he told himself to chalk up to wishful thinking. People saw what they wanted to see and more often than not the mind was only too happy to dance along. It didn't take much fancy footwork to make music out of a stray fragment of noise.

And anyone who didn't believe that could check out the millions of people who had been sold all those magic beans: beachfront in Kansas, the true Hope Diamond, a deposed king's hidden gold, the blessing of never-ending good luck, the Deity's unlisted phone number. Or the absolutely-positively-not-fake-not-a-simulation-but-real conversion code for the Out Door, derived by a scientist using the secrets of the Pharaohs and the Mayans, giving you unlimited access to everything you wanted and more—contact your more successful self in another timeline and see where you went right, ascend to a higher plane of being, join God's private club! Or just go to Japan.

"To be honest, I felt sorry for her."

The small round object in the bottom of Goku's cup opened out into a blossom under the stream of boiling water from the spout of Emmy Eto's fancy electric kettle. It amused him that most Americans referred to it as a teapot, even though they only heated water in it.

"That was why I gave her a freebie in the first place," she added, pouring water into her own cup before replacing the kettle in its stand on the coffee table and sitting down on the couch beside him.

"A freebie?"

Emmy Eto chuckled. "On the house, *gratis*. You don't have to pay."

"Yes, I know. I'm just not sure what you mean by *you* gave *her* a freebie."

"That's a delightful accent. London, am I right?" Emmy Eto chuckled again, eyes twinkling in a way that made him think of Celestine's smile, although there was no resemblance between the two women. Emmy Eto was ninety-five, with short, silvery hair carefully styled to look unruly and bright green contact lenses. Goku suspected her eyes would have been just as bright without them; no doubt she could be quite unruly too.

"Please, Ms. Eto," he said, taking a sip of tea. The flower waved at him from the bottom of the cup.

"You'll want to spoon that out," she told him. "Unless you're a typical Brit and like your tea thoroughly stewed."

The flower went from graceful to drowned as he removed it to a saucer on the table. "Please, Ms. Eto?" he said again.

"I'm a professional relative," she said. "Isn't it in the case file?"

Goku felt his face grow warm. "I'm sorry, I obviously missed that."

"Because you figured I'm just retired. Oh, don't have a cow, dude," she added, waving one hand as he started to apologize. "You want to know the truth, I'd have figured that too if I were in your place. Most of the people who live here are *at leisure*, shall we say. They've had two, three, even four careers—and that's not counting all the McJobs for rent money in between. And they've had about as many families, formal and informal. Worked their asses off—well, their hips, knees, and shoulders anyway. There's so much titanium around here we get more spam from salvage firms than funeral homes.

"Anyway, most of my neighbors are tired. They just want to hang out, spark a few bowls of medicinal, and watch a movie. With or without actually putting one on."

Goku sipped some more tea, even though it was too hot, to keep himself from grinning.

"And I gotta admit, I do that too now and again. Careers and McJobs—I had 'em back to back. I traveled a lot, lived in a lot of different places. But I only ever had one family. One husband, one child, and I had the bad grace to outlive both of them."

Goku blinked away the definition of McJobs that had popped up in the lower left-hand quadrant of his vision and said, "I'm sorry."

"It was a very long time ago," she said, waving away his words again. "You don't set out to be a widow, but you live with the possibility and what happens is what happens. But surviving your child is an unnatural act, especially when she's an actual child. Takes a long time to make up for it. So I rent myself out to people who need a nice old lady relative. Grandma for the kids, auntie for the grown-ups. Sometimes both at once, in which case I give them a special rate rather than just double-dipping. Anyone who has to hire a nice old lady relative in the first place deserves a break. And you'd be surprised at how many people that is."

She picked up a small remote and pointed it at a large painting of wild horses running through a countryside under a stormy sky on the wall opposite. The image faded away to a white background, where color photos of various shapes and sizes began to appear. The people in them were various shapes, sizes, and colors as well. Many of the pictures had been taken at special occasions—birthdays, weddings, anniversaries, graduations, and holidays, big elaborate parties and smaller, more intimate get-togethers. But there were also plenty of Emmy Eto sitting with a toddler on her lap or walking in a park holding hands with a couple of small children. And a few not-so-small children.

He was grinning from ear to ear, Goku realized, and tried to tone it down without sobering too abruptly. "That's quite a lot of people," he said, "but if we could get back to—"

Nodding, she used the remote again. "You're just lucky I didn't cue up the soundtrack." She chuckled. "You'd have sat through the whole six hours, weeping nonstop. Big, manly, silent tears, of course." She put a hand to her lips. "Oh, no, wait, I forgot, it's all stiff upper lip with you Brits."

The words were out of his mouth before he'd even known he was going to speak. "But I'm also Japanese. Like you."

"And?" Emmy Eto blinked at him. "Meaning what?"

"I was just thinking that you're old enough remember Japan, the actual land, before the quakes—"

"Yes, we both existed at the same time, but I never went there." She sighed heavily. "I'm as much a *sansei* as you are in that respect. What does that have to do with Pretty Howitzer?"

"It's part of the special circumstances attached to the charges against her. She targeted you not only because you're elderly but also because you're Japanese."

Emmy Eto sighed. "We've been vaccinating against plaque and vascular dementia and schizophrenia and all kinds of other head bugs for, what, seven decades? Almost eight? And everyone still thinks that if you're over eighty, you got nothing above the neck but moths and cobwebs."

"I don't feel that way," Goku said, hoping he sounded kind rather than defensive. "And neither does anyone I know at I3 or—"

Emmy Eto shooed his words away with both hands. "Yeah, yeah, yeah, it's always some other, much less enlightened dude." Abruptly, she grimaced. "Oh, hell. I'm sorry, Agent Mura, I'm taking things out on you and I shouldn't. I just get *so fucking cheesed off* sometimes. You have no idea, the crap aimed at people my age. Nostalgia and religion, religion and nostalgia, like no older person is interested in anything else. Well, I'm all about today, *right* here, *right* now, and then what's on for tomorrow. You know what I did yesterday?

Went to the farmer's market and bought green bananas. That's right, you heard me, I'm ninety and I *bought green bananas*—in your *face*, mortality! Woke up this morning—in your face again, mortality! Just because I'm not concerned about getting pregnant—or *not* getting pregnant—and what the hell is it with all that pregnancy hoo-ha anyway? Pregnancy isn't the permanent centerpiece of *every* woman's life, even if they're actually pregnant! It's ageist, it's sexist—" Putting a hand to her mouth, she looked down at her lap, smiling with embarrassment.

"Damn, I'm *so* sorry," she said, laughing a little. "Once I get started, I can't seem to stop, and it's so rude. Please forgive me again, Agent Mura."

He waited for her to look up, but apparently he'd have to forgive her first. "There's no need to apologize, Ms. Eto. When you're the victim of a crime, it's quite normal to feel like the whole world is against you."

Now she did look up, her face a mixture of surprise and relief. "Oh?"

He nodded. "It's bad enough dealing with the complications, anything from overdue bills to repo men. Or losing something that means the world to you but has no monetary value to the shithead who took it and probably threw it away." Emmy Eto gave a surprised giggle at the profanity. "But then there's the indignity of how people keep referring to you as *the victim* rather than using your name. It adds insult to injury."

Emmy Eto put both hands over her face for a long moment. Goku thought she was crying and looked around for some tissues, but when she lowered them, her face was dry and composed. "I thought I was being childish."

"Were you not offered counseling?" Goku asked, making a mental note to ask Celestine.

She made another shooing motion with both hands. "Bitch, puh-*leeze*." Her cheeks suddenly turned pink. "As we used to say in my day, if you'll pardon my Hungarian. That little bitch Pretty Howitzer, *she* needs therapy. I need my money back." Pause. "Or am I just shit outta luck on that one?"

Goku made another mental note to follow up on counseling for her anyway. "No, these days we can trace where the money went," he told her. "But that takes time. And it takes more time to convert it back to liquid form."

Emmy Eto's hopeful smiled faded. "Convert it from what?"

"People like Pretty Howitzer love to buy themselves presents, goods or services. Property is usually straightforward, services are trickier."

"Which means I can't count on getting *all* my money back."

"No, but you'll get most of it. I3's recovery team seldom recoup less than seventy-five percent of the original monetary value, and it's usually closer to ninety percent."

This information didn't cheer her as much as he'd hoped. "And how much time are we talking about?" she asked.

"Well…longer than anyone would like." He hesitated, then plunged ahead before he could think better of it. "May I ask you a personal question, Ms—ah, Auntie Emmy?"

"You can ask." Suddenly a little of the old twinkle was back in those unequivocally green eyes.

"Is this the first time you've been the v—ah, on the receiving end of a criminal act?"

"Nice save." She twinkled some more. He started to wonder if it was a special effect in her lenses. "And to answer your question, no, but it's been a very, *very* long time since my last brush with the underworld. All I usually have to worry about are drive-bys and snipers. No matter how much 'proofing you've got, something always gets through."

Goku frowned. "But this is a residential building."

"But not a completely residential *area*. Lots of stores means lots of shopping and lots of shopping means lots of advertising—*active* advertising that lots of people engage with. There's enough activity to reveal the local market segments. It's *almost* spam but not quite." Emmy Eto shrugged. "My filters update every other day. Whatever gets through, I trash without really seeing it."

"Any ill effects—headaches, mood swings, increase in episodes of déjà-vu?"

Emmy Eto shook her head. "Get to be my age, you're inured to a lot. It takes more to make an impression than when you're thirty. Or even sixty." She laughed suddenly. "Listen to me. What was I saying about ageism?"

Goku chuckled. "It's not ageism to understand your own characteristics, is it?"

"I dunno, dude. Maybe. Stranger things have happened."

The words echoed in his head, but in Konstantin's voice. *Stranger things have happened. If I had a family crest, that would be on it. Stranger things have happened—they'll carve it on my tombstone.*

Emmy Eto was staring at him. "Is something wrong, Agent Mura?"

"My calendar's just reminding me of an appointment." He stared off to one side for a moment, hoping he looked like he'd just had a pop-up from his to-do list, then pretended to blink it away. "Now, where were we?"

"In the middle of your very busy day," Emmy Eto said. "Sorry, I know I'm just one of a gazillion cases. Tell me what else you want to know, I'll try not to ramble. More tea?" Without waiting for an answer, she took his cup into the tiny kitchenette, rinsed it out and brought it back with a fresh blossom in the bottom.

"You mentioned feeling sorry for Howitzer," Goku prompted as she flipped the kettle's on switch. "In what way?"

Emmy Eto laughed. "That name, for one thing. What kind of person could look at their newborn baby and think, *Pretty Howitzer*? Either her parents hated her or had a cruel sense of humor, or both."

"You never thought it was a made-up name?"

"Sure, at first. But it isn't."

"You're pretty—ah, very certain. What ID did she show you?"

Emmy Eto chuckled. "A card of origin, but even I know those can be stolen or forged. What convinced me was—" She took a pair of oversized sunglasses out of a case lying on the coffee table and put them on. "Goku Mura?"

Then she hooked a finger over the frames, pulling them down her nose to stare at him over the tops of the lenses. He kept his expression neutral.

"Well, *that's* a surprise," she said, her gaze even sharper than her tone. "I had no idea Interpol 3 allowed an agent to work under an assumed name."

"More like a *nom de plume*, actually," he said, hoping he didn't sound sheepish. "Or *nom de guerre* might be more like it. For the protection of family members as well as ourselves. It keeps the professional completely separate from the personal. Tell me, how did you come by that particular bit of software?"

She folded the sunglasses and put them back on the table, well out of his reach. "Oh, I know a dude who knows a dude who knows a dude. It's not one hundred percent accurate. If you'd been on your guard, I wouldn't have caught you. And in answer to your question—" Suddenly her face was sad. "My daughter cooked it up. She was very bright, my girl, a prodigy. Eccentric—she straddled the border between Asperger's and autism. She was fascinated by the physical characteristics of human emotion. She created the program to measure the response when you called someone by name. Well, by *a* name. You know there are people in this world who believe on a gut level that their name is Lover or Darling. Or—" She gave a short, soundless laugh. "—I'm sorry to say, Asshole. Fortunately, there aren't many of those." She laughed again, more heartily. "Well, actually, there are plenty of those, but only a teeny-tiny minority would answer to the name, at least in here." She put one hand to her chest and covered the glasses possessively with the other. "You aren't going to confiscate them, are you?"

"Not unless you've used them to commit a crime," he said, shifting uneasily on the couch. "Not invading people's privacy, are you? Stealing their life savings?"

Emmy Eto smiled demurely. "I've been a good girl, Agent Mura."

"I'm sure. Now, about your relationship with Pretty Howitzer—"

"Believe it or not, I'm not a total mark, Agent Mura." The sadness returned to Emmy Eto's face. "Like I said, I only talked to her in the first place because I felt sorry for her. I could see she was lonely." A corner of her mouth twitched in a brief half smile. "But I suppose being a con artist is a lonely way to make a living. Anyway, I always enjoyed a good Easter Egg and I really thought it was all she had. I'd have overpaid for it—not as much as she ended up getting out of me but still, too much. Just because I thought it would make her happy and I can't take it with me."

"Then she disappeared and reappeared?" Goku prompted. This was usually the trick that scammers like Pretty Howitzer used to seal the deal.

But Emmy Eto shook her head. "Oh, please. I know how camouflage and encryption works in Augmented Reality, how it's just the surroundings prerecorded and interpolated. Even the cheapest AR+ cover-ups work fine as long as whoever or whatever you're covering doesn't make any sudden moves. Or if *you* don't, because you'll get that lag with the perspective.

"Personally, I don't bother with anything cheap—my mother always said cheap was dear in the long run—but some people aren't fussy. They don't care if the perspective doesn't shift perfectly or the resolution gets a little chunky. One lady I know says she likes it that way. She says it reminds her that there's less than meets the eye. But I say if you're going to use AR+, then use it. Go big or go home. That's another of my mother's sayings."

She stared silently down at the cup in her hands before she set it on the coffee table. "The disappearing act was pretty good. She even managed to fix the log so it looked like there was missing time. Maybe that might have convinced me, I don't know."

"If that didn't," Goku asked gently, "what did?"

"I saw my girl." Emmy Eto gazed at him for a long moment as if expecting some reaction. "I saw my girl and I called her by name and it was her. I didn't have the software from those sunglasses, of course, but I'd seen her through them often enough that I could tell. She knew her name. And she knew me."

He nodded. "I see."

"And I certainly did. That's how they get us, isn't it? Not by what they show us but by what they can get us to see. Because we see what we want to see. You'd think we'd live and learn, but we never do. I remember hearing all about the Virtual Homeland scams. People fooled into believing they could actually inhabit a whole new world or a whole new universe. Or an old one, lost to earthquakes and radiation. I never understood how people could fall for that. Not until there was something I wanted to see."

His conscience pounced on him the moment he left Emmy Eto's apartment building (the brushed metal plaque over the main entrance declared it was a retirement community in emphatically no-nonsense letters). No surprise—as soon as he'd known he wasn't going to confiscate Emmy Eto's sunglasses, he'd felt it getting ready. Simply tagging the glasses for collection after Emmy Eto's eventual death wasn't enough to satisfy what Konstantin called his inner Boy Scout.

I could go back inside and see if Auntie Emmy would be open to sparking a bowl of medicinal. Just as a favor to a stressed-out free-range cop. They only use top-grade stuff for medicinal—

Some part of him—a surprisingly big part—thought that was

the best idea he'd had all day. But he knew that if he did go back to Emmy Eto's apartment, it wouldn't be to get high but to take her dodgy sunglasses, the way he should have if he'd been going by the book. He'd be very apologetic and explain that while the software was not *exactly* against the law, it was in a gray area that almost always resulted in expensive legal problems for the average citizen, who of course didn't mean any harm, but still. She would argue that lots of people had lenses with add-ons that were just as sketchy, not to mention stuff that actually *was* illegal, and he'd tell her, yes, that was true, but he didn't know about anyone else, only her. She had used the software not just in his presence but as part of their interaction, while he was on duty and without his consent. And then—

And then nothing. He was spinning his wheels imagining a conversation he'd decided not to have. He cleared his mind and focused his attention on his surroundings—the line of flowering shrubs that went the length—width?—of the building on either side, the recently repaved sidewalk parallel to it, the convenience shop—no, they called it a store here—on the corner. Diagonally opposite was another convenience store from a competing chain. The two stores seemed to be having a price war, but he wasn't sure on what; maybe everything. The four-lane traffic-way that ran past the building was restricted to local and electric, except for emergency vehicles. It was so empty he wondered if it had been closed off for some reason before five two-seaters appeared several blocks in the distance. Scan-vees, he saw as they approached, from the World Within project. He turned his back as they passed him, although he didn't actually care. He had walked through so many World Within scans, his mannequin was probably one of their standard placeholders. Facial features scrambled so he was unrecognizable, of course.

Or perhaps not. Perhaps someone who knew him well enough would recognize him anyway. Emmy Eto's semilegal sunglasses.

He was waiting to cross the street in front of the convenience store when he finally noticed a message light in the lower left-hand corner of his vision blinking. It was a short note from Ogada, saying he might as well use Konstantin's office while he was here.

The offer took him by surprise. It hadn't even occurred to him to ask because he hadn't thought about staying any longer than it would take to arrange Pretty Howitzer's transfer to London. He hadn't given any thought to that either, but it didn't really require any—all he'd have to do was fill out a form, then go home and wait for a couple of prisoner transport marshals to arrive with her a day or two later.

He didn't have to be in such a hurry. Ogada had thought being handed over to I3 would make Pretty Howitzer more cooperative, though she had been more rattled by the prospect of hard time underwater. If he gave her more time to think about it, let her sleep on it, she might be only too happy to work out a deal with the local authorities. In which case, he could sign it back to Ogada or Celestine or whoever had caught it to begin with and save I3 the expense of airfare plus accommodations for two prisoner transport marshals. No, he definitely didn't have to be in such a hurry.

Something moved in his peripheral vision and he automatically focused on it, thinking it was another message. But there was no blinking light. The movement came again, something moving just out of his visual range. He turned his head. Across the street, two people were coming out of a café and holding the door for two other people going in. Again, motion fluttered on the far side of his vision. This time, he relaxed his focus and let himself see rather than actively looking.

It was the barest flicker, over almost before it registered on him. There had been an image of some kind, he was sure of it, but the only thing that came to him was Konstantin's face.

Emmy Eto's own security system was usefully elaborate, more so than he had expected. Combined with surveillance from the building as well as standard public records, Goku had nearly minute-by-minute accounting for Pretty Howitzer and Emmy Eto together, and not much less separately, but only for the period leading up to the crime. The actual crime itself was documented in and out of AR+ by the bank records showing the transfer of money from Emmy Eto to Pretty Howitzer.

Studying the transaction, Goku wondered if Emmy Eto knew how lucky she was that she had done everything in Augmented Reality. Had the scam occurred in Artificial Reality, it would have been harder to make a case against Pretty Howitzer. Not impossible—there had been a number of successful prosecutions against people who had scammed the elderly, all predicated on the claim that the offenders had deliberately used techniques and FX to confuse and disorient their aged victims to the point where they became incapable of distinguishing between AR and an unenhanced, nonaugmented offline environment. A few less-than-elderly people had tried using the same argument for civil actions against scammers who had relieved them of money or property or both while in AR. Results had been mixed, especially across international boundaries, and even successful plaintiffs learned that the difference between winning a judgment and actually collecting was a lot like the difference between AR and unenhanced, nonaugmented offline reality.

He didn't think anyone would believe Emmy Eto had been confused and disoriented by Pretty Howitzer. The old lady wore several layers of AR+ routinely and nonstop during her waking hours—in a typical day, she probably didn't see the unenhanced, nonaugmented offline world for as long as sixty seconds. If that—he revised the estimate downward when he saw how often she slept with her lenses in. She did a lot of swapping too, as well as layering. Between her assorted glasses and contact lenses, she probably changed the world half a dozen times before lunch. After which she probably napped for an hour, waking to butterflies and honeybees.

She would never come off as someone who could be confused or disoriented to a jury. He wouldn't have believed it himself. And yet, when he had asked her if she really thought Pretty Howitzer had an out door—an actual, no-fooling portal to a different reality—she had said yes.

"Of course, I don't believe it now, Agent Mura, and if you're anything like me, you probably don't understand how I ever could have. Do you think I'm wondering how I could have been so gullible? Well, I'm not. I know why I fell for it. I saw because I was looking for it, and it was as real as anything else I see with my very own eyes." She had looked around, moving only her eyes, a tiny smile on her lips. "And if I saw it again tomorrow, it would be déjà vu all over again."

The recording stopped and Emmy Eto vanished. Goku found himself sitting sideways at his desk, the way he would have been had he still been sitting next to her on her couch. There was a slight crick in his side from the awkward posture he had unconsciously assumed to keep his elbow from touching the arm of his chair; it would have ruined the illusion.

And there it was, practically on cue: a faint flutter at the limit of his peripheral vision, but this time on the left rather than the right. He made a note to find out if Emmy Eto had noticed her daughter's image on one side more often than another or whether it just popped up in the middle.

His phone chimed with a message from Ogada, telling him he could visit Konstantin this evening.

At first Goku thought he was in the wrong room. There was a wire-frame contraption rather than a bed, and the figure suspended in it looked more like a large doll than a living person, a sexless, featureless mannequin in an elaborate hotsuit meant for a programming engineer or a Foley editor rather the standard end-user. Then he realized and looked away.

"It's always so hard when people see someone they know in a condition like this." The nurse's low, kindly voice had a hint of the Caribbean. Goku wondered how far removed she was from it, whether she ever went there, and if so, did they welcome her home or as a tourist.

"I didn't think there were many people in this condition," he said, still not looking at Konstantin.

"I meant a condition *like* this—incapacitated. If I gave offense, I apologize."

"You didn't, not at all." Goku winced inwardly. "One of her staff told me about the, ah, incident and that it was an unusual injury. She had a hard time explaining. I ran into her boss and I thought maybe he could tell me more. But all I got from him was something about laser pointers and burned retinas."

The nurse raised her eyebrows. "Hmph. Pretty good."

Pretty Good—Pretty Howitzer's overachieving cousin, the one she could never live up to; the thought blew through his mind, a scrap of absurdity. Konstantin had talked about sometimes feeling a sense of unreality or surreality. He'd never been quite sure what she meant, but now he thought he had an inkling.

"Too simple, of course," the nurse went on. "If it really were that basic, they might have made some progress with her. But as an analogy, it's pretty good. Better, though, for the neuros to accept that a person is more than a mind driving a body."

"Greater than the sum of her parts?" He suppressed the urge to mutter something sarcastic about platitudes.

She made a disgusted noise. "Oh, don't give me that."

"Excuse me?" Goku stared at her.

"People who say that think they *know* all the parts. What they are, how many."

He shook his head, baffled.

"People are a *lot* more complex. Can you trace the exact shape of the hole she left when she fell out of her life?" The nurse looked at him with grim amusement. "Work on that, maybe you'll be getting somewhere." She went over to the framework holding Konstantin and peeled back the right sleeve of the suit, exposing a pasty but still firm-looking forearm. She bared Konstantin's hand as well and Goku started to turn toward the door, thinking the nurse was going to bathe her.

"No need to go," the woman said. "You came to visit, stick around." She laid her own arm along Konstantin's, intertwining their fingers, and gently moved Konstantin's hand back and forth as if trying to retrain her movements. Next to the nurse's dark brown skin, Konstantin's looked as white as paper, but it wasn't the contrast that struck him.

After a couple of minutes, the nurse switched the position of her arm so that it was now on the outside of Konstantin's. It didn't look like any physical therapy he had ever seen, but he resisted the temptation to say as much. Instead, he asked, "Does that help?"

The nurse smiled. "Can't hurt."

"Do you ever try that with both her arms at once?"

"Takes two people. If you're volunteering—" she tilted her head toward Konstantin's other arm.

"Actually, I was thinking five more people at least. There's a form of Japanese theatre called *bunraku*—"

"I know what bunraku is. Those big puppets. It's not a bad idea," she said, still manipulating Konstantin's arm. "But now it's getting complicated."

"So? You just said people are complex."

"I mean legally—permissions. Which would be all right, but…" She gave him a Look. "The lieutenant told me you were in from England. You want to help with this, you can't phone it in. We don't do AR or AR+. You planning to stick around?"

He nodded and immediately there was another flicker on the left. Definitely right on cue, too perfectly timed to be more than that fancy footwork all human brains were so partial to, even his. In this case, especially his.

But what the hell, he thought. He didn't have to believe one way or the other. In which case, he would stipulate for the record— whatever record that was—that yes, he wanted to see Konstantin. And he would come here and see her tomorrow, and the next day, and the day after that, for as many days as he could wheedle out of I3.

If he saw her every day, the odds were good that sooner or later she might catch a glimpse of him.

Golden Bread by Issui Ogawa
Translated by Takami Nieda

A tray was set next to the futon where Yutaka lay.

There was an earthenware bowl filled with a hearty soup. But what was in the soup left little to be desired. The broth was an inky brown color he'd never seen before, and floating in it were oddly shaped brown balls and white pasty-looking lumps, and even what appeared to be tentacles of some kind.

This was clearly the staple food of an uncharted, uncivilized territory, a far cry from the beef stew, borscht, and *pot-au-feu* to which Yutaka was accustomed.

Yutaka sat up on the futon and cast a wary eye on the blonde-haired woman in the kimono who had brought him the tray. The woman knelt down on the tatami mat, flaring her nostrils as she looked down at him. She appeared to be in her mid-twenties and had sharp features, which, at the moment, made her look all the more intimidating. About ten local kids peered in from the shadow of the sliding fusuma door. All of them had bright blond or red hair and green or blue eyes that seemed otherworldly to Yutaka. They all stared curiously at the black-haired, black-eyed visitor.

He didn't sense any hostility in his captors. It was clear that the meal set before him wasn't a barbaric attempt at murder or execution, or even human experimentation. At the same time, he wasn't sure what to make of their food hygiene awareness. To put it bluntly, the soup was liable to give him food poisoning.

Nevertheless, Yutaka was a prisoner here. His priority was to heal his wounds and keep up his strength so he could return to his squadron.

He leaned over the bowl, mindful of the cast on his left hand, and with the right hand, shoveled the soup into his mouth with the strange wooden sticks.

The soup had a rustic flavor and tasted like seawater in his mouth. The potatolike balls were slimy, forming sticky threads when he bit them in half, and the white pasty lumps stuck to his teeth as he chewed. There was no way he could bring himself to eat the tentacles.

So horrid was the soup that he covered his mouth with the back of his hand, beginning to feel as if he were being subjected to some absurd method of torture. With tears in his eyes, he fought back his gag reflex and swallowed what was in his mouth, but could eat no more.

"What is this?" Yutaka muttered to himself. "Is this what you call soup?"

"How's that for gratitude?" said the woman. "I made that soup!"

Yutaka stared in shock. It was the first time anyone had spoken to him since the crash.

"You...understand what I'm saying?" he asked.

"What do you think?" she said, her voice dripping with sarcasm. "We bumpkins may not know how to build starfighters, but we *do* talk."

"No, I meant that you understand my English. I didn't expect it to be spoken in the backwoods of Kalif."

"Ahem! This is the language we've always spoken in these *backwoods*."

Yutaka watched the woman look away. She pouted like a child.

"You wouldn't have something more...real to eat?" he asked.

"I doubt you'll find much better than that potato and squid *suiton*. Eat up because that's all there is."

"Doesn't this colony abide by the laws?" The Interstellar Laws of Warfare dictated the humane treatment of prisoners of war.

Hearing this, the woman sneered. "Why do you think I'm sharing what little we have to feed you? Or did you forget what you've done?"

Yutaka flinched and shook his head. "I don't remember."

"Don't play innocent with—"

"No, really," he interrupted. "I lost consciousness soon after I bailed out. I really don't remember."

The woman fell silent for a moment. "Well, that's too bad," she mumbled. "Your fighter crashed into the storeroom, sending all of the rice flying out into space. All that's left to feed the village are the vegetables in the fields and some nonperishables. Although I guess I can't blame you if you're saying that it was an accident."

"That sounds...serious."

"The will of Andromeda. There are four hundred ninety-seven of us in this village, and for a while, we thought half of us would have to go hungry. But after poring over the books, checking the drums, and counting every last provision in the vacu-room for three days and nights, we calculated that the village should hold out until autumn. That was just this morning. Consider yourself lucky! If you had come to yesterday and some of the others heard you talking like that, they would have tossed you into the composter!"

The words flooded from the woman's mouth in a torrent. When she was done, she was breathless and red-faced. Her blue eyes glowed like jet burners; sparks danced around her blonde hair that was tied back in a bun.

Although he recognized that it was the spring rays spilling in through the shoji screen that cast her in this light, Yutaka could not help but admire her beauty even as he was overwhelmed by her fierce tongue. Yutaka was from Yamato, an aggressive nation that valued advancement and expansion, where assertiveness was a respected trait.

As far as Yutaka could gather, he was at fault. The young pilot had only happened to engage an enemy fighter near Kalif territory. The Kalif Federation was a neutral nation and not an enemy of Yamato.

Yutaka decided it was best to apologize. He sat upright with his legs folded beneath him like the woman before him, pressed his hands firmly against his waist, and bowed his head deeply. "I regret the damage I've caused. I'm sorry."

When he raised his head, the woman was staring at him dumbstruck, and then her cheeks ballooned until she burst into laughter.

The pilot would later learn that the proper prostrate gesture in Kalif was one where you pressed your head against both hands brought together in front of you on the floor. However, Yutaka had unwittingly bowed down having combined the *attention* and *sitting* positions. Such a gesture did not exist in Kalif culture. It was no surprise the woman had laughed.

"What's so funny?" shouted Yutaka.

"You are." The woman smiled and wiped the tears from her eyes. Yutaka was taken aback by the kind expression that came over her face. "I wondered if you had any manners when you started eating without saying anything. But maybe you aren't a completely bad seed. My name is Ainella Burbanks. I'll be looking after you until a rescue comes for you. What's yours?"

"Second Lieutenant Yutaka Kubuki of the Yamato no Yasoshima Interstellar Expeditionary Fleet, 3rd Carrier Strike Group, 34th Fighter Squadron."

"That's a mouthful. How old are you? You look awfully young."

"Eighteen in Earthian years."

"You're just a young pup," said Ainella, blinking.

It was the villagers of Lakeview, which was located on a tiny unnamed asteroid, who had saved Yutaka and taken him in. After thanking them, he took the necessary course of action that any stranded starfighter pilot would take and contacted the mother ship.

Lakeview had an interplanetary communicator. Despite the difficulty of hailing a military vessel through civilian channels, Yutaka succeeded in making contact by devising an encryption code. But what he learned was grim. After several days, the mother ship had determined there was no chance of his survival and had departed the sector.

Most interplanetary spacecraft traveling inside the solar system were incapable of changing course due to the current limitations in orbital science and nuclear fusion engines. Once a spacecraft passed a certain point, it was unable to turn around unless it refueled at the next port.

It had taken the carrier group three months to reach this sector. Even if the mother ship were to turn right around after reaching Yamato, it would take over six months to return for him.

Not that the military was going to mobilize a carrier vessel to retrieve a lone pilot in the first place. In other words, Yutaka would not be able to rejoin his squadron as quickly as he'd hoped.

The Yamato military drilled its striker pilots with the standards of conduct and skills for just this type of situation. The first survival protocol, as far as Yutaka could remember, was "Don't panic." The second was "Return to the fleet by any means necessary."

Yutaka attempted to carry out the second protocol.

But before long, he realized that it was easier said than done.

Lakeview was a subsistence village on a tiny asteroid off the beaten path. A shuttlecraft arrived from a heavily populated planetary hub once a month, but it was run by the very enemy nation that Yutaka had been deployed to attack.

Relying on an enemy vessel to get off this asteroid was out of the question. In fact, he had to assume that the enemy was looking for him.

Yutaka had no choice but to follow the first protocol of survival. He would have to lie low until he saw his chance to escape.

"Anything but this!"

Day fifteen since Yutaka had come to live in the Kalif-style wooden house. Scowling, he shoved as much of the vegetable stew called *suiton* into his mouth as he could. The peculiar taste of fermented soybean along with the pasty lumps that stuck to his teeth made his skin crawl, and it was all he could do to force the stuff down his throat.

"Have some *ohitashi*."

Ainella, sitting across from Yutaka with her legs folded, coldly slid the dish of boiled greens across the tea table. There was also some smoked fish and pickled red berries of some kind. As meager as the portions were, Yutaka tried to pack away as many calories as he could. And yet, he couldn't help but ask, "Do you have any meat?"

A rump steak twice as thick as your palm? Some bread and milk, potatoes, ice cream, pork and beans? Pasta?

"We slaughter the livestock in autumn," Ainella said curtly, bringing a small fry up to her mouth. She was frightfully dexterous with chopsticks. "You fatten them up during summer and autumn when there's plenty to graze on and slaughter them before winter— everyone knows that. Just how do you people live on Yamato?"

"That's what I'd like to know," said Yutaka, clumsily trying to pick up a small fry with his chopsticks. When the fish fell into pieces on the table, he tried to pick it up until he remembered the cast on his left hand. "I don't understand why you people have to grow grass during the summer and suffer the cold in winter. That kind of thinking is from an era when we were still constrained by Earth's axial tilt. Your asteroid doesn't experience seasonal changes. Why haven't you standardized your energy resources year-round? Why haven't you industrialized your meat production?"

"Oh, stop with your whys! Because it's Kalif tradition!" Ainella shouted. "This is the way the Kalifornia people have always lived. It's always been our custom to live off of the healthy, natural foods according to the changes in seasons. These foods are our tradition and have been scientifically linked to our longevity. Meat, on the other hand, is fattening and smelly, inefficient to produce—there's nothing good about it!"

Ainella, with her tall and sturdy frame, cut quite an imposing figure when she was angry. Despite feeling a bit intimidated by the Kalif woman, the very embodiment of the Anglo-Saxon character he'd learned about in school, Yutaka drew up one knee and said, "Since you brought up tradition, now it's my turn. The Yamato people are a race that once gathered the world's delicacies. Diverse foods from a hundred countries lined the streets and were cooked in oil brought in on enormous ships. We are a people that require calories. We were born to consume meat and flour and sugar, so we can build a powerful military and contribute to Yamato's prosperity. That is our birthright, and if you knew that, you'd understand that I'm not asking for much."

"The spite coming out of your pretty little mouth!"

"It's basic history every Yamato kid learns in grade school. If you don't like it, I guess you shouldn't have saved me and taken me in."

Ainella squeezed the chopsticks in her hand so hard they might have snapped in two. Yutaka watched a frightening smile come over her face and—

Psshh!

She struck his raised knee with three rigid fingers.

"Ouch!"

"Mind your manners! Don't raise your knee at the table! Hold the bowl in your hand! You didn't even say *itadakimasu* before you started eating."

"I refuse for religious reasons. Besides, how do you expect me to hold a bowl with *this*?" said Yutaka, raising his cast-wrapped left hand.

Psshh!

A terrible pain shot through his broken hand, and Yutaka let out a groan. Ainella drew back the hand that had struck his cast, but she did not apologize.

Yutaka sat up straight, trying to ignore the pain, and went back to eating what was left of the meager meal. "The Yamato people and Kalifs are genetically different to begin with. Do you have any idea why rice tastes good to you?"

"What are you talking about? Rice tastes good because it's rice," said Ainella, nonplussed by the question.

Yutaka shook his head. "It's because you secrete a specific enzyme that breaks down starches called amylase. The number of copies of the salivary amylase gene or AMY1 varies widely according to ethnic groups, and groups with traditionally grain-rich diets have more copies of the gene. If you favor the taste of rice and suiton and other starches, you probably have eight or ten copies of AMY1 in your genome. The reason I can barely stand the stuff is because I lack the gene. So you can't force me to digest something that I can't."

For several minutes, Ainella said nothing. Yutaka continued to eat, satisfied at having argued the woman down.

After they finished their meal, Ainella straightened her posture and said, "Yutaka Kubuki of Yamato, it's been fifteen days. How is your broken hand mending?"

"Huh? Oh…it's better, I think," answered the pilot, holding out his left hand. "It doesn't hurt if I don't touch it."

"Fine, then I'll shut down gravitational rotation."

The room slowly moaned to a halt as if someone had slammed on friction brakes. For the first time, Yutaka realized that an artificial force had been acting upon the house the entire time.

Suddenly, the weight of his body left him and he felt as if something heavy hung inside his nostrils. The familiar sensation he experienced upon boarding the mother ship. He was weightless.

Ainella went out to the open corridor facing the azaleas in the yard and gestured for Yutaka to follow. Yutaka floated down the wooden planks of the corridor until they came to a hidden door. Once through the door, Yutaka found himself inside an enormous tunnel dug out of the gray rock.

Looking behind him, he discovered that he had come out of a massive metal drum laid on its side. Perhaps it was ten meters in diameter. The entire house was contained inside the drum, and the landscape scenery was likely a holographic image of some sort.

But this was no surprise to Yutaka; in fact, he was insulted that Ainella would bring him here as if she were pulling back the curtain to some big revelation. None of the asteroids in the asteroid belt produced enough gravity to tether anything down. That Yutaka was able to sit on the tatami mat with his legs folded was evidence enough that he was inside a rotating centrifuge.

Shifting his gaze from the drum to Ainella, he said, "Yeah, so?"

"It isn't my intention to brag. I'm only trying to show that we were operating the centrifuge in the sanitarium to speed your recovery."

"Hmph!" Yutaka snorted indignantly. The presence of gravity did indeed help osteoblast function to heal bones. If the Kalifs had operated the sanitarium for his sake, then perhaps he owed them something.

"Come with me," said Ainella.

Yutaka followed the woman into a narrow access tunnel.

They navigated several forks until they emerged into a cavernous passage. Ainella looked expectantly at Yutaka.

"Whoa…" he said, unable to hide his awe.

It was a long, straight tunnel stretching as far as the eye could see, over five hundred meters perhaps. It was without a doubt the longest tunnel Yutaka had ever seen and perhaps would ever see again.

Building an underground structure of this length would have been impossible on Yamato. And it would certainly be no mean feat to build more than one of these tunnels inside this asteroid either. The passageway likely cut clear through the center of the asteroid, in which case this must be the main tunnel that served all of Lakeview.

But this was not what Ainella wanted him to see. The true marvel of this place were the structures built equidistantly up and down the main tunnel.

"One-tan drums," said Ainella.

Numerous lidless drums about ten meters in diameter were laid on their side.

"*One tan?*" Yutaka asked.

Ainella kicked off the ground and flew away. Her white calves peeked out from the hem of her kimono. Yutaka floated after her.

"Yes, the drums are thirty-one meters deep and nine hundred ninety-one square meters inside, which is exactly *one tan*, the Kalif unit of area for agricultural land. Each drum can provide a year's rice for five people. These are our rice fields."

The metal drums rotated slowly on rollers on the floor, creating enough centrifugal force so that a thick layer of mud caked their interiors.

Bright green grass sprouted out of the mud in neat rows, and light tubes supported by spokes affixed to the central axis of the drum shone in every direction. The Kalifs had seemingly devised a rather elaborate but primitive system to make the grass distinguish between up and down and to stimulate its growth.

Countless drums lined the length of the tunnel. Ainella and Yutaka floated past tens of drums to the right and left as well as above and below. Summer-lit fields—or rather, rice paddies surrounded them.

One villager planted seedlings, while a pint-sized contraption ran up and down the mud like a faithful dog. There were others painstakingly pulling weeds by hand. A young man pushed a horrendously rank container down the rails running along the side of the tunnel. Chattering children flew past and dove into the drum up ahead, where a couple removed their straw hats, wiped the sweat off their faces, and took the lunches that the children brought them. A ruddy-cheeked old man smoking a pipe sat on the edge of the drum and spun slowly round and round, the smoke from the pipe drawing a loose spiral like the Milky Way.

A flight of brown birds twittered overhead and flew past Yutaka in a spiral. As he watched them disappear into the distance, a frog came twirling out of nowhere and smacked spread eagle against his cheek. An impressively sized green and black frog.

Yutaka heard giggling from inside the drums.

It was a far cry from the sterilized starch factories on Yamato's Stanford Torus colonies, which prohibited human entry. A perfect plant and animal system, the likes of which Yutaka had never imagined, flourished here. At this rate, it was reasonable to assume that there was a fully functional ecology from the atmospheric and aquatic layers and to the microbial and viral levels.

As Yutaka drifted and twirled in the air in awe, he felt a tug at his collar.

"This way." Ainella grabbed him by the scruff of the neck and pulled him backward until the rows of drums along the ceiling and walls of the main tunnel disappeared, the drums on the left and right receded from sight, and finally, they arrived at a dead end.

Perhaps they had traversed the length of the asteroid and come to the end of the tunnel.

That was when it struck Yutaka that this peculiar colony had a fundamental flaw.

"How do you expand the colony?" he asked, turning around to face Ainella.

Without a word, the woman dragged him down another narrow tunnel.

Yutaka was taken through a thick insulated door. Unlike the well-ordered area he'd come from, this place was in utter ruins. Cinder blocks, rocks, sacks, and containers of all types lay on top of each other in heaps, which suited men in masks were trying to shovel into some order.

Before he could ask where he was, Ainella shoved various items into his arms: a dust respirator, a jumpsuit, and Velcro shoes. Then she quickly proceeded to dress him before Yutaka had any time to protest.

"What is all this?" he finally shouted.

Ainella smiled and said, "You're cleaning up the mess you made of this storeroom." She pointed to the twisted rubble and debris ahead. "The area has been sealed off, but we haven't touched that dangerous toy you crash-landed in case there were weapons and explosives on board. Your first job is to neutralize all that. And when you're done with that, you can get to work fixing this place."

"My hand—it's broken, remember?"

"That's why I asked if it was better." But the gleam in her eye revealed that she couldn't care less about his hand. "If you're well enough to blather on about genes and such, you can at least show them how to work their way around your fighter. Oh, and you can take your lunch with the crew. You'll be working here starting today. I'm sorry I've been such a shrew."

Two brawny men, pausing from their work, came behind Yutaka and grabbed him up by the arms. Although the Kalifs had attended to his wounds, it had been overly optimistic of him to assume that he was welcome here after he'd destroyed their storeroom and food supplies.

That Ainella is one tough customer, Yutaka thought.

Yutaka couldn't escape. Instead, he was integrated into life in Lakeview as prison labor.

The labor was hard work. With the storeroom sealed off by nothing more than a tarp, air pressure was constantly fluctuating, creating a dangerous environment where workers got their hands caught in the rubble and were hit by flying bits of concrete. But the meals were no heartier than the ones at the sanitarium. They were lacking in both calories and taste, and Yutaka's stomach growled constantly.

One incident very nearly broke Yutaka's recently healed hand. The fighter engine came off the mount and drifted toward an unsuspecting worker, trapping his leg against the wall. Yutaka, who happened to be nearby, jammed his casted arm into the gap and twisted.

In the same moment the man pulled his leg free, Yutaka's cast cracked and fell away in pieces. Even after he pulled his arm back, Yutaka was so shaken he was unable to speak for several moments.

Scowling as he rubbed his sore leg, the young man glanced over at Yutaka standing in shock, pale-faced. "Hey, you finally got your cast off," the man deadpanned.

"Oh, yeah…" Yutaka said, nodding. "Saved me the trouble of going to the hospital."

Later during lunch hour, the young man introduced himself to Yutaka as Dewey and offered him the first chocolate bar the pilot had laid eyes on in Lakeview. Yutaka took the candy bar and thanked him.

In time, Yutaka began to talk to Dewey about this and that. Like

Ainella, Dewey revealed himself to be quite talkative for a country bumpkin.

"Tell me, Yutaka," he said one day. "Why do your people like to instigate war?"

"We're not instigating wars, we're colonizing. And if we were, we wouldn't be the only ones."

"Oh, so the Yamato people call riding in on someone's planet in battle destroyers *colonizing*."

"Yamato doesn't attack populated planets. We only move in on unsettled asteroids. Planting a flag on a planet doesn't make it yours unless it's been populated. The concept of territory has always gone hand in hand with actual occupation since Earthian days."

"The Kalif Federation has scores of people who were driven off their home planets by Yamato forces. The way I hear them tell it, your attack probes appeared out of nowhere and chased them off."

"Well, those people had probably just arrived at whatever planet they were driven from and built temporary bases there. In neither case could you say that they had settled the planet."

"So if a Kalif or another foreign vessel were to drive out the residents of a Yamato outpost, you'd be all right with that?"

"Well, no…you have to consider that on a deeper level. The Yamato race is outward looking, such as in the way they favor meat. Other ethnic groups aren't this way. The reason why we colonize space is because we are destined to do so."

"Really? I thought everyone—not just the Yamato people—have a natural predisposition toward war."

"You're wrong."

"But that's what a certain Yamato pilot told me just now," Dewey said, grinning.

Yutaka looked down, unable to find the words. No one told him how quick with the tongue these country folk were. Or perhaps Yutaka wasn't quick enough.

Several days later, it was Yutaka who approached Dewey.

"Listen to me, the difference between the Yamato and Kalif people is evident in the composition of the nations' territories. I can explain to you Yamato's inclination for expansion that way."

"Oh?"

"Do you know how Yamato—er, not just Yamato, but how many nations other than Kalif expand their territory?"

"Can't say that I do," said Dewey. "I was born and raised in Kalif."

"Spacefaring people are essentially known as *spinners*. Yamato is nothing more than one of many nations of spinners."

"What does that mean?"

"It's just like it sounds." Yutaka made his best attempt to repeat the history lessons he'd been taught. The myriad races inhabiting the solar system all had their reasons for leaving the confines of Earth, but there was only one practical method for accomplishing it. They had all been flung into space by the orbital elevator using Earth's centrifugal force. Then the evacuees found asteroids with the requisite resources and daylight in the belt between Mars and Jupiter and built colonies.

"So they're called spinners because they were spun into space," said Dewey.

"That's not all."

Early space colonists that first settled outside Earth's orbit soon learned that humans and other organisms required a certain measure of gravity to live in relative stability. The only celestial bodies able to provide any meaningful amount of gravity were Earth and its moon, Venus, Mars, and the dwarf planet Ceres. If humans were going to settle anywhere else, they had to figure out a way to produce artificial gravity.

The challenge was in stabilizing the rotations of space habitats. Any spinning object experiences gyroscopic precession, a wobbling on its axis like a gyroscope. Scientists also needed to devise a way to connect the rotating sections with the stationary parts of the colony.

After various designs for rotating colonies were proposed, the model that came to be widely used was the concentric Stanford Torus.

The CS Torus was not a megatechnology. It was nothing more than a disc-shaped colony about five hundred meters in diameter capable of housing ten thousand inhabitants at most. But the advantage of the CS Torus was not its population capacity, but in its ability to provide for the necessary numbers of people at any given point to support its construction.

The construction of the CS Torus began with three sections: the non-rotating axis and two gravity chambers that revolved around it from suspension tethers. The central axis was typically built from the hull of the spacecraft that the first settlers arrived on. In fact, that was the method of construction that had been proposed from the start.

Expansion was undertaken from the two opposing and tethered gravity chambers. Pieces were added to what initially resembled a humble mobile and was supported by four spokes and then eight spokes until the rotating ring called the torus was complete. Afterward more rings were added around the first; at the same time, the rotational speed was dropped to maintain optimal gravitational acceleration at the outer circumference.

Once the inhabitants added as many rings as the spokes could support, the construction was complete.

"The CS Torus is considerably smaller than this asteroid. Do you understand the advantage of building on that scale?" Yutaka asked.

"No," said Dewey, shaking his head.

"Mass production. The CS Torus is habitable even as it's being built. Which means as soon as the inhabitants are ready to expand, they can move on to building the next habitat. Since the habitats are small, they're quick to build and it's easy to pause construction if necessary. The parts and construction have been standardized from start to finish, so the design is all set. You just have to repeat the same process. Once you create an assembly line, you can build as many colonies as necessary."

"Mass production, eh?"

"It was Yamato that employed this method on a large scale. Thanks to the decision to employ the CS Torus as its habitat, Yamato has expanded and grown into a major power, boasting a population of five million!"

Yamato no Yasoshima had risen to become a superpower governing nearly four hundred CS Torus colonies in the asteroid belt. Yutaka recalled the constellation of silver-colored discs that he'd seen from the carrier vessel upon leaving Yamato and could not help speaking with some pride.

Dewey rubbed his angular jaw and glanced at Yutaka out of the corner of his eye. "And you're saying that the Kalifs are of no comparison."

"That's right. Take this village, for example. Lakeview has virtually no way to grow."

"You're right, once we dig as far as we can dig on this asteroid, that's it. We can't move the drums to the surface because of the cosmic radiation, which is the reason we have to live underground in the first place."

"Exactly. Plus you don't have a way of moving to the next asteroid when this village reaches capacity. This is what I'm getting at."

While Yutaka continued to argue emphatically, Dewey listened with the same composed smile. This villager, one of a population of only five hundred, didn't seem at all humbled by the existence of a nation of five million. Furthermore, he was not reacting out of ignorance.

Seeing this, Yutaka grew irritated, uneasy even. *How old was he anyway?* he thought. *He is older for sure.*

"The Yamato people are great because they've built a great nation, and the Kalif people aren't because they've not. Is that what you're getting at?"

"Well…I wouldn't say that…"

"But you are, Yutaka." Dewey smiled, patting Yutaka on the shoulder. "One question," he continued, raising a finger. "Did the Yamato become outward-looking people because they built the Torus colonies? Or did they build the Torus colonies because they were outward-looking people to begin with?"

"What?" Yutaka frowned and answered, "We chose this efficient method of expansion because it's in our nature to think outwardly."

"Nature before nurture, eh? Then one more question."

"What is it?"

"You have many friends back at Yamato?"

Yutaka faltered for an answer. Upon seeing this, Dewey let out a belly laugh and returned to work.

Even after being consigned to hard labor, Yutaka was ordered back to the sanitarium at night.

That evening, he was eating the bland Kalif dinner in the usual tatami-mat room, when Ainella said, "I hear you and Dewey are friends now."

"Did Dewey tell you that?" Yutaka said, surprised.

Ainella chuckled. "Do you think Dewey is the type of man to say something like that?"

After thinking for a moment, Yutaka replied, "Well, no…and I wasn't trying to be friends with him either. In fact, I said some rude things. Someone must've seen us talking and assumed we were."

"Actually, I lied. It was Dewey who told me." Noting Yutaka's surprise, Ainella nodded reassuringly. "So you *do* know when you're being rude. Maybe that's what he likes about you."

"What's Dewey like?"

"No one knows. He's a bit of a cynic, a contrarian," Ainella said, shrugging, without any hint of irritation. "That's why everyone's so shocked to hear he made a friend."

"I never said that we were friends."

"So you were having a long talk with just a random person?"

Yutaka had merely been trying to expound on the Yamato identity. But was that truly the only reason? No one back home listened to him as thoughtfully as Dewey did. As long-winded as Yutaka had been, he wasn't necessarily expecting Dewey to agree with him. In fact, he knew the Kalif would come back at him with some clever reasoning.

Ainella gathered the empty plates onto a tray. "Looks like the food is going down a little better," she said, even though Yutaka had not touched the lumpy dumplings in the suiton.

Ainella rose from the table with the tray. Yutaka watched her calves peek out of her kimono as she disappeared into the kitchen.

Suddenly he realized how uncommonly close he was to other people and felt stifled. On Yamato, members of the same family ate their meals according to their own schedule. In that sense, dining in such close proximity to others was unthinkable.

Standing up, Yutaka slipped on some sandals and went out into the yard. "Don't go out past the flower bed!" Ainella called out.

An old atmospheric image of a pastoral landscape spread out before him. Looking up, he found a familiar satellite: Earth's moon.

Sticking his hands inside the *samue* sleeves, Yutaka stared up at the moon without knowing why.

The cleanup of the demolished storeroom was completed in ten days, after which rebuilding began. When the bulk of the labor was finished, Yutaka was sent to the fields for weeding.

Inside the rows of one-tan drums spinning in the main tunnel, the fields had grown darker and greener with grass, and a small-seeded plant had also emerged from the soil. Though this species of millet was edible, it was considered a weed since it robbed the rice crop of nutrients. While it was standard to kill the weeds with chemicals on Yamato, spraying chemicals was prohibited on Lakeview in order to avoid atmospheric contamination.

The weeding took place with the aid of what was called a belly plank, a kind of scaffolding laid across the length of the thirty-one-meter drum. When Yutaka and the villagers lay flat on their bellies on top of the plank, their hands could just reach the bottom of the paddies. Since the drum rotated as the plank stayed in place, the weeds appeared before them, ready for plucking. As Yutaka and the villagers pulled weeds out of the soil one after the next, their hands and faces were spattered with mud.

In some of the drums, the villagers released ducks that fed only on the weeds. Their manure also made for good fertilizer, and once they served their purpose, the ducks could be eaten. Upon hearing this from Dewey, Yutaka had to concede their usefulness.

"I have to admit, the ducks are a good idea. Are you going to raise more of them and put them to work in all of the drums?"

Shaking his head, Dewey said, "Too much manure can over-nitrogenize the mud. Ruins the flavor of the rice. There aren't plans to use any more of those noisy birds. Besides, they smell horrible."

"So you're going to get rid of them?"

"Not exactly."

Dewey explained that he wasn't about to propose either raising more ducks or ending their use. Despite being bothered by this ambiguous response, Yutaka decided to let it go, knowing that any discussion with Dewey would escalate into an ugly debate.

It was around this time that the scheduled shuttlecraft docked at Lakeview for the second time since Yutaka's arrival. He did not know of its existence the first time. Yutaka contemplated commandeering or stowing away on the shuttle, but the dock was so congested with people that he couldn't get close enough. To the villagers, the arrival of the shuttle was an event worthy of a festival. If Yutaka were going to escape, he would have to come up with another way.

The villagers, suspecting nothing, gave him an equal portion of the limited food supply and allowed him to freely roam the community. In fact, he soon came to realize that their treatment of him was strangely improving. Oftentimes, he was handed sweets and fruit during breaks, and villagers talked to him more. One day, after Yutaka had helped tend to the livestock in the barn, a freckled girl bashfully gave him an earthenware jar. It was filled with fresh cow's milk.

Yutaka took the jar back to the sanitarium and dutifully handed it to Ainella, thinking better of initiating a romantic relationship or keeping the encounter a secret. But the woman laughed and returned the jar, saying, "You're free to do what you want."

After drinking down the raw milk, Yutaka suffered an upset stomach and had to be examined by a doctor, who scanned his genome with an outdated DNA reader.

Whatever the case with the freckled girl, it appeared the villagers had forgiven Yutaka for the damage he'd done thanks to his endless toil in the rice fields at their side. In Lakeview, it wasn't so much that the economy revolved around raising rice but that the entire world revolved around it.

One morning the following week, Yutaka was awakened in the morning by shouting.

"Snails!"

"I see snails!"

Yutaka ran out to the paddies with Ainella and found bright pink egg sacs resembling berries or tiny grapes stuck to the rice grass above the waterline in every drum.

"What are these things?" asked Yutaka, looking down at the grass in disgust.

"Here," said Ainella, handing him a hand shovel. "They'll eat the rice if they hatch."

The work of scraping off the eggs that the pesky mollusks had laid in one night continued past noon. When the eggs broke, they gave off a rotten smell, the fluid causing the skin to itch horribly.

The labor required every last villager, young and old. Even Ainella, usually housekeeping this time of day, hiked up her kimono hem and sleeves and pitched in next to Yutaka.

"They're descended from a species called the channeled apple snail, which originally inhabited the Amazon. They were taken out of there as a possible food source, causing them to spread all over Earth."

"Did someone bring them into this village?"

"Not out of malice, mind you. The snails were just one of many things we tried as a food source to survive on this asteroid. But the result was about the same as on Earth. You just have to accept the fact that these things happen."

"If this were Yamato, we'd eliminate the pests chemically or mechanically."

Ainella stopped her work and shot him an icy look. Yutaka ignored her, but he couldn't hide his discomfort.

"Haven't you gotten used to this place yet?"

"What do you mean *yet*?" shouted Yutaka. "I'm a pilot of the Yamato military, understand? Don't expect me to get used to—" Suddenly he started coughing, choking on the force of his own voice.

Far from anger, there was a tranquil light in Ainella's blue eyes. The woman removed the towel covering her head and wiped the egg fluid from Yutaka's cheek with the edge of the cloth. "Why would you want to go back to a place that forces eighteen-year-old kids to fly fighters…"

Apparently some people didn't recognize the honor of flying a fighter at eighteen. Yutaka felt offended and oddly unsettled at the same time.

The eggs were gone by afternoon. Only some pink fluid, spoor of the removal process, remained on the edges of the drums. Just as Yutaka was heading back, spent from the unexpected labor, he happened upon a strange sight.

Several of the drums in one corner of the main tunnel had not a trace of the pink fluid splattered along their edges.

When he approached one of the drums to investigate, a plump duck swam past him leaving a V-shaped wake.

There were more of them gathered against the far wall, eating something.

Yutaka looked around for someone to whom he should report this finding. Diagonally across was the ruddy-faced old man with the pipe spinning on the edge of the drum.

There was no one else looking in his direction. Both Yutaka and the ducks were past the point of drawing any concern from the village.

Along with hotter weather came more weeds. As the temperature on Lakeview rose, Yutaka and the villagers spent much of the day weeding. Yutaka realized that the summer weather was not something this village was simulating; it was caused by the external environment. He decided to ask Dewey about it.

"Does it get hot here because the asteroid has an elliptical orbit or because the sun's rays hit the asteroid at a more direct angle?"

Hearing this, Dewey laughed and patted Yutaka on the shoulder. "You're going to tell me that it's different where you came from, right? That on Yamato the temperature is the same year round because the planet rotates on a perpendicular axis and has a circular orbit."

"How did you know?"

"Why would you assume that we didn't? The Yamato government is a thousand times more industrious about publicizing how great they are than you."

"I didn't know...We don't see the external reports. No, I don't mean to compare this place to Yamato. Just tell me, am I on the right track?"

"Why are you asking?" said Dewey, his face clouding suddenly.

"Why? I guess I'm just curious about the temperature on Lakeview, that's all."

"Oh." After a beat, Dewey said, "It's both. The asteroid isn't quite a spheroid—it's deformed. Even if it doesn't have a perfectly circular orbit, we have no choice but to go on living here."

"But if you've been able to continue to grow rice in spite of all that, you must be able to maintain the temperature somehow. How are you buffering the external effects when it gets too hot or too cold? Do you have some sort of heat exchanger somewhere?"

"You'll find out soon enough." Dewey walked away, saying nothing more. So curt was his response that Yutaka felt as if he'd been brushed aside.

Later, Yutaka learned of the existence of giant water tanks near the surface, and that in addition to providing water to the village, they also acted as radiation barriers and heat buffers. Since this was not necessarily a matter of public record, he had come upon this discovery through some old-fashioned footwork—or jumpwork.

Yutaka could not let go of the feeling that Dewey had tried to conceal the existence of these water tanks.

As July passed into August, the water was drained out of all the drums to dry out the soil. Then the drums were shut down one by one so the rollers could be inspected.

Once the one hundred or so drums stopped spinning for the first time since spring, the hitherto omnipresent low hum also disappeared. Only the light tubes remained on, blazing down over the crops to coax their growth, and a suffocating silence and light filled the main tunnel. Yutaka stripped down to the sleeveless shirt and short pants he knew not the names of and sweated in the fields as he scattered manure. Several of the men working in the fields, who had taken a liking to him, invited him to the summer festival, and on two separate occasions he was approached by women with romantic interests.

Yutaka grew more troubled by the day.

The summer festival began in mid-August. Four of the drums were removed from the main tunnel. Three different drums filled with booths and refreshment stands were installed in their place, and another empty drum served as the main stage, in the center of which was an enormous drum—the percussion instrument, that is.

When the drum began to rotate along with the beat of the drum, the villagers jumped in at once, and with their feet planted against the wall on a higher gravity setting, began to dance.

Boom! Boom! Badoom! What a thrill it would be to join these Caucasian men and women dressed in their best clothes and dance to the thunderous drumbeat, Yutaka thought. Unable to bring himself to do so, Yutaka roamed the darkness away from the festivities. When he returned, he took up a corner of a concession drum and idly played with a chocolate-colored puppy that was inexplicably named after a Hindu god.

"Shiva!" Yutaka said, waving a straw bundle shaped like a bone in front of the eager pup. "Shiva, fetch!"

When Yutaka threw the bundle, the deviating force sent the toy in a strange direction and smacked Ainella, who peeked around the corner, in the face.

"Ouch!" she cried. "Some thanks I get for looking for you."

"Sorry, it was an accident."

"What are you doing over here? Why don't you come and dance? No one's going to get mad if you're a bad dancer."

"I don't think so, Ainella. I'm an outsider here."

"Well, everyone knows that."

"No, what I mean is that I'll eventually leave this place. I appreciate that everyone here's made an effort to accept me, but I can't. Maybe it's a matter of national character, but the way you Kalifs try to welcome outsiders into your community feels foreign to me. I'm scared, Ainella. On Yamato, everything begins with setting ourselves up in opposition to others. We resist blending in with others and willfully expand outward. That's just the way the Yamato people are. You shouldn't be accepting me. You're better off driving me away."

Hearing this, Ainella bent down next to the young man and took his head in her arms. The woman's sweet floral scent wafted into his nostrils, and Yutaka's body tensed.

"You told me what was in your heart. I'm so glad. I didn't know Yamato men could be that way," Ainella said tenderly. "Tell me, do you want see your family back home?"

"I told you, the Yamato are pioneers. We've been prepared to leave our families behind since we enlisted."

"Then why don't you stay here? I have a feeling you're not like the other Yamato people."

Before he knew it, Yutaka was pressing his nose against her skin. Pulling away after several undeniably long seconds, he said, "I am Yamato, whether I like it or not." He pushed Ainella away, fighting back the desire to embrace her. "This isn't about the psyche. It's a physical and biological issue. I still can't stomach the suiton or that taro dish you make. I don't have the digestive gene. For a meateating Yamato like myself, the rice culture of the Kalifs is too alien. I can't live here."

"Yutaka." Brushing her fingers through his black hair, Ainella drew him close and kissed him. The sensation was so unimaginably sweet that it triggered a sharp pain in his chest at the same time. Yutaka pushed her away and broke into a run. The puppy barked noisily at his back.

"Yutaka, I'm sorry!"

But the pilot couldn't understand what she was apologizing for. After all, no one was to blame here. The stars had just not aligned for them.

The same day the radio broadcast reported that the Yamato no Yasoshima Interstellar Expeditionary Fleet would resume its "expedition" of the sector, Lakeview held its annual harvest festival.

At this year's thanksgiving ceremony to the cosmos, Kingston, the head of Lakeview, cut a shaft of rice with a dull knife made of condrite and offered it to the shrine at the far end of the main tunnel, along with tilapia and ham and all manner of vegetables and mushrooms.

"We made it," said Dewey, giving away his relief. "When you crashed your fighter into our food cache, I didn't know if we'd survive to see this day."

"If your food supply had run out in the summer, what would you have done with me? Sliced me up like a ham?"

"Yeah, how'd you know?" When Yutaka shot him a dubious look, the Kalif smirked. "But the discussion did come up. Not about eating you, of course. About how we'd have one less mouth to feed if we just tossed you out on your ass."

"So my life was spared?"

"That was Ainella. She was the one that found you, so she insisted she'd look after you out of her own food rations. You better have thanked her for every meal."

"Yeah," said Yutaka, wincing. "I thanked her all right. More than she cared to hear."

"Good. She'd be upset if you left without saying a word."

"Left? Me? I've just about given up about getting off this rock," Yutaka said and sighed. When he looked up, Dewey had fixed a hard stare on him.

"The Yamato fleet is on its way here. You're planning to jump on the next shuttle to get back to your squadron."

"Come on, how the hell do you expect me to do that with all the commotion every time a shuttle arrives?"

"You're going to wait in near-space and hitch a ride on the shuttle's hull. You stashed away an EV suit on the night of the summer festival."

Yutaka stared down at his feet. He was no good at lying.

Dewey let out a sigh. "You should stick around, Yutaka. We don't want any trouble, but we've been ordered by the Kalifornian Federation to apprehend any suspicious characters."

"Dewey, you're not—"

"It's not what you think," said Dewey. "I'm not a spy or anything. I was born and raised in this village. I just had some training in that sort of thing. I'm only trying to protect this village."

"So you thought I was a spy…?"

Yutaka felt a sudden weariness come over him, when Ainella in red hakama pants over a white kimono floated over in their direction and lit down in front of them.

"Were you two watching the ceremony? Oh—" she said, glancing at Dewey. "So is he…?"

"Yeah," Dewey said. "He's leaving Lakeview."

Ainella turned toward Yutaka. The pilot had to look away. Ever since he'd run away from her that night a month ago, Yutaka could hardly look at Ainella.

But it wasn't out of guilt.

"I see…" the Kalif woman said coolly. "Are you sure? Is it really so unthinkable living in a foreign culture?"

"Yeah…I'm sure."

"Then fine, go. I won't stop you."

Yutaka looked up. Ainella had turned her back. Though he wanted to say something, Yutaka lost the nerve to speak after glimpsing her wipe her cheek with the back of her hand.

"At least taste the *shinsen* before you go."

"Shinsen?"

"It's an old word that refers to an offering to God. But it's also what we call the first meal from the year's harvest. I want you to have a real taste of Kalif food, not the stuff we've had to survive on these last few months. Just once, I'd like to hear you—"

Ainella stopped mid-sentence, but Yutaka knew the rest. He was well aware of the words he'd never uttered.

Nodding, Yutaka said, "Sure."

The new rice was cooked in an enormous cast iron pot and served on bamboo plates. Following the serious ceremony, the mood was cheerful as villagers laid straw mats around the harvested rice field and eagerly took turns ladling the steaming rice into their bowls. It was an entirely foreign sight to Yutaka. Neither the taste nor smell did anything to stimulate his appetite.

A silver tray was set in front of Yutaka.

"This is the shinsen," Ainella said.

On the tray was a mountainous loaf of bread.

The fragrant smell wafting up from the golden crust told him immediately it was fresh-baked. The chief priest brought a slender knife down on the loaf and a slice fell away revealing the fluffy crumb inside.

Yutaka lacked the will to wonder how such a thing could be made in the first place. After six months of forcing down the disagreeable suiton and soy sauce-flavored meals, it was the first food that he recognized from home. No doubt Lakeview had a supply of flour that he didn't know about. Perhaps he was being told about it now as a parting gift.

"Eat," said the chief priest.

At the old man's urging, Yutaka took the slice in his hand. Although usually eaten with butter and jam back on Yamato, the bread smelled so sweet that he didn't dare spread anything on it.

Yutaka brought the bread up to his mouth.

When he bit off a piece of the soft, chewy bread, the taste of the moist flesh filled his mouth.

He worked his jaw. It was good. As he chewed, the bread tasted sweet.

Yutaka began to devour the bread.

He gulped down the first and second slices in big mouthfuls, he took his time to savor the third slice, and it wasn't until he stopped for a breath halfway through the fourth slice that he noticed the villagers staring at him. Ainella nodded as Yutaka blushed.

"Something tells me you like it. Is it good?"

"Yeah," answered Yutaka with a mouthful of bread. It was the taste his DNA had been craving.

"This bread represents the pioneering and expansionist spirit of the Yamato people, while this rice represents the insular and conservative nature of the Kalifs. Is that about right, Yutaka?"

"Yea—yeah." Yutaka nodded, acknowledging the unbridgeable rift between the two races.

"That's rice you're eating," said Ainella, smiling.

For several seconds, Yutaka continued to chew, and after swallowing, he asked, "What was that?"

"The bread you're eating—it's made of rice. You knead the dough made of rice flour, let it rise, and bake it."

"What are you saying? This is bread made from wheat. It tastes like bread—"

"Made out of rice, I tell you," said Ainella. "Tastes just like wheat bread when you bake it. They're both starches, after all."

"This is rice...? But how?"

"I'm afraid your Yamato education has failed you." Ainella took a bite of the bread and nodded her approval. "The number of copies of the amylase gene or AMY1 differs according to the ethnic group to which you belong, and those with fewer copies of AMY1 are better suited to a meat-based diet than a starch-based one—yep, that's what the research suggested in the past, and I suppose it's true, in part. The only problem is that your body doesn't support that theory at all. We had a look at your genome, Yutaka. You have nine copies of AMY1, which is more than Kalifs possess. Shocking, isn't it?"

"You're lying! Just what evidence—"

"And while we're at it," Ainella interrupted, "you seem to be lacking the gene for the lactase enzyme, which breaks down milk sugars. It's best you don't live a nomadic life."

Yutaka fell silent. He quickly recalled the time when he had a stomachache and the doctor had scanned his genome with a DNA reader. Since it wasn't all that difficult to pinpoint a specific gene in the genome, the doctor must have been able to do it with the outdated equipment he had.

He gritted his teeth. "So what if I'm off by a gene or two! Our ethnic identity and culture are closely linked to history. There's no denying it!" Yutaka shouted defiantly.

"Actually they aren't linked at all. In fact, everything here was borrowed from Yamato culture two hundred years ago." Ainella spread her arms, indicating everything from the harvest festival to the harvested fields inside the drums to the rice-growing Caucasians of Lakeview. "Before that, we used to live very much in the way the Yamato live now. Now I don't know how or why this change came about, but I can only imagine a lot happened. You can check it out for yourself if you don't believe me. You can even access the network outside Kalif and Yamato from this village."

"B-but you saw how my body reacted."

A smile escaping her lips, Ainella replied, "You have a lot of likes and dislikes. But aside from the milk, you never once felt sick to your stomach, did you?"

Rendered speechless, Yutaka dropped his shoulders in defeat.

Seeing this, Ainella crouched down next to the young man and put a hand on his shoulder. "Yutaka."

"Let go of me."

"I thought you might be able to accept this, Yutaka. It's ridiculous to decide your fate based on genealogy. I know you can adapt to our way of life, and I wish you would stay. But I won't lie to you. Just as you can choose to stay, you can find a way out of here. The shuttle will arrive in three days."

Yutaka continued to stare down at the straw mat for what seemed like an eternity. Sensing the eyes of the village upon him, he glanced up to find Dewey and the head priest and the young men and women of the village smiling bashfully at him.

Finally, the Yamato pilot shifted his gaze toward Ainella. "You said you slaughter the livestock in autumn?"

"Yes, soon," answered Ainella, her blue eyes narrowing.

Then Yutaka said a bit brusquely, "I'm not crazy about soy sauce flavoring."

One Breath, One Stroke by Catherynne M. Valente

1. In a peach grove the House of Second-Hand Carnelian casts half a shadow. This is because half of the house is in the human world, and half of it is in another place. The other place has no name. It is where unhuman things happen. It is where tricksters go when they are tired. A modest screen divides the world. It is the color of plums. There are silver tigers on it, leaping after plum petals. If you stand in the other place, you can see a hundred eyes peering through the silk.

2. In the human half of the House of Second-Hand Carnelian lives a mustached gentleman calligrapher named Ko. Ko wears a chartreuse robe embroidered with black thread. When Ko stands on the other side of the house he is not Ko, but a long calligraphy brush with badger bristles and a strong cherrywood shaft. When he is a brush his name is Yuu. When he was a child he spent all day hopping from one side of the house to the other. Brush, man. Man, brush.

3. Ko lives alone. Yuu lives with Hone-Onna, the skeleton woman; Sazae-Onna, the snail woman; a jar full of lightning; and Namazu, a catfish as big as three strong men. When Namazu slaps

his tail on the ground, earthquakes tremble, even in the human world. Yuu copied a holy text of Tengu love poetry onto the bones of Hone-Onna. Her white bones are black now with beautiful writing, for Yuu is a very good calligrapher.

4. Hone-Onna's skull reads: *The moon sulks. I am enfolded by feathers the color of remembering. The talons I seize, seize me.*

5. Ko is also an excellent calligrapher. But he is retired, for when he stands on one side of the House of Second-Hand Carnelian, he has no brush to paint his characters, and when he stands on the other, he has no breath. "The great calligraphers know all writing begins in the body. One breath, one stroke. One breath, one stroke. That is how a book is made. Long black breath by long black breath. Yuu will never be a great calligrapher, even though he is technically accomplished. He has no body to begin his poems."

6. Ko cannot leave the House of Second-Hand Carnelian. If he tries, he becomes sick and vomits squid ink until he returns. He grows radish, melon, and watercress, and of course there are the peaches. A river flows by the House of Second-Hand Carnelian. It is called the Nobody River. When it winds around to the other side of the house, it is called the Nothingness River. There are some fish in it. Ko catches them with a peach branch. Namazu belches and fish jump into his mouth. On Namazu's lower lip Yuu copied a Tanuki elegy.

7. Namazu's whiskers read: *In deep snow I regret everything. My testicles are heavy with grief. Because of me, the stripes of her tail will never return.*

8. Sazae-Onna lives in a pond in the floor of the kitchen. Her shell is tiered like a cake or a palace, hard and thorned and colored like the inside of an almond, with seams of mother of pearl swirling in spiral patterns over her gnarled surface. She eats the rice that falls from the table when the others sit down to supper. She drinks the steam from the teakettle. When she dreams she dreams of sailors fishing her out of the sea in a net of roses. On the Emperor's

234 CATHERYNNE M. VALENTE

birthday Yuu gives her candy made from Hone-Onna's marrow. Hone-Onna does not mind. She has plenty to spare. Sazae-Onna takes the candy quietly under her shell with one blue-silver hand. She sucks it for a year.

9. When Yuu celebrates the Emperor's birthday, he does not mean the one in Tokyo. He means the Goldfish-Emperor of the Yokai who lives on a tiny island in the sea, surrounded by his wives and their million children. On his birthday he grants a single wish—among all the unhuman world red lottery tickets appear in every teapot. Yuu has never won.

10. The Jar of Lightning won once, when it was not a jar, but a Field General in the Storm Army of Susano-no-Mikoto. It had won many medals in its youth by striking the cypress roofs of the royal residences at Kyoto and setting them on fire. The electric breast of the great lightning bolt groaned with lauds. When the red ticket formed in its ice-cloud teapot, with gold characters upon it instead of black, the lightning bolt wished for peace and rest. Susano-no-Mikoto is a harsh master with a harsh and windy whip, and he does not permit honorable retirement. This is how the great lightning bolt became a Jar of Lightning in the House of Second-Hand Carnelian. It took the name of Noble and Serene Electric Master and polishes its jar with static discharge on washing day.

11. Sazae-Onna rarely shows her body. Under the shell, she is more beautiful than anyone but the moon's wife. No one is more beautiful than her. Sazae-Onna's hair is pale, soft pink; her eyes are deep red; her mouth is a lavender blossom. Yuu has only seen her once, when he caught her bathing in the river. All the fish surrounded her in a ring, staring up at her with their fishy eyes. Even the moon looked down at Sazae-Onna that night, though he felt guilty about it afterward and disappeared for three days to purify himself. So profoundly moved was Yuu the calligraphy brush that he begged permission to copy a Kitsune hymn upon the pearl-belly of Sazae-Onna.

12. The pearl-belly of Sazae-Onna reads: *Through nine tails I saw a wintry lake at midnight. Skate-tracks wrote a poem of melancholy on the ice. You stood upon the other shore. For the first time I thought of becoming human.*

13. Ko has no visitors. The human half of the House of Second-Hand Carnelian is well hidden in a deep forest full of black bears just wise enough to resent outsiders and arrange a regular patrol. There is also a Giant Hornet living there, but no one has ever seen it. They only hear the buzz of her wings on cloudy days. The bears, over the years, have developed a primitive but heartfelt Buddhist discipline. Beneath the cinnamon trees they practice the repetition of the Growling Sutra. The religion of the Giant Hornet is unknown.

14. The bears are unaware of their heritage. Their mother is Hoeru, the Princess of All Bears. She fell in love with a zen monk whose *koans* buzzed around her head like bees. The Princess of All Bears hid her illegitimate children in the forest around the House of Second-Hand Carnelian, close enough to the plum-colored screen to watch over, but far enough that their souls could never quite wake. It is a sad story. Yuu copied it onto a thousand peach leaves. When the wind blows on his side of the house, you can hear Hoeru weeping.

15. If Ko were to depart the house, Yuu would vanish forever. If Ko so much as crosses the Nobody River, he receives a pain in his long bones, the bones that are most like the strong birch shaft of a calligraphy brush. If he tries to open the plum-colored screen, he falls at once to sleep and Yuu appears on the other side of the silks having no memory of being Ko. Ko is a lonely man. With his finger-nails he writes upon the tatami: *Beside the sunlit river I regret that I never married. At tea time, I am grateful for the bears.*

16. The woven grass swallows his words.

17. Sometimes the bears come to see him and watch him catch fish. They think he is very clumsy at it. They try to teach him the Growling Sutra as a cure for loneliness, but Ko cannot understand

them. He fills a trough with weak tea and shares his watercress. They take a little, to be polite.

18. Yuu has many visitors, though Namazu the catfish has more. Hone-Onna receives a gentleman skeleton at the full moon. They hold seances to contact the living, conducted with a wide slate of volcanic glass, yuzu wine, and a transistor radio brought to the House of Second-Hand Carnelian by a Kirin who had recently eaten a G.I. and spat the radio back up. The Kirin wrapped it up very nicely, though, with curls of green silk ribbon. Hone-Onna and her suitor each contribute a shoulder blade, a thumb bone, and a kneecap. They set the pieces of themselves upon the board in positions according to several arcane considerations only skeletons have the patience to learn. They drink the yuzu wine; it trickles in a green waterfall through their rib cages. Then they turn on the radio.

19. Yuu thanked the Kirin by copying a Dragon koan onto his long horn. The Kirin's horn reads: *What was the form of the Buddha when he came among the Dragons?*

19. Once, Datsue-Ba came to visit the House of Second-Hand Carnelian. She arrived on a palanquin of business suits, for Datsue-Ba takes the clothes of the dead when they come to the shores of the Sanzu River in the underworld. She and her husband Keneo live beneath a persimmon tree on the opposite bank. Datsue-Ba takes the clothes of the lost souls after they have swum across, and Keneo hangs them to dry on the branches of their tree. Datsue-Ba knows everything about a dead person the moment she touches their sleeve.

20. Datsue-Ba brought guest gifts for everyone, even the Jar of Lightning. These are the gifts she gave:

A parasol painted with orange blossoms for Sazae-Onna so she will not dry out in the sun.

A black funeral kimono embroidered with black cicada wings

for Hone-Onna so that she can attend the festival of the dead in style.

A copper ring bearing a ruby frog on it for Yuu to wear around the stalk of his brush-body.

A cypress-wood comb for the Noble and Serene Electric Master to burn up and remember being young.

Several silver earrings for Namazu to wear upon his lip and feel mighty.

21. Datsue-Ba also brought a gift for Ko. This is how he acquired his chartreuse robe embroidered with black thread. It once belonged to an unremarkable courtier who played the koto poorly and envied his brother who held a rank one level higher than his own. Datsue-Ba put the chartreuse robe at the place where the Nothingness River becomes the Nobody River. Datsue-Ba is very good at rivers. When Ko found it, he did not know who to thank, so he turned and bowed to the plum-colored screen.

22. This begs the question of whether Ko knows what goes on in the other half of the House of Second-Hand Carnelian. Sometimes he wakes up at night and thinks he hears singing or whispering. Sometimes when he takes his bath the water seems to gurgle as though a great fish is hiding in it. He conceived suspicions when he tried to leave the peach grove, which contains the house, and suffered in his bones so terribly. For a long time that was all Ko knew.

23. Namazu runs a club for Guardian Lions every month. They play dice; the stone lions shake them in their mouths and spit them against the peach trees. Namazu roars with laughter and slaps the ground with his tail. Earthquakes rattle the mountains in Hokkaido. Most of the lions cheat because their lives are boring and they crave excitement. Guarding temples does not hold the same thrill as hunting or biting. Auspicious Snow Lion is the best dice player. He comes all the way from Taipei to play and drink and hunt rabbits in

the forest. He does not speak Japanese, but he pretends to humbly lose when the others snarl at his winning streaks.

24. Sometimes they play Go. The lions are terrible at it. Fortuitous Brass Lion likes to eat the black pieces. Namazu laughs at him and waggles his whiskers. Typhoons spin up off the coast of Okinawa.

25. Everyone on the unhuman side of the House of Second-Hand Carnelian is curious about Ko. Has he ever been in love? Fought in a war? What are his thoughts on astrology? Are there any good scandals in his past? How old is he? Does he have any children? Where did he learn calligraphy? Why is he here? How did he find the house and get stuck there? Was part of him always a brush named Yuu? Using the thousand eyes in the screen, they spy on him but cannot discover the answers to any of these questions.

26. They have learned the following: Ko is left-handed. Ko likes fish skin better than fish flesh. Ko cheats when he meditates and opens his eyes to see how far the sun has gotten along. Ko has a sweet tooth. When Ko talks to the peach trees and the bears, he has an Osaka accent.

27. The Noble and Serene Electric Master refused to let Yuu copy anything out on its Jar. The Noble and Serene Electric Master does not approve of graffiti. Even when Yuu remembered suddenly an exquisite verse repeated among the Aosaginohi Herons who glow in the night like blue lanterns. The Jar of Lightning snapped its cap and crackled disagreeably. Yuu let it rest; when you share a house you must let your manners go before you to smooth the path through the rooms.

28. The Heron verse went: *Autumn maples turn black in the evening. I turn them red again and caw for you, flying south to Nagoya. The night has no answer for me, but many small fish.*

29. Who stretched the plum-colored screen with silver tigers leaping upon it down the very narrow line separating the halves of the house? For that matter, who built the House of Second-Hand Carnelian? Sazae-Onna knows, but she doesn't talk to anyone.

30. Yuki-Onna came to visit the Jar of Lightning. They had been comrades in the army of storms long ago. With every step of her small, quiet feet, snowflakes fell on the peach grove and the Nothingness River froze into intricate patterns of eddies and frost. She wore a white kimono with a silver obi belt, and her long black hair was scented with red bittersweet. Everyone grew very silent, for Yuki-Onna was a Kami and not a playful lion or a hungry Kirin. Yuu trembled. Tiny specks of ink shook from his badger bristles. He longed to write upon the perfect white silk covering her shoulders. Hone-Onna brought tea and black sugar to the Snow-and-Death Kami. Snow fell even inside the house. The Noble and Serene Electric Master left its Jar and circled its blue sparkling jagged body around the waist of Yuki-Onna, who laughed gently. One of the bears on the other side of the peach grove collapsed and coughed his last black blood onto the ice. Yuu noticed that the Snow-and-Death Kami wore a necklace. Its beads were silver teeth, hundreds upon thousands of them, the teeth of all of winter's dead. Unable to contain himself, Yuu wrote in the frigid air: *Snow comes; I have forgotten my own name.*

31. Yuki-Onna looks up. Her eyes are darker than death. She closes them; Yuu's words appear on the back of her neck.

32. Yuu is unhappy. He wants Sazae-Onna to love him. He wants Yuki-Onna to come back to visit him and not the Noble and Serene Electric Master. He wants to be the premier calligrapher in the unhuman half of Japan. He wants to be asked to join Namazu's dice games. He wants to leave the House of Second-Hand Carnelian and visit the Emperor's island or the crystal whale who lives off the coast of Shikoku. But if Yuu tries to leave his ink dries up and his wood cracks until he returns.

33. Someone wanted a good path between the human and the unhuman Japans. That much is clear.

34. Sazae-Onna does not like visitors one little bit. They splash in her pond. They poke her and try to get her to come out. Unfortunately,

every day brings more folk to the House of Second-Hand Carnelian. First the Guardian Lions didn't leave. Then Datsue-Ba came back with even more splendid clothes for them all, robes the color of maple leaves and jewels the color of snow and masks painted with liquid silver. Then the Kirin returned and asked Sazae-Onna to marry him. Yuu trembled. Sazae-Onna said nothing and pulled her shell down tighter and tighter until he went away. Nine-Tailed Kitsune and big-balled Tanuki are eating up all the peaches. Long-nosed Tengu overfish the river. No one goes home when the moon goes down. When the Blue Jade Cicadas arrive from Kamakura Sazae-Onna locks her kitchen and tells them all to shut up.

35. Yuu knocks after everyone has gone to sleep. Sazae-Onna lets him in. On the floor of her kitchen he writes a Kappa proverb: *Dark clouds bring rain, the night brings stars, and everyone will try to spill the water out of your skull.*

36. At the end of summer, the unhuman side of the house is crammed full, but Ko can only hear the occasional rustle. When Kawa-Uso the Otter Demon threw an ivory saddle onto the back of one of the bears and rode her around the peach grove like a horse, Ko only saw a poor she-bear having some sort of fit. Ko sleeps all the time now, though he is not really sleeping. He is being Yuu on the other side of the plum-colored screen. He never writes poetry on the tatami anymore.

37. The Night Parade occurs once every hundred years at the end of summer. Nobody plans it. They know to go to the door between the worlds the way a brown goose knows to go north in the spring.

38. One night the remaining peaches swell up into juicy golden lanterns. The river rushes become *kotos* with long spindly legs. The mushrooms become lacy, thick oyster drums. The Kitsune begin to dance; the Tengu flap their wings and spit *mala* beads toward the dark sky in fountains. A trio of small dragons the color of pearls in milk leap suddenly out of the Nothingness River. Cerulean fire curls out of their noses. The House of Second-Hand Carnelian empties.

Namazu's Lions carry him on a litter of silk fishing nets. The Jar of Lightning bounces after Hone-Onna and her gentleman caller, whose bones clatter and clap. When only Yuu and the snail-woman are left, Sazae-Onna lifts up her shell and steps out into the Parade, her pink hair falling like floss, her black eyes gleaming. Yuu feels as though he will crack when faced with her beauty.

39. The Parade steps over the Nothingness River and the Nobody River and enters the human Japan, dancing and singing and throwing light at the dark. They will wind down through the plains to Kyoto before the night is through, and flow like a single serpent into the sea where the Goldfish Emperor of the Yokai will greet them with his million children and his silver-fronded wives.

40. Yuu races after Sazae-Onna. The bears watch them go. In the midst of the procession Hoeru the Princess of All Bears, who is Queen now, comes bearing a miniature Agate Great Mammal Palace on her back. Her children fall in and nurse as though they were still cubs. For a night, they know their names.

41. Yuu does not make it across the river. It goes jet with his ink. His strong birch shaft cracks; Sazae-Onna does not turn back. When she dances she looks like a poem about loss. Yuu pushes forward through the water of the Nothingness River. His shaft bursts in a shower of birch splinters.

42. A man's voice cries out from inside the ruined brush handle. Yuu startles and stops. The voice says: *I never had any children. I have never been in love.*

43. Yuu topples into the Nobody River. The kotos are distant now, the peach-lanterns dim. His badger bristles fall out.

44. Yuu pulls himself out of the river by dry grasses and berry vines. He is not Yuu on the other side. He is not Ko. He has Ko's body, but his arms are calligraphy brushes sopping with ink. His feet are inkstones. He can still here the music of the Night Parade. He begins to dance. Not-Yuu and Not-Ko takes a breath.

45. There is only the House of Second-Hand Carnelian to write

on. He writes on it. He breathes and swipes his brush, breathes, brushes. Man, brush. Brush, Man. He writes and does not copy. He writes psalms of being part man and part brush. He writes poems of his love for the snail-woman. He writes songs about perfect breath. The House slowly turns black.

46. Bringing up the rear of the Parade hours later, Yuki-Onna comes silent through the forest. Snow flows before her like a carpet. She has brought her sisters the Flower-and-Joy Kami and the Cherry-Blossom-Mount-Fuji Kami. The crown of the Fuji-Kami's head has frozen. The Flower-and-Joy Kami is dressed in chrysanthemums and lemon blossoms. They pause at the House of Second-Hand Carnelian. Not-Yuu and Not-Ko shakes and shivers; he is sick, he has received both the pain in his femurs and the pain in his brush handles. The Kami shine so bright the fish in both rivers are blinded. The Flower-and-Joy Kami looks at the poem on one side of the door. It reads: *In white peonies I see the exhalations of my kanji blossoming.* The Cherry-Blossom-Mount-Fuji Kami looks at the poem on the other side of the door. It reads: *It is enough to sit at the foot of a mountain and breathe the pine mist. Only a proud man must climb it.* The Kami close their eyes as they pass by. The words appear on the backs of their necks as they disappear into the night.

47. Ko dies in mid-stroke, describing the sensation of lungs filled up like the windbag of heaven. Yuu dies before he can complete his final verse concerning the exquisiteness of crustaceans who will never love you back.

48. Slowly, with a buzz like breath, the Giant Hornet flies out of her nest and through the peach grove denuded by hungry Tanuki. She is a heavy, furry emerald bobbing on the wind. The souls of Ko and Yuu quail before her. As she picks them up with her weedy legs and puts them back into their bodies she tells them a Giant Hornet poem: *Everything is venom, even sweetness. Everything is sweet, even venom. Death is illiterate and a hayseed bum. No excuse to leave the nest unguarded. What are you, some silly jade lion?*

49. The sea currents bring the skeleton-woman back, and Namazu who has caused two tsunamis, though only one made the news. The Jar of Lightning floats up the river. Finally the snail-woman returns to the pond in her kitchen. They find Yuu making tea for them. His bristles are dry. On the other side of the plum-colored screen, Ko is sweeping out the leaves.

50. Yuu has written on the teacups. It reads: *It takes a calligrapher one hundred years to draw one breath.*

Whale Meat by Ekaterina Sedia

Ever since I was six, I believed that a divorce necessitated trans-atlantic travel—ever since my mom bundled me into my warmest coat and took me to the US, while dad was left behind, small and sad. He saw me off at the Sapporo Airport; Mom and he never talked to each other, and in my memory, my father is always like this—forever receding behind me. I'm an adult now, so I can visit him whenever I want. Still I always end up leaving, and he seems to get smaller every time as if my guilt eats away at him.

My guilt is a complex thing; the fact that I usually stop in Tokyo rather than flying directly to Hokkaido is a contributing factor. I could be spending more time with my dad, but Tokyo is where I earn a good chunk of my living, and so I go, because without it I would probably have to get a regular job rather than waking up at noon and typing chai-fueled nonsense in my PJs.

All the clothing companies are in Tokyo, BabyStar and Luxe and a million others. I guess they are running out of aging *gosuroris* and forest girls to peddle their clothing to and are desperate for the US markets.

So in exchange for ad space and articles and product placement on DISPARASIAN, my blog, they ply me with their outfits, which are pretty enough; I would be tempted if any of them ever fit over my size 6 thighs. "You're built like an American," their tiny reps tell me. I'm actually thin in the US, but not here.

I thank them politely in my first-grader's Japanese (I stopped talking Japanese at home when I went to school) and gather armfuls of petticoats and capes, jumper dresses, pleated skirts, lace-sleeved blouses and silk sashes. All of them will be worn by someone who isn't me, styled and photographed and given away or auctioned off on my blog. I have no problem with shilling—it gives me the ability to write about serious stuff, like identity and guilt and politics and environmental protection.

But before I can return home to New Jersey (I lie that I'm in New York for blogging glamour purposes), I have to visit my father in Sapporo. When he sees me at the gate, he manages a two-second stoic smile before his face crumples and he cries, like he cries every time—eyes suddenly hot and face twitching, and I hold him and wish him not to grow old. And then I cry too.

After all the emotion at the airport, he leads me to his under-sized old Toyota and drives toward Soseigawa Dori. This two-hour trip north is usually what it takes for me to get used to everyone driving on the wrong side, until my heart stops swooping in my chest as he pulls to the left side of the road.

This time, however, we go west.

He explains on the way. There is a new assignment, he says, and he will be traveling out of the country—to the Kurils, to be exact. Well, Sakhalin. "You never get proper news in the US," he tells me. "There was a fisherman from Hokkaido killed in the waters by Sakhalin. Russians let us fish there—well, that's the treaty anyway.

But there were a few…a few cases in the past ten years. I will go and investigate this last one."

My father is a prefect, and as far as I understand Japanese law enforcement (not very), he really is not in the position to travel abroad and investigate anything. I mumble something to that effect.

He laughs. "The Russians won't extradite. And I go…as a private citizen. I have relatives there—not very close ones, but plausibly close. I'll go, see what I can find. Undercover, like in a Hollywood movie!"

I laugh. "Oh Dad." It must be so hard for him, to have an American child. "Can I come with you? For plausibility?"

"Your Japanese passport still valid?"

I nod and feel a bit peeved that he anticipated my saying it. That he really left me no choice—either go with him or head back to the US a week early. "When are we leaving?"

"In two days," he says. "I figured we can spend time in Sapporo, maybe go shopping? All the fashions that you like so much?"

"My suitcase is pretty full," I say. "But sure, we can spend time here. And I'll probably need some cold weather clothes."

"You can put some of your stuff in my suitcase. Then we take a train and a boat," he says. "It'll be an adventure!"

I don't particularly care, but I'm glad to see him so happy. Things we do for our parents, especially the ones who read our blogs. The ones we feel we ought to have been nicer to.

I don't know what to expect from Sakhalin, and just in case I buy an extra sweater and a windbreaker, even though my father reassures me that Septembers there are balmy. He really tries hard—I started going to Japan when I turned eighteen, and there's that void of twelve years when all I knew of him was an occasional letter and a parcel. My mom was not a bitter person, but as far as she was concerned, my father was over—done and in the past and no reason to Skype or email or keep in any meaningful touch with. After these twelve years—most of my childhood—we'll never catch up. But he tries anyway.

"What are your friends like, back in the States?" he asks when we're back to the hotel after a day of awkward silences and shopping for sweaters and parkas. I get clothes from the men's department, and my father is cool with that. "Do they ever ask you about going to Japan? What do you tell them?"

I shrug. "Mostly that it's not all about businessmen eating sushi and buying panties from the vending machines." Only after I wish him good night do I realize that he wanted to know if I ever mention him.

Sakhalin turns out to be fairly cold but surprisingly beautiful. We are staying in a small town, mostly Japanese still, although the language they speak is so peppered with Russian I imagine myself trapped in some weird *Clockwork Orange* production. It's located on the shore, like any good fishing town ought to be, and there are hills—*sopki* the locals call them—round and blue, dressed in steam escaping from some dormant but dangerous-seeming volcano underground. There are trees there too: they look like firs of some sort, except they're bright yellow. "Larches," Dad says to me in English.

The sea there is gray, and there's a cold wind blowing from it. I'm glad for my sweaters and leggings and parkas, as I throw a cape over them for good measure and go to explore all by myself. I want some nature and quiet for a change, and the talk in our hosts' home is depressing and alienating; they and my father seem to want nothing more than to complain about Kurils being Russian, and Russians deporting Japanese families, and how everyone is worried. I suspect that no one remembers that this town even exists.

I stand by the shore and watch the dirty lace of the surf flow over the rocks, lingering for moments in creases between them and flowing back, until my attention is distracted by some people a few dozen yards from me. They seem to be tugging on a net of some sort and yelling at each other. I wander in their direction, hopeful that this place is too small for any egregious crimes. Then I remember the fisherman.

The men with the net are all Russian—I'm guessing from their blond beards and cable-knit sweaters under their canvas hoodies. When I approach them, they all look at me without any particular hostility, but not friendly either.

"Hi," I say. "I'm just visiting here. Any of you speak English?"

One of them nods—he seems to be in his thirties, wispy-bearded, with a face windburned to an intense brick color. "I speak English," he tells me. "Where are you from?"

"The United States."

He perks up. "Santa Barbara?"

"New York...well, New Jersey."

"Oh." He tries to hide his disappointment.

"Fishing?" I ask.

He shakes his head. "Dead whale," he says. "Fresh, Japanese were hunting here yesterday—they take blubber, whale's mustache...its teeth, yes? Leave everything else behind. All the meat. Have you ever tried whale?"

I shake my head.

"Come to the shop tomorrow," he says, just as his fellows heave the net and I finally see: black and red, torn raw, revolting. They wade into the chilled water, and I see then that they all carry knives strapped to their legs in cracked wooden sheaths. They take out the wide, flat blades and hack at the mound of flesh, which doesn't even look like anything that used to be sentient. And I cannot get mad at them because they didn't kill it—they were merely salvaging what they could from someone else's crime.

The next day, our hosts take my father and me grocery shopping. The whale meat is there already, labeled in Russian and Japanese, and it is cheaper than anything else in the store. My yesterday's acquaintance is working behind the fish counter, and the variety of fish really is impressive—or would be, if I could only look away from the bright red mammal flesh that doesn't belong with the fish. Whales are seafood though, I suppose.

"I want to try whale," I tell our hosts. "May we?"

I feel like a cannibal when I say it, but the pull of the forbidden and the secret is way too strong. Although it won't be secret for long—I will probably blog about it, because this is just how it is.

"Sure," says Yumi, the old woman my father keeps calling "Aunt" even though the degree of their relatedness is nowhere that close. "Would you like some *toro* too?"

The word is unfamiliar to me, but my father tenses and lights up. "It's legal here?"

Then I remember that toro is the belly of a kind of tuna, bluefin, now a globally protected species with even the Japanese unable to harvest it. When the law first went into effect, Mom and I were already living in the US, and her decision to give up national affectations apparently included tuna as well—at least, I don't remember her saying much about it.

"Yes," his dubious aunt says. "It's farm-grown."

My father sighs. "Does it taste the same?"

"You'll see," Aunt Yumi says slyly.

Sakhalin is severe and beautiful, and I take picture after picture every day: steaming ground and rounded hills, evidence of silent geothermal activity everywhere. In fact, Russians are building a power station nearby, run entirely on geothermal power. When it is finished, it'll supply power to fully one quarter of Sakhalin. I take notes for my blog. My father leaves in the morning—on business, he tells me very seriously. Our relatives have jobs and things to do, so I'm left to entertain myself.

I spend my days wandering about taking pictures and speculating about my father's secret mission. Perhaps, I think, the fisherman was killed as revenge for a dead whale. Or maybe he was not a fisherman but an industrial spy, trying to find out secrets of geothermal technology—although I'm guessing it's not like nuclear power, and there're probably not many secrets. Still, it is fun to pretend.

I return home by supper, which takes place about eight o'clock, just as the sun is beginning to set. I forget how long summer nights are so far north, and even now they're dwindling. For supper, we eat rice, steaming in round bowls, and dumplings, and thin slices of locally grown toro. My father loves it, clearly, even though he does say that it's not the same as wild-caught fish. But he puts it away as if his life depends on it. I try not to think of bioaccumulation as I eat it too—and it is delicious.

The whale proves to be a disappointment though: it turns gray when cooked and smells sour, and it tastes like fish but has a confusing beef texture to it. It tastes like the ocean tinged with blood. It tastes like sin.

I call my mom three days in because she is probably wondering why I haven't emailed her. Roaming charges here are ridiculous, but I can afford a phone call, so I do.

"Sakhalin?" she says. "Have you heard about the whale?"

It's as if she can see my soul, and I blanch and feel grateful that there's no one but yellow larches and the pale, lemon meringue sun to see me here. "What whale?

"The one that Japanese whaling ship harpooned off the coast. They said it was the last representative of the species—what was it, a sperm whale?"

"I don't know," I whisper. "I haven't heard—I can't read the newspapers, they're all in Russian."

"Everyone's talking about that," she says. "Be careful."

I hang up, and my stomach feels hollow. I cannot understand how they manage to protect tuna and not whales, and familiar rationalizations pop up: whales are the only source of whale oil, and there are many species of tuna, and whaling is traditional, and I cannot understand it at all.

That night, after dinner, I tug at my dad's arm as if I were a child, and he looks up at me as if startled from slumber. Our hosts' house is small but somehow it feels spacious, with such small, spare furniture and a tiny TV permanently tuned to some backwater Japanese channel—the only one that reaches all the way here into the Russian territory. It seems to air mostly variety shows and an occasional vintage eating contest. I try not to develop too much affection for Kobayashi.

"What's the matter?" he asks.

"I want to go for a walk," I say. "Come with me."

He does, and we stroll along the main street, a dirt path already frozen—it freezes after dark but thaws again in the morning—flanked by rows of the ubiquitous larches, to the shore. The oceanic susurrus is ever present, and I grow oblivious to it and then aware again all the way from the village.

There are flashlights bouncing along the shore and disappearing around the bend one by one by one. "Have you found anything?" I say, watching the disembodied lights. "About the dead fisherman?"

My father shakes his head. "Even the Japanese don't know, and the Russians wouldn't even speak to me. There are rumors of another Japanese repatriation, and everyone knows better than to say anything. Even if they know nothing and have nothing to hide."

"It's about the Kurils?" I ask.

"It's...it's hard to explain. They used to be ours, and after the war...they weren't won, see. They were a toy your parents gave away to punish you. No one wants to be treated like a child."

"Do you think we'll be leaving soon?"

"Yumi doesn't want me to go. And she wants me to tell her that it'll be okay."

"Just tell her that Japan is a thousand times better than this backwater." As I say it, I realize it's stupid because there is no better or worse when it comes to things like this; I too might think that Japan is better, but New Jersey is where it's at.

"Let's see what they're doing there," my father says diplomatically. "I think this is where they have those tuna pens."

The lights have all disappeared and it's growing darker, and the moon is full and is reflected in the oily black water. "Russians call it the moon road." My father points at the ladder of moonlight running across the lazily sloshing ocean.

"Do they raise tuna like this in Japan?" I ask.

He nods. "It's not the same though. Young people like it, but those who remember the real thing...everything is different."

"You like the toro here."

He smiles. "Here, I can pretend to be something else."

We round the bend, and the moon road breaks into crescents and vortices of light, churning. We come upon the same groups of fishermen as before, and the one who speaks English smiles at me.

"Late walk," he says.

"This is my father," I say, and they shake hands gingerly. Other men watch, neither interested nor impatient.

"You're working late," my father says politely.

"It's beautiful at night." The man points at the churning water and follows his gesture with the beam of his flashlight. I see bulky dark sides rubbing against each other with a slight metallic whisper, as the enclosure by the shore comes alive with fish—they crowd together, every one at least as long as me, and the sharp ridges of their gill covers flash silver. The beam snatches their reddish eyes as they meet mine, and their maws open with a soft kissing sound as they swallow air. The men toss buckets of small herring at them, and the water boils white. "Have to feed them all the time now, so they get fat enough for winter," the man says. "Then, we move the pens away from the shore, into the deeper water for the winter. Protect from the storms."

"Does it get really cold here?" I ask.

He nods. "Very cold. Cold is not bad though. It's the winter—when you know you're alone in the world. Here…very alone."

The dorsal fins of the fish slash the water like knives, drag traces of moonlight behind them. I think of the dead fisherman and whether he knew he was going to die alone. I watch my father watching the jostling fish, his face narrow and suddenly old in the moonlight, and I wonder if he ever expected to find out anything here, or if it was his way of being something else, alone, among the yellow larches when the winter is coming. Most of all, I wonder if I'll ever manage to forget how this night feels, with thrashing giant fish in the black water and the taste of dead leaves in the moonlight. In my knotted stomach, the last whale begins to sing.

Mountain People, Ocean People by Hideyuki Kikuchi

Translated by Takami Nieda

The launch platform was a five-minute walk past the grave-yard. Kanaan wondered why a platform was necessary in the first place.

You could fly from just about anywhere as long as you strapped on a glider. Kanaan's first flight had been off a bluff in the west, and his father's from atop a stone wall in the east.

Though they'd just finished breakfast, the children had already taken to the skies.

The largest group, in their crimson uniforms, was from Ararat.

The platform here was about the same elevation as Ararat's summit, so the visiting children must have found the steep drop to be a challenge.

The green-uniformed children from Anyemaqen, who were but blurs in the distance, appeared to be getting used to the current here. There were several instructors accompanying them as the children flew in a steady formation, but Kanaan disapproved of their technique. They were never going to master the current around Everest flying like that.

The children of Everest also visited Anyemaqen and the

Matterhorn, but fewer than one in a hundred learned to ride the currents in those parts.

Kanaan looked up.

Puffy cumulus clouds dotted the ultramarine sky. *Maybe now's my chance,* Kanaan thought.

"Hey down there!"

A figure wearing a sky-colored uniform swooped down from above. Kanaan instantly recognized Domino's smiling face.

With a slight tug of his hands, the young man applied just the right amount of drag to the white membranous wings stretched between his wrists and ankles and brought himself to a full stop in midair. As effortless as hovering looked, it was a maneuver that only veteran gliders could execute.

"Don't do it, Kanaan," said Domino. "Your job is to protect the village. You can think about going up later."

"Leave me alone. Then *you* go."

"Not on your life. Being an instructor suits me just fine. I don't want anything to do with Lascaux's nonsense about how we were born to fly higher. I just don't want to lose our best hunter, is all."

"I'm not going anywhere." Kanaan grimaced in an effort to hide his shock that Domino had read his mind.

Domino dropped his right shoulder, tilted slightly to the right, and glided several meters in that direction.

"I'll catch you later," said Domino. "The mornings are just too crowded with students. I know the current here is perfect for lessons and all, but it's a little annoying."

And with that, Domino dropped like a stone out of sight.

"Careful you don't fall in the ocean!" Kanaan shouted and then went back to take in the view before him.

The mountains, shrouded in patchy clouds, resembled mortar bowls set atop cylinders. Seen from above, the mountains measured about a hundred kilometers in diameter. Several settlements were scattered about the emerald green forest; river threads cascaded down, turning into waterfalls at the lips of the bowls. The water glistened like gold in the morning sun, and it was this scene that children liked to draw most at school. Penetrating those waterfalls tumbling into the void below was apparently considered a feat even among the children.

In fact, there had been plans to connect the mountains and waterfalls with a suspension bridge, but they had come to nothing. It was far easier to fly than to build the bridge and traverse the fifty-kilometer distance on foot.

Kanaan went up to the edge of the launch platform and looked down into the ocean, when, suddenly, an old man wearing a silver uniform ascended from below and glided to a halt just three meters above Kanaan's head. Behind him were several security guards, all of whom Kanaan recognized.

"You scared me," Kanaan said to Tsukua, the village chief. "Is something the matter?"

"There's been an intruder." Tsukua's silver beard quivered as he spoke. His voice came down upon Kanaan like a proclamation.

"Aron spotted someone during his morning patrol in the grave-yard north of the village," Tsukua continued, pointing over his shoulder at one of the guards. "The intruder slipped into a crevice when Aron tried to approach him. If you find anyone suspicious, you are to notify me immediately."

"I understand, Chief Tsukua," Kanaan said, a bit overly formal.

The old man glared. Barking "Let's go" to the guards behind him, he paddled the air with one swift breaststroke and disappeared into the clouds.

"That makes six," Kanaan muttered to himself.

He had heard about four through legend, and the fifth had come when he was four years old. Had this intruder come from above like the others?

"Kanaan!" Someone called out from behind.

He recognized the voice without turning around. "What is it, Benes?"

"Are you busy?"

"I was about to go for a glide."

"Pretty crowded up there today." The teen girl shifted her gaze upward before Kanaan's eyes could find hers. Framed by her short-cropped hair, her round eyes sparkled, their brilliance at times obscured by the silver shadows gliding above.

"I hear we had an intruder."

"From where?"

"From above, of course. Below us is the ocean."

"The ocean…"

Kanaan detected a change in Benes's voice when—

"Kanaan, look!"

Benes pointed to a dark patch of sky.

An ominous black swarm descended toward them. The siren from the observatory blared.

"Sky sharks! Get inside!"

The wail of another siren nearly drowned out Kanaan's voice. The guard in the watchtower had discovered the threat, but too late. The devil worked faster than even the heightened senses of the guards.

Kanaan turned to the long sword affixed to the side of the launch platform. He unchained the sword with the hunter's key fastened to the tip of his index finger, gripped the hilt and leapt off the platform. In an instant, the thick white mist below filled his field of vision—the ocean.

The guards and adults would protect the children. It was the young man's job, the hunter's job, to turn back the threat.

After Kanaan plunged his sword into three of the monsters' flanks, the villagers joined the aerial battle and soon the sky sharks fell into a retreat.

All told, ten sky sharks went down in a spectacular spray of blood, three escaped, and the rest were captured and sent to the factory for processing. The villagers of Everest would not go hungry for at least five days. Ararat and Anyemaqen would likely ask for a share of the catch, but Chief Tsukua, ever the crafty one, would no doubt ably dodge their requests.

Shortly before noon, Kanaan paid a visit to Old Man Lascaux. Extolled as the greatest hunter before Kanaan's father's time, the old man had been furnished with a house in retirement.

"Benes told me," said the old man. "You are a fine hunter, Kanaan. Took down three sky sharks all by yourself and not a scratch on you. You're more skilled than your father and I ever were."

Kanaan shrugged. He didn't know how else to respond.

"How many did we lose?" the old man asked.

"Eight. None of them children, thankfully."

"Anyone from the other mountains?"

"Two."

"They were killed in our airspace. We'll hear about it later."

"I know it," Kanaan replied a bit sullenly.

Lascaux grimaced but quickly regained his usual kindly expression. "Looking at you just now...I see so much of the old man in you."

"Yeah?" Kanaan quickly changed the subject. "Brought you some lunch." He took out rations of bread and ham from his satchel and set them on the table.

"I'm much obliged, Kanaan. But this is your share."

"Forget it. There's a woman at the factory who always slides me a little extra. Besides, I still have a ton of things I want to ask you."

"Just like your old man," said Lascaux, after giving the boy a long look. "Kanaan, don't you want to go up?"

"...No. Domino was going on about the same thing earlier. Why're you asking?"

"Because your old man wanted to go. He was about your age when he first attempted it."

"Not me. Chief Tsukua said there's nothing up there anyway."

"That's because he can't afford to lose you. Not when you're finally becoming useful to the village."

"So I'm finally old enough that they can work me to the bone. That's understandable, I guess. There's sky sharks, balloon whales, air octopi, wind spiders—plenty of nasty monsters to fend off and not enough hunters to fight them."

Then the old man uttered something completely unexpected.

"Just so you know—the only way isn't up."

There was a moment's pause before Kanaan could respond. "What did you say?"

"Thanks for lunch," said the old man, squeezing the boy's hand with both hands. "Now go. There'll be trouble if they find out you've been sharing your meals with me."

"Let's go."

Urged on by the instructor's voice, a tiny uniformed figure leapt off the bluff.

After plummeting halfway down the twenty-meter drop, the student spread both arms. The membranous wings gave a bit against the force of the wind. After falling another five meters, the figure began to rise with the instructor trailing behind.

They were not alone.

One after the next, students accompanied by their instructors jumped off the edge of the bluff toward the one-kilometer-wide crater below. Although all of the children were trained at this site, the shadows soaring the skies now were mostly those of adults. It was evidence of how few children there were in the village.

Kanaan let out a sigh and lay down in the grass. This was Kanaan's favorite place to go for a little peace and quiet.

The ultramarine sky filled his vision. Soon it would take on a purple tint, and the world would be shrouded in darkness with only the stars flickering in protest.

A swirl of emotions welled up inside Kanaan.

That's where I want to go.

I want to know what lies beyond that blue sky.

Even if it turns out there's nothing.

Memories of his father crowded in on him.

Kanaan's father had been a hunter; he'd been lauded as having no equal in the region. He had retired after destroying both wings in a deadly fight against a swarm of sky sharks. The village, however, did not consider his past achievements when distributing rations. The family managed to eke out a living from the meager pay Kanaan's mother earned at the factory and from the discreet support of fellow hunters.

A year after his retirement—the morning after Kanaan's first flight—his father disappeared.

"Your father was a weak man."

Kanaan recalled the words of his unbending mother.

"That's why he threw himself in the ocean."

"No," said Kanaan. "Father went up to heaven."

"How would a child like you know that?" his mother scoffed.

Kanaan explained.

Years ago—the night six houses near the southern ridge had been swept up into the void—Kanaan had watched his father by the fireplace listening to the wind howl.

"A good wind," his father had said. "How I've longed to be swept up in that wind. It is a wind that goes up to heaven. The villagers swept away in that current have all glimpsed heaven. I couldn't attempt it when I was a hunter. The village and your mother and you have no use for me now, and for that, I am glad. Now I am free to go."

Kanaan's father scooped up the little boy in his arms. He had the broadest chest and the biggest heart of anyone in the village. And then he bequeathed to his son a prophecy.

"Your mother will denounce me as a coward. I want you to believe her when she does. That's what is best for your mother and the village."

"You want to go up to heaven?" Kanaan asked. "Have you always wanted to, Father? But why?"

"That's hard to say. Your grandfather and your great-grandfather have also felt it. It may be because this village is where our mountain civilization began. But remember this. There are others who have wanted to climb higher."

"Others?"

"Your friends, Domino and Benes—their fathers and grandfathers felt it. We've never talked about it, but I've seen them looking up at the sky. Perhaps all the men of the village—no, of all the mountains have felt it."

"Why?" asked Kanaan.

Kanaan's father shook his head. "I don't know. That is a mystery, as much as why our people live in these mountains."

The raging wind had died down. Kanaan's father took the boy by the hand and opened the stone door. Outside, they could hear the sound of people crying in the distance. Perhaps it was the families of those that had been killed by sky sharks.

"Look up at the sky."

Kanaan's father covered the boy's ears. The loss of one of his senses instantly sharpened the others.

Kanaan gasped. The sadness he'd felt upon hearing the mournful cries left him.

All the stars that had been obscured by the night sky came into definition. How brilliantly they shone!

"Look, then forget," said Kanaan's father. "Forget if you can. If you take after your grandfather and me, in time, you will become a hunter. And in time, you will cease to be a hunter. Then remember what you and I saw on this night."

"Oh, is that so?" his mother had sneered. "That's hardly a reason to throw yourself in the ocean. Without saying so much as a word of thanks to the hunters and others who supported us so we could live. Imagine my shame."

Kanaan's mother had died the year he turned seven, having said nothing more about his father.

Kanaan concentrated on the blue sky above him.

What could be up there?

Do you really want to find out?

Even if the answer may be nothing?

Suddenly, the sky took on a different complexion. Two faces appeared.

"I thought you'd be here," Domino said with a chuckle, while Benes bared her white teeth in mock anger. "We were just at Old Man Lascaux's. He said you'd been by earlier."

"Making a delivery?" Kanaan asked, looking away.

Though many thought of Lascaux as a has-been, both Domino's and Benes's families had not forgotten that the old man had once been a superior hunter.

"He was crying about how lucky it was that a useless codger like him had us looking after him. It was enough to get me misty-eyed."

"You lie!" Benes glared at Domino. "You weren't crying. You're just trying to make yourself look good."

Domino shrugged.

"And another thing," continued Benes, "Lascaux practically begged us not to tell Kanaan that he'd been crying. Or did you forget, blabbermouth?"

"Aw, shut your yap, you sky sharkette."

"What did you just call me—"

"What do you two want?" Kanaan interrupted.

"Oh, yeah," Domino said, remembering. "I've got something to show you." He patted the inside pocket of his fur coat and shot a look at Benes. "Why don't you get lost?"

"Don't talk to me like that! If you must know, I have something important to tell Kanaan too, so why don't *you* get lost?"

"I've had enough of both of you," said Kanaan, jumping to his feet. "I don't need to know anything you can't tell each other. It'll be dark soon. Go on home before the wind spiders get you."

"Okay, okay." After scanning the area to make sure no one was around, Domino reached into his pocket. "Take a look at this."

The metal fragment that Domino laid on the grass was ten centimeters long, two centimeters wide, and less than a millimeter thick. It looked like a piece of silver leaf.

Kanaan brought it up to his face. "It's heavy. What's it made of?"

"Beats me. Ask me where I found it," Domino said excitedly.

"Wipe that stupid grin off your face and just tell us," Benes demanded.

Noting Domino's bitter expression, Kanaan asked, "All right, where?" But when Domino was slow to respond, he snapped, "Well?"

Finally, Domino pointed above his head.

"No way," Benes said, staring agape at the sky.

"Uh-huh." Domino looked triumphantly at Benes. "You know my uncle that works at the observatory? He was on duty ten days ago when *this* fell out of the sky. Nearly sliced off his shoulder before it stuck right into the stone floor."

Benes flicked a finger against the metal surface.

"This looks man-made. So what are you saying—that there are humans up there?"

"I guess I am."

Kanaan examined the foreign object in his hand. "Did you do anything to it?"

"Sure," answered Domino. "I tried putting it over a flame, I tried cutting it with a knife—didn't leave a mark on it. Ruined a perfectly good knife though."

"There must be people with more evolved brains up there," said Benes.

Kanaan nodded and returned the metal fragment to Domino. "I guess so." His cheeks quivered with an excitement he could barely contain. "So what's *your* news, Benes?"

The comely girl gave Domino an exasperated look, then relenting at last, said, "Come with me. Don't worry about the wind spiders. There's a person I want you to meet. At least, I think it's a person."

Benes led Kanaan and Domino to the church ruins in the eastern forest. Ever since a swarm of sky octopi had attacked and taken nearly a hundred worshippers fifty years ago, the church had sat empty. The interior, reputed to be able to withstand the passing of a thousand years, remained impregnable to the elements.

When Kanaan entered the room that had once been the priest's study, he quickly discerned that the visitor was not human.

The mysterious figure was covered head to toe in a shiny yellow fabric. Dark glass lenses bulged out of the eye sockets, and a ridged tube stretched from the black cylinder tank on its back to the back of its head. It had no wings. Kanaan wondered how it had come here without them.

It raised what appeared to be a small pickaxe upon seeing Domino and Kanaan.

"Who are you?" it said sharply. Kanaan relaxed a bit at the sound of a human voice.

"It's all right," said Benes. "These are the friends I was telling you about."

The visitor lowered the pickaxe. "You've already helped me, so I'll have to trust you."

"Good. This is Kanaan and Domino."

"I'm Takamura. Call me Taka."

Benes sat down on the only available chair while Kanaan and Domino leaned against the wall.

"Benes filled us in on our way over here," began Kanaan. "She told us you came from the bottom of the ocean."

"That's right. I climbed the cliff face with this." Taka nodded and slapped the handle of the pickaxe. "I came from beneath what you call the ocean—that's where my world is."

"Is that why you're dressed like that? What's the bottom of the ocean like?"

"Just a second—" Taka put a hand on top of his head.

There was a pneumatic hiss and the head split down the middle in two.

"Whoa," Domino let out upon seeing the face of a middle-aged man around the same age as his own father.

Furrowing his brows, Taka took a moment to steady his breathing. "The temperature is about the same, as expected, but so little oxygen at nine thousand meters. It's no wonder you're all so barrel-chested. Excuse me—"

Taka covered his face once again with the fabric suit.

"Finally made it up here thanks to this suit," Taka said between gulps of breath. "Nine thousand is tough."

"Nine thousand—what does that mean?" Benes asked, tilting her head.

"The distance between your world and mine. You live almost ten thousand meters up in the air."

The three teens looked at one another in disbelief.

Several seconds passed before Benes could ask, "In the air? You mean, up there?"

Taka looked up in the direction Benes pointed. "I suppose that's right coming from your perspective. But where I come from, everything above ground is considered up, including your world."

Taka gave the teens a moment to absorb his remarks. "I should start by explaining how our worlds are connected. I'm glad the language has remained the same after ten thousand years."

"Ten thousand years?" said Kanaan. When he stroked his chin, his hand came away shining with sweat.

"That's right. There was a time when we all lived in what you call the bottom of the ocean. Then ten thousand years ago, a violent shift in the earth's crust caused catastrophic destruction to the world. That's when a small contingent of the population fled for the mountaintops. Those people were your ancestors."

Taka went on to explain how when the ground sank and massive waves swept across the earth, all the homes and structures—and half of humanity—had been lost.

The three teens asked why they didn't just fly to safety. Taka answered that wings had not yet been invented.

The fractured mountains spewed fire into the atmosphere, the heat from which turned water into vapors that blocked out the sun. The thick smoke layer wreaked havoc on the weather; deadly chemical substances that had leaked from destroyed plants were spread by raging winds and rained down on the earth.

For better or for worse, the capricious winds had spared the people that had fled to the highlands.

There were also survivors who emerged from the rubble where seemingly all had been lost. They were the people that had gone underground in shelters—built by the government who'd foreseen the apocalypse—along with the technology and machines needed for the rebuilding effort.

But restoring the earth poisoned by deadly chemicals to a habitable state took a thousand years longer than expected, and much of the technology that humanity had come to rely on was lost. Flight was one of them.

"We, thanks to our ancestors, were aware of the people that had fled to the highlands. Whether we went up or you came down, we always believed that we would reunite—although I don't think anyone would have imagined it would take ten thousand years. But we didn't forget. We knew of your existence, in part, because every so often, a mysterious creature or one of your people fell out of the sky. It took ten thousand years, but having had the fundamental skills needed for rebuilding, we have managed to achieve much of what we set out to accomplish. Which is when our curiosity turned to finding you and your civilization."

Taka pressed a button on a panel on his left forearm. The teens could hear the sound of slurping from Taka's facemask.

Letting go of the button on his arm, Taka explained, "Hot cocoa. It's a drink that helps clear the mind and warms the body." Staring at the three teens, he asked, "Care to see what's down there?"

"No, not me," answered Benes, looking down at her feet.

"Me neither," said Domino.

Taka gave Kanaan a good look. "What about you?"

"Any sky sharks or wind spiders down there?"

"No, the only large animals you're likely to see are the livestock we raise for eating. There are some dangerous monsters, but they rarely if ever encroach upon civilization."

"That's good enough for me."

"Kanaan..." Benes's voice was filled with anguish. It was the moment she realized her beloved friend was about to cause trouble.

"Your friend here told me about all the monsters up here," Taka said, nodding toward Benes. "The cloud layer you call the ocean was once a radiation belt—a layer of hazardous gases that no longer poses a threat. We sent up a balloon to measure the radiation levels. It poses no risk to the human body. You're all free to come down anytime you'd like. But—"

"But what?" This time it was Kanaan's turn to stare at this strange visitor.

"It appears the leader of this world doesn't want to acknowledge that reality."

"Taka was attacked," Benes said, "even after he introduced himself as a friend."

"I wouldn't put it past the village chief," Domino said.

"Chief Tsukua hates change," said Kanaan. "He thinks his only duty is to maintain the life they have now. He'll probably kill you no matter what you have to say."

Taka stared dumbly at Kanaan, then at the others. "Do you

really believe that? You seem so much more mature than the kids back in my world. Is that really what you believe?"

Kanaan nodded. He could not lie to a man who'd risked his life to come here.

"I think you'll find that everyone shares our opinion," said Benes. "Actually, I *know* so."

"I'd like to talk to someone of influence—someone who is as powerful as your chief. Will you take me to him?"

"If anyone finds out, we'll all be severely punished," Domino said.

Taka slammed a fist against his knee. "But surely once the chief realizes that there are others like you down below, he'll want to at least talk, no matter how resistant to change he may be."

"He's already heard what you have to say. To the chief, you're a foreign threat that could destroy this world. If he finds you, he *will* kill you." Kanaan recognized the despair in his own voice.

"This is horrible…"

Suddenly, a shadow came over the room. Kanaan instinctively looked out the window and spotted a white mass just as it swooped into the room.

"Air octopus!" shouted Kanaan. "Damn, only wind spiders are supposed to come out this time of day."

Domino pulled out the folding bow stuck in his belt. But before he could nock an arrow, the octopus slithered from the window and onto the floor and extended its three-meter-long tentacles. The dark green eyes between its massive head and tentacles reflected the images of its prey.

The bulbous heads of more octopi appeared in the windows.

"Get out of here!" shouted Kanaan, readying his own bow. "I'll get the door!"

The octopus's tentacles stretched out toward him. Twirling out of their grasp, Kanaan somersaulted in the air. *Twang! Twang!* One arrow pierced through the beast's head and another through the eye.

The octopus writhed violently in pain. Kanaan slipped past its flailing tentacles, dashed out of the study, and kicked the door shut.

He turned to the others waiting for him. "Downstairs to the basement. No octopus or spider will get through the iron door."

"There's a spider now!" said Benes, looking down to the end of the hall.

An enormous reddish-black spider with legs resembling those of a crab was scuttling straight toward them.

"My bow is useless against that thing," said Domino, unleashing an arrow nevertheless. He fired, and the arrow bounced off the hard shell of the spider's cephalothorax.

"I think I pissed him off!"

The spider lurched toward them.

"The basement! Now!" yelled Kanaan.

"The door is rusted shut!" Benes cried. "It won't open!"

"Help her!" Kanaan yelled in Domino and Taka's direction as he glided toward the study door.

The spider's long pincer legs were fast on Kanaan's heels.

Would he make it in time?

Kanaan grabbed hold of the door handle and yanked with all his might. The door flew open and out tumbled the octopus—only for its head to be harpooned by the spider's legs. Before the spider could claim victory, however, the octopus wrapped its tentacles around the arachnid and crushed its cephalothorax.

"It's open!"

Turning around, Kanaan flew in the direction of Benes's voice.

"Did they get out all right?" Taka asked.

Kanaan nodded, after having returned from seeing Domino and Benes safely out of the church. Domino and Benes both had families to go back to. If they didn't return, their families were sure to send out a search party. Then it would only be a matter of time before their meeting with Taka came to light.

"Yeah. The monsters don't come out at night."

"Airborne organisms born out of cataclysmic meteorological changes…" Taka mused. "You've had to deal with them all your life and you never thought to seek refuge in the so-called ocean?"

"I grew up hearing about hundreds of people drowning in that ocean. And besides I much prefer looking over my head than down at my feet."

"Over your head?" asked Taka, frowning.

"I know you can't tell while cooped up here in this basement, but try looking up sometime. It'll make the hairs on the back of your neck stand up."

"Aspire to go higher, is that it? That figures."

"What's that supposed to mean?"

"Would you say that your life here is easy?" Taka asked.

"Not at all. It's nothing if not hard. The air is too thin, the sun is too intense, the sky is swarming with monsters, and sometimes the Mad Wind kicks up and sends dozens of villagers tumbling into the abyss."

"So that explains the people falling from the sky from time to time. They must not all make it down to our world because some of them get stuck somewhere along the way." Taka nodded, satisfied. "And you still believe in the sky's magnificence?"

"I do."

"And you want to fly higher?"

"Yeah."

"And see what's beyond the sky?"

"Yeah."

"It is said that when the world began to crumble, your ancestors were led up the mountains by a world-class alpinist. You may well be a descendant. No, I'm convinced of it."

"I suppose I'll have to go on living in this world," Kanaan said. "My duty as a hunter is to this village. But if these wings ever fail me or I'm banished from the village, I might give it a try."

"How would you like to go down first?"

"Huh?"

"Seeing is believing. Take a look for yourself. Then you tell everyone all about how there's a better life for them below."

"A better life…"

"You can still go up afterward. Surely not all of the others share your aspirations."

"Well, no." Kanaan had to smile despite himself. Whenever he had spoken of his dream to others, they had laughed and looked at Kanaan as some sort of kook. The only ones that had not laughed were Domino and Benes.

"An alpinist…" Kanaan muttered. And then they heard the echo of footsteps overhead.

Chief Tsukua and his guards burst through the basement door before Kanaan and Taka had time to react. Turning a deaf ear to his exhortations, the guards tied Taka up and led him away. Tsukua and Kanaan followed closely behind.

"I'll deal with you later," Tsukua said to Kanaan.

"Who told you?" Kanaan asked, glancing over at Taka.

"Domino told his family," Tsukua answered. "Don't be angry with him. You should have known better than to involve him."

"I know. What are you going to do with Taka?"

"He has disrupted the peace of the village. He will suffer the heaviest penalty."

"I hear the bottom of the ocean is a good place to live, Chief."

"That's enough!"

"Yeah, okay," muttered Kanaan.

Taka and Kanaan were escorted out of the church, and the party began to walk back to the village with only the guards' torches to light their way.

Taka racked his brain for a way to escape his captors.

Nothing.

He could think of nothing else but to sigh.

And then—a mighty wind blew in his face.

"The Mad Wind! Get down!" someone yelled, as the wind sheared through their path.

In a split second, Kanaan reared back and took flight. Taka alone stood helplessly while the guards, having forgotten about their prisoner, took cover.

Kanaan surrendered his body to the wind. Twisting his upper body, he glided toward Taka and wrapped his arms around his torso.

The wind howled in his ear.

Suddenly, the wind shifted. For an instant, Kanaan's legs skimmed the ground. A grove of trees up ahead. Kanaan raised his right arm high over his head. Deftly controlling the angle of the wind lashing against the wings, Kanaan, carrying Taka, began to climb. The thin membrane of his wings was stretched to its limit.

"Woooahhhhh!"

The spine connecting the wings began to buckle, and then—

They were through!

The violent current was behind them.

"I guess I'm going to your world after all, Taka."

"Are you sure? It's nine thousand meters down."

"No worries."

"Never mind me. What about you?"

"I guess we'll find out. Hang on!" Kanaan said.

It took less than a minute to reach the nearest ridge.

From there, Kanaan grabbed hold of Taka once again and dove into the dark night.

The white sea of clouds soon came into focus, and Kanaan dove into the mist. It was quiet. What a peaceful world the ocean was.

When the altimeter on his arm read five thousand meters, Taka said, "We'll be through the cloud layer soon. Take a good look."

"Here we go!" shouted Kanaan.

The blue ocean—the real one—glittered below them. The surface shone with the brilliance of a million lights that would take an eternity for a mere mortal to arrange.

"Is *this* your world…?" Kanaan asked, and then he began to cough violently. His chest felt as if it were burning.

"Don't talk. The oxygen level is too high for you. Your lungs will melt!"

Kanaan felt himself fading, but managed to touch down with Taka somewhere in the middle of town.

Beasts with beaming eyes crisscrossed before them. Kanaan found himself standing under a tiny moon he'd never seen before, surrounded by imposing buildings.

"This is our world," Taka said. "You'll get used to the burning in your chest soon enough. No Mad Wind to worry about, and few monsters. Well? Wouldn't you and the others like to move here?"

"Yeah, it looks like a great place to live," Kanaan said quietly. Beautiful strains of music floated in from somewhere. Kanaan looked around, but unable to locate the source, he closed his eyes and allowed the sweet sound to wash over him.

"That's someone playing the piano," Taka said, looking at Kanaan. "If you came here, you'd be able to listen whenever you liked. You *could* come here alone."

"It *is* very beautiful," Kanaan said. After a moment, he opened his eyes and made a request of Taka.

Kanaan hoisted the rucksack containing the pictures of this world Taka had gathered for him and said goodbye. The first rays of dawn began to peer out from behind the buildings.

"You'll be back, won't you?" Taka asked, to which Kanaan raised his right hand. The right membranous wing was torn.

"The next flight will be my last."

"It's my fault," said Taka, his face pale.

"It's okay. I've made up my mind, thanks to you, and I got to see a pretty special world. I never imagined that such a peaceful place could exist."

"I hope you'll be back."

"Maybe, if I'm able. I'll be sure to deliver the contents of this rucksack to the leader of the antiestablishment group. I hope you'll come again."

"You have my word."

"I'll see you."

And then Taka finally realized. "You said *deliver*. Wait a minute, you *are* staying once you go back to the village, aren't you?"

"Nah, I'm headed for someplace higher."

"Now wait—"

"I'm just better suited to climbing. Maybe you can pray for me— pray that I find something wherever I end up."

Taka looked at the young man before him and then shifted his gaze up at the heavens as if in prayer. Finally looking back at Kanaan, he said, "Take care of yourself."

Kanaan shook Taka's outstretched hand and went out onto the street.

Just one more time…

Benes woke up to the sound of tapping at the window and jumped out of bed. It was already light outside.

"Kanaan?"

Benes went outside and found a rucksack by the windowsill.

Opening it, she cried, "Kanaan—why?"

The girl looked up at the sky, sensing where her dear friend had gone.

The photographs clutched in her hand fell at her feet.

Tears streamed down her cheeks.

"Why did you have to go? You just got back…"

Kanaan's breathing was labored. The right wing was nearly completely torn in two. *Will I make it?*

He felt a kind of affection for the two worlds he'd left behind.

But the world Kanaan wanted to glimpse began here in this rarefied air.

Climb higher and farther. Reach for the skies—for the stars.

The sky was no longer blue.

Countless stars sparkled in the violet-colored world.

Kanaan spotted one star that flickered a different color than the rest. Maybe it was his imagination. Nevertheless, adjusting the angle of the wings, Kanaan rode the fading current and ascended toward the pulsating glow.

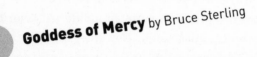
Goddess of Mercy by Bruce Sterling

Miss Sato left the hostage compound. Her liaison was waiting in a rusty Toyota pickup.

Miss Sato's guide in Tsushima was the star reporter of a local broadsheet called *Truth Dawn*. Yoshida was a gangling twenty-two-year-old with a broad bamboo hat, a dirty undershirt, cargo shorts, Brazilian flip-flop sandals, and a pet terrier.

Yoshida helped Miss Sato into the back of the truck as the frisky dog barked a greeting. "So, how's the old woman doing?"

"The 'old woman' looks twenty years older from her sufferings," Miss Sato declared. She knotted a scarf on her head and grabbed the pickup's roll bar. "She used to look so pretty on television. I campaigned for Mrs. Mieko Nagai, you know. That was part of my political awakening."

Yoshida removed his big conical hat, examined the bright autumn sky, thought better of the exposure to surveillance, and put the hat back on. "You campaigned for the hostage? That's an interesting angle to your story."

The Toyota jounced along the crumbling roadbed. Miss Sato and Yoshida had to ride standing because a bulky Russian antiaircraft gun took up most of the room in the truck bed.

This rugged Russian gun had arrived on Tsushima with two Russians, bored young mercenaries from Kamchatka. Bumper stickers on their truck made the absurd claim that Tsushima was a Russian island, but since the stickers were in Cyrillic, nobody noticed or cared.

Yoshida spoke up over his terrier's excited yapping. "I hope you assured Mrs. Nagai that my newspaper's party line is firmly against hostage-taking. Mrs. Nagai does read my work, right? *Truth Dawn* offers free subscriptions to all political prisoners."

"Where are we going?" Miss Sato hedged. She had seen a land-mine crater scarring the road ahead.

Miss Sato had experienced close calls on Tsushima, but thanks to due caution and her steady alertness, she had never been blown up. Miss Sato had learned to read the wreckage on Tsushima the way one might read tea leaves. The neat round holes in roofs and walls were American naval artillery. The shattered palm trees and big dirt craters were aircraft bombs from the mainland provisional government. All the other bombs had been built and exploded on Tsushima itself.

The pirate island of Tsushima had wireless belt-bombs and miniature pocket grenades. Tsushima had head-breaker cell-phone bombs. Leg-breaker land mines. Car-breaker bike bombs. House-breaker car bombs. Every once in a while, in particular fits of malignant frenzy, Tsushima had truck bombs that could demolish a city block.

The center of this story, the Gojira of this transformation, was "The Bomb." That half-forgotten monster of Japanese history, "The Bomb." "The Bomb" had entirely smashed Tokyo. "The Bomb" remade Japanese history. Even when The Bomb was just a crude, barely ballistic, North Korean bomb.

With Tokyo in ruins from the North Korean sneak attack, Nagoya became the emergency center of southern Japan. Northern

278 ★ BRUCE STERLING

Japan rallied around Sapporo. In the chaos, the obscure rural island of Tsushima had been abandoned to its own devices. Its esoteric, electronic devices.

The first pirates to settle in Tsushima came from North Korea. These wretches were starving North Korean refugees, Asia's latest boat people, fleeing the vast, searing, vengeful blast zones of the many American hydrogen bombs. The North Korean refugees had quickly overwhelmed what passed for law and order on the sleepy little tourist island.

In the wake of the Korean invasion came all of Asia's waterborne criminals: Taiwanese arms dealers, South Korean drug merchants, and Hong Kong triads. Even the Russian mafia drifted south from the Kuril Islands. These network-savvy global marauders shared a single goal. They all came to rob Japan, a land without a government or a capital, the world's richest and newest "failed state."

The Americans observed this development with grave concern—because the Americans had already much seen the like in Iraq, Somalia, Afghanistan, Columbia, Mexico, Pakistan, and Nigeria. "Boots on the ground" rarely triumphed against "global guerrillas." The insurgents merely scattered, regrouped, and left their roadside bombs to kill soldiers.

The Americans, much overstretched in Korea, Iran, and elsewhere, could not invade and pacify the rugged pirate island of Tsushima. But the Americans did possess tremendous air power and precision satellite targeting. So the Americans pounded Tsushima. They pulverized the island's harbors, bridges, power plants, and telecom towers.

A great and lasting silence and darkness descended on the island. A silence broken only by bombs.

That was what always impressed Miss Sato about her life in Tsushima: not the bombs, but that deep, lasting darkness. Mainland Japan was not dark. North Japan and South Japan had restored their shares of the broken power grid. Everyday life in post-atomic Japan was about as bright and busy as life in Argentina. But Tsushima was dark to its core.

Tsushima's darkness was damp, dense, and mystical. No neon, no traffic. No electrical power, and no Internet. No light, no heat. No banks, no credit cards. No passports. The pirates of Tsushima were stateless, anarchic, gun-toting marauders from all over the world. They had no documents, no official identities. No marriage, no religion. No police and no priests. No running water. They didn't even have clocks.

Tsushima was haunted by bombs and by a head-bending swoon of illegal narcotics. The ragged coasts swarmed with fast, small boats full of hard, scarred men of every shape, size, and language. They rushed ashore to raid the fat and peaceful coastal villages of Japan, and they ran off with anything and anyone they could grab.

Tsushima had newfangled global crimes that hadn't been named yet. This was Miss Sato's island of Tsushima. She spent much more of her life here than she ever did in her cheerless little relief office in Nagoya.

"So, what can you tell me," said Miss Sato to Yoshida, as the war-truck squeaked and rattled, "about a blind man, some kind of pilgrim or gambler, who visits the Mechatronic Visionary Centre?"

"Oh, that poor old guy's not news to anybody." Yoshida grabbed the rusty roll bar welded to the Toyota's roof. "He's like the Mechatronic janitor. They let him in and out because he's blind and he can't steal the precious hardware stored there. He used to live in there, before the Tokyo Bomb."

Miss Sato grew alert at this intelligence. "What kind of role did he have in that laboratory?"

"The role of some helpless blind man, I guess," Yoshida said with a shrug. "That 'Visionary Centre' was supposed to be the research lab for a Japanese camera company. We all knew that was just the cover story. So many weird people coming in and out of that place...Foreign scientists, the military, politicians, bankers...spies, yakuza gangsters. They were up to no good in there, and every weekend, we Tsushima people had to get them drunk and find them women. And we did that for them too. But was that news story ever in the mainland Japanese media? Never! Not at all! Not one word!"

"The women's movement knew about the military lab on Tsushima," Miss Sato objected. "We women were aware that the Japanese Self-Defense Forces were contravening the Constitution. They were reacting with covert violence to the pirate attacks on Japanese shipping in Somalia. They used offshore, deniable proxies."

Yoshida scowled. "That's the problem with you peacenik feminists: you have no ideological insight! Pirate, anti-pirate, that is just pure dialectic! A covert War on Terror is the same as the Terror itself. It all becomes the same in the long run! Once you abandon the quest for social justice, it just becomes a matter of market price."

Miss Sato tactfully overlooked this Marxist tirade. "I'm sure your readers agree with you, so, then, may I ask, can you please introduce me to this Zeta One? I need to talk to him. Mrs. Nagai says that whenever he visits the labs there, he always brings the hostages steamed buns and pickles. He can't be that bad a person if he feels such pity for other human beings."

Yoshida nodded impatiently, his bamboo hat wobbling. "Yes, I interviewed your Mrs. Nagai. You know what? She has Stockholm Syndrome. She's gone crazy in her head."

"It isn't crazy that Mrs. Nagai sympathizes with her pirate oppressors."

Yoshida bent down and unclipped his dog's leash. "Yes it is. She's in chains, but she spends all her time crying about pirates in prisons on the mainland! What a joke!"

"Mrs. Nagai wants to arrange a prisoner exchange. She wants to go home to her family. She wants all this mutual suffering to end. Tsushima should be at peace with Nagoya. We're all Japanese, even if we have no capital city anymore."

"Well, that's just not going to happen," said Yoshida, grinning with conviction. "If Nagoya ever released those pirates, they'd just jump back into their speedboats and seize more Nagoya politicians, just like they grabbed her. No government is that stupid—not even your sorry little emergency government."

"It's true that our hostage negotiations have progressed rather slowly to date," said Miss Sato, restraining herself. "But progress might go very quickly if I could find an authority who could release Mrs. Nagai."

"Forget that," scoffed Yoshida. "If there was anyone in charge here, the Americans would kill him with a drone bomb. That's what they always do."

"Well, since this blind pirate is allowed inside the prison with the hostages, he must have some political influence. Maybe he can lead me to Khadra the Pirate Queen. I've received certain signals that Khadra the Pirate Queen would respond positively to my peace initiatives."

"I can't believe you've been in Tsushima this long and you still have such harebrained ideas," Yoshida said. "Zeta One is useless! Half his head and both his eyes were blown off by a mobile-phone bomb. Zeta One is poor, he's in rags, and he's a drunk. Plus, he smells. And Khadra is not the 'queen' of anything. Nobody's seen Khadra for months. She'd hiding or she's dead. So, forget all about them. Zeta One is not a story, and today I got a hot new lead on a great story. We're going to find a buried treasure today!"

The Toyota rambled past a motley mess of black-market shacks. These shabby hovels had been built to blow over, in storms, or fires, or car bombs, or drone strikes. The pirates who manned them looked just as makeshift and temporary as their shacks.

The Tsushima pirate shacks featured a great many cardboard signs, hand-daubed in English, Korean, Japanese, Chinese, even Tagalog, Malay, and Filipino. They offered the various products of a boat people's theft-based economy.

Used clothing appeared in ragged heaps, with plenty of used Chinese shoes. Also beans, dried tofu, dried fish, bark, roots, seeds, fried insects, anything remotely edible: seaweed, boiled taro stems, acorns scrubbed with soap. Big "wood ear" mushrooms were growing from clear plastic bottles stuffed with wet sawdust.

Also, hand-forged bicycle parts, useless power tools all gone to bright red rust, handwoven bamboo baskets, rusty radish graters, little clay stoves with tall chimneys. Gloomy pirate molls and their ragged pirate children had some bundled stacks of fuel for sale: straw, reeds, and twigs.

Then, in bursts of relative prosperity, came whitewashed concrete-block hovels, which sold all kinds of things made from dismantled Japanese cars. These long-dead vehicles yielded chairs, big glass windows, mirrors, wire jewelry, engine-block anvils, and muffler oil lamps.

The truck began weaving back and forth uphill.

Gripping the Toyota's roll bar in the crook of his bare arm, Yoshida unfolded a yellowing sheet of old-fashioned notebook graph paper. "You're good at reading English, right? Kindly read this pirate treasure map for me."

The folded graph paper held a map of the city of Tsushima, a modest village that stretched along the island's eastern coastline. This fiendishly detailed diagram was spotted and dotted all over with bomb craters, skulls, and furious hand-scribbled notes in the English language.

"Maps are always so complicated," said Miss Sato, squinting in dismay. "I can read some names of dead men and the dates when they died…This says 'whacko,' in English. Here it says 'wacko,' which is a different English spelling. Also, here it says 'wako,' but that word is in Japanese."

"Yes, a computer-vision genius drew that map," said Yoshida aloud, tapping the side of his close-cropped noggin under the hat. "Computer hackers love puns! When there's no electricity, and their computers are all dead, programmers get touched in the head. My source used to snort Korean speed and stay up for days drawing this map. With nothing but paper and a pencil!"

The Toyota loudly crunched over a broad scattering of bricks and shattered glass. "So is this truly a real map of pirate treasure?" Miss Sato said. "It certainly looks mysterious!"

"Well, this map is mine now, but I'm bad with English," Yoshida said.

"But what does it mean, this map?"

"Well, any treasure map is always news to my readers. I believe this map leads to the sniper death-robot of Boss Takenaka. Boss Takenaka was a 'King of the Pirates' for a while. Takenaka is dead now, of course. A drone strike wiped out his whole gang with one blast, just slaughtered everybody. But three years ago, Boss Takenaka was the scariest gangster this island ever saw."

Yoshida shook his treasure map triumphantly. "My job today is to write the last big news story of Boss Takenaka's career. Everybody's going to read my great scoop too. I'll sell out that whole issue all by myself." Yoshida tucked the folded map in his wallet and rubbed his hands with anticipation.

"Can you stop this truck, please? I need to find this blind pilgrim pirate person. Can you tell me the real name of Zeta One? Where does he live?"

"Look, Zeta One is so brain-damaged that he doesn't remember his name! Nobody on Tsushima has any legal identity. Nobody, never! My real name's not even Yoshida."

Miss Sato was hurt. "Your name isn't Yoshida?"

"I had a legal identity once, but I'm a Tsushima native. The Americans blew up our city halls and destroyed all our legal records."

"Why do they call him 'Zeta Number One'? A name that strange must mean something."

"It's a pun. It's a pirate pun. The Zetas were Mexican drug cops who turned into Mexican drug crooks. Pirates here love that idea, of being a pirate, but also a state privateer. All the biggest pirates in history had some state support. Every pirate thinks he's a master criminal, but he also thinks he's some kind of superspy cop."

Miss Sato wasn't entirely surprised to hear this. She read every issue of *Truth Dawn*, and the newspaper always featured splashy glamour stories about Tsushima's wickedest pirates. Since the tabloid lacked any cameras, the stories were always illustrated with woodcuts.

"Just remember Osama bin Laden," Yoshida said, "the world's most-wanted criminal, living in his mansion as a rich Pakistani spy. This Tsushima story is really an Osama bin Laden story. This is Osama's world now, and the rest of us just live in it."

"I'm getting confused," Miss Sato admitted.

Yoshida nodded as he caught a flea with his thumbnails. "You should read this very important pamphlet that I wrote about the 'Global Pirate Heritage.' My nonfiction pamphlet is full of reveal-ing facts and figures on the subject. I'm gonna write a whole book someday: 'Inside Global Piracy.' Because that's my ticket out of here. My pirate book will make me world famous someday because, unlike most soft sissies who just write about piracy, I'm a skilled reporter who has really been there where piracy happens."

Miss Sato bounced bruisingly from the cab of the Toyota as the wheels hit a fresh patch of rubble. "I can't afford to buy your 'impor-tant pamphlet on pirate heritage.' Can you loan it to me?"

"No! Absolutely not! You have to pay! No sharing and no steal-ing! My pamphlet is totally analog, a privately printed limited edition! It's published only here on Tsushima, with a metal press and handmade local paper! My pamphlet is a precious cultural artifact! Now, if you told your sponsors back in Nagoya to give me a mainland bank account, like I said before…"

"My relief society does not engage in any offshore money laundering."

Yoshida sighed. "I keep thinking you'll 'wise up' someday, but you sure are a 'pill' and a 'stick-in-the-mud.' Never mind—that's pirate slang. You wouldn't understand."

The Toyota was climbing uphill. The slopes on the spine of the island were treacherous, precipitous, rocky, and commonly mined. Little terraced patches thick with the weeds of neglect, here and there. Feral fruit trees burst through the tumble-down walls of dead vacation homes.

"When will we return to Tsushima City?" said Miss Sato at last.

"Well, my story deadline for *Truth Dawn* is Wednesday. But I could push that to Thursday morning if I'm willing to set type myself."

"But I have much more important things to do than hunt for some pirate treasure!"

"What are you, crazy? There's nothing more important than treasure! Besides, Boss Takenaka was ten times more important than your stupid female politician hostage from Nagoya. Takenaka was the pirate captain who grabbed your hostage in the first place! Takenaka was a major kingpin—a criminal millionaire warlord wanted in twenty different countries. He was bigger than Chapo Guzman."

"What are you talking about?"

Yoshida sighed. "After they killed Osama bin Laden, Chapo Guzman was the world's second biggest pirate. Since you haven't read my famous pamphlet, you just have no sense of heritage. Boss Takenaka became the warlord of Tsushima, just like bin Laden in Afghanistan and Guzman in Sinaloa. And you know how Takenaka did that? With Japanese high technology. With an augmented computer-vision system from the Mechatronic Visionary Centre. That's how he did it."

Yoshida retrieved the paper map from his wallet and passed it over. "Look at all these lines and angles and geometric viewpoints. That's what computer vision looks like when you draw it with a paper and pencil. Takenaka had high-tech killer hardware; he stole it and he deployed it here. And this map shows where it still is. Buried on Tsushima. Just waiting to be dug up."

Miss Sato glanced reluctantly. The patient fanatic who had hand-drawn the map, annotating it with icons, Japglish puns, and at least ten thousand geometric lines, was obviously out of his mind. What could drive a person to such fits of unnatural intensity? Revenge.

Yoshida scratched his whining terrier behind the ears. "So many dead men in this story already—and not one of them dead on Takenaka's own turf. That was my best clue, see? That's how I broke this story wide open. Listen! Everybody thought that the Americans were killing those pirates with drones. Just more Americans shooting more terrorists with their robot airplanes. That was a lousy story for *Truth Dawn* because that story's so boring, so old-fashioned, so obvious to everyone. Nobody would want to read about that, trust me."

Yoshida drew a breath. "But—it turns out—and this treasure map proves it—that story's not even true! The truth is, Boss Takenaka had a Japanese robot-vision system. He stole it from the Mechatronic Centre and hot-wired it to a machine gun. Then, Takenaka planted that killer thing up in the hills, and that robot vision just watched for pirates, all day and night, like a security camera. So if you carried a gun or a rocket grenade, anything that made you look piratical—pow! Bang! A fifty-caliber round right through the center of your silhouette."

"But why would a pirate like Boss Takenaka kill the other pirates?"

"Because that system was anti-pirate technology. He stole that from the Mechatronic Centre, he didn't invent it himself! Pirates are stupid, they can never understand high technology! It's the journalists like me who are smart and always on top of these trends."

"Oh."

"Takenaka wiped out his competition by remote control. That

machine gave him a really good alibi too because he was never around when they died. Boss Takenaka used to go to their funerals with big heaps of flowers, that yakuza hypocrite. We even published his eulogies in *Truth Dawn*, but I finally figured out the truth about Takenaka, and today, I'm going to prove it! I'll inform every subscriber! That's what my career as a trusted newsman is all about."

"Some very smart man must have given you that map," Miss Sato concluded.

"Oh no, don't you dare try that with me," said Yoshida airily, pulling a Korean candy bar from the baggy pocket of his army-surplus shorts. "I will never betray a source." He broke the bar and tossed a sugared morsel to the terrier. "Me and the pup here are gonna sniff out the robot of death! We'll bring it back into town as our trophy. An exclusive scoop! Think how great a machine gun will look next to our big mechanical printing press. Now you see why this matters so much, don't you? Military high tech is always a fantastic story!"

Miss Sato was meekly quiet for a while. Distant thunder rumbled to the west—a big storm brewing over mainland Korea, or possibly Korean artillery. "Yoshida, can I wait for you back in your newspaper office? It sounds like you might be some time."

Yoshida stared at her. "What urgent task do you have now—taking bento boxes to your jailbirds? You'll never understand Tsushima if you don't go up into the hills. Sea pirates may seem strange, but wait till you meet those Afghan misty-mountain monsters up in their opium patches."

Miss Sato smiled politely at this bluster. She was older than Yoshida. Furthermore, she had seen stranger things than the blue shores and green hills of his little island. Miss Sato had worked with salvage crews in the ruins of Tokyo. She had even seen what the furious Americans had done to North Korea in their vengeance for Tokyo.

That was why Miss Sato was not afraid of the pirates of Tsushima. Everyone back in Nagoya assumed that she must be very brave to do her relief work among savage pirates. But pirates were merely people, evil people, and evil was a weakness. Miss Sato feared no evil, but she did fear the righteous wrath of the just. Pirates merely robbed and then fled. The vengeance of the just lasted seven generations.

The Russian Toyota forged from a steep track onto an abandoned parking lot, all thigh-high weeds. Up here at the makeshift rendez-vous, some hapless pirate drug trucks had been surprised by American missiles. To judge by the shiny bits of scattered high technology, the bombs had cost ten times as much as the trucks.

Miss Sato endured a further hour of smelly engine-gunning, scary skidding, drunken maneuvering, and much cursing in Russian. The precipitous slopes were daubed with feeble lines of mildewed cardboard and spray-bombed graffiti tags. These were long-departed pirate gangs, ferociously warning other dead marauders never to cross the line.

Then a more serious boundary appeared: a kind of pirate Chinese Wall. This barricade was all cheap cement and poorly stacked concrete cinder blocks, but it was as tall as a man could reach and topped with razor wire. There were guardhouses too. Once upon a time, someone had clear-cut the forest to create clean lines of fire along the wall. Now crooked weed trees were engulfing all of that.

The Russian driver carefully unfolded an ancient paper map of Tsushima Island. He conferred with his colleague, a scarred and helmeted global guerrilla who was even drunker than he was.

"We're lost," said Yoshida with relish. This was an exotic, pirate-island thing to say, because people in the rest of the world never got "lost." The rest of the world featured smartphones and tower antennas and satellite locators. But not dark little Tsushima, where all such things had been bombed back to dust and mud.

"Takenaka's walls aren't on any maps," said Yoshida. "Look what he did to that precious old-growth forest, that rascal. You know what? I'm gonna get my Russian friends here to level a chunk of this wall with their antiaircraft gun. Then we can just drive through it."

"Maybe there are mines in that death strip," said Miss Sato.

"You're always carrying on about mines. Takenaka's smart mines ran out of batteries long ago. Why do you think *Truth Dawn* hires these Russian guys? Takenaka's long dead, nobody's gonna mind. Let them limber up the Russian artillery there, this will look great in my story."

Yoshida engaged in some pidgin shout-and-gesture with his mercenaries. The Russians, who were no older or wiser than Yoshida, had no trouble catching on to his idea. They were very proud of their big gun. They whooped with glee as each deafening round punched a massive hole in the pirate barricade.

Every bang from the jolting gun blew through Miss Sato's scarfed head. It made the very hills ring. From somewhere in the sullen hills came answering blasts. Protest? Celebration?

Yoshida's terrier leapt from the back of the Toyota. The dog bulleted off through the weeds, his furry legs a blur. He disappeared through a freshly blasted hole in the pirate wall.

Yoshida reached down and hooked up a stack of his newspapers, bound with a thick hemp string. "Now we follow the dog," he said, dismounting from the truck.

"Why?"

"Because he's my dog. You want to stay here breaking bricks with Yuri and Leonid? Give them my best!"

Miss Sato followed Yoshida as he pursued the eager dog. They ducked through the fresh rubble of the blasted barricade. No human foot had stepped here in years. The three of them were in utter wilderness, snagged by briars, scratched by weeds, and bitten by whining mosquitoes.

"You told me once you could get me an audience with the Pirate Queen," Miss Sato called out, groping at damp boughs and stepping over wet nettles. "Khadra may be 'hiding underground,' but that doesn't mean that she can hide from you. Not if you really want to find her."

"Look, you need to stop trying to be clever," said Yoshida absently. "Khadra is just a gangster moll. Khadra's boyfriend Takenaka was a 'King of the Pirates,' but he got blown to bits. Khadra's just a Somalian hooker. She takes her men as they come along, and there's always some new one."

Miss Sato ignored this impropriety. "But the Americans, the Chinese, the Koreans, they uniformly agree—she's the 'Pirate Queen of Tsushima.' They all agree that if an act of mercy can resolve my hostage crisis, then Khadra would be the key actor."

"That's the lying mainstream media! They just say that for their own political advantage. Khadra doesn't rule this island, she is just some pretty Somali girl who got mixed up with pirates! Every man she ever kissed gets killed. And I'll tell you why—it's because Khadra is a police informant. She rats out her lovers to the Chinese, or the Koreans, or the Americans—whoever pays her most."

Miss Sato considered this assertion. She and Yoshida were both lost in the tall grass.

"Doesn't anyone in this world have any sense of decency?" Miss Sato said at last.

"It's the truth! Think about it. Once you're a pirate's woman, you can't just divorce your pirate and walk away. He's evil, he's a killer, and to be free of him you have to have him killed." Yoshida insistently stamped a path through some windblown, rotten bamboo. "It was Khadra who betrayed Boss Takenaka. Khadra got him blown to bits, eighty men dead in one night. A real massacre. Someday I'll find the proof that Khadra herself did that. Then I'll write that story and publish it. People will be totally amazed!"

"Maybe Khadra isn't a pirate queen or a police spy or a hooker or a gangster moll, or any of those cruel things you say about her," Miss Sato offered. "Maybe Khadra's just a refugee woman who is cruelly exploited by violent men. At least, Khadra would know what that means to a woman. And why that oppression should end."

"Oh no, Khadra's evil, all right," said Yoshida. "But I'm not in any hurry to denounce Khadra. That's because Khadra is such great copy. Hot news stories about exotic, promiscuous pirate beauties will practically write themselves. Hey, hey, wait, look at this, look what my dog just found here! Good boy!" Yoshida fell to his bare knees in his cargo shorts. "This is Tsushima ginseng! Still growing up here in the good old mountain wilderness, imagine that! Wild ginseng is as rare as a Tsushima wildcat! This must be my lucky day."

"You could sell that ginseng to a rich Korean," Miss Sato said, "if there were any rich Koreans to eat ginseng anymore."

"That was a joke of yours, wasn't it," said Yoshida, rising to his feet with a scowl. "Ginseng is Tsushima's truest buried treasure. I could dig up this root right now if I had a shovel instead of my newspapers. Ginseng roots are shaped just like buried men, you know. They're full of mystical vitamins."

Miss Sato reached into her woven handbag and produced a half-empty bottle of multivitamin pills. "You don't need any dark, ancient roots."

Yoshida wiped wet dirt from his hands and dry-gulped a vitamin. "Well, let's dig up one pirate treasure at a time. Boss Takenaka's robot gun is buried somewhere on this hill. My map says we're standing near it right now." Yoshida waved his hands around the rugged woods, which had a commanding view of the island's eastern slopes. "This was Takenaka's favorite turf. He wanted to dig in deep, up here, with secret forts and pillboxes. Dig in and fight it out to the bitter end, Pacific-War style. Just like the kamikazes from World War II, a hundred years ago."

"The kamikazes flew airplanes," Miss Sato corrected him. "They didn't dig any secret forts in hills."

"Well," said Yoshida, offended, "I meant to say the original kamikazes—the samurai who fought Mongols here on my island, one thousand years ago."

"Weeds are pirates, while pirates spread like weeds."

"That's pretty clever," said Yoshida.

"I read that in your newspaper."

"I've got a real way with words," Yoshida agreed. He gazed around, alertly smiling. "It's incredible how fast the weeds grow during climate change. Turn your back, and the weeds just take over the world! Post-atomic Tokyo is one huge vacant lot now, a vast dead city full of weeds. Fukushima has mutant trees ten meters high!"

"Fukushima is not so bad as that," Miss Sato said. "I've been to Fukushima. Fukushima is very peaceful and pretty. Fukushima has no people, but it is full of wildlife."

Yoshida scowled. "What kind of wildlife is in Fukushima? Glowing, three-eyed dolphin mutants?"

"Whales are in Fukushima. Siberian cranes. Wild monkeys even." Miss Sato laughed. "Monkeys are so funny. Monkeys are much kinder to each other than people are."

Yoshida glanced up at the clouding sky and shifted his bundle of newspapers. "Now it's trying to rain on us. All you have to do is talk about the 'sacred wind,' and here it comes to get you, the kamikaze! Did you ever notice that, when you speak the words 'climate change,' the weather will actually change?"

Miss Sato nodded. "Oh yes. Everybody says that nowadays. Even on the mainland."

"I spotted some roofs on the far side of that ravine," said Yoshida. He picked up his dog in one arm and hefted his newspapers in the other. "So I bet there's a village where I can deliver my newspapers. We'll be uphill of the sniper nest too. So maybe we can see it by looking down at it from a position of vantage."

Yoshida was young and energetic rather than reasonable, but

his thrashing through the tall weeds was soon rewarded. He led her from the choking, tangled overgrowth into a clearer area.

Boss Takenaka had built a concealed guardhouse here to defend his mountainside drug farms. Faded warnings of land mines were nailed to the larger trees.

A warm, sticky drizzle began to fall. It was the premonition of much worse weather to come.

"Land mines," Miss Sato murmured.

"Those signs are probably lying," Yoshida advised. He scampered forward along with his yapping terrier. Miss Sato followed, treading with care in his footsteps.

The pirate guardhouse was almost invisible, built to fool aerial surveillance by military drones. The big hut was roofed with a dense thatch, thoroughly smeared with mud and festooned with flourishing gourd vines. Crooked sniper holes allowed a few rays of daylight.

The yawning door was hung all over with lucky pirate amulets. Superstitions had arrived here from all over the planet: wreathed anchors, topless mermaids, see-no-evil monkeys, marijuana leaves, hooded skeletons. Crossed revolvers, hypodermics, bloody dice, Taoist yin-yangs, lightning bolts, ninja masks...

Inside the guardhouse were three stone steps leading downward. Dried herbs and spider webs dangled from the rafters. The uneven floor of the hut—just simple, damp, pounded earth—was strewn with rotting tatami mats.

The terrier trotted down the steps and barked at a pile of damp hay in the hut's darkest corner. The hay-pile sat up. It revealed itself as a slumbering derelict under a thick straw raincoat.

"Nice dog," the blind man said mildly, grasping at a long stick. "I know your voice, doggie! If you are here, then your master, that journalist, must be nearby."

"That's right," Yoshida admitted, "and fancy meeting you in here, Zeta One."

"The sacred wind always makes me sleepy," said Zeta One. He crowned his dented head with a rain hat. His conical hat was the size of a bicycle wheel and, from above, made him resemble some harmless patch of weedy island sod.

Zeta One sniffed aloud. "So, what brings you to this lonely place, with your pretty female friend, who is standing there? Should I ask that?"

"She is not my girlfriend," said Yoshida. "She is Miss Sato from the Federation of Nine Relief Societies. She's a peace activist from the mainland."

"So then you're from Nagoya, Miss Sato," said Zeta One, fingering his pilgrim's sacred cane. "I can tell that by the way you talk."

"But I haven't said a word," Miss Sato said.

"See, you really are from Nagoya."

"Are you living inside this shack these days?" asked Yoshida. "I haven't seen you in Tsushima City lately. At least, not since that gambling house exploded. The casino that kicked you out."

"Ah, well then," said Zeta One, smiling blindly into the dim air lit by sniper holes, "a fine young gentleman like yourself doesn't frequent the brothels and gambling dens where a reprobate like me passes his time."

"Well, yes, being a journalist, I do spend my time in there, actually. I was lucky not to get killed."

"We keep different hours," said Zeta One. "Poor, blind wretch that I am, I can't tell any difference between night and day. It's only due to the kindness of strangers that I get by on humble charity bowls of sweet-potato porridge."

A flicker of irritation crossed Yoshida's youthful face. "So—what exactly are you doing in here?"

"I am sleeping the big storm away," said the blind man with a tender, confiding smile. "I can't see the lightning, so the lightning might kill me. The sound of thunder on my poor blind ears, that always makes me jump with fear."

"I don't believe a word of that," Yoshida objected. "Miss Sato and I were just discussing you, not one hour ago. And yet here you are, 'like the daughter-in-law who ate the autumn eggplants.'"

"No one believes in your old proverbs anymore."

"My old proverbs have nothing to do with it! Obviously you knew that we were coming here! You were lurking in here, waiting for us."

"You're such nice people," said Zeta One, "that this must be a blessing from the Goddess of Mercy. You see, in penance for the many past sins of my wretched former life, I have vowed to visit all six temples of the Kannon on Tsushima. Now that I'm on my sacred pilgrimage to the east, west, north, and south of this island. Meeting you is how the Goddess rewards me for my piety."

"What a sweet thing to say," Miss Sato interrupted. "I'm glad to hear of such a blessing! Because I've been searching for you, Mr. Zeta One. I bring you some personal greetings from Mrs. Mieko Nagai. Mrs. Nagai is an unfortunate hostage who is held captive in chains, as you know. And she told me you were kind to her. That's the truth, isn't it?"

"Well, that's all for you to judge, miss," said Zeta One, adjusting a twisted leather thong on his huge rain hat. "This poor old bean of mine took quite a pounding in the old days. So I'm afraid I don't remember any Mrs. Michiko what's-her-name…Never saw one glimpse of that lady, can't remember what I don't see, please forgive me." He briefly bowed where he sat.

"Oh stop all that," Yoshida objected. "You wouldn't fool a ten-year-old child!"

Zeta One meekly and silently rubbed at his long cane.

"You got that cane from the Mechatronic Visionary Centre," said Yoshida. "You did, didn't you?"

Zeta One chuckled. "What, a poor blind wanderer like me, who can't even read a computer screen? Whatever would I know of your fancy technology?"

"You're in and out of that damn lab all the time, you big faker! You wrapped that metal antenna in leather, and you smeared it with dirt, but that thing's packed with circuitry. That cane has got some kind of radar."

Alarmed by the anger in his master's voice, the terrier began barking furiously at a spider. The spider, disturbed by the rain, was inching up the timber of a ridgepole.

Without looking at the spider—without listening, without even turning his much-battered head—Zeta One hefted his staff, reached out, and precisely mashed the spider into paste.

"You shouldn't scold a blind man about his cane, Mr. Yoshida," said Miss Sato, in the rising patter of rain. "That isn't decent."

"I can tell by your sweet voice that you're a kindhearted lady, Miss Sato," said Zeta One as he levered himself to his huge, callused, straw-sandaled, and malodorous feet. "Not like this nosy young man with his Communist scandal sheet. I'll be on my way to the local temple of mercy. No one cares if an old blind man is soaked to the skin by the typhoon."

"You're not leaving until you tell us why you were waiting here for us," Yoshida said.

"Who, me? But I want nothing from you!" said Zeta One. He shook a leather bag on a belt under his shaggy raincoat. "Unless you want to give me a few gold coins to gamble away at the dice house. That's my only amusement—to listen to the rattle of the dice and the cries of the yakuza gamblers."

"I'll go with you to the temple," said Miss Sato at once.

Yoshida was scandalized. "You can't wander off with this sleazy character! You can't trust him. How can a blind man gamble with dice? He can't even see the spots!"

"You might as well ask why this pirate island has gold coins!" Miss Sato shouted. "Nobody wants Tsushima's stupid coins. Mint all the fake treasure you want, your gold has no legal value with any government! Pirate gold is worse than trash!"

Zeta One rumbled with laughter. "I do so enjoy the witty chatter of clever people. Sadly, since my brain was damaged, I can't keep up with the likes of you. Goodbye." He tapped his way toward the stairs of the guardhouse.

Yoshida blocked his way. The two men confronted one another for a moment, Yoshida glaring and Zeta One mildly turning his ravaged face to the dirt floor. Then, reluctantly, Yoshida stepped aside.

Zeta One found the yawning door of the hut with the tip of his stick. Then he left.

Miss Sato followed him. The forest trail was a sinister maze of briars, loose rocks, and rain-slick muddy slopes. Also, it was raining. But Zeta One moved at quite a brisk pace, setting his huge, sandaled feet with firm decision, like a man placing go stones.

"I'd appreciate it if you stopped following me," Zeta One said at last, stopping but not turning to face her.

"Now that I've finally found you," said Miss Sato meekly, "I'm so afraid to lose you."

"Maybe you're falling in love with me." Zeta One chortled. "Young ladies often do that, you know."

"I might do that," said Miss Sato. "Because I'm a woman with so many troubles, and you're such an interesting man."

The sun emerged from between two swirling fronts of the oncoming storm. Birds sang out in relief, and the trees dripped. "There are land mines all around us here," said Zeta One. "Even your dainty little feet can set one off."

"Oh, that's quite all right. I'm not afraid when you're here. I'll just come along with you."

"Maybe you'd like it if I sang you a song as we walk through these land mines."

"A song? That might be nice."

"Yes, I know an old song from old Tsushima. When it was just an innocent island, long before any satellite positioning or any bomb-targeting maps. You see, my girl, back in the good old days on Tsushima, the trails in this island's great forests were dark even at midday. So every Tsushima boy, and most every girl, knew a song of all the roadmarks. That's what I sing to myself as I make my pilgrimage."

The blind man sang in time with his sandaled steps. Every dozen paces, he would whirl the cane above his head. He poked it about from one side to the other, tilted his rain-hatted head this way and that, sniffed at the air, muttered, and sang. The Korean-flavored, Japanese island dialect was impossible to understand.

"How did you learn such songs?" Miss Sato said at last.

"From old wind-up Victrolas," Zeta One said. "Those old songs were collected by Mr. Miyamoto Tsunekazu, for whom they made the famous Daffodil Festival. But of course stupid old island songs are of no interest to a fine Nagoya girl like yourself."

"I can sing," Miss Sato volunteered.

"That would be a kindness, since we blind men are so appreciative of music. What songs do you sing?"

"I sing protest songs," said Miss Sato. "Peace songs, resistance songs, nuclear disarmament songs, and civil rights songs. Also, many personal singer-songwriter songs about how difficult it is to be a contemporary Japanese woman."

Zeta One cocked his head. "Don't you know any happy songs?"

"You mean children's songs? Yes, I still remember a few."

Zeta One reached under his baggy straw cape and grubbed around through a set of pockets on a bandolier. He munched a brown handful of shredded squid. "Would you like some?"

"Yes," said Miss Sato, plucking the tangled mess out of his hand but not eating it.

"I want you to do something for me."

"What is that?"

"There are solar panels concealed somewhere near here. Those are great treasures because they have power…but I can't remember where I put them. The panels are hung high up in the trees. People never look up when they search for pirate treasure. They always think it must be under the ground." He chuckled.

"How can a blind man climb a tree?"

"I'd like you better if you didn't ask questions," Zeta One said simply.

Miss Sato obediently gazed at the tops of the forest trees. It took a while, but she was patient and persistent. At length she spotted a gleam in the canopy. Two solar panels were visible. A monkey couldn't have carried them any higher. A man of Zeta One's bulk, and blind, clambering so high up there while carrying solar panels? Incredible.

However, she asked no more questions. She guided Zeta One to the tree trunk.

The power cable's plastic sheath was dappled with forest camouflage. It had been hidden with devious cunning—writhing through leaf litter, ducking under thorn bushes.

This power cable led, dodging and wriggling, to a spider hole buried in the hill-slope. This cunningly hidden death trap was all vine-covered sandbags, with just one wide leafy slit, like a mouth in an eyeless skull.

The vision-slit commanded an impressive view over the bay of Tsushima City, a splendid vista of East China Sea blue, with a lacy, roiling storm front stretching toward distant Japan.

The spider hole smelled of damp earth and ruin. Inside it squatted a stark mechanism, a long muzzle with legs, cogs, and exposed wiring. The rains and island damp had been at the robot machine gun. It had rusted to junk.

"You built this," said Miss Sato. "You knew it was here, so you're the one who built it."

"I don't remember about that," said Zeta One, "but it would be a good idea if it wasn't here anymore. It would bad if someone sullied the memory of Boss Takenaka, that yakuza man-of-honor.

Also, Boss Murai; Murai was killed too, so one shouldn't speak ill of him. Boss Shosuke was never a friendly man, but after the way he perished, it's better to say nothing about that."

Zeta One heaved and pried at the heavy sandbags. After much grunting, hand-groping, and ripping of snarled vines, he hauled the sniper gun from its camouflaged lair. He patted the lethal mechanism from stem to stern, muttering to himself.

Then he briskly dismantled the big, rusty gun, like a sushi chef boning a tuna.

Miss Sato spoke up. "My friend, the journalist, says that this robot gun killed many pirates. They died in the streets of Tsushima City, far away, far downhill there. Farther than a human eye can see."

"I wouldn't know about that," said Zeta One, "as I was never here or there when that happened. I'm always far away when bad men come to bad ends." He bundled up the gun's stripped components, wrapping them with rotten strips of sandbag. "Now, I need some deep water. Even a blind man knows that water always runs downhill…" He chuckled to himself. "But I can't carry this gun because I need my staff to walk."

"I'll carry the gun for you," Miss Sato volunteered. "Getting rid of guns is always a good thing to do."

"Don't carry the muzzle like that," he said, gripping her hand. "If you show any silhouette with a heavy weapon, we might both be struck by a drone. Stay below the ridges, because your body might be outlined to a flying robot. Don't walk like a human being walks. The flying machines know what that gait is like. Bend down. Walk like an animal."

Miss Sato's clumsy efforts to skulk didn't please him. He unknotted his shaggy straw cape and wrapped her up in that disguise. His cape reeked of sweat and mildew.

Beneath his cape Zeta One wore crossed webbing bandoliers. Most patches on the bandoliers were empty, and others smelled like rotting squid, yet among this derelict jumble was a personal belt-bomb. A clipped-together set of wires, a battery pack, and seven little cartons of plastique.

She knew better than to ask him about that.

The two of them lurked and skulked downhill until she spotted the slumped ruins of a vacation house. "I can see a big swimming pool over there," she told him. "It's full of mosquitoes and mud."

"When it comes to buried treasure, mud is even better than dirt," said Zeta One. "I'm sure a dainty lady like you doesn't want to touch any filthy mud. But if you will kindly help me into that smelly morass and give me that robot gun, then I'll wallow about a bit and bury it."

Zeta One carefully leaned his long cane at the rim of the dead swimming pool. Then, splashing and snorting like a walrus, Zeta One buried the ruined weapon. He trampled it deep into the all-obscuring muck.

"Can you see anything of the treasure now?" he asked her at last.

"No. No one could possibly see it."

"You're sure," he said. He slapped at a few hungry mosquitoes.

"I'm sure. You are waist-deep in that mud, and the robot monster is deep under your big feet. No one will ever see."

"It's always good to hear," said Zeta One, "that everyone else is just as blind as me." He chuckled. "That means that everyone will forget. My work here is done, and now I have to get out of this mud. For a tired old man like myself, that's not so easy." He stretched out one mud-caked hand.

"I can't reach you," said Miss Sato.

"Why not? Where are you?"

"If I get any closer, I'll get stuck in there myself."

"Just reach out to me with my staff."

"I don't believe I can see your staff," Miss Sato said, picking it up. "It's gone. I can't remember where you left it."

Zeta One stirred about in the wallow of mud. He removed his straw hat and threw it outside the swimming pool. His skull was curiously scarred and thin gray hair grew in patches.

"This situation is so very much like the sad fate of Mrs. Nagai," Miss Sato remarked brightly. "For four years, I've been promising to release her from that jail. She is an elected official of my government, and I helped to elect her. When I visited her, this time, and she told me about you and how kind you are, well, I swore I wouldn't leave the island. Not unless I can take her home with me."

Zeta One muttered in disbelief.

"That was my sacred vow," Miss Sato said casually.

"Your friends in Nagoya can solve your hostage problem," Zeta One said. "It's always foolish for a government to be trapped by sentimental feelings for the innocent. Tell them to bomb the hostage compound. Kill them all, and level the Mechatronic Visionary Centre to the ground."

"I'm sure there's some better plan that's rather less cruel."

"I don't make strategic plans." Zeta One shrugged. "Living from day to day as I do. You should listen when I tell you to destroy my own home. That's where they put me when they brought me back from Somalia. They stitched me back together in there. They did amazing things to me. They were cruel things, but I volunteered for the cruelty."

"I volunteered for all this too," said Miss Sato. "That's why, unfortunately, you're not getting free unless Mrs. Nagai also gets free."

Time passed after this declaration. Zeta One struggled to extricate himself from the clutching mud. He made some small progress, but he had to pause periodically to ward off the mosquitoes. Their fierce, annoying whine seemed to bother him far more than their bites.

Miss Sato shared the bites of the mosquitoes. They were painful and possibly infectious.

"I have another plan," said Zeta One at last. "Visit the hostage and leave her a metal file. She could saw the chain off her leg. Then, one dark stormy night, a friend throws a rope ladder over the wall. The escaped captive would use standard escape-and-evasion techniques to reach Teppu Point at the southern tip of Tsushima. Then, swim to the Australian navy base on Naiin Island."

"Mrs. Nagai isn't a global commando. Mrs. Nagai is a sixty-year-old female socialist politician."

"It's a pity my tactics are so inadequate," said Zeta One as he killed another mosquito. "It seems I'm doomed to drown in mud."

"It's bad enough that we have an Australian naval base in Japanese waters!" said Miss Sato, slapping her own mosquito-bitten cheek. "Where is your pride? Where is your decency and honor? All we have to do is liberate one innocent Japanese woman from a terrible situation, and you're carrying on like that's the end of the world! Do we all have to blow ourselves up?"

Miss Sato paced back and forth, rapping the rim of the swimming pool with his heavy cane. "When I think of all the money we Japanese wasted on our soldiery, you men who should have been our roof tiles and instead cost us more than jewels. And for what? What safety and security did you soldiers ever bring us? After all your strutting and boasting and shouting through megaphones and waving of your big, striped, fascist flags, we lost our own capital to a sneak attack! Now we're beset by bandits, and the more we bomb them, the crazier they get!"

"Japan was a pirate island," rumbled Zeta One. "Tsushima was the biggest pirate island in the world for three hundred years. When the pirates ruled Tsushima, there was no Japan, just warlords who killed each other every spring. Evil men came here to rob Asia from as far away as Portugal."

"You sound proud of these evil, wandering men."

"Proud of them? I'm one of them."

A white terrier leapt over a tumbledown wall and began yapping in frenzy.

"I should have blown up that kid's stupid newspaper a long time ago," Zeta One said. "No target is softer than a reporter...But since he was born here on Tsushima, well, none of this was really his fault. Yes, yes, I feel true regret for his native family."

Miss Sato watched as the terrier scampered back and forth, yapping till it drooled in sharp distress. "I hate all dogs, but there's something quite wrong with this dog's behavior. I think he wants us to help his master."

"Who, us? How?"

Pirates arrived. They were mountain pirates, the creatures of the backwoods. There were forty of them, and their mood was evident by the fact that they had the severed heads of the two Russian drivers, Yuri and Leonid, stuck onto two sharp steel poles.

These mountain pirates were mostly teenagers, fearless youth who had never spent a day in school. To judge by their angry, pidgin jabber, they had no language in common either. They had only three great commonalities among them: scars and bad tattoos were two of them.

Fresh, bloody wounds were also common because Yuri and Leonid, being Russians, had battled to their last breath.

A few older pirates lurked among the bloodstained crowd of feral teens, veterans of thirty who looked about sixty. They were jittery, twitchy, red-eyed, heavily armed, and very high on drugs. No pirate gang was a family, so these were not motherly, fatherly, older people. The older pirates had the timeworn look of prison trustees, bad people grimly burdened with the task of keeping even worse people in line.

The Toyota's antiaircraft gun was their latest trophy, lashed to a shoulder-borne tote pole. The same fate had befallen Yoshida. The captured journalist had been lashed to a pole with leather thongs at his wrists and ankles.

"Don't you worry, Miss Sato!" Yoshida called out. "I sold all my newspapers!"

Miss Sato picked up Zeta One's metal staff and threw it to the blind man. This quick gesture made little sense, but she knew they would steal the cane from her, and she didn't want that to be her fault.

Irritated by this gesture of defiance, the pirates fell upon Miss Sato and beat her up. Miss Sato limply dropped to the damp earth and offered no resistance. They kicked her, punched her, dragged her around by the hair, tore her clothes off, crudely tied her arms and legs, urinated on her, shouted many insults, and threw mud in her face.

Miss Sato shouted with pain at appropriate times and guarded her vital organs from the blows. Being young people, they soon grew bored with the trouble.

The pirates dumped Yoshida next to her, bound hand and foot. Yoshida rolled in the mud to face her. "My newspaper has comic strips," Yoshida confided. "They can't read the words, but even illiterates love comics."

Miss Sato searched with her tongue for any broken teeth.

"Modern global pirates are a simple people at heart," said Yoshida.

These backwoods Tsushima pirates were studying Zeta One, who was mired in his mud but clutching his cane alertly. They were genuinely puzzled about what to do about him. He was too poor to have anything they wanted to steal, and nobody wanted to jump in the mud and attempt to haul him out. Likely they had noticed his mud-smeared personal belt-bomb.

"What are they going to do to him?" said Miss Sato to Yoshida.

"Well," said Yoshida, "they could shoot him and leave him there."

"If they shoot him, he's going to explode. I'm sure his belt-bomb has a dead-man's switch. He likely has a hidden second bomb, timed to go off when rescuers come to investigate the first bomb. That is rather standard."

"You know," said Yoshida, craning his neck to investigate her bound and naked body, "for a feminist peace campaigner, you're a lot tougher than you look. Where did you get all those scars on your body? You've got more scars than some of these pirates do."

"These pirates never did any salvage work in Tokyo. Skyscrapers fell down in Tokyo. Buildings that big, they fall down even long after they fall down."

"You'll rebuild your Tokyo someday, I suppose."

"No, Tokyo is over. But Japan isn't. Pay attention now. If they shoot him, he will explode. You and I will be deafened and wounded by the blast. But these pirates will all be dead because they're standing up. They're in blast range."

Yoshida's terrier arrived. It tenderly licked Yoshida's face as he lay there bound hand and foot. "Stop briefing me about bombs," Yoshida complained. "I know all about bombs. I wrote a hundred bomb atrocity stories for *Truth Dawn*, and they're always just the same."

The pirates fell silent at the rumble of an approaching jeep. This ex-military American Humvee was a psychedelic wonder of feathers and fronds, all fuchsia, hot pink, magenta, and vermilion. It bore a large and silent uniformed driver and, in the back, a statuesque, very pregnant African woman.

Khadra the Pirate Queen dressed as if a treasure chest had been emptied on her gravid body. She wore necklaces, bangles, rings, hammered gold badges, ropes of pearls, a towering crown of leather and feathers half a meter high, and not much else.

"Stop here," Khadra told her driver in Japanese. She studied the scene before her. "Well! What a good opportunity to get rid of three trespassers and put their bones in this mud pit."

"So, what's new with you, Khadra?" the journalist called out. "Who's the new father?"

"If I wanted you to know about my lovers," said the gorgeous Queen of Pirates, "I wouldn't be living underground. Yoshida, who is this ugly, naked, skinny woman?"

"Miss Sato is a peace activist from the mainland. She is a hostage negotiator."

"Well, well," said the pirate queen, "another mainland captive, that's so nice. Why isn't she chained in the compound with the others? Take her there right away. Wait—untie her and put some clothes on her first, she looks ugly. Also, pull those severed heads off those poles. Those always look vulgar. Can you talk?"

"Yes," said Miss Sato, standing up shakily as four or five pirates gripped her bruised limbs. "Yes, I can talk to you."

"Are you from North Japan, or are you from South Japan?"

"I came here to Tsushima from Nagoya."

"That's really too bad for you," said the pirate queen serenely. "If you'd been one of my dear friends from North Japan, then I would have released you now with all courtesies. And even given you rich gifts of gold and silk and exotic drugs. Whatever you like. But since you're an aggressive corporate criminal who comes from evil South Japan, then I must charge you with overfishing in Tsushima's territorial waters. Also, you are guilty of abusing our beautiful island republic as your toxic waste dump. That's why you're my hostage. You understand that? All right? Good! Now! How much do you think your family would pay for you? In American dollars."

"Khadra," Yoshida protested, "Miss Sato can't be your hostage. She's an official hostage negotiator from the Nagoya regime. It's because of her that the people in South Japan know that we still hold hostages here. See, that's all been settled. That was all printed in the newspaper."

Yoshida's terrier yapped triumphantly.

"Untie that journalist," Khadra said. "We can't shoot a journalist. We need his newspaper to publish our demands and communiques. Also, all the foreign intelligence agencies read his newspaper. He's valuable. That's a cute dog."

An obedient teenager sawed through Yoshida's leather bonds. "Thanks," Yoshida said, rubbing his skinned wrists.

"Now shoot the cute dog," Khadra commanded. Her burly driver pulled out a chromed sidearm and put a round through the terrier. Galvanized with a final spastic fit of animal vitality, the dog ran shrieking in a tight circle and died coughing blood.

"Now throw that bloody dead dog into that dirty mud pit. Dead dogs are so disgusting. You there, big dirty blind man, yes, you, stuck in that mud like a hippopotamus. Bury that dog in the mud for me now. I don't like the way that dog looks."

"I can't see any dog," said Zeta One reasonably. "I'm a blind man."

"Blind man, what are you doing there, stuck in that mud?"

"Your highness, ma'am, your great and beautiful ladyship, I'm on a pilgrimage to the six sacred shrines of the Goddess of Mercy," declared Zeta One. "I seek forgiveness for my many past crimes. But I'm so blind, so stupid and clumsy, that I slipped and fell in here. In my pitiful efforts to thrash my way out, I just sank in deeper and deeper, until, well, I almost lost my cane. If you would graciously help me out of this predicament, I would pray for you until my last days."

"I love this blind man," Khadra said. "I always loved him, because he has the proper humble attitude. All of you should be more like him. He's sweet. Jump in there now and pull him out of that muck."

None of the pirates showed any signs of obeying Khadra on the issue of the mud. They'd been a little startled by the pirate queen's sudden advent in her jeep festooned with seashells, fake pearls, and rhinestone jewels, but they had rapidly lost interest in her. The pirates were a shell-shocked people by nature. They were up to the things that any very ill-organized crowd would do when lost in the woods. They were swatting mosquitoes, aimlessly gathering firewood, scrounging for edible herbs, crouching pantsless behind trees, and so forth.

Miss Sato realized that she was not going to be immediately killed. Although she had been stripped and beaten, she was neither surprised nor afraid. "I'm proud to meet the Queen of the Pirates," she called out in a loud, even voice. "Because I've asked to meet you many times! People often spoke to me of your good temper, your good sense, and your sincerity, and now I can see why."

"Are you talking to me now, you ugly, skinny old woman?"

"Of course! I want to ask you a favor."

"Well, you're not allowed to talk to me in your disgusting condition! Somebody put some clothes on the ugly peacenik witch there. You there, yes, you, the girl with bones in your dreadlocks. Take all your clothes off, put them on the hostage, you're the right size. Yes, your shoes too, especially your shoes, and the rest of you, stop fooling around! It's important when the Queen of the Pirates negotiates with organized governments! You should pay attention to my maneuvers—you'll learn something. Now, hostage, or hostage negotiator, whatever, how many hostages do you want to buy from me? What treasure did you bring me? You didn't bring me very much, unless someone else already robbed you."

Miss Sato knotted a dirty straw skirt around her waist. Then she slipped her bare arms into the girl-pirate's rough canvas coat. "I'd hoped," she said, "that a leader of your great qualities would release one innocent woman for me as an important moral gesture."

"Oh, right, you're one of those, are you?" said the Queen of the Pirates. "You think I've never met your kind before? I know all about you people and your 'moral gestures.' Well, listen to this, bitch: I didn't capture those hostages. I didn't grab them any more than I blew out the eyes of this poor blind man here. It's not my fault that they have to be kept there so that you won't destroy our precious high-tech cultural compound."

"The Federation of Nine Relief Societies never blows up anyone."

"Yes you do. You are dropping bombs on innocent women and children here just like that man Guernica and his painting of Picasso. I should have that beautiful painting tattooed on your ugly, skinny back, you penniless hypocrite. If you want this woman released, why don't you agree to take her place yourself? Ha!"

"I already agreed to take the place of Mrs. Nagai," said Miss Sato. "I agreed to that condition four years ago. Let's do that right now. Let Mrs. Nagai go home, and I will stay in her place."

"Oh my God how boring!" protested the Queen of Pirates. "What a bother to have to put up with this crazy, ugly woman when that poor blind man there is almost drowning in his mud! Every week I'm harassed by arrogant demands from you stinking mainland bureaucrats, when the loyal subjects of my island, like the blind man there, suffer your oppression." She turned to her enormous, mute brute of a driver. "I want him out of there. Get the big towing chain."

Miss Sato turned her attention to Yoshida. "Well," she began, "we're making some good progress here," and then she broke off because, to her surprise, Yoshida was racked with silent sobs.

"What's wrong?" she said.

"The pirate queen killed my dog," Yoshida choked out.

"What? But you're a journalist in a conflict zone. You see bodies every week!"

"He was my best friend," said Yoshida, writhing with woe and shaking like a leaf.

A pirate approached and slapped Yoshida on the back. "Don't take that so hard," he urged in English. Miss Sato hadn't spotted this English-speaking pirate among the group before—he was dressed with particular oddity.

This new interloper was dressed in land mine-removal armor. He wore the big ceramic helmet with its platelike tinted blast shield, which gave his hidden head an angular, turtleish appearance. He also wore big blast-sloping epaulets that guarded his neck and shoulders, samurai-style. Ridged overlapping plates nestled around his back and belly, but this peculiar gear simply ended at his skinny ass. He wore ragged shorts and rubber wading boots.

"Where's the damn robot gun?" he demanded from Yoshida in

English. "You were supposed to fetch down that machine gun for me today."

"I can't talk English to you," Yoshida said in Japanese. "I'm too upset!"

"What the hell good are you, then?" said the faceless man in the armor. "I gave you this important news leak on a plate! All you had to do was dig that circuitry out of its hole and bring it back to me."

"I don't know where your robot gun is," said Yoshida in anguish. "Leave me alone."

Everyone was leaving the interloper alone. This seemed odd for a group of aggressive pirates. Then Miss Sato noticed that, along with his de-mining gear, the stranger was carrying a muddy satchel full of freshly grubbed-up land mines. He had disinterred these treasures somehow and now carried them around like so many daikon radishes.

"I know where your robot gun is," said Miss Sato to the faceless man in English. "Who are you?"

The faceless man casually waved his bare left hand, which was missing the tips of three fingers. "I am in deep background, lady," he said. "I am strictly off the record in this story of yours. You never saw me around here. In fact, you are not even talking to me."

"You must have some kind of name," said Miss Sato practically.

"Look," said the faceless man, "you're Japanese, right? So, did you ever see Noh drama? Where there are all these, like, brave samurai and ghosts and lords and ladies being all super-traditional Japanese? Then there are these other black guys in black costumes. Guys so deep-black they make ninja look too obvious. Well, that's me. I was one of those deep background guys of yours."

"You're his confidential source," Miss Sato concluded. "You made that treasure map for him. You're a hacker from the Mechatronic Visionary Centre."

"Yeah, but I haven't been in there in years," the faceless hacker said. "My lab is boarded shut and full of your chained-up dorks from

312 ★ BRUCE STERLING

the mainland. That's a dirty shame too, because that place was so perfect. We had creative freedom in there. We had our freedom to build anything we could dream up."

"I have a hostage friend in there who also longs for freedom," said Miss Sato at once.

"What, you want some kind of deal from me then?" scoffed the faceless man. "You, a no-budget peacenik who hangs out at the fringes of a provisional government? What are you gonna do for me, write me a trillion-yen personal check to 'Mickey Tronic'? You have no idea what we accomplished in there. We were fantastic. We were beyond your world."

"I know that you were top secret."

"No, no! First, we were top secret. Then, second, we were war-on-terror secret. Third we were anti-nuclear-missile-proliferation secret. And then the whole lab was officially run by a sleazy private contractor—a crooked Japanese camera company in hock to the yakuza to keep its stock price up! They just paid our bills and never asked a word. That's how great my situation was. Then some North Korean secret bomb-lab morons had to ruin the whole arrangement."

"My hostage is still a hostage," said Miss Sato patiently, "and she still has a shackle on her leg. Nothing you said has changed that."

"We pulled in cool mil-spec hackers from every garage in the world," said Mickey Tronic mournfully. "Most of us couldn't speak a word of Japanese. I still can't speak any Japanese. '*Yoroshiku onegai itashimasu*,' that's about it."

"That is a good thing to say to me," Miss Sato admitted. "But the prisoner is still in chains, even though you say that to me."

"Just check out that guy stuck in the mud pit over there," said Mickey Tronic. "He was one of us! Terrific guy, never knew his real name, of course, but he was our ideal lab subject. Imagine building a tactile, augmented interface for a blind soldier. An interface so he can literally feel every centimeter, practically every cubic micron of the 3-D spaces around him…Do you know what 'prioperception' is?"

"No," said Miss Sato, gazing at the stir of pirates reluctantly gathering around Zeta One. "I don't know that. I do know that they'll never pull him out of there with that chain."

"Yeah, he's pretty well mired in there like a water buffalo," Mickey Tronic admitted. "That's a shame, because once that guy was a true Japanese Special Forces ninja. Superb martial artist, totally dedicated, complete devotion to the Japanese nation—if Tokyo existed, he'd still be saluting his emperor. I have to say, I always liked him."

"I should admit that too," said Miss Sato. "I like him myself."

"That brave guy—he lost everything that mattered to him in two bomb blasts, but he never says one word about his past. He just lives for the now. Very Zen. He wanders this island, pretending to pray—hell, he's probably really praying—and whenever people annoy him, they blow up. This whole section of the island is painted in infrared targeting lasers, right now. These cannibal Peter Pan children can't see that, but they'd be stone-dead if he twitched a finger."

"Is that true?"

"Isn't it obvious? The guy is the one-man focus of death from above. The thing that's great is that, after he liquidates the bad guys, he never attempts to assert any law and order on the ground! He's too soulful for that! That's what I love about him, that's why I never…you know…put a land mine under his tatami mat. There's something rare and magnificent about him. It'd be like poaching a tiger."

"If there's going to be an airstrike on these coordinates," said Miss Sato, "then we should leave right away."

"What is your hurry? I need my machine-gun robot back," Mickey Tronic said. "I mean, I don't need the gun itself, I'm happy if this weepy clown here mounts that gun in the office of his commie rag. But I need the visual coding for the microcontroller of the gun.

Five of us worked on that project for three years, and we were so busy that we never commented the code! You know how much hard work that is, computer-vision coding? No, you don't get that, do you?" Mickey Tronic sighed within his blast helmet. "Why am I talking to you?"

"If you had the software code you want so much," said Miss Sato, "could you get a prisoner released from that computer lab of yours?"

"Let me share the big secret with you here," said Mickey Tronic. "Your hostage, Mrs. Nagai, she doesn't have any jailer. All her jailers are dead. They all got wiped out by mud-pit boy there. That's why you never got anywhere around here, and you're never going to get anywhere. It's not in the interests of anybody anywhere to straighten your situation out."

"So that's it," said Miss Sato. "Then the truth is, I am facing anarchy."

"Not really," said Mickey Tronic. "I'm an anarchist, but your problem is red tape. A setup like yours is just very Japanese. Everybody just ignores your uncomfortable problem till it turns impolite to mention it."

"Well, I am Japanese," said Miss Sato, "and if nobody talks about Mrs. Nagai staying in the prison, then nobody will talk about her if she leaves."

Mickey Tronic shrugged beneath his plate armor. "Go ahead, be all Japanese like that, I never said any different. Be Japanese, just let me have my true hacker freedom, all right? That's all I wanted. Freedom. Not 'free as in beer,' not 'free like free speech.' I mean total hacker freedom, like, completely free of any obligation to any other person, ever. And that's what I've got here on Tsushima. Still." He sighed. "Even when I'm down to a goddamn paper and pencil."

"If you give my treasure—Mrs. Nagai—to me, then I promise that, in return, I'll give your treasure to you."

Drizzle was falling again. Mickey Tronic wiped the smoked glass of his faceplate. "I'm supposed to believe that strange promise of yours?"

"Yes," said Miss Sato, "because I am an honest woman of moral principle, and when I make a promise, I never lie."

"Every tough guy thinks he's bulletproof," said Mickey Tronic, "just like every honest woman thinks she'll never be a whore. But the truth is, people break. They break whenever life gets hard enough. The only guy who will never break is that guy stuck in the mud over there, and that's why he's not human." He sighed. "I didn't even mention all that cyber-stuff we installed in his brain. That was just technical."

"So, do we have an arrangement?" said Miss Sato. "Because you won't see the last of me on Tsushima until I get what I want."

"Yeah, well, you never saw me in Tsushima in the first place. I'm so deep-black budget that I don't even exist. Nobody sees me at all."

"All right," said Miss Sato.

"Then we might, actually, have some kind of deal," admitted Mickey Tronic. "Just, don't ever try to find me. Because, believe me, I can easily locate you."

The Queen of Pirates suddenly loomed upon them in her furious majesty. At close range, her headdress towered over them like a feathered gun turret. The pirate queen had golden rings, silver bracelets, pearl buttons, and spangled, sequined sashes wrapping her grand, pregnant belly.

The pirate queen shouted at Mickey Tronic in very broken English. "Why you talk to this woman so much like that? You betray me now?"

Mickey Tronic gave an indifferent tilt to his smoked-glass faceplate. "Look, lady, don't try to boss me around. If you're the Queen of Pirates, then I'm the Witch Doctor of Pirates. I got your stepping razors, your whipping sticks, I got tech voodoo that would scare you so bad your grandchild will be born two-headed. So back off."

"I never understand this stupid computer man," said the pirate queen to Miss Sato, her regal face wrinkled with dismay. "Why does he speak English to me like that?" She pointed east, with a rattling clatter of bangles. "Does he think that is England over there? That is Japan!"

"Tell the Third World mother-of-eight here," said Mickey Tronic, "that I don't need any geolocation lessons. Tell her to get lost. Tell her that the ninja in the mud pit there is about to liquidate her the same way he did to pirate boyfriends one, two, and three."

"I'm a woman of honor! I hate disrespect!" shrieked the Pirate Queen. "A quick death is too good for this no-face turtle man! I will kill him now in such an awful, terrifying way that everyone will be impressed! Tell me, you, peace woman, you're always crying about the people suffering! What is the very worst thing in the world that ever happened to anyone? Tell me that! Tell him I'll do that to him."

"She claims she's going to torture you," said Miss Sato in English.

"Hell, this is Japan," shrugged Mickey Tronic. "Her torture's no good around here. Tell her I'll commit an agonizing hara-kiri just to spite her."

Miss Sato wisely said nothing.

The pirate queen glanced behind her, where half-hearted attempts to haul the blind man from his mud were getting nowhere. "Talk to him in English and make him scared of me, and I'll reward you richly. Don't make that face, because I'll give you back your real clothes. You'll be just like you were before we beat you. I will, you'll see, I'll do that now."

The pirate queen turned and raised her voice to harangue her scattered minions, but a rolling peal of typhoon thunder blotted out her commands.

This was the season of the sacred winds, and a huge storm front was rolling in from continental Asia. The kamikaze was serious, world-scale weather, a storm front big and black and presumably radioactive. The kamikaze was full of tainted rain from the city-sized craters of North Korea. A tremendous rain was coming, the kind of rain that would scatter a horde of Mongols the way Mongols scattered civilized nations.

"Oh what a bother," said the pirate queen. Gathering her robes in the patter of thumb-sized raindrops, she waddled to her jeep and fled the downpour.

The tempest bent the trees. Howling, ship-killing winds roared across Tsushima with salvo after salvo of thunder.

No one could remain in rain of this kind, so everyone simply left the scene.

Miss Sato and Yoshida found some shelter under the leaning roof of a dead vacation home. This stately family mansion had died not long after Tokyo had perished, as a collateral casualty. The house had suffered a fuel shortage, a water shortage, an electrical blackout, abandonment, a fire...

The beautiful island house had just fallen over in that strange mysterious way a civilization decays when nobody champions it. The dead house was a filthy mulch of fire-blackened memorabilia, wise books, tasteful paintings, meaningful photographs, important and civilized things.

These civilized things were so entirely gone now, so entirely flaked to nothingness and debris, that they lacked even the *mono no aware* of a cherry blossom. They were like an entire cherry orchard blown flat by a giant storm. With a loss of such scale, one could not even start over. One could not even vow to persist. One could only, in some halting but seismic fashion, come to identify with the storm winds.

Winds lashed and rain fell in buckets for four hours. When the tempest finally faded, the island landscape was foggy, silent, dark, and very cold. The swimming pool had flooded to its brim. When the evening sun flashed on it, it looked pretty and sweet again, a place of leisure and pleasure.

Zeta One had vanished. A blind aircraft had ditched in his swimming pool. It was perfect and sleek, pearl-white above and, from below, as blue as a sunlit sky.

Autogenic Dreaming: Interview with the Columns of Clouds by TOBI Hirotaka

Translated by Jim Hubbert

1.

<I> am watching a movie.

A bleak country road in a foreign land.

A truck moves along the unpaved track. It stops in a village. Castile, Spain. The 1940s. A sign, screen right—HOYUELOS. That must be the name of the village. Children run toward the truck. High excitement. The men are wearing caps. They open the rear of the truck. The children shout.

"Movies in a can!" Film cans. The men are traveling cinema operators.

"What kind of movie?" "Cowboys?"

The men answer. "A great movie." "The best you'll ever see."

The children's shining eyes open wide.

<I> am watching a movie. Let me put that differently. The film I'm watching—along with countless other works—is already part of me. I can access any scene in it instantly. Or maybe it would be better to say that this movie has incorporated me. That I'm swimming in it. That would not be wrong, but it's not quite right either. Anyway, I selected a movie—and I've dropped into the opening scene.

The movie proceeds. The men put up a poster on the wall of the town hall. A man's deformed face with a stitched-up wound across his jutting forehead. His eyes are half shut. Thick bolts protrude from his neck. The title is AUTOR DEL MONSTRUO.

Right, Dr. Frankenstein is the "author of the monster." It makes a strange kind of sense and I move farther in. Japanese burn-in subtitles. This must have been a print for distribution in Japan. Maybe it was the print Jundo Mamiya saw when he was a boy.

Villagers gather in an empty room in the town hall. Children, women, old men, each bringing a chair.

A black frame painted on a white stucco wall. That must be the silver screen. The stains, cracks, and finger marks on the wall are part of every movie people see in this village. Faces float in the dim reflected glow. Two children, sisters, stare raptly at the screen. The younger girl's enormous eyes are wonderful.

The movie proceeds. A black-and-white film comes up on the stucco screen. A man and his young daughter. The shore of a lake. Flowers everywhere in full bloom. The man says something to the girl and leaves her. She plays innocently, picking the flowers.

Frankenstein's monster steps out of the shadows. The children in the audience freeze. The little girl on the screen shows no fear at all. She speaks to the brute. Do you want to play with me? The monster is mute. The girl presses flowers on him. He kneels and starts to play with her. The carefree child seems to free him from the terror of his pursuers. He smiles, plucks a blossom, plucks another, tossing them onto the water. The lake dances in the sparkling sunlight. The children stare, wide-eyed, mesmerized by the tranquility and suspense.

A new scene. The father we saw earlier walks stiffly through the village, cradling the girl. His eyes are empty, his heart is clearly broken. Her arms and legs dangle limply. They testify wordlessly that she is dead.

The children gasp. Their expressions are real, without a trace of pretense or artifice, especially the little sister. Her awestruck eyes seem to swallow the film's light.

#*Introduction*

This story—leaving aside the question of whether this is in fact a story—is the record of an extended interview with that renowned man of letters and murderer, Jundo Mamiya. I can't post the complete transcript, please bear with me. The interview can't be related in a sequence of orderly sentences. It's not even an interview in the usual sense. The subject—Jundo Mamiya—died thirty years before the conversation took place. And the interviewers—<I> and <I>—are not human either, in the ordinary sense of the word.

The interview was also, in and of itself, the struggle with Imajika. At its peak, this epic confrontation commandeered three percent of humanity's total computing resources. Those untold myriads of calculations make up the substance of this interview.

I can already picture you wincing, but I must impose on your patience and add one more thing.

<I> and <I> are not first-person pronouns. You'll be very close if you think of them as proper nouns temporarily allocated to a specific program. When the subject is <I>, it doesn't automatically mean singular. Let's just say that <I> is a placeholder for the subject of the sentence.

Naturally you're going to end up reacting to <I> and <I> as the first person; no harm done. I won't even object if you assign a male voice to <I> and a female voice to <I>. Allowance has been made for that too.

What follows is the tumultuous story of how Jundo Mamiya, a notorious killer who harried scores of victims to the grave, returned from death to strike down a monster. But on the surface, it's nothing more than a quiet conversation. Even an action-packed novel is written out on a silent monitor—or on paper. This story is no different.

That's enough prologue, I think.

You're free to go now.

If you do, I'll ask you not to return. And I'll say, Go in Peace.

2.

The elevator descends quietly. <I> am trapped within my sensation of movement, falling toward an underground prison, closing in on a single prisoner confined in the bowels of the earth.

There are two elevators only. The indicators display no floor numbers. Individual digits and letters flash by and vanish with dizzying speed. The Justice Ministry officer who brought me as far as the elevator told me this was how they keep escapees from finding out which floor they're on. Other than knowing that I'm in a prison built into an abandoned mine, I have no clue where I am.

Faint vibrations penetrate the soles of my shoes. The weight I gave up earlier is returned. I straighten my collar, smooth the hem of my skirt, and cough lightly. Two corrections officers wait in the corridor. An elaborate procedure verifies my identity. The older one says, "Thank you for your patience. Do you want to see him right away?"

His misgivings seep through the politesse. It's not because of my youth, lack of experience, or slim build.

We walk down the corridor. A barred gate slides open, metal grating on metal, an atavistic sound. The younger officer steps me through the rules. Do not approach the barrier. Do not accept anything from him. Anything you need to give him goes into the cell through the sliding meal tray. No pens, no pencils. No paperclips. And no conversations of a personal nature under any circumstances.

I almost laugh in his face. Personal? That's right. I have to act like a "person" in here.

My houndstooth jacket is tacky. My bag clashes with my shoes. This dungeon is so overdone. Do I have to explain the meaning of every one of these things?

"Well then." My escorts pull up short before the final gate. "This is as far as we go."

I walk on. The gate rumbles shut behind me. Barred cells line the left side of the corridor. All of them are empty. Farther down, a steel pipe chair stands in the middle of the corridor, facing Jundo's cell. He is the only prisoner here.

I sit down and face the cell. Jundo is directly across from me. Between us stretches a heavy glass barrier.

He sits cross-legged on the bed with his back against the stone wall, staring at me.

Jundo Mamiya. Forty-five years old. Novelist, playwright, poet, critic. At the pinnacle of his fame, the inexhaustible fount of a staggering oeuvre, each work without peer. A year from now, he'll confess to seventy-three murders and pass sentence on himself, a sentence with no possibility of appeal.

He killed himself.

Jundo Mamiya. Just over five feet, heavily muscled like a judoka. Round face atop a thick neck, hair cropped close to the scalp. He's utterly motionless, but he seems capable of sitting in this cross-legged posture for hours and then instantly breaking into a sprint. I'm certain he could reach me in a single motion. I can't relax. Even with the barrier—

I erase that from my mind very quickly. Just the thought is dangerous.

"You needn't worry. I won't move from this spot."

Jundo speaks. It's like my thoughts are transparent to him.

"You were observing my posture. You're right; my body is idling. It's a technique of mine. But I repeat, you needn't worry. I've no intention of harming you. I've been craving someone to talk to."

Coming from Jundo, nothing is more terrifying than *you needn't worry*.

"It's nice to meet you."

"Welcome. Why are you here?"

"I want to talk with you."

"Conversation. I've been dying for it. What's the topic? Concerning what I did? Or what I'm going to do?" Jundo asks.

"Neither. People have been grilling you about your actions since you were a child. Criticism from parents and teachers. Fawning counselors interviewing you. I'd like to keep discussion of your past history to a minimum today. Just so you know, I already know everything about you. I've read your novels and essays, all several hundred of them."

Jundo rarely blinks. His face is a mask. He fixes motionless, half-closed eyes on me. "Nothing."

"What?"

"I don't smell anything." He points to the small round openings in the barrier. "When I have a guest, the trace aromas tell me whether the weather is fine or if it's raining in the world up above. I can infer your brand of soap. Perfume. Skin lotion. But—" The slightest hint of wariness crosses his face. "There's no odor about you at all. Fascinating. All sorts of airborne particles stick to people's clothing and hair as they move. But not to you."

Jundo was a master profiler. He could characterize someone accurately from the smallest detail, even on first meeting. Casual conversation was all he needed. Invariably the other person would end up spilling his secrets without intending to. In such situations, Jundo often used his sense of smell as a guide.

Which is why I made sure to erase any odor.

"Are you really human?" he asks.

I pause. "Are you really human?"

A beat. Jundo is silent. He's usually very verbal, but he can use

silence strategically. This is different. He's thinking, vast compu-
tations. The response comes back after a lag. Does he suspect the
meaning of my question?

"Intriguing. I'd have thought I was thoroughly tired of that
question. But in this context, it's refreshing."

"Mr. Mamiya—"

A gesture cuts me off. "You haven't told me your name."

I shake my head and smile. "I don't have a name."

Jundo's narrow eyes close. "No scent. No name. You're far more
interesting than a riddle. And that…that ensemble! That truly
makes me want to hold my nose. It reeks—the rube jacket, the
shabby pumps. Completely beyond redemption. It's not what you
usually wear, is it?"

"What do you think?"

"Did someone put you up to this?" Jundo asks.

"I wonder."

"There'll be a motive of some sort. You planned that getup. And
the subtext?"

I'm at a delicate juncture here. If all I had to do was guide his
attention to the truth, things would be straightforward. But I have
to get him to notice the significance of the situation on his own by
feeding him tiny hints that are hardly even clues.

"Ah, yes," says Jundo. "Now that I think of it, I recall a scene just
like this. From a movie?"

"Yes."

"I see."

Jundo turns his face toward the wall. The rough-cut stone
trapezoids are like the wall of a fortress. A fortress buried in the
earth, tens of meters deep. Captivity with no possibility of escape.

"Mmm, very impressive. Yes." He considers. "And what was it
you wanted to talk about?"

"I'd like you to take a look at this." I take a book from my bag, an
old, heavy book. *Moby-Dick*. The tome is large and thick. The surface

of the massive leather cover is a jumble of bulges and furrows: tree roots, knots, an old man's veins. The pages are swollen, bursting from the covers.

"Waterlogged?" asks Jundo.

"You'll take a look?"

I put the book in the meal tray and slide it into the cell. As Jundo opens the book, the pages separate with a sickening, gelatinous sound. His face contorts with disgust.

"What is this, the work of some author who thinks he's an artist?" He holds the book out to me. The letters multiply, spill out of their lines, overlap, devour each other, get bigger, turn pages black, metastasize to the cover, penetrate it, fuse into knots.

"No. It's an ordinary book. No gimmicks. One day it changed. In the end, it became what you see. No outside agent did that. The letters did it themselves.

"Mostly it starts unnoticed. Letters in a line multiply. Closer examination shows the letters overlapping and replicating. Spaces open up in words, splitting them into terms with unknown meanings. The process accelerates. Soon the letters spill into the gaps between lines. They can't be contained. The letters begin to overlap. Words join and swallow each other up or divide into new words."

The phenomenon manifests in a variety of forms. Sentences on a page might intertwine into a helix. Chapters shrink or explode. Letters expand or flake off the page. New pages form, letters invade the new space and breed there. Further detail would be pointless. That corpse of a book sprawled in Jundo's cell—that tumor-devoured carcass—testifies to this bizarre destruction more eloquently than anything. But the carcass is not the final stage.

"And you ask me to believe that?"

I shrug my shoulders and glance at *Moby-Dick*. "Why would I come all the way here just to lie? You can see what's happening yourself. And you already believe, don't you."

Jundo's confidence in his senses is absolute. If he can see it and smell it, it's real. That's his creed. His calm is unshakeable.

"It's not just this book, is it?"

"Unfortunately no. Thousands, tens of thousands of books have been infected by the same disease. And not only books."

I take a plastic case from my briefcase. A movie disc. The jacket photo shows two little girls in white standing side by side. An endless red-brown plain stretches into the distance behind them.

"I don't see the anomaly," says Jundo.

"At a certain point in visual works, a catastrophe occurs. The content changes."

"May I see it?"

"Certainly." I pass the disc through the slot.

"Oh, that's right." He gives me an elfin wink. "Now you just need to send through the equipment to let me watch this."

"Very easily done."

"How are you going to get it in here?"

I don't answer immediately.

"The person who designed and built this cell—that was you, wasn't it?" says Jundo. "No, this jail, this whole prison is probably your creation. And you created me too, didn't you? Created and 'loaded' me here."

I sigh, satisfied. Jundo's acuity is truly marvelous. Not totally accurate, but still outstanding. I should mention that he was never held in a prison like this when he was alive. This is nothing more than an imagined location, generated from moment to moment.

"I'll prepare a viewing device now." I gesture. A fully equipped screening setup appears in the corner of the cell, but Jundo shows no trace of surprise.

"So why are you here?"

"I wanted you to know that this phenomenon exists. We call it Imajika. All you have to do is talk to me, like we're doing now."

One of Jundo's eyes closes very slowly, then opens again. "And the reward?" Apparently that was a wink.

"I know you'll like it."

I take a small cassette tape player out of my bag. Its shell is cast as a single unit, completely enclosing the cassette. All risk has been carefully eliminated.

"Magnetic tape. Very contemporary." Jundo happily accepts the machine and presses one of its buttons. They're in a line, like a keyboard. "Let's hear what we've got."

The *Goldberg Variations* flows from the toylike speakers. The sound quality is superb.

"Thank you. It's not Gould, is it? But still, a wonderful performance. So—how should I say? So human." A satisfied smile spreads over his face. He quietly hums the melody.

I don't trust that smile.

Yet even Jundo's smile is nothing more than my creation, a product of literal technology.

Jundo Mamiya.

A monster, fashioned from our corpses.

#Imajika

Alice Wong's status as Imajika's first victim is debated, but we won't try to settle that here. Without a doubt she was an early example, one so sensational and tragic that it was carved into our memory as a crime for the ages. That much is certain.

Alice was a celebrated poet. That morning, about three weeks after her thirteenth birthday, she was out on her daily run, working out ideas for new poems. No one else was on the streets at that hour. Her family was still in bed when she left the house. The wind carried a foretaste of the winter to come, and Alice loved the bracing feeling of cutting through it as she ran. The road was nearly dry, but the air still held the fragrance of rain from the night before.

#Like eyes purified by tears #Autumn's fair daybreak unfolds, crystalline

This verse was left behind by the swarms of CASSYs that Alice used to propagate her apparently endless streams of poems. With their stripped-down feature set, restricted message size, and bare-bones AI, these unsophisticated CASSYs were blunt tools, but they could piggyback toll-free on the city's pervasive services net, and they acted as useful assistants. Alice's generation of women used CASSYs as personal secretaries to continuously convert their thoughts and actions into text. Users could choose from a wide range of expressive styles, all of them awful. But for Alice and her friends, that quirky AI style was part of the fun.

CASSY-generated text—with location data, timestamp, ambient temperature, street views, and user browsing history—were routed to GEB, which stripped out personal ID tags and absorbed the text into its resources. GEB's archive of anonymous murmurs and actions from people all over the world expanded constantly, from moment to moment.

Alice often wove worthless CASSY snippets into her own poems. Her touch transformed these childish phrases into something compulsively appealing.

#Long black hair in a pony tail/effortless acceleration/sugar maples by the road/crimson leaves splinter morning sunlight

Alice's voice and movements were recorded from tens of different distances and angles. Physiological data generated by bloodstream and nervous system sensors, links to the dozen or more literary works she was consulting, the music she was streaming, observation data from satellites in the orbits of Mars and Jupiter—the fresh data streaming over her from the pervasive services network was like an energizing wind as she ran that morning.

Was her existence unraveling into untold strands of data? Or were strands of data weaving her into existence?

As she focused on her run, she began to feel body and spirit funneling into the narrow borderland between weaving and unraveling. Far off within the vast space of her mind she saw a horizon, a mind regarding itself. Something reverberated there. She strained to make it out.

Along that horizon, her poems were born.

#Humanity in this era has nearly abandoned poetry #Since the Entangled Bookshelf and literal technology absorbed human knowledge, literature has not made a single creative impact #Alice Wong was one of the doves that landed on that blasted plain with an olive branch in her beak #A genius who limned herself anew in the tension between clashing character strings, cascading from all directions

#The run was going great #Her horizon was sharper than ever, she felt the stirrings of several poems #She was in such good form, she wanted to start outputting them as soon as she got home

#Feeling refreshed, she glanced up at the bright sky #She stopped to look at something strange in the sky #Her streaming hair fell to her back

#Pebbles floating in the sky

#Definitely there, floating high off the ground #But then they would be more than ten meters across #Shape and texture, smooth, like something from a stream bed #Ordinary pebbles, floating in the sky #Alice rubbed her eyes in surprise

#Then there was just one pebble, as if there wasn't a sky at all #No sense of illusion, no Magritte feel, just a realistic pebble

#And

#In an eye blink, the stone disappeared

Alice craned her neck, peering upward. Whatever had been there a moment ago was nowhere to be seen.

By now, Alice had already been subjected to an intrusive, destructive contact from Imajika. In a split second—from her point of view—the contact ended and Imajika was gone. Alice resumed her run without realizing what had happened. She went back to planning her next batch of poems, completed her usual circuit, and returned home. Her selfhood had already been destroyed, but she had no awareness of it.

As the maid served breakfast, Alice turned to her mother to tell her about the strange sight she had witnessed. She searched for a word, cocked her head.

And froze.

She was trying to remember how to say something she had never said before, but Imajika had already destroyed the retrieval pathways. The features that made Alice distinctively herself, personal settings she had fashioned over thirteen years, were corrupted; her search function was disabled. Her awareness had lost its way. But because there was no return path, she dropped.

Living organisms are highly flexible systems. The brain can recover from sleep, lapse of consciousness, or corrupted aware-ness as though nothing happened. Before her family even noticed, Alice's awareness moved smoothly to reboot itself.

But her settings were corrupted. No one knows what Alice saw when those settings were read into her mind on startup. The maid's CASSYs recorded the entire tragedy. Alice screamed throughout the incident. She was the fearful exterminator, but she was also the one who was most fearful, the most ravaged by terror. Two people died and three were slightly injured in the Wong Family Dining Room Incident. Her mother, mortally wounded, crawled into the kitchen. A falling refrigerator—she had toppled it to create a barricade—killed her daughter. The mother was declared dead two hours later at the hospital.

That was as far as it went, at least at the scene of the crime.

The problem was that Alice Wong was a poet.

Alice's poems were not written by putting pen to paper. Such poems were already extinct. Her poems were a typhoon of words run amok on GEB, the "Golden Eternal Bookshelf," as she thought of it. With CASSY support, Alice often generated up to a hundred poems a day. When new poems were entered into her archive on

GEB, the words were deployed according to their potential, mixing with previous poems, multiplying and dividing repeatedly, keeping her works fresh and new. GEB was home to several thousand collections of poetry, but Alice's poems were the most full of life, the most introspective and sensual, and her readers were hungry for more. As her collection detonated other works and devoured them whole, it grew to almost unequaled size.

If typhoons are like living organisms metabolizing heat and water, Alice's poems were a life force that metabolized the freshness of language. Alice was nearly always online, connected to her collection of poems, and although she and her CASSYs were contributing new poems all the time, the typhoon was never the same from moment to moment, yet never anything but distinctively Alice Wong.

Some people are excited by typhoons. Others chase tornados. Alice's poems were accessed by a vast audience that loved her gale force winds.

This morning was no exception.

The corruption of her settings spread to this typhoon of words, sending it spinning out of control. Some who surfed in to rubberneck at the explosion of language were killed instantly. Hundreds of others had their settings totally corrupted. The impact varied, but a few of these victims were driven to acts that closely matched Alice's.

That was only the first-order damage. At least it was restricted. The real damage occurred several seconds later, when the countless secondary works linked to Alice's typhoon took the impact, precipitating a cascade effect.

All at the whim of Imajika.

3.

<I> am watching a movie.

An overwhelming plain stretches across the frame. A dry land, blanketed with small stones. The sparse grass is white-brown, but I can't tell if it's dry or just looks that way on the screen.

Two small figures sit in the foreground. Sisters, the girls who were watching *Frankenstein* in the town hall. They're wearing matching white clothes, holding book satchels, looking out over the endless plain from a small rise. The ground slopes gently down to the gigantic plain at their feet, with nothing to break the line of sight all the way out to the distant, blue-shrouded mountains. A featureless waste you would only see in Westerns.

The wind is blowing. I feel the sound of the wind gradually merging with the clicking of the projector at my back. In fact, that uniform plain is getting hard to distinguish from the screen itself.

Tiny waves of movement seem to envelop the screen. Is it waving grass? Is it film grain? Maybe it's just noise in the audience's vision?

"That house. With the well."

The older girl points below them. A small building comes into sight and disappears again, half buried in the waving of the plain. There seems to be a well next to it.

"Is he there?" says the younger one. Her sister has told her that the house shelters Frankenstein's monster from the movie—actually, it houses the Spirit of the Beehive.

The girls stand and walk down the slope. Their receding forms quickly grow smaller, then tiny, melting into the wind, into the film grain and the visual noise. They pass into the screen itself—into the source of the movie.

I lean forward. Something terrible is coming.

This location, this movie that was released in 1973, is also within Imajika's reach. The presence gets stronger. I clench my fists on my knees. My hands tremble violently. I feel the urge to get up and run.

But escape is forbidden.

The figures finally disappear. The waving of the plain is violent now. The sand-colored film grain runs amok.

Then it happens.

On the undulating surface, at the center of the plain, a hemisphere pushes up like soft candy, a huge bubble. The hemisphere grows with uncanny speed and spreads its footprint. It expands faster and faster, pulling the landscape along with it, and in a moment covers more than half the plain. But its footprint, its diameter, keeps expanding. More than half of the sphere is still below the surface.

I am resigned to my fate. The sphere dwarfs everything on the screen. It's bigger than the screen itself. The swelling quickly reaches the edges of the screen, spreads beyond them and engulfs the row of seats in front of me.

I can only look up and away. When I look back, the sphere has fully emerged. A sand-colored rock now floats where the movie was, in an utter void, like a small, incongruous, sandy moon.

Then the surface of the sphere crumples inward, as if unable to bear its own weight. Chasms form and rumble inward, collapse upon collapse, altering the surface contours with a violent roar.

I watch as scene after scene from the movie, scenes in motion, are sucked into that parched avalanche. I listen as fragments of soundtrack—dialogue, music, and effects—rumble in a last dying convulsion. Then the rumble is cut off, the collapse stops, and suddenly the orb morphs into the very image of Méliès's weeping moon.

Again the chasms collapse and the moon's surface is reshaped and transformed, and now it is not a moon, but a fist—a fist clenched so tightly, I'm certain the fingers have fused.

4.

The walls in the high-ceilinged room are lined with bookshelves that are filled with dark, leather-bound volumes. The books absorb the light, pushing this study a long step past four PM, the time it is now, toward night. The gold-inlaid titles on the spines have flaked off and the dyed leather has darkened. What little light there is comes through a tall, narrow window. The window is floor to ceiling, about a foot and a half wide. It can't be opened, and the light coming through it is enervated, scattered by the complicated layout of the courtyard beyond.

A large, old-fashioned chair stands next to the window. Its legs and armrests are elegantly curved. The seat back is broad. <I> place—I placed—Jundo Mamiya in that chair.

Jundo clears his throat and blinks his slitlike eyes. The expression in those tapered, hooded eyes is hard to read. His eyebrows are slender. His head is shaved. Jundo strokes his face from cheek to chin. He strokes his ears and shakes his head slowly. His neck is thick with muscle. His body seems to be bursting from its short frame. Jundo Mamiya in his late thirties, vigorous and robust. His shirt has a standup collar. His pants are silk. On his feet, leather slip-ons.

"Nice to meet you. Is this room suitable?"

Jundo looks dissatisfied. "What are these clothes? I can't take them off."

"Your clothes have no buttons. No metal clasps or strings. No belt, of course, and no seams. Everything woven to fit your body. You can't take them off, unless you rip them off."

Jundo's clothes were generated along with the rest of him moments ago.

"There's something rather peculiar about this situation. You have me at an overwhelming disadvantage, I take it."

"The clothes were a hint, yes."

"And you can erase me anytime?"

"Yes. And I'm afraid you can't influence me with words."

You are completely at my mercy. That's sure to get a rise out of Jundo. Maintaining the right degree of resistance is part of my role here. Extremely dangerous, but unavoidable. We need as many Jundos as we can generate, and we need a wide range of variation.

"There's something I really must object to." Jundo gestures toward his left ear. "This. I certainly can't accept this."

Jundo's left ear is smaller and less mature than his right. It is his ear at age thirteen.

"I'm sure you know I cut this off when I was in elementary school."

"I'm aware of that. You had two last names then, didn't you? At school you used Mamiya, your mother's name. Your father's name was on your birth certificate. You were living with your mother in a provincial town of about thirty thousand. You cut off your ear in order to murder your teacher during a home visit."

"I didn't kill her. She did it herself," Jundo says.

"She used your knife to stab herself in the throat."

"That's right. Mrs. Tsuge used my knife. Thank you—I hadn't thought of that name for a long time. Yukiko Tsuge."

"Your teacher had no reason to kill herself, of course. She had a warm family life with a husband, a daughter in fourth grade, and a son in kindergarten. She was happy."

"She had her reasons. We all do. I just gave her a little encouragement."

"You manipulated her. No threats, no hypnosis, just conversation—"

Jundo had the ability to drive people to suicide with nothing more than conversation. This he confirmed in writing before his death. If it struck his fancy, he could make you take your own life, no matter who you were.

Seventy-three victims. His final testament contained a list of their names.

Each one had proved to be a real person. They each had had a relationship with Jundo, just as he stated. He knew the time and manner of each death. Yukiko Tsuge was his eighth victim, which meant Jundo had already wielded this power as a child. His first victim was the father of a classmate, a man widely known for making violent threats. On his way to work, he jumped the center divider and plowed head-on into several other cars, dying instantly. The evening before he was killed, he had been talking to Jundo.

Some victims took their own lives on the spot, others committed suicide months or years after their conversation with Jundo. According to his testament, he found it amusing to force people to recall long-forgotten personal secrets and sins. Then he would bore in and finish them off.

Jundo's testament reproduced an example, a fragment, of one of these exchanges. It ended in the suicide by poison of a fellow writer his age. Everyone who read the account was struck by a physical conviction that it was genuine. It was as if the letters Jundo used to record the conversation began to move like insects on the page, crawling under the nails of the hand holding the document. The quiet abuse he unleashed on his victims is still under analysis by more than one organization.

"—just conversation."

"Not always." Jundo looks annoyed. "Words weren't enough for Mrs. Tsuge. She was obstinate. She wouldn't go over the edge until I gave her my ear. It was never that difficult before. That was my biggest disgrace. The worst stain on my record. I made up my mind never to repeat such a blunder. So you see, my missing ear is the core of my identity. But you've grown it back. You mock my dignity."

He doesn't look as angry as he sounds. His eyes are a mix of boredom and irritation with a trace of interest. A viscous look, something slowly mixed together and congealed, like the film on a bowl of porridge gone cold. That disturbing gaze, the one that comes to mind when anyone hears the name Jundo Mamiya.

"The ear of a child on an adult's head. The technology to do that without the slightest effort is the core of what I am. You regard yourself very highly, but you can't even escape this room with no locks. From where I sit, you're a nonentity."

Jundo's eyes smolder. "I want this ear gone."

"Then maybe you'd like to do it again? I can't give you a razor, but you can always tear it off."

"Tell me to tear it off. I'll probably use all my strength to do it."

This surprises me, frankly. Jundo is nearing the core. No, he's already there.

"I'm sure you would. You are completely in our power."

"'Our power'? I see." Jundo never misses a detail. A man who can kill with a few words. Superhuman profiling ability. "This is some sort of project, isn't it? And I'm one of the inputs."

"Exactly."

"You regenerated my ear. You control me completely. Dress me in clothes I can't take off. How can such technology be?"

"You yourself are the proof of its existence." I manage to force that much out.

"At minimum, I seem to have no physical existence. Are you using some kind of emulator?"

"In a sense. But you know that simulating a real person's body and their mind and actions would be impossible. It's far too complex. Especially when the person you want to simulate has been dead for thirty years."

My function is to draw Jundo's attention to the fact that he's dead. That he is not of this world. That nevertheless, our literal technology has given him a brief resurrection.

We agents—thousands of us deployed throughout GEB—are each delineating thousands of Jundo Mamiyas. I am speaking to one of them. I speak to spark awareness.

You are one of the dead.

A patchwork monster.

A botched Ahab.

Then—

"And what if I'm not a simulation?"

The dead man, the monster, the Ahab, gets out of his chair and faces me. Small and tough. He stands relaxed, like a veteran judoka. The tall, narrow window behind him is turning the color of boiled pine pitch. Night is flowing in. Night air seems to rise from Jundo's body. I try to speak, but I only mumble. Is he controlling my will? Jundo takes a step forward.

"In that case, what are you doing?"

"I—"

I sense that Jundo has already reached this conclusion, but I speak anyway.

"I am 'writing' you."

#The Letter

Those happy hours we all spent together will never return
I have been praying to God to reunite us

I have prayed every day since we parted in the civil war
In this remote village
Where Fernando, the girls and I struggle to survive

Except for the walls, this house has changed completely
What could have happened to all the wonderful things we had
I say this not out of nostalgia
That is something I have not been capable of feeling for years

So much that we knew was lost, so much has been destroyed
Only sadness remains
Along with the things we lost,
I think we have also lost the strength to live life fully

I don't know if this letter will reach you
The news from outside is so sparse, so confusing
Please let me know that you are alive

All my love
—Teresa

5.

\<I\> am in a decaying apartment. It's a three-story public housing block surrounded by farmland on the outskirts of a small provincial town. The tatami mats are sun-bleached, scuffed, and gritty with dust. I see paddy fields through grime-clouded windows. It's been years since anyone cleaned them. The golden rice stalks lie flattened by yesterday's typhoon, as if some gigantic dog shed its fur all over the fields.

I turn away from the sliding window and shut the paper screen. The paper is spotted with round stains. A young boy is sitting on the floor, kneeling on a cushion with his heels under his buttocks. Black shorts, a white shirt. His left ear is already gone. His shirt is dyed crimson from shoulder to chest. The cushion is squishy with blood, but not his blood. His teacher faces him in the same formal posture, torso thrown forward. Her forehead touches the tatami. Her hands are pinned beneath her throat. The point of a knife protrudes from the left side of her neck. She probably died less than an hour ago.

I hear the musical sundown announcement from a distant PA system, a distant melody. A child's voice speaks over the music. "All primary school students, time to go home now." The voice belongs to Yukiko's daughter, but the boy may not know it. He moved here less than two months ago.

"Niwahiko? You're Niwahiko Taira."

The boy glances up sharply. He'd locked the door from the inside.

"Who…?"

Niwahiko's last name will not formally change to Mamiya for five years. Jundo is a pen name he'll use when he publishes his first collection of works in his second year of middle school. Right now he's Niwahiko Taira. His arms and legs are skinny. He's still just a child.

"Don't move. You don't want to start bleeding again."

Of course, healing him would only take a moment, but I feel it would be better to avoid that. The tatami is gritty with dust. The paper screens are missing random sections like gapped teeth. The room is so littered with plastic supermarket bags and cast-off clothing that it's hard to avoid stepping on them. An old game console. Unopened mail scattered about. A black coat hanging from the stump of a broken light fixture.

Standing there, I feel the poverty that fettered Niwahiko.

"All you all right? That's a terrible wound."

Of course he's not all right. Niwahiko actually fainted from shock and loss of blood within a few minutes of severing his ear. What I am "writing" now embellishes the truth to render Niwahiko Taira with crystal clarity.

"What were you and your teacher doing?" I sit next to Niwahiko.

"We were just talking."

Yukiko Tsuge is a thickset, tanned woman with a broad back in a short-sleeved pink polo shirt. The skin on her elbows is thick and dry. Her wiry hair is short.

"Do people stab themselves in the throat just because of something someone said?"

Niwahiko doesn't react.

"This is the eighth time, isn't it?"

The boy's pupils dart sideways, but he quickly conceals his panic.

"Did you have to go this far?"

He stares at the floor. A new emotion wells up that he can't hide. He looks terribly discouraged—almost despondent. He's here because he was craving something. It was a craving he couldn't fulfill. A frail, delicate boy. This is so unexpected that I had to sit next to him.

"You had to do it, didn't you?"

Niwahiko is silent.

"You wrote a composition right after you came to your new school. 'Mrs. Tsuge is always smiling, and she has a loud voice, and her hand was so strong when she shook hands with me, and her skin was so rough that I was surprised. Later I heard it was from playing softball. I've never seen such a sunburned teacher in all the schools I've been to.'"

Plain, unadorned sentences. That's important.

During his life, Jundo Mamiya wrote over a hundred thousand pages of text, every sentence a superflux of expressive power and weird technique, with an abnormal kinesthesia that seemed to burrow deep inside the reader. That style was his signature, right from his first-grade composition about a school outing. He wrote using plain language only once.

"You liked Mrs. Tsuge, didn't you?" I put my hands on Niwahiko's. His hands are very cold. "I don't mean as a woman. But you felt something when you touched those strong hands, didn't you?"

Niwahiko clenches his small hands into hard fists, like his heart.

"You have a talent that frightened you. And you thought she had the strength to stand up to it. But you couldn't control your power. The more she resisted, the more you sent it back at her. You finally had to cut your ear off before you could push her over the edge."

Then I notice something.

Niwahiko has no fingers.

Or more accurately, his fingers have fused. His fists are as hard as stone. I reflexively try to pull my hands away. It doesn't go so well.

I look again. My hands are embedded in Niwahiko's fused fists.

A low, small voice says, "You're stuck now."

That's not possible. In the graphiverse, I—we—possess absolute, unrestricted license to delineate worlds any way we please. Worlds appear just as we write them. Therefore, I should easily be able to withdraw my hands from these fists of stone. And that's when it finally hits me. There is no one who can write "My hands are embedded in Niwahiko's fused fists" except me.

Or is there?

I don't know. I don't know.

"Would you listen to what I have to say?" Niwahiko's voice is serene. "I found out something nice. If I hold on to your hands, it means you won't die like my teacher. You can't run away from me either. You can't cover your ears. I can talk forever and you'll listen."

Who is writing Niwahiko's words?

Is it me?

Is it Imajika?

Or is it Niwahiko himself?

"You'll listen no matter how long I talk. Won't you."

6.

Three space cruisers commanded by Jundo Mamiya attack a sentient rock in orbit around Mars.

Or: *Jundo the Barbarian leaps atop the monster as it rises out of the water. He plunges the stone point of his spear into its slimy back.*

Whatever <we> write happens as soon as we write it. That is the unique feature of this cathedral we have built in the graphiverse, with Gödel's Entangled Bookshelf and literal technology. We don't have to write the details. All we need is an outline of the basics, even a single sentence. The fine details are built up by legions of CASSYs.

GEB's CASSYs are more sophisticated than commercial agents.

Their sentences are more varied, more apt, and more original than anything a human might come up with—styles from the burning roughness of rotgut bourbon to the sensual swirl of whipped cream.

That's why <I> am here, in the captain's cabin of an old sailing vessel, sitting across from Jundo Mamiya. The age of steam is in the future. The cabin reeks of seaweed and whale oil. Everything is damp from sea spray.

"So? What new indignity is this?" Jundo scowls. I've written him with a wooden leg, like Ahab.

"I don't want you to run away."

"That's not it. I mean the food." The captain's dinner is salt pork and potato gruel.

"This ship left port a year ago," I remind him. "You're the captain. If you want something fresh, work harder. Catch a whale and you can dine on fluke steak."

No one on a whaling vessel yearns for whale meat. Even a fresh bloody steak wouldn't tempt the crew of the *Pequod*.

The sperm whale's massive head contains a prodigious cache of oil for candles and lubricants. The blubber under the hide also yields huge quantities of oil. Before petroleum distillates and cheap vegetable oil, the limits of civilization were practically defined by the availability of this single resource. Whales! Living oil fields, roaming freely across the world's oceans. To hunt them, humans perfected a system—huge winches to raise the carcasses, specialized knives to flense them, precise techniques for coiling harpoon rope, the surest ways to con men into joining the crew, when and how much to pay them, protocol between ships. Every facet served one goal: hunting whales. Humans always do this. They overadapt.

"You're the captain, go ahead and eat. You don't have to worry about appearances."

"Captain, am I? Do you expect me to bellow orders to the

crew? And in the final act, lash myself to Imajika as he dives for the depths?"

I smile. "No need to follow the movie script. Do as you like. This ship isn't searching for Imajika anyway."

"By the way—" The meat is so tough that Jundo gives up and throws his fork across the room. "You're quite a talker. Are all the rest of you like this?"

"Interviewing is our job. We talk to you. You respond. We output your responses immediately. We use a certain method to integrate your responses and generate virtual Jundo Mamiyas in other locations. We're compiling all the fine details. Calculating a complex mega-Mamiya."

"Interesting. I ask a simple question and you bury me with information. Aren't you worried that I might be the one who's interviewing you?"

Jundo sure knows how to get right under your skin. "It doesn't matter, actually. It won't affect our process."

"So you're out of reach. Well, it's nice to be confident. But I have one question. I hope you can give me an answer."

"Fire away."

"If you're writing me, I don't see how the 'me' you're writing can be Jundo Mamiya. It can't be anything more than 'you.'"

"That's a valid question. May I give you a slightly roundabout answer?"

I can hear the waves striking the prow. The creaking of timbers and the noises made by the crew flow beneath our voices. Everything is rocked by the ocean swells.

Everything surrounding us at the micro level is nothing more than text generated with blinding speed.

<I> am a composite generated by extended-feature CASSYs. I am outside this cabin. Whenever I write something I have to exit this setting.

First I have to explain how GEB originated. It's critical that Jundo understand this. Otherwise, "Jundo Mamiya" won't be able to fight Imajika on equal terms.

"Jundo, I assume you remember Gödel?"

"Don't mock me. I know what Gödel is, and CASSYs too. Gödel is the company that developed a totally new search algorithm. What was it called? PageRank? They stood the industry on its head."

"Correct. Gödel laid its foundations as a clever fusion of search and advertising. Their mission was to 'organize the world's information and make it universally accessible and useful.' Their business exploded—automated news editing, maps, photo albums, video upload, OS development. In 2009, they reached a settlement with authors to digitize the holdings of the world's libraries and make the content available to users.

"The official name of that new service was Gödel Entangled Bookshelf."

"I remember. They wanted to make money by digitizing everything published, complete with illustrations, then slice them up, ferment the slices, and create a data cloud like strands of sauerkraut. It didn't interest me at all."

"Really? Why not?"

Jundo actually wrote about this.

"I rarely read books. When I left middle school I'd read exactly seven hundred, and that was quite enough. Reading books was merely basic training, like pushups or marathon running. Very boring."

"Training for what?"

"To hold myself back. My words are too powerful. In first grade I wrote about getting carsick on the bus during a field trip. A teacher read it and vomited. Reading books taught me how much I had to dial back that power so people could read my works. It was truly mind-numbing."

"You had your power on a leash with everything you wrote?"

"Of course. Using my raw strength would hardly have been art. But no one noticed."

Indeed. If Jundo hadn't held back, who knows what might have happened to his readers.

"Well, I suppose it was useful. I didn't go to high school, but I could make as much money as I wanted. No need for academic credentials or family wealth."

"And the books you wrote were caught up in Gödel's project."

"I told you, I didn't care whether it helped my book sales or hurt them."

"I see. Then let's set this aside for the moment.

"So GEB was launched, and as expected, it generated huge amounts of red ink. First it focused on the world's libraries. Then it gradually expanded its net. Finally it started swallowing up any kind of printed material. Government and corporate publications. Handwritten manuscripts from before the invention of the printing press. Everything ever written anywhere in the world.

"Of course, the project included moving images, music too. Advanced analytics tagged images and musical effects with linguistic data that was fed into GEB's archives—to borrow your image, it became part of the sauerkraut. At first there were conflicts over author rights, but ultimately that hurdle was easily surmounted.

"GEB's real significance is that it put a vast amount of the world's 'paper' information into Gödel's belly."

"Its belly?" Jundo asks.

"People thought they were searching the Worldwide Web via Gödel, but they were searching a mirror of the web built up in Gödel's belly. Gödel used unique metaheuristics to parse and analyze the content: finding relationships, ranking them, performing countless iterations of the same operations on the metadata, and incorporating every search query into its evolution, moment by moment."

"And the 'paper' data went into the same belly."

"The sentences stored in GEB become, in a sense, anonymous.

Of course, they're tagged with author and publisher data, but parsed into phrases. The process of cross-linking starts immediately, and when users encounter a book's content, it's in the form of search results triggered by a key word. In GEB's library, the books are shelved with the spines facing inward."

"What's wrong with that? Authors and their obsession with rights bored me to death."

"There's more to the story," I say. "For one thing, there's far more information buried in paper data than even Gödel realized at first—enormous volumes of information, written down and recorded once, never read or understood by anyone.

"For example, say there was a minor conflict fought in some remote corner of nineteenth-century Europe. The only records might be trivial. A diplomat's expense report for a banquet. A procurement slip for a single overcoat or a knapsack. Hundreds of revisions to land registers after territory was surrendered. Pension records for thousands of soldiers. There are mountains of this kind of information. And people's memoirs, from best-selling works by politicians to the recollections of a private in the army, privately printed for some library."

"So by subjecting large volumes of mundane data to Gödel-style analysis," Jundo says, "and with the freedom to relate it to any other data on the Worldwide Web, one could gain unheard-of knowledge? Well, I suppose so. What else?"

"The development of LEBAB 1.0 and CASSY software agents."

The candlestick sways as a big swell passes. Our shadows lurch across the cabin wall. I haven't filled in any of the exterior details. A cabin and the motion and sounds of the sea are all there is. A captain's cabin suspended in the void.

"So what is LEBAB an acronym for?"

Now it's my turn to smile. "Not an acronym. It's just BABEL spelled backward. Gödel threw all of its resources into developing it. A unified, multi-language translation engine. But LEBAB is not just a tool for business and communication. It's deeper than that. It was developed to preserve languages in danger of extinction—and maintain them even after the last speakers died—and for languages that are already dead, or archaic forms of modern languages. It covers around ten thousand languages. In other words, one sentence added to Gödel immediately gives birth to ten thousand versions in other tongues.

"As long as they're locked up in libraries, books are nothing more than paper and ink. Until the stacks are opened and the books are opened, their voices will be silent."

"But once they're digitized, they can't remain silent," Jundo says.

"Correct. Texts that have never been read will reach out to form connections with other texts. Or with visuals. With music. CASSYs—Complex Adaptive Software Systems—are the intermediaries that make that happen. They're programmed to respond in different ways to meaning, seek out sentences that stimulate those responses, and build a higher intellectual synthesis through the connections they create."

"And these are your ancestors?"

"Yes. Driven by search queries, we till GEB's fields without a moment's rest. But GEB grew too complex. No human knows what GEB holds. They can calculate its size and structure, but that's all. GEB's substance, and the nature of the meanings being generated there, are beyond them. GEB is a gigantic synthesis of meaning, mentation, and correspondences that far exceed anyone's comprehension. It's almost as if another natural world has come into being. People know it's there. They can use it. But to actually understand it? That day will never come."

"Even for you?"

"Does an ant grasp the structure of the anthill? We agents are just as restricted by our functions. CASSYs infer the intent behind a user's search request, consult multiple texts, and write best-fit results. We're extremely advanced for the purpose, but we're still nothing more than text searchers. Our lives are very short."

"You're generated each time someone initiates a query. You output the answer and that's it for you?"

I nod. "Generated on demand, then we're gone. We are a collective, designed to fulfill one purpose."

"A collective?"

"<I> am a temporary collaboration between thousands, sometimes tens of thousands, of micro agents. They return their search results. I synthesize them and write everything out according to specific policies. That's the simple version, anyway."

"It sounds complicated to me."

"Are humans any different?"

Jundo smiles cynically. "So all this, what you're writing now, our conversation—this is all search results?"

"Exactly."

"Then let me ask you—" Jundo leans forward slightly. Just this gesture changes the atmosphere. "Who ordered the search? And where did you search within GEB?"

"Mr. Mamiya. Can we return to your original question?"

"Hm?"

"What you're asking is, if the Jundo Mamiya sitting here is merely being 'written,' and CASSYs are doing the writing, and if you're not a simulation, then where is the wellspring for Jundo Mamiya?"

"Well yes, I suppose."

"That's the question. Where we searched would be your answer.

"<We> searched your works, more than a hundred thousand pages of text, and other works you cited or mentioned, and all ten thousand translated versions, and works with strong associations to your works. Your favorite films and music too."

Jundo laughs. "You mean to say that you compiled words from my works and the works of others? And this cabin, this candle and this meal, and me with this wooden leg, this is a pastiche?"

"Yes. The words you just spoke all trace back to real sources, of course. Assembled word by word from different sources, that is."

"I see. You're 'writing' my speech by stitching dead words together. I'm a collected corpus, or maybe a collection of corpses. But is that really all it takes to make me Jundo Mamiya?"

"One Jundo wouldn't be enough. But <we> are simultaneously running tens of thousands of searches on texts with associations to Jundo Mamiya and returning huge volumes of results. Further calculations take place elsewhere at the individual text level. Tens of thousands of Jundo Mamiyas and Niwahiko Tairas are superimposed to create a Jundo Mamiya more complete than even the real Jundo himself could have comprehended."

"I'm still not convinced." Jundo licks his lips, as if his appetite has been thoroughly whetted. He searches for the words. "And if I should be lucky enough to find Imajika, what can I do? Imajika mutates humanity's intellectual assets, whatever their form. Correct? I'm nothing more than text. How could I possibly win? Though of course it is you who will lose, not me."

"The terms are even. Imajika itself only manifests as text."

"How's that?"

This is hard to absorb, even for Jundo.

"Imajika always appears as some kind of mineral—stone or pebbles, even a small moon—but that's not necessarily its true form. It may exist as an entity outside GEB. But Imajika may also be a phenomenon that arises spontaneously from within words themselves.

"What's certain is that Imajika always manifests via GEB, in the same way that music can only manifest as vibrations in a medium, regardless of its character. The way novels only manifest through language.

"Imajika does not so much rewrite words as it exists within that movement of being rewritten. In that case, we must write faster and with more effect than Imajika. You see?"

Jundo looks disgusted. "That means I'm expected to preach very fast, in a very loud voice."

"That's exactly what we expect."

#Alice Wong

Alice woke even earlier than usual that morning. It was dark outside. Even as a small child she had never lingered in bed, but today she was up immediately for a different reason.

She went to the beautiful writing desk that had been her mother's and her grandmother's before her, opened her laptop, and turned the sound low as she connected to Gödel Videoscope. A second screen, like an old cathode ray tube, appeared on her monitor. The screen showed a man fastened to a cross. Wong's large eyes had not completely lost their innocence, and they were transfixed by the man's image. A childlike, solemn gaze.

The man was covered with blood. His entire body had been flayed. The torso was divided midline, from sternum to pubic bone, and two large, symmetrical flaps of skin had been peeled upward like a pair of wings. The man was still alive.

This was not torture. The man was using a medical robot to methodically dissect himself. As suicide, this was so absurd as to be almost a joke. But the figure on that embedded TV screen was tinged with a startling majesty—and something else, something so unforgiving that Alice had to understand it. For three days, she had been watching this suicide unfold.

In point of fact, the suicide was consummated thirty years ago by a writer at the peak of his fame and wealth. He left an extensive written confession outlining his ability to murder just by speaking to his victims. Then he disappeared—until he suddenly surfaced on Gödel's video service to broadcast his self-mutilation to the world.

When Alice reached her thirteenth birthday, some of the parental controls were unlocked. She was engrossed in browsing previously forbidden sites when she stumbled across this video. What a contrived, exhibitionist suicide! The robot itself was the cross on which the man had bound himself. Ten or more automated arms moved independently, performing a programmed procedure upon the programmer himself. Of course, Alice had heard about this notorious performance before she found it on the web.

She had also read many of Jundo's works. His discursive style, like power held in check, made her wince sometimes. But beneath the bizarre embellishments, the lyricism and touching poignancy of his imagery were unmistakable. Alice loved the undercurrent of loneliness that pervaded his writing like the coolness of new sheets.

Before he mounted the cross, Jundo had said, "I want to disappear from this world, slowly but surely. I regret my crimes. Now the sentence must be carried out. Layer by layer I will be pared away, stripped away, and gradually I will diminish. I will die at some point, but I don't want you to know when that happens. When the last shred falls from this cross I will be gone, but my sins will not go with me. That is why I want to inflict suffering on myself that is commensurate with my crimes."

Bullshit.

Alice was certain of that instinctively. He is *so* lying.

Not like this public suicide was fake, and he's actually alive someplace. Saying he wants to disappear—that's phony. I'm surprised he didn't stick his tongue out at the end to let everyone know he was bullshitting them.

It's not that he wants to disappear. It's more that he doesn't want to. As an equally gifted writer, Alice had a feeling she understood.

He wants to escape to somewhere, she thought. He's not giving up, but he's not running away from anything either. Is this—dispersion?

It's no use, that's the way it is with words. Look away for a moment and they fall apart. Try to ditch you.

"But still…You left us a little too soon, Jundo," whispered Alice.

The figure's winglike flaps of skin had by now been carefully detached, and the pectoral muscles were being dissected. The massive chest, like a martial artist's, convulsed in agony.

Alice stopped the video, stood, and took off her pajamas. Clad in her underwear, she went to the window. The day promised fine weather. The sky was already light.

This was the one time of day when Alice shut down her CASSY links. Silently she watched as the sky brightened. Far above her, a long contrail caught the sunlight coming over the horizon.

That high up, the wind must be strong. As she watched, the contrail twisted on itself and morphed into illegible handwriting.

When she was a little girl, her parents told her, you used to pester us no end to read the contrails to you.

Little Alice had been certain they meant something.

Those were words up there, twisting in the wind.

6.

The flat-panel monitor in the corner of the cell now shows only the rock and the void.

At the halfway point, the movie buckled inward and became a pulpy mass, a weeping moon, and finally a tightly clenched fist, floating in utter solitude.

"That is Imajika."

<I> am explaining to a jumpsuit-clad Jundo Mamiya.

"The phenomenon isn't limited to text. Any GEB-readable work may come under attack. Often Imajika isn't satisfied with attacking a single work but propagates to any content with associations to that work. The damage spreads very fast, then stops, as if Imajika is trying to decide what to do next. The attacks keep happening. They're eating holes in GEB's data that can't be repaired."

Jundo doesn't seem too interested in either the video or my

explanation. He's fiddling with the tape deck. He played the tape twice; he must be rewinding it again.

"Christening it 'Imajika' was inspired. Whose idea was that?"

"GEB's system software did the naming. But Mr. Mamiya—it's the title of one of your works." I must look ecstatic. "Remember? The series of short stories about a book that has a different plot each time you read it. You started by quoting the narration in the movie we just saw. The letter that the mother of those little girls was writing to someone who doesn't appear in the movie."

"Hm. I forgot that one." Jundo's listless tone is mystifying. "But just because these works are being attacked, like this video here—it's only within GEB, right? Is that worth panicking about?"

"Many works now exist nowhere else. But the situation is more complicated than that. As a business entity, GEB was dissolved long ago. Now it's a shared public space, jointly maintained and administered by lots of nonprofit entities.

"GEB has huge numbers of CASSY-enabled users, all trailing data wakes after them in the course of their activities, the services they like, you name it. CASSY search results are stripped of personal data, so they're of no individual interest to anyone. But more than ten billion users are on the system, and everything gets translated. GEB generates networks of relationships between data. It takes in fresh, living detail about things happening all over the planet. Over time GEB has become the body of the world, free from notions of artistry, self-consciousness, or celebrity.

"That's what GEB is for people today—a garden where vast numbers of data trails are stored up. CASSYs are the gardeners, tilling their 'output' to make multitudes of flowers bloom.

"If the garden falls into ruin, the human spirit will wither as well. No—GEB is already part of the human spirit, the way sunrise and the sea and mountains of cloud used to be. The way the hustle of crowds or a warm fire or books and plays used to be. We've got to protect GEB from Imajika, whatever the cost."

Once more Bach flows from the deck in Jundo's hand. The work opens with a quiet theme—the aria—followed by thirty variations, and finally the aria again.

"There's something I just need to confirm."

Jundo finally speaks as the opening aria draws to a close. I expect the first variation next, but what I hear is number thirty, the so-called quodlibet.

"Wait a minute…"

"I tried reversing the playback order. What you just heard was the closing aria."

I'm about to explain to him that magnetic tape can't be played back that way. Then my jaw drops.

It can.

If we write it that way.

But who…?

I keep my voice calm. "What did you want to confirm?"

"Everything you write is in response to search queries, correct?"

"Yes…" This final variation combines melodies from different German folk songs. What were they titled…?

"Answer me. Who is the searcher?"

I don't intend to respond. I should conceal the truth to the end. But for some reason my mouth opens. The words flow.

"The searcher is Imajika."

<I> is not a first-person pronoun. Within GEB there is no subjectivity, no self, no awareness. Nothing but chains of letters, numbers, and symbols. <I> am not writing <I>. <I> am—is—simply a proper noun—according to—yes, according to something written somewhere.

"Imajika is querying GEB?" Jundo's calm hints that he had it figured out from the beginning.

"Yes…"

"Properly speaking, what you CASSYs decided to do was to try interpreting Imajika's contacts as queries. You surmised that the damage he was doing was questions—search queries—and you responded to them.

"I'm not surprised. Everything on the *Pequod* was optimized for whaling, and everything in GEB is designed to handle queries. Any system stimulus you detect evokes a search-and-results response. As many substructures—agents like you, all of you—as needed can be generated on demand, like an organism's immune cells. Imajika queries, you answer.

"Therefore everything written until now, including this little speech of mine, is Imajika 'interviewing' GEB."

Then Jundo gives me the order.

"Recite the emergency escape passcode. The one you were given when you came down here."

The red mishmash of letters and numbers that flashed by on the floor indicator. I recall them. In order. Jundo commits them to memory.

"Thank you."

The prison morphs, and somehow I'm trapped behind the glass barrier. Jundo is standing in the corridor in a trimly fitted suit.

"I'm very grateful to you, all of you. You've completed me as Jundo Mamiya. But not because you searched my works. *Because it was you who did the searching.*"

I can't find the words. Is it possible that he knew? About us?

"Of course I knew. Don't you think I'd know my own characters? They are all only myself. You probably analyzed my novels and absorbed my narrators' speech patterns. Which makes you my alter egos. I am you, searching my works.

"I think I also recognize the novel and the character. It's a pleasure to see you again."

If only CASSYs would let me feel emotion.

"Incidentally, that shabby outfit was what my mother wore to my first day of elementary school. Hand-me-downs from my grandmother, unfortunately."

An unbelievably gentle smile crosses Jundo's face.

The quodlibet flows again from the cassette deck in his hand.

Quod libet: What pleases.

My body suddenly feels light. I return to the position of narrator.

Jundo turns away and gestures lightly in farewell. The variations play back in reverse order as he walks off down the corridor. I'm guessing that about now, multitudes of Jundo Mamiyas are commencing their escapes from their respective domains.

But we anticipated this too.

By reading Imajika's contacts as search queries, we've already output a huge volume of results—so huge that individual works are spontaneously interacting to build a complex structure. By joining that structure, the sequence where I am now can be stable without writing Jundo.

Alone in the cell, I turn to the display panel again.

Imajika floats in the ash-gray void.

If I had known Jundo was that compassionate, perhaps it would have been okay to reveal Imajika's true nature to him from the beginning. Or perhaps his compassion is precisely why it was better that I didn't?

Embedded within this stone is a thing people have long yearned to understand but could never reach out and grasp. Something strong enough to overwhelm humanity's works. The works that humans created could not endure that force. They metamorphosed, crumpled, and transformed to stone.

That is why it has no name.

Not Hate, not Love.

Neither Life nor Death.

No one can read this stone. Not <I> or <I> or anyone alive.

Except—

Except, just maybe, this structure that is slowly coming to life can read it. Like an embryo weaving a new organ, in that space, with Imajika's queries as its pulse.

An indestructible, Intelligent Textual Organ.

This is our project.

#*The Spirit of the Beehive*

Alone, Alice trudges along. Suddenly she emerges into a huge open space. She's at the top of a small rise. The ground below slopes gently away to a broad plain with the dim peaks of mountains in the distance. The scenery reminds her of a film she saw once, with one big difference. The ground beneath her feet is not exactly ground. It flexes. There's a grain to the surface, like knit material. It almost feels like flesh, and it covers the surface as far as she can see. The slope, the plain, the mountains—everything is made of the same material. If she were to look closely, she would see that the surface is a lattice of tiny hexagons.

"Jundo, how could you?" Alice purses her lips with frustration. "This was my poetry collection!"

Managing Alice's collection required an immense calculation space. An educational foundation recognized her gifts and helped her borrow the necessary server capacity. But Imajika was growing more dangerous when Alice died, and afterward her space was appropriated to help deal with the threat.

Now thousands of "Jundo Mamiya" emulators are arriving here from all over GEB. Recursive correlation across incalculable volumes of Jundo Mamiya tweeting is slowly generating an exquisite structure of minute hexagons and truncated octahedrons. A honeycomb structure.

Our textual organ—spawned and ripened by Jundo's ideas, desires, and literary genius intertwined with the framework of Alice's collection—is generating this awesome landscape. "You're around here somewhere, aren't you? I promise I'll find you."

Alice felt sure that the landscape's resemblance to the famous sequence in *The Spirit of the Beehive* must mean something.

The heroine, a little girl, finds a fugitive soldier hiding in the house with the well, not far from the foot of the hill. And later, she has her encounter with Frankenstein's monster in the woods, by the lake, in a place where dreams and reality are indistinguishable.

In the center of the plain, where the little house should be, is a sphere half embedded in the ground, a gigantic Imajika.

"So you're here too? Just you wait."

Alice runs down the slope, digging her heels in to get traction on the soft ground, arms flung wide to keep her balance. Imajika is a deformed sphere that looks carved from a mountain's worth of rough stone, flinty and dense. Its rocky skin is cold and still. Alice doesn't sense danger here, for the moment at least.

From a distance the sphere appeared to be buried in the plain, but now Alice sees that the ground around it has buckled and risen up, as if it were slowly pulling the sphere down into itself. Ropelike strands of some mineralized material extend from the ground to the sphere, like mooring lines holding it back. The strands end in massive hooks that bite into the stone. The rock is riven and gashed around the hooks, traces of a mammoth struggle before the sphere was finally contained.

Those mooring lines are probably more remains of Imajika's victims, turned to stone. The ground around the sphere is slowly fossilizing the same way. Imajika might burst its bonds and run amok again at any moment. As she realizes this, Alice's eyes travel warily across the rock.

As she works her way across the undulating terrain, she finds herself on the other side of the sphere. What she sees makes her gasp with surprise. She stops in her tracks.

A battered wooden sailing ship leans against Imajika as if run aground. A man stands on the deck.

Jundo Mamiya.

But Jundo is not the reason Alice gasped.

From where she stands she now sees that Imajika, which looked at first like a stone sphere, is without a doubt the head of a gigantic whale, lunging from the ocean.

"Didn't Ahab have a wooden leg?"

"You think I'd put up with the way I was written?" Jundo Mamiya stamps loudly on the oil-stained deck with his thick, short legs. "See? I'll do this the way I want."

"Well, you go right ahead. Listen, this thing isn't going to wake up, is it?"

"I don't know. It's quiet now. Spooky."

"But why does Imajika appear in the form of stone?"

"This outer structure is not Imajika. It's an aggregation of all the works Imajika has vandalized, the mutated corpses of books and films. Imajika is inside. It armors itself with the corpses of its victims. Some of the original texts might still be readable if you look at the surface carefully."

"Texts like my poems?"

"Your poems…?" Jundo stares up at this young girl who is taller than he is. "By the way, who are you?"

"Allow me to introduce myself." Alice smiles, flashing those white teeth. "I'm your landlady. Except, as you can see, I'm a ghost."

If Jundo Mamiya is a monster stitched together from the corpses of words, this Alice Wong would have to be described as a ghost without even a dead body.

After contact with Imajika killed the physical Alice, the multiple Jundo Mamiyas that were written into this space acted on one another to create a complex new structure.

But then Alice's poems—poems too precious to be dispersed—where have they gone?

"Wouldn't you like to harvest Imajika's oil?"

"Oil?"

"I mean Imajika itself, under this armor. There's so much buried in what people have written, meanings they never even noticed were there. The reason is simple. Hundreds of people separated by hundreds of years have been writing about the same things in hundreds of languages. And there was no way to connect those dots until GEB's algorithm—its high-speed, multilanguage intertextual semantic relationship generator—stumbled across them.

"But GEB couldn't deal with these relationships because there was no way to assign them names. Whatever GEB can't deal with, it discards, and GEB discarded millions and millions of these relationships. It just went on finding and discarding them—until they returned, bringing a dynamic system with them. Imajika.

"That's what the head of this whale holds. Without names, they are outside the 'written' domain. The only alphabet that can write them is the wind.

"The wind is invisible. You can only see it when it leaves its imprint in a twisted contrail. It's the same with Imajika. You can't see it, but when it twists texts and turns them to stone you can see that power. You can see that yearning."

Alice points to the stone. "What do you think, Jundo? You can't find that anywhere these days. It ought to be amazingly valuable.

"I suppose it would. As valuable as an oil field," Jundo says.

"Even if that treasure is wasted on GEB, I bet the people who created this domain are hoping you'll extract that oil and bring a barrel of it back for them." Alice smiles her best smile.

"I see. And what's the next interview question?"

"Hm?"

"Drop the pretense. I'm not your enemy. Alice Wong—you're here to help Imajika, aren't you?"

Imajika devoured Alice's poems. For the embryonic Imajika, Alice's collection—huge and always powerfully moving forward—must have been a towering presence. And Alice herself became collateral damage.

As Imajika absorbed them, Alice's poems were deformed, crushed, and fossilized. Now they were probably part of this wall of stone.

Jundo Mamiya walks to the gunwale, stretches out his hand and puts a fingertip against the frozen rock.

"I told you," Alice says. "I'm a ghost. Your words were laid safely to rest in GEB, muscle and bone. CASSYs can dig them up and drench them with electricity. But my words got turned into whale hide."

Jundo had phenomenal profiling ability. He could draw inferences from almost any behavior and assemble them into a complete personality profile. That gift was now distributed throughout this plain, throughout the Intelligent Textual Organ. With Imajika lashed securely into place, Alice can be read directly from the surface of the stone.

"Jundo, please pay attention."

"What now?"

"I need to ask you something." Alice looks up at the sky. *The heavens are clear, but they're the same material as everything else.*

Humanity's words gently embrace Imajika.

Alice hesitates for a moment. "Did you really kill a bunch of people?"

"Yes, I did. After a bit of conversation with me, they all chose death. They had to."

Alice winces, exasperated. "You're so stiff-necked. Okay. Different question for you. You wrote that you talked to them because you wanted to murder them. You said you had a natural urge to kill. But that was a lie, wasn't it?" Alice is certain. "You wouldn't have cut your ear off just to push your teacher over the edge. You didn't have to. You had more than enough power. You wanted to restore her sanity. Or you wanted to amputate your own power. I'm right, aren't I?"

Jundo is silent.

"I knew right away when I read your books. You were a little Imajika. The people who talked to you—those seventy-three people? Afterward they realized what kind of people they really were, didn't they? It's like you put that powerful profiling ability of yours inside of them. Their everyday behavior, their little speech habits, their secret vanity, the sins they'd rather forget, the things they chose to remember—everything went into the profile, until their true makeup was staring them in the face. Everything they did and everything they said came back at them, completely transparent, totally decoded. Twenty-four seven. It must've been like being in hell."

"And that was only the beginning." Jundo finally speaks. "The transformation is progressive. It doesn't end with mere self-realization. Ultimately it can go far broader and deeper than that. The psychic structure collapses completely. Very few make it that far, but in the end I could never predict who could possibly survive so long."

"Weren't you ever afraid, Jundo? I mean, when all you had to do was talk to someone you were close to, and they died?"

"It's strange. I could never destroy my own inner structure. Like the hammer that can't hit itself."

"Jundo. In GEB, authors are anonymous, but CASSYs still found your works. Imajika wanted to read you, I'm sure of it. It had to be your words or nothing. I guess that shows how precious they really were."

Again, Jundo is silent.

"You died too soon. You know?"

"I suppose. Yes, too soon. I blundered. I spent years preparing carefully, but if I had known I'd be a witness to such fascinating events, I think I would've wanted to go on and on."

Like a gigantic monument, the whale seemed to be leaping toward the sky, as if it wanted to sink its teeth into it. Alice wondered if the time might come when it would succeed in doing just that to this tender organ.

That would be the end of humanity's words. They would be drenched in whale oil and vanish.

"What are you going to do now?" asks Jundo.

Alice is silent now.

Only as long as Imajika is captive can these two converse like this.

A monster and a ghost.

"Can I sit here a little longer?" she says finally.

"As long as you like."

Alice smiles impishly. "Thanks, I owe you."

Jundo Mamiya reaches out to touch Imajika again, when he suddenly sees that his hand is tightly clenched into a fist.

How long has he been clenching it? He hadn't even noticed he was doing it. That was because no one wrote him to notice it, but now he has a feeling he's been doing it all along, even when he was alive.

He tries to spread his fingers. The tendons and joints are contracted and stiff. His fingers are frozen. Jundo tries to pry his fist open with his other hand. Alice helps. She tries to worm her slender fingers into Jundo's fist. She tries using her teeth. They keep at it for a long time, until they're both covered in sweat, trying to force that fist open. And finally it does open.

They both cry out in surprise.

There in Jundo's palm is Niwahiko Taira's little ear, like the petal of a flower.

I would like to thank Sinjow Kazuma and Jyouji Hayashi for their helpful comments regarding my depiction of GEB.

COPYRIGHT
ACKNOWLEDGMENTS

CONTRIBUTORS

PAT CADIGAN sold her first professional science fiction story in 1980 and became a full-time writer in 1987. She is the author of fifteen books, including two nonfiction books on the making of *Lost in Space* and *The Mummy*, a young adult novel, and the two Arthur C. Clarke Award-winning novels *Synners* and *Fools*. In 1996, she emigrated to the UK and now lives in gritty, urban North London with the Original Chris Fowler, her son, the musician and composer Rob Fenner, and Miss Kitty Calgary, Queen of the Cats. She can be found on Facebook and Google+, and tweets as @cadigan. Most of her books are available electronically via SF Gateway, the ambitious electronic publishing program from Gollancz.

TOH ENJOE was born in Hokkaido in 1972. After completing a PhD at the University of Tokyo, he became a researcher in theoretical physics. In 2007 he won the *Bungakukai Shinjinshō* (Literary World Newcomer's) Prize with "Of the Baseball." That same year brought the publication of his book *Self-Reference ENGINE*, which caused a sensation in SF circles and which was ranked No. 2 on *SF Magazine*'s list of the best science fiction of the year. Since then, EnJoe has been one of those rare writers comfortable working in both "pure literature" and science fiction. In 2010 his novel *U Yu Shi Tan* won the Noma Prize for new authors. In 2011 his "This Is a Pen" was nominated for the Akutagawa Prize, and he won Waseda University's Tsubouchi Shouyou Prize. In January 2012, he won the Akutagawa Prize with "Doukeshi no Cyo" (Butterflies of a Harlequin). His other works include *Boy's Surface* and *About Goto*.

KEIKAKU (PROJECT) ITOH was born in Tokyo in 1974. He graduated from Musashino Art University. In 2007, he debuted with *Gyakusatsu Kikan* (*Genocidal Organ*) and took first prize in the Best SF of 2007 in *SF Magazine*. His novel *Harmony* won both the Seiun and Japan SF awards, and its English-language edition won the Philip K. Dick Award Special Citation. He is also the author of *Metal Gear Solid: Guns of the Patriots*, a Japanese-language novel based on the popular video game series. All three of his novels are available in English from Haikasoru. After a long battle with cancer, Itoh passed away in March 2009.

HIDEYUKI KIKUCHI was born in Chiba in 1949. He graduated from the Aoyama Gakuin University of Law and, inspired by H. P. Lovecraft, began publishing supernatural fiction in the early 1980s. One of the most prolific authors in the field, Kikuchi has published over three hundred books and still produces approximately one per month. He has enjoyed international success as a novelist, and much of his work has been adapted for manga and anime. Kikuchi is the author of the ongoing series *Vampire Hunter D. Wicked City*, *A Wind Named Amnesia*, and *Dark Wars: The Tale of Meiji Dracula* number among his works available in English.

KEN LIU (http://kenliu.name) is an author and translator of speculative fiction, as well as a lawyer and programmer. His fiction has appeared in *The Magazine of Fantasy & Science Fiction*, *Asimov's*, *Clarkesworld*, *Lightspeed*, and *Strange Horizons*, among other places. Ken's work was nominated for the 2011 Nebula Award in two different categories. He lives near Boston, Massachusetts, with his wife, artist Lisa Tang Liu. They're collaborating on their first novel.

DAVID MOLES spent six years in and around Tokyo near the end of the twentieth century. He currently lives in San Francisco.

ISSUI OGAWA is known as one of Japan's premier SF writers. His 1996 debut, *First a Letter from Popular Palace*, won the Shueisha JUMP Novel Grand Prix. *The Next Continent* (2003, Haikasoru 2010) garnered the 35th Seiun Prize. A collection of his short stories won the 2005 Best SF Poll, and "The Drifting Man," included in that collection, was awarded the 37th Seiun Prize for domestic short stories. Other works include *Land of Resurrection*, *Free Lunch Era*, and *The Lord of the Sands of Time* (Haikasoru 2009) and a ten-volume epic called *Tenmei no Shirube* (Sign of the Heavens and the Underworld), the fifth volume of which was published in 2011. Ogawa is a principal member of the Space Authors Club.

FELICITY SAVAGE is an American fantasy author. Born in South Carolina, Savage lived until the age of two in rural France and then in the west of Ireland. At six, she moved with her family to the island of North Uist in the Outer Hebrides, where she joined the Girl Guides and appeared in productions of Robin Hood and Peter Pan at the RAF base on Benbecula. Her first novel, *Humility Garden*, and its sequel, *Delta City*, were published by Penguin ROC in 1994 and 1995, while she was still at Columbia University. Her *Ever* trilogy was published by HarperCollins in 1995, 1996, and 1997. Savage was a finalist for the John W. Campbell Award for Best New Writer in 1995 and 1996. She currently lives in Tokyo, Japan, with her husband, daughter, and two cats (one fat and one insane). When not writing, she works as a Japanese translator, sings Gregorian chant, and moonlights as a serial houseplant killer.

EKATERINA SEDIA resides in the Pinelands of New Jersey. Her critically acclaimed novels, *The Secret History of Moscow*, *The Alchemy of Stone*, *The House of Discarded Dreams*, and *Heart of Iron* were published by Prime Books. Her short stories have sold to *Analog*, *Baen's Universe*, *Subterranean*, and *Clarkesworld*, as well as numerous anthologies, including *Haunted Legends* and *Magic in the Mirrorstone*. She is also the editor of *Paper Cities* (World Fantasy Award winner), *Running with the Pack*, and *Bewere the Night*, as well as the forthcoming *Bloody Fabulous* and *Wilful Impropriety*. Visit her at www. ekaterinasedia.com.

BRUCE STERLING is a Texan science fiction novelist who unites his time between Austin, Belgrade, and Turin. His most recent work is an introduction to a volume of Mexican fantastic short stories.

RACHEL SWIRSKY's short fiction has appeared in numerous magazines and anthologies and been nominated for the Hugo, the Locus, the Sturgeon, and the World Fantasy Award. In 2011, her novella "The Lady Who Plucked Red Flowers beneath the Queen's Window" won the Nebula Award. She lives in Bakersfield with a fluctuating number of cats.

TOBI HIROTAKA was born in 1960 in Shimane Prefecture. He was the winner of the Sanseido SF Story Contest while a student at Shimane University. From 1983 to 1992 he actively contributed short stories to *SF Magazine*. After a hiatus of ten years, he returned in 2002 with his first full-length novel. *Grande Vacance: Angel of the Ruined Garden I* took second prize in *SF Magazine*'s Best SF of 2002. In 2004, *Kaleidoscape*, his collection of revised and new works, took top honors in that year's Best SF in the magazine, and the 2005 Japan SF Award. One of the stories from the collection, "Shapesphere," also won the 2005 Seiun Award for Best Japanese Short Story of the Year. "Autogenic Dreaming: Interview with the Columns of Clouds" earned TOBI his second Seiun Award for Best Japanese Short Story in 2010. He is also the author of *Ragged Girl: Angel of the Ruined Garden II*.

CATHERYNNE M. VALENTE is the *New York Times* bestselling author of over a dozen works of fiction and poetry, including *Palimpsest*, the Orphan's Tales series, *Deathless*, and the crowd-funded phenomenon *The Girl Who Circumnavigated Fairyland in a Ship of Her Own Making*. She is the winner of the Andre Norton Award, the Tiptree Award, the Mythopoeic Award, the Rhysling Award, and the Million Writers Award. She has been nominated for the Hugo, Locus, and Spectrum Awards, and the Pushcart Prize, and was a finalist for the World Fantasy Award in 2007 and 2009, and a finalist for the Nebula Award in 2012. She lives on an island off the coast of Maine with her partner, two dogs, and an enormous cat.

WHAT IS HAIKASORU ?

SPACE OPERA.

DARK FANTASY.

HARD SCIENCE.

MAGICAL REALISM.

AND MORE...

With a small, elite list of award-winners, classics, and new work by the hottest young writers, **Haikasoru** is the first imprint dedicated to bringing Japanese science fiction to America and beyond. Since our launch in 2009, our books and editors have been nominated for or won the Hugo Award, Shirley Jackson Award, and the Special Citation for the Philip K. Dick Award, and have placed on several best-of lists.

Featuring the action of anime and the thoughtfulness of the best speculative fiction, **Haikasoru** aims to truly be the "**high castle**" of science fiction and fantasy.

HAIKASORU

THE FUTURE IS JAPANESE

COMING IN 2012 AND 2013!

METAL GEAR SOLID: GUNS OF THE PATRIOTS BY PROJECT ITOH

From the legendary video game franchise! Solid Snake is a soldier and part of a worldwide nanotechnology network known as the Sons of the Patriots System. Time is running out for Snake as, thanks to the deadly FOXDIE virus, he has been transformed into a walking biological weapon. Not only is the clock ticking for Snake, nearly everyone he encounters becomes infected. Snake turns to the SOP System for help, only to find that it has been hacked by the SOP's old enemy Liquid Ocelot—and whoever controls the SOP System controls the world.

GENOCIDAL ORGAN BY PROJECT ITOH

The war on terror exploded, literally, the day Sarajevo was destroyed by a home-made nuclear device. The leading democracies transformed into total surveillance states, and the developing world has drowned under a wave of genocides. The mysterious American John Paul seems to be behind the collapse of the world system, and it's up to intelligence agent Clavis Shepherd to track John Paul across the wreckage of civilizations and to find the true heart of darkness—a genocidal organ.

BELKA, WHY DON'T YOU BARK? BY HIDEO FURUKAWA

When Japanese troops retreat from the Aleutian island of Kiska in 1943, they leave behind four military dogs. One of them dies in isolation, and the others are taken under the protection of US troops. Meanwhile, in the USSR, a KGB military dog handler kidnaps the daughter of a Japanese yakuza. Named after the Russian astronaut dog Strelka, the girl develops the psychic ability to communicate with canines. A multigenerational epic as seen through the eyes of man's best friend, the dogs who are used as mere tools for the benefit of humankind gradually discover their true selves and learn something about their so-called "masters."

VIRUS: THE DAY OF RESURRECTION BY SAKYO KOMATSU

In this classic of Japanese SF, American astronauts on a space mission discover a strange virus and bring it to Earth, where rogue scientists transform it into a fatal version of the flu. After the virulent virus is released, nearly all human life on Earth is wiped out save for fewer than one thousand men and a handful of women living in research stations in Antarctica. Then one of the researchers realizes that a major earthquake in the now-depopulated United States may lead to nuclear Armageddon…

SELF-REFERENCE ENGINE BY TOH ENJOE

Toh EnJoe's prize-winning fiction crosses the streams—from hardcore science fiction to bizarre surrealism—and has found an audience across the genre divide. *Self-Reference ENGINE* is a puzzle of a book, where vignette and story and philosophy combine to create a novel designed like a concept album.

CURRENTLY AVAILABLE:

THE OUROBOROS WAVE BY JYOUJI HAYASHI

Ninety years from now, a satellite detects a nearby black hole scientists dub Kali for the Hindu goddess of destruction. Humanity embarks on a generations-long project to tap the energy of the black hole and establish colonies on planets across the solar system. Earth and Mars and the moons Europa (Jupiter) and Titania (Uranus) develop radically different societies, with only Kali, that swirling vortex of destruction and creation, and the hated but crucial Artificial Accretion Disk Development association (AADD) in common.

THE NAVIDAD INCIDENT: THE DOWNFALL OF MATÍAS GUILI BY NATSUKI IKEZAWA

In this sweeping magical-realist epic set in the fictional south sea island republic of Navidad, Ikezawa gives his imagination free rein to reinvent the myths of the twentieth-century Japan. The story takes off as a delegation of Japanese war veterans pays an official visit to the ex-World War II colony, only to see the Japanese flag burst into flames. The following day, the tour bus, and its passengers, simply vanish. The locals exchange absurd rumors— the bus was last seen attending Catholic mass, the bus must have skipped across the lagoon— but the president suspects a covert guerrilla organization is trying to undermine his connections with Japan. Can the real answers to the mystery be found, or will the president have to be content with the surreal answers?

HARMONY BY PROJECT ITOH

In the future, Utopia has finally been achieved thanks to medical nanotechnology and a powerful ethic of social welfare and mutual consideration. This perfect world isn't that perfect though, and three young girls stand up to totalitarian kindness and super-medicine by attempting suicide via starvation. It doesn't work, but one of the girls—Tuan Kirie—grows up to be a member of the World Health Organization. As a crisis threatens the harmony of the new world, Tuan rediscovers another member of her suicide pact, and together they must help save the planet…from itself.

YUKIKAZE BY CHŌHEI KAMBAYASHI

More than thirty years ago a hyper-dimensional passageway suddenly appeared… the first stage of an attempted invasion by an enigmatic alien host. Humanity managed to push the invaders back through the passageway to the strange planet nicknamed "Faery." Now, Second Lieutenant Rei Fukai carries out his missions in the skies over Faery. His only constant companion in this lonely task is his fighter plane, the sentient FFR-31 Super Sylph, call sign: YUKIKAZE.

GOOD LUCK, YUKIKAZE BY CHŌHEI KAMBAYASHI

The alien JAM have been at war with humanity for over thirty years…or have they? Rei Fukai of the FAF's Special Air Force and his intelligent tactical reconnaissance fighter plane Yukikaze have seen endless battles, but after declaring "Humans are unnecessary now," and forcibly ejecting Fukai, Yukikaze is on its own. Is the target of the JAM's hostility really Earth's machines?

LOUPS-GAROUS BY NATSUHIKO KYOGOKU

In the near future, humans will communicate almost exclusively through online networks—face-to-face meetings are rare and the surveillance state nearly all-powerful. So when a serial killer starts slaughtering junior high students, the crackdown is harsh. The killer's latest victim turns out to have been in contact with three young girls: Mio Tsuzuki, a certified prodigy; Hazuki Makino, a quiet but opinionated classmate; and Ayumi Kono, her best friend. And as the girls get caught up in trying to find the killer—who just might be a werewolf—Hazuki learns that there is much more to their monitored communications than meets the eye.

TEN BILLION DAYS AND ONE HUNDRED BILLION NIGHTS BY RYU MITSUSE

Ten billion days—that is how long it will take the philosopher Plato to determine the true systems of the world. One hundred billion nights—that is how far into the future Jesus of Nazareth, Siddhartha, and the demigod Asura will travel to witness the end of all worlds. Named the greatest Japanese science fiction novel of all time, *Ten Billion Days and One Hundred Billion Nights* is an epic eons in the making. Originally published in 1967, the novel was revised by the author in later years and republished in 1973.

THE BOOK OF HEROES BY MIYUKI MIYABE

When her brother Hiroki disappears after a violent altercation with school bullies, Yuriko finds a magical book in his room. The book leads her to another world where she learns that Hiroki has been possessed by a spirit from The Book of Heroes, and that every story ever told has some truth to it and some horrible lie. With the help of the monk Sky, the dictionary-turned-mouse Aju, and the mysterious Man of Ash, Yuriko has to piece together the mystery of her vanished brother and save the world from the evil King in Yellow.

BRAVE STORY BY MIYUKI MIYABE

Young Wataru flees his messed-up life to navigate the magical world of Vision, a land filled with creatures both fierce and friendly. His ultimate destination is the Tower of Destiny where a goddess of fate awaits. Only when he has finished his journey and collected five elusive gemstones will he possess the Demon's Bane—the key that will grant him his most heartfelt wish…the wish to bring his family back together again!

ICO: CASTLE IN THE MIST BY MIYUKI MIYABE

A boy with horns, marked for death. A girl who sleeps in a cage of iron. The Castle in the Mist has called for its sacrifice: a horned child, born once a generation. When, on a single night in his thirteenth year, Ico's horns grow long and curved, he knows his time has come. But why does the Castle in the Mist demand this offering, and what will Ico do with the girl imprisoned within the Castle's walls? Delve into the mysteries of Miyuki Miyabe's grand achievement of imagination, inspired by the award-winning game for the PlayStation® 2 computer entertainment system, now remastered for PlayStation® 3.

ROCKET GIRLS BY HOUSUKE NOJIRI

Yukari Morita is a high school girl on a quest to find her missing father. While searching for him in the Solomon Islands, she receives the offer of a lifetime—she'll get the help she needs to find her father, and all she need do in return is become the world's youngest, lightest astronaut. Yukari and her sister Matsuri, both petite, are the perfect crew for the Solomon Space Association's launches, or will be once they complete their rigorous and sometimes dangerous training.

ROCKET GIRLS: THE LAST PLANET BY HOUSUKE NOJIRI

When the Rocket Girls accidentally splash down in the pond of Yukari Morita's old school, it looks as though their experiment is ruined. Luckily, the geeky Akane is there to save the day. Fitting the profile—she's intelligent, enthusiastic, and petite—Akane is soon recruited by the Solomon Space Association. Yukari and Akane are then given the biggest Rocket Girl mission yet: to do what NASA astronauts cannot and save a probe headed to the minor planet Pluto and the very edge of the solar system.

USURPER OF THE SUN BY HOUSUKE NOJIRI

Aki Shiraishi is a high school student working in the astronomy club and one of the few witnesses to an amazing event—someone is building a tower on the planet Mercury. Soon, the enigmatic Builders have constructed a ring around the sun, and the ecology of Earth is threatened by its immense shadow. Aki is inspired to pursue a career in science, and the truth. She must determine the purpose of the ring and the plans of its creators, as the survival of both species—humanity and the alien Builders—hangs in the balance.

THE LORD OF THE SANDS OF TIME BY ISSUI OGAWA

Sixty-two years after human life on Earth was annihilated by rampaging alien invaders, the enigmatic Messenger O is sent back in time with a mission to unite humanity of past eras—during the Second World War, in ancient Japan, and at the dawn of humanity—to defeat the invasion before it begins. However, in a future shredded by love and genocide, love waits for O. Will O save humanity only to doom himself?

THE NEXT CONTINENT BY ISSUI OGAWA

The year is 2025 and Gotoba General Construction—a firm that has built structures to survive the Antarctic and the Sahara—has received its most daunting challenge yet. Sennosuke Touenji, the chairman of one of the world's largest leisure conglomerates, wants a moon base fit for civilian use, and he wants his granddaughter Taé to be his eyes and ears on the harsh lunar surface. Taé and Gotoba engineer Aomine head to the moon where adventure, trouble, and perhaps romance await.

DRAGON SWORD AND WIND CHILD BY NORIKO OGIWARA

The God of Light and the Goddess of Darkness have waged a ruthless war across the land of Toyoashihara for generations. But for fifteen-year-old Saya, the war is far away—until the day she discovers that she is the reincarnation of the Water Maiden and a princess of the Children of the Dark. Raised to love the Light and detest the Dark, Saya must come to terms with her heritage even as the Light and Dark both seek to claim her, for she is the only mortal who can awaken the legendary Dragon Sword, the weapon destined to bring an end to the war. Can Saya make the choice between the Light and Dark, or is she doomed—like all the Water Maidens who came before her...?

MIRROR SWORD AND SHADOW PRINCE BY NORIKO OGIWARA

When the heir to the empire comes to Mino, the lives of young Oguna and Toko change forever. Oguna is drafted to become a shadow prince, a double trained to take the place of the hunted royal. But soon Oguna is given the Mirror Sword, and his power to wield it threatens the entire nation. Only Toko can stop him, but to do so she needs to gather four magatama, beads with magical powers that can be strung together to form the Misumaru of Death. Toko's journey is one of both adventure and self-discovery, and also brings her face to face with the tragic truth behind Oguna's transformation. A story of two parallel quests, of a pure love tried by the power of fate, the second volume of Tales of the Magatama is as thrilling as *Dragon Sword and Wind Child*.

SUMMER, FIREWORKS AND MY CORPSE BY OTSUICHI

Two short novels, including the title story and *Black Fairy Tale*, plus a bonus short story. *Summer* is a simple story of a nine-year-old girl who dies while on summer vacation. While her youthful killers try to hide her body, she tells us the story—from the point of view of her dead body—of the children's attempt to get away with murder. *Black Fairy Tale* is classic J-horror: a young girl loses an eye in an accident, but receives a transplant. Now she can see again, but what she sees out of her new left eye is the experiences and memories of its previous owner. Its previous *deceased* owner.

ZOO BY OTSUICHI

A man receives a photo of his girlfriend every day in the mail...so that he can keep track of her body's decomposition. A deathtrap that takes a week to kill its victims. Haunted parks and airplanes held in the sky by the power of belief. These are just a few of the stories by Otsuichi, Japan's master of dark fantasy.

ALL YOU NEED IS KILL BY HIROSHI SAKURAZAKA

When the alien Mimics invade, Keiji Kiriya is just one of many recruits shoved into a suit of battle armor called a Jacket and sent out to kill. Keiji dies on the battlefield, only to be reborn each morning to fight and die again and again. On his 158th iteration, he gets a message from a mysterious ally—the female soldier known as the Full Metal Bitch. Is she the key to Keiji's escape or his final death?

SLUM ONLINE BY HIROSHI SAKURAZAKA

Etsuro Sakagami is a college freshman who feels uncomfortable in reality, but when he logs onto the combat MMO *Versus Town*, he becomes "Tetsuo," a karate champ on his way to becoming the most powerful martial artist around. While his relationship with new classmate Fumiko goes nowhere, Etsuro spends his days and nights online in search of the invincible fighter Ganker Jack. Drifting between the virtual and the real, will Etsuro ever be ready to face his most formidable opponent?

BATTLE ROYALE: THE NOVEL BY KOUSHUN TAKAMI

Koushun Takami's notorious high-octane thriller envisions a nightmare scenario: a class of junior high school students is taken to a deserted island where, as part of a ruthless authoritarian program, they are provided arms and forced to kill until only one survivor is left standing. Criticized as violent exploitation when first published in Japan—where it became a runaway best seller—*Battle Royale* is a *Lord of the Flies* for the twenty-first century, a potent allegory of what it means to be young and (barely) alive in a dog-eat-dog world.

MARDOCK SCRAMBLE BY TOW UBUKATA

Why me? It was to be the last thought a young prostitute, Rune-Balot, would ever have…as a human anyway. Taken in by a devious gambler named Shell, she became a slave to his cruel desires and would have been killed by his hand if not for the self-aware Universal Tool (and little yellow mouse) known as Oeufcoque. Now a cyborg, Balot is not only nigh invulnerable, but has the ability to disrupt electrical systems of all sorts. But even these powers may not be enough for Balot to deal with Shell, who offloads his memories to remain above the law, the immense assassin Dimsdale-Boiled, or the neon-noir streets of Mardock City itself.

THE CAGE OF ZEUS BY SAYURI UEDA

The Rounds are humans with the sex organs of both genders. Artificially created to test the limits of the human body in space, they are now a minority, despised and hunted by the terrorist group the Vessel of Life. Aboard Jupiter-I, a space station orbiting the gas giant that shares its name, the Rounds have created their own society with a radically different view of gender and of life itself. Security chief Shirosaki keeps the peace between the Rounds and the typically gendered "Monaurals," but when a terrorist strike hits the station, the balance of power is at risk…and an entire people is targeted for genocide.

MM9 BY HIROSHI YAMAMOTO

Japan is beset by natural disasters all the time: typhoons, earthquakes, and…giant monster attacks. A special anti-monster unit called the Meteorological Agency Monsterological Measures Department (MMD) has been formed to deal with natural disasters of high "monster magnitude." The work is challenging, the public is hostile, and the monsters are hungry, but the MMD crew has science, teamwork…and a legendary secret weapon on their side. Together, they can save Japan, and the universe!

THE STORY OF IBIS BY HIROSHI YAMAMOTO

In a world where humans are a minority and androids have created their own civilization, a wandering storyteller meets the beautiful android Ibis. She tells him seven stories of human/android interaction in order to reveal the secret behind humanity's fall. The tales that Ibis tells are science fiction stories about the events surrounding the development of artificial intelligence (AI) in the twentieth and twenty-first centuries. At a glance, these stories do not appear to have any sort of connection, but what is the true meaning behind them? What are Ibis's real intentions?

VISIT US AT WWW.HAIKASORU.COM